THE DEADMAN'S PEDAL

THE
DEADMAN'S
PEDAL

ALAN WARNER

JONATHAN CAPE
LONDON

Published by Jonathan Cape 2012

2 4 6 8 10 9 7 5 3 1

Copyright © Alan Warner 2012

Alan Warner has asserted his right under the Copyright, Designs
and Patents Act 1988 to be identified as the author of this work

First published in Great Britain in 2012 by
Jonathan Cape
Random House, 20 Vauxhall Bridge Road,
London SW1V 2SA

www.randomhouse.co.uk

Addresses for companies within The Random House Group Limited can be found at:
www.randomhouse.co.uk/offices.htm

The Random House Group Limited Reg. No. 954009

A CIP catalogue record for this book
is available from the British Library

ISBN 9780224071703

The Random House Group Limited supports The Forest Stewardship
Council (FSC®), the leading international forest certification organisation.
Our books carrying the FSC label are printed on FSC® certified paper.
FSC is the only forest certification scheme endorsed by the leading
environmental organisations, including Greenpeace.
Our paper procurement policy can be found at
www.randomhouse.co.uk/environment

Typeset in Bembo by Palimpsest Book Production Limited,
Falkirk, Stirlingshire
Printed and bound by
CPI Group (UK) Ltd, Croydon, CR0 4YY

for Mike Moorcock and for all the boys of the old station

A commodity appears at first an extremely obvious, trivial thing. But its analysis brings out that it is a very strange thing, abounding in metaphysical subtleties and theological niceties.

Karl Marx

Still lightsome and unheartbroken
Their stories only beginning.

'Hallaig', Sorley McLean
trans. Seamus Heaney

Now and for always, Simon will be moving through the night, up on those diesel locomotives — a stable of just thirty or so as familiar as his home — crossing these lone territories between stations in a blackness as complete as outer space.

The windscreens of those driving cabs are endarkened — as if the cell within is dedicated to the most profound contemplation. Invisible earth all around — docile sheep sometimes glimpsed on the lowest slopes, still as white boulders marking some ancient way. Offended deer high above, their heads slowly following the molten orange rectangle of exhaust. Under his Clarks brogues and through the bossed metal of the deadman's pedal, the wheels are regularly reporting where the rail lengths just kiss at their joins.

These scoured mountain flanks and these bare summits; slopes wrinkled by mile-long cables of narrow down-burns whitened by the rush of their own excited froth. Ten thousand winters and not much changed except rail or road cuttings and bridges threading the miles between a few skeletal settlements. Cross-mountain electricity pylons helicoptered in; the imperceptible growth of hardy pine forestry commission. Rivers run between the mountains and birds sit in the trees above the beasts of the woods while the yellow summer sheep trails meander, showing like threaded blood vessels on the land. Some winter lochans so still the reflected sky can be mistaken for ice.

The rail line and the road down to Glasgow follow the glens and straths by all those lochs and those rivers; they sometimes part where the railway climbs alone, tucked into the lower slopes of mountainside, marked by parasite bushes and birch saplings along its lee.

Where track and tarmac have agreed to come so close together, a night train can be accompanied, suddenly sharing adamant headlights: a Vauxhall, or a Bedford truck as outrider, briefly adjacent. Between the two types of driver are drooping and lifting telegraph wires, ceramic ranks of insulation caps aglint up on the poles. Then moon-rail and road centre-line peel off

I

as train and vehicle move yonder, like nocturnal things who blundered together, spoors acknowledged and the parting accepted.

A dozen train drivers, six guards – relaying down and back through lifetimes, out of the Port terminus and along the eight-station, sixty-mile run to Ardencaple Glen, then back again and again. Seasons changing, trees growing from saplings, cross birds, foxes, pine martins, deer on the high hills, even true wildcats glimpsed with their fat tails. In the few heatwaves the cab doors of their diesel locomotives are lashed open onto the bulkhead pipes, the noisy air around the drivers festered with clouds of bankside foxglove seeds swirling before their faces and sticking in their grey hair.

Ardencaple signal box and passing loop is one thousand feet up, no station and no passenger platform. Still remaining from steam-engine days are rotting coaling staithes of wooden sleepers and a redundant water tower, the raining sky constantly reinvigorating its rusty drip. Ardencaple box is run by a family of all ages – in through the dirty windows you'd see a boy of twelve pull a red signal lever on the frame, while his little sister waves her doll.

A worn path leads from the signal box, on up through open heather to their modest bungalow, portable Calor gas bottles strapped to the exterior wall. Often a dapple of snow in a shaded place as late as June.

Drivers or secondmen pull up their diesels expertly in the dark – the cab interior is suddenly lit yellowish – and the cab door opens; two men holding flasks or sandwich boxes and metal-cased torches step out onto a brief wooden platform with steep stairways and banisters – like some hastily assembled gallows. The city footplate men and their guard take the train southbound while the rural crew take the other train back up northward and west, over the familiar route.

Night driving, these northbound enginemen have full knowledge of the invisible road. There are no headlights on these diesels, so drivers move forward in a spectacular blindness through the starless dark, using trackside landmarks, platers' huts or numbered bridges and viaducts to triangulate their location so the land exists in their minds more than to their senses. That ancient dark comes smothering close around the trains in the inhuman places.

Short rust-topped check rails on the inside of the running rail strengthen the cant on the tightest curves and the wheel flanges grate, creaking and *shooting high metallic screeches. The train feels on ahead, held on brakes by the drivers — some who have been forty years just on this line and could drive with their eyes shut, which they might as well do, chins lit from the minimal light of the five gauges on the dash before them. The sway of every familiar bend and brief straight, felt and intuited rather than seen; blunt-snouted locos, always shaking home towards that outlying station terminus in its little bay; that glass-roofed Victorian station of fretted wood with four platforms and four freight sidings run out by the ferry pier which serves the islands.*

Wednesday 19 April 1961

Some stars still showed in uncertain bleats of light. It was dark at the Pass mouth and the limited sky to the east only began to indicate an uneven top of the ridge above.

They had watched the car headlamps sliding up the driveway, pushing vast, ghostly blocks of dusty light through the glossed metal fence; then showing through the thickest, snaking rhododendron boughs. The tyres crunched the gravel, over behind the different angles and high elevations of the slated roofs and the two towers. As the men feared, in just minutes a house door opened. The Gothic arch into the utility room. The doorway shape showed above the head of that human figure who stood there, a naked bulb behind him.

As the door had swung open, a bore of light widened and yawed across the lawn, showing the ground's unevenness and those higher clods threw shadow. For the season, there was an odd breath of glistening frost upon the land, covering the area of grass under open sky which was free from the heavy, overhanging dark of the pine trees. The edges of the frosted patch were shown to be in a kind of uneven retreat.

The figure came out the doorway towards them, quickly covering the hundred yards of grass, his long shadow jerking and pulling. The four men stood stock-still, their location only confirmed by the brightening and the fading tips of cigarettes which they all smoked. There was a singular, quick orange bead as one man whipped a cigarette from his face, dropped it down to his thigh to exhale and then quickly brought it back up to his mouth once again. None of the men threw their cigarettes to the ground though; things weren't that bad.

They could hear the crunchy, slight resistance of the lawn under the approaching man's heels.

4

'I cannot see a damn thing. Who's here?'

'George, sir.'

'Who else?'

The other men would not speak.

George's voice answered, 'Calum and his son. And Fitz.'

There was silence in the cold air.

'He's the new groom.'

'What's with the blackout, Dod? We both know fine the war's long over. Is it the Russians you think are coming?'

'Just waiting for that wee touch daylight, sir. Did you drive through the night?'

'You're out early enough, I'll say that.' He suddenly seemed to mellow. 'It's going to be a beautiful day. Not a breath of wind.' The voice paused. 'I'm pleased you've finished the stones and railings on the driveway but why in the name of Christ have you started in here when we've just talked about it? I didn't give the go-ahead on this at all.' As he spoke he walked on past them. 'Not at all.'

'We started yesterday, after the painting,' George's voice said.

'Oh God, no . . .'

'Yes, sir.'

The figure stopped at the edge of the excavation. 'What a mess. What a bloody mess. George.'

'Yes, sir.'

'Do you not read a single decent paper, you clowns? The house is littered with *Daily Telegraph*s. The dogs eat off them in the scullery but yous lot won't read them.'

'Sir?'

Wondering why the man's two dogs had not followed him from the doorway, the youngest man turned back to the big house, then three small windows lit up, where young Fiona and the nanny bided – high in the staff heavens. He noted that smoke had begun to drift in the windless sky. It was coming from the east chimney stack which he knew meant either the huge hall fire had been lit – despite the season and early hour – or even that the billiard-room fire had, which seemed an impossibility.

'How far down have you gone?'

'We just took the top off.' Despite the dark George noticed light reflecting on polished leather at the man's feet. The figure hadn't even paused to pull on his wellington boots and was still in city shoes – uncaring as to the muck.

'Tell me that the top turf's cut and neatly stacked at least.'

'Oh aye, sir. Stored in the lean-to, by the tack room. Apart from at the edges where the bank started. The turf was too thin.'

In a more thoughtful and tolerant tone, the figure asked, 'Many roots?'

'Some. No as bad as we'd feared. You always did suppose it might kill one of the pines.'

The figure nodded. 'So you were going to dig on it today?'

'Aye. Yes, sir. Even thought of burning it.'

'Ah, Christ. That would have been a sight.' He chuckled to himself. 'Well, I caught yous in time. If Edinburgh wasn't Edinburgh I would have asked for you on the telephone. It's my fault. If I don't do something myself then it goes wrong.' They could see he was still nodding, the neck moving above the check of the tweed jacket. He turned and the closest to him was young Fitz.

'Know much about badgers, boy?'

'No, sir.'

'From Kirkintilloch are we not? The town that Mr Johnston made dry. You've the Campsies all round you, man!'

'Kirkcaldy, sir. Right in the town.'

'Kirkcaldy?' The figure turned to George. 'Kirkcaldy.' The voice was mannered Scots – more so, it seemed, after his two-day trip to Edinburgh, and it was pronounced Kir-Call-dey. 'Since when did you seek your young horsemen from fucking Kirkcaldy, Dod?'

George did not answer. With too jocular a tone, the young voice confessed, 'Never clapped a horse till I came through your gates, sir. I'd betted on them right enough.'

There was a tense silence but the man in the tweed jacket laughed. 'Maybe so. But you can shovel shite as good as any Highlander? Eh?'

'Aye, Mr Bultitude.'

Three chuckles came out of the dark and the cigarette ends all danced a little.

The man carried on looking towards the lad's vague location. 'A badger sett can be three hundred year old, son. It can go down and down and down and down. And across too. Like a Fife coal mine. Understand?'

'Yes, sir.'

'You can see it's way out under the lawn but they're not as bad as the moles. You could dig out badger tunnels for a month here and not get down to the den. Or find it's an old one and they've moved to another, deeper down.' In a quieter voice, Bultitude went on, 'The badgers are civilised; they pass the sett from generation to generation. Like a great house. And they've been here as long as my family has. My own father tried to dig this one out when I was little. Then they'd be snouting up round the door to the kitchens a month later. When the kitchens were still big, you went down to the old door at the basement level. You'd hear the badger's claws scratching on the stone steps. At night I used to think they were monsters come up from the graveyard, when I was a wee fellow.' He laughed brutally but none of the others did. 'Maybe I like the badgers more than the lawn. It's bad luck to shift them, Dod. It's a miracle they stay with the dogs about anyway. Leave them be.'

'Yes, sir.'

Suddenly the figures were weakly picked out by pale and buttery light. All five of the French windows on the ground-floor dining hall – with the fanned panes above each – lit, yellow and tall along the wing. The figure of young Fiona the maid, pulling a black cardigan over her shoulders, walked across the vague reflection of polished parquet.

In a dark voice Bultitude announced, 'So, Elsie and the wee lassie are no bothering to draw the curtains at night now. When I'm away. And then they greet to me about the cold in the house. Might there have been cards in the scullery with my good wife last night?'

'Aye. I think so, sir.'

'Do you not know any more when Elsie's in your bed, Dod?'

Fitz sniggered.

'I'm paying that fucking English nanny to play cards with my wife.'

The men all laughed.

'So I trust the wee ones slept sound?'

7

'I heard no different, sir.'

'Alexander sleeps like the blessed, but Varie's a crier.' He seemed to say to himself in a tired voice, 'And today's a big day for them both, but I doubt they'll even remember it.'

A distant clicking sound came clear as anything, through the two miles of night to their north.

'What train is yon, at this hour?' George's voice asked, deeply concerned.

'I don't know,' said Bultitude – curious himself. He bent up his arm and brought the top of his hand right to his eyes, trying to look at the face of his wristwatch.

'It's coming over from the town, that one,' another man told them.

'Perhaps the timetable is changed because of the train today?' Bultitude asked it with an edge of satisfaction.

The men all stood listening for a long time as the train engine came closer – as if it were the harbinger of some occult certainty.

A man now said, 'That's just an engine on its own, a wee newfangled diesel; always breaking down, so I hear.'

In a voice of scorn Bultitude said, 'Of course. British Railways. The business I've given them down the years. And no one profits.'

Still the men listened as the light engine came from across the river bridge then out on the horseshoe curve, across the Broken Moan garage and its single petrol pump. There was a nasty snarl – a sound of powerful modernity – as the engine opened up with a burst then shut off very soon after, so the exhaust stuttered and the heavy, repetitive double-wheel clicks became more dominant as they moved on and receded away down the catch of the Pass.

Bultitude said, 'So not a single one of you saw today's *Telegraph* then, my bonnie laddies?'

This was an impossibility. He was building up to something. The newspaper came with the milk in the grocer's van each morning and it wasn't there yet – as Bultitude knew fine well.

All the same, George obediently replied, 'No, sir.'

'But the Queen's coming.'

'Aye. We've knowed that for a good while now.'

'Not just to open the Barrier. She's coming here to Broken Moan. It's in the London *Daily Telegraph* today, boys. The name of the house and my name too. I've a fresh copy inside. I'll shows yous all. The *Port Star*'ll be coming to take the pictures.'

There was a long silence.

They heard the wicked satisfaction when Bultitude said, 'Bloody old Argyll himself will need to come up the driveway to my house and this time his car won't be first either. That's for sure, boys.'

The voice of George sounded heavy – and you could mistake this for reverence, rather than weariness. 'To the house? Argyll *and* the Queen?'

'Yes, Dod. The Queen is coming to Broken Moan this afternoon.'

'Oh my goodness.'

'You've got to know what strings to pull in Edinburgh, boys.' His voice got stern. 'It's my right. Due dignity. She wasn't getting this close and escaping.' He turned to bring them up to date. 'The Royal Train leaves the Waverley this morning up through Callander. She's away into the town first, opening this new bloody council building and meeting that councillor mob. But then, on the way back, the train will stop specially at the Back Settlement. The Holyroodhouse Rolls is coming up and that'll take her down to the Barrier for the ceremony. But then, bonny laddies, the car will stop off here on the way back to the train for a wee half-hour or so. Christ, I hope it's a good steam engine on that Royal Train and not one of your diesels that break down. That would be a sign of the times, eh?'

He paused to let all this sink in.

There was a sharp squeaking sound from the house and they all turned to look across the lawn. One of the French windows had been opened; the doors swung outward and remained there – they saw young Fiona stoop to kick in the small wooden chocks against the usual wind. Then the process was repeated for the next window, and the next. Elsie – George's old wife – was there as well as young Fiona.

'I'm getting the silver cleaned. Every bloody bit of it and the formal table will be laid. You never know, boys, she might fancy a light lunch on our own salmon. Or is it the Hydro's?'

They chuckled cautiously.

'You, Kirkcaldy, and another of yous. Get yourselves into the house in two minutes. Make sure your feet are clean and help the lassies get the trestle tables out onto the lawn. The tables we used for the wallpapering men. They're right in at the back of the cellars on the left. It's going to be a braw day but they're to light every single fire downstairs, so make sure the coal shed's well stocked with logs. The girls are going to clean all the silver, laid out on the lawn like we did every bloody year in my father's time. It makes a grand sight, boys, Calum here'll tell yous – the silver all laid out and polishing up in the open air, shining and reflecting the colours back. Next.' He turned directly to the young Fitz. 'Kirkcaldy.'

'Yes, Mr Bultitude?'

'Clean every downstairs window. Don't you be worrying about the upper floors, just clean every window on the ground floor. Every one. Make sure you clean behind the ivy now, where it's grown in at the sides, over the glass. Clean the new wing and the old and especially the French windows to the very top. Get this mess turfed over again and rolled. Turned good, so it doesn't show. Here now?'

'What, sir?'

'Are the posts-and-rails in the paddocks painted nice and fresh? White?'

'Aye, sir. Could you no see from the road? We did them a week ago before we started the driveway.'

'Good lads, good lads. Bloody good timing. For once.' Then in a small childlike voice, Bultitude nervously said, 'She might want to see the stables. She's a horsewoman.' The voice became hard again. 'You call it a stud, boys. You don't say the stables. You say the stud, if any of the the staff or officials ask. Understand?'

'Yes, sir.'

'Make sure your groom's cottage is decent inside, Kirkcaldy. And the tack room ordered as well. This all needs done by two o'clock – sharp. All of it. Is that understood?'

'Yes, sir.'

'Aye, Mr Bultitude.'

'Very well, Andrew.' It was a man called old Calum who replied, in his slow island voice.

'A proud day, Calum, eh?'

'Aye, Andrew.'

Only old Calum would have dared use the Christian name. He'd been on the estate, working for the father, since Bultitude was a wee boy.

'Father would have been proud, eh?'

'Aye. He would that,' old Calum's voice said.

Now the elocution – only hours out of Edinburgh – had turned more broad and cheery, so he almost spoke like them. 'Right, boys. They'll be drams the night if it goes off well. Get yourselves bathed and into Sunday best before three o'clock. I can't see in all this, but clean-shaven too.' He turned to Fitz. 'If you've started to sprout a beard yet.'

The other men all laughed as Bultitude held out a hand and ruffled the young boy's head of hair.

'Calum.' Bultitude nudged his head and walked forward with the old man, bringing him away from the others with a tweed sleeve around the shoulders of Calum's dirty donkey jacket. As they moved together, Andrew Bultitude put his mouth down to Calum's ear. 'Get time to go down the chapel yard, yes? Get some jute sacks and cover over the graves, yes?'

'Oh aye. I understand.'

'We've done it before. You put a layer of sacking on the graves, then sprinkle some soil and you cover them over in plants or something. There's all those ferns, potted up in the greenhouse for the rockeries. Anything to make them look normal. You understand?'

'Aye. Of course.'

'I mean, I can't imagine the Sovereign wants to go look at Father and my rotted grandad, but it would be just my fucking luck. You know?'

'Aye. Aye. No, I'll personally get them covered up, Commander. You needn't worry on that account.'

'It's no so much her as these, well, her bloody retainers. London flunkeys and pressmen and the rest with cameras snooping all around the place. You know what rumours are like and they might be nosing all over?' Bultitude slapped the old fellow's shoulders once. 'Good, Calum.'

Bultitude walked ahead towards the big house alone. The group of men still stood and watched him detour, heading for the open doors of the French windows, but just before he reached them, Bultitude lifted each leg from the knee and peeled off his shoes as if he were about to leap in a river and rescue someone. The shoes were handmade by Lobb's in London and sent up annually on the train, but he abandoned them in the grass and walked ahead in his stocking soles to where he entered the dining hall and began shouting and waving arms at old Elsie and young Fiona.

Old Calum walked back to the group.

'Aye aye.'

'All that by fucking two. Every windae. That's impossible.'

'Aye.'

'Another day of it.'

The one called George said, 'Nay greeting now. It is the Queen, lads.'

'Keeping her up at the Barrier doing her business seemed like a decent distance to me.'

'That's treason,' George said, but with a half-humorous tone.

'Away and shite, Dod.'

The other men chuckled out in the dark and lit more cigarettes.

'It's all better than digging out fifty yards of badger runs.'

'He's full of it the day though, eh, boys? He'll be as high as a buzzard the day,' Calum nodded.

'Fancy a queen coming here.' Young Fitz blew out air. 'Will there be any — what is it? — debutantes with her?'

And the men chuckled. Even George.

Old Calum's long and angular face appeared in the tangerine light of his match as he lit another cigarette. 'You're the closest we have to a debutante these days, boy.'

They chuckled as the match was waved out and near darkness resumed.

George said, 'It's his big day, right enough.'

Calum nodded the tip of his cigarette. 'Aye. He's drowned a whole village and that man'll no be satisfied till the waters part for him.'

'What was he saying to you there?' George deferred his tone to Calum.

'To cover the graves.'

'Oh aye. Of course.'

It was beginning to grow lighter all around the men, and the big house and grounds were starting to emerge from the darkness. As if the world was just an idea, slowly being thought up by some great imagination.

Friday 8 June 1973

Simon and Andy Galbraith were up the railings above the main entrance and a rush of escaping pupils – mostly wee first years – burst down past them and below. There was the sound of shoes scuffling and of tackity heels scraping on tarred surfaces.

'I'm leaving, Galbraith. I'm telling you.'

There was a gap in the queue down the stairs but two very long-haired sixth years from the town were approaching from the closed tuck shop. Simon and Galbraith naturally let them pass. Galbraith shoved his mouth up to the hair at the side of Simon's head, his breath right there. 'Mind that hairy ape when we's were back in the old 1B1? The Rector belted him six with the lash.' Then they stepped in to descend the stairway – Galbraith first.

'I can work with my old man any time I want to.'

'Aye, aye. That'll be right; flushing the trailers with a hose but you can't drive a lorry till you're eighteen.'

'I drive lorries all the time.'

'Aye. Round and round your old man's garage like the dodgems; you got up to over five mile an hour yet?' Galbraith laughed and made the strange animal sound of his. Simon noted how big and loose the shoulders of Galbraith's school blazer still were – bought for another year's use yet.

Galbraith said, 'Check it out, man. Nikki Caine's down the gates there, yah jammy bass. Bet it's you she's waited on too. Fucking fancies you like anything, man.'

'Does she fuck.'

'She does. Seen her big sister, Karen, man? Another pure ride.'

'Her big sister's over eighteen now.'

'I know that fine. I'd lick her fanny bare of the hairs. Training to be a nurse up the hospital. Whoa. When we was second years,

14

Karen Caine went to End-of-Year Dance dressed up as fucking Alice in Wonderland. Ponytails and a skirt up to here, man.'

'Aye, I know. I heard all that.'

'We should've gone this year, Crimmo.'

'And what? Get off with our own shadows in different corners?'

Galbraith dropped his voice even lower. 'Goan get Nikki up the road, man.'

'A lassie is no going to be seen going up the road. With both of us. No a lassie like her.'

'Why no?'

'Just won't. Not with both us.'

'Imagine riding it. Legs. Little shoes with wee heely things. Telling you. There's no fucking ways Nikki Caine's a virgin, Crimmo.'

'Shut it, Galbraith. She's dead nice.'

'Crimmo's in love. Aww. He's in *love*.'

It was jammed up with blazered bodies at the turn to the gate; everyone bunched and talking. But sure enough, Nikki Caine was still stood there as they both shuffled into the crush. She held something in both arms. They funnelled out among the shoving and excitement of all the years. Pupils were dodging across the road in bluff dashes, ignoring the lollipop man who periodically yelled at them.

Simon looked straight at Nikki Caine and he nodded. She smiled right back at him. Simon cleared his throat. 'Aye, Nikki.'

'Hello there. Hi,' she said – all directed at Simon. 'Hello, Galbraith.' She added his name with brief coldness. She turned her face back to Simon. 'Pleased to be finished?'

'Aye.'

Galbraith blurted, 'Crimmons says he's leaving.'

'Shut it, Galbraith.'

'Are you?'

'Look. Crimmo's getting a big huge massive brassing beamer. He's no allowed to leave the school. Cause his dad's a big shot.'

'Shut it. I am.'

'Are you just thinking about it? You shouldn't; no ways. Mrs Peters would miss you.' Nikki Caine turned to Galbraith. 'Simon's in English with me.'

'Aye, I know. Peters' swotty English.' He'd criticised her by implication. So he shut up.

Nikki Caine turned back to Simon. 'Should wait till you get your results.'

'Och, it's not that, it's just – school. You know?'

Held to her navy jersey in both hands with gold rings on two fingers – but not her Engaged finger – was a large and filled brown paper bag.

'Want some of these?'

'What is it?'

'Peaches. Apples. Mrs Robb in Home Economics gave them me. Just sat and did nothing for two whole periods. It was brilliant. Mrs Robb said they were only going to get thrown out.'

Galbraith boldly moved closer to the girl and looked down into the paper bag, so Simon copied, pretending to examine the blushy fruit but actually trying to peer between the big knot of her tie and low-hung tartan scarf, studying her small collarbones showing through the fair skin where her shirt was unbuttoned.

'Aye, I'll take one, thanks.'

'I don't like fruit.'

She showed her teeth. 'Who's asking *you*, Galbraith?' But after Simon selected a peach and looked at it suspiciously, Nikki turned, silently offering the open top of the bag to Galbraith.

'I'll take,' he glared, appalled at the peaches, 'an apple. Ta.' He immediately bit into it and looked around, perhaps spying to see if a gaggle of Nikki Caine's pals were anywhere – spying.

Simon smiled and grandly told her, 'We're no getting the school bus home. We're getting a bus or a lift in one of my dad's lorries.'

'Are yous?'

Galbraith nodded, crunching the apple.

'I'll get you up the road then.'

The sounds of Galbraith's chewing ceased.

'Aye, but we're going to Dad's garage first.'

'I can get home round that way,' she shrugged – but Simon and Galbraith knew fine this was a substantial detour for her, from up on the Brae Estate.

They were crossing the road as the lollipop man barred traffic. Nikki to Simon's left but Galbraith on his right.

'So what are you going to be doing for the summer then, Nikki?' Simon's voice was dry with a nervousness.

'Dunno. Well. Now I've turned sixteen, working in the Scotch Wool Hosiery with my auntie. Three days a week and all the old grannies,' she tutted.

'Oh aye.'

'If I see another ball of wool.'

Galbraith and Simon laughed.

'You can sword-fight with knitting needles. I do it with my cousin. And you've got the name for it. Nikki the Knitter.' He laughed.

'Watch it, Galbraith.'

They were walking with the uniformed crowd, on the muddied pathway by the burn, towards the blaise playing fields and bus park. Up ahead, a bunch of first years – they were from Nine Mile House – feigned to shove another of their party from the bank and down into the shallow burn water below; the flat brown boulders beneath the clear surface were fustered with brown silt laverings. Two guys forced the other into the verge but it was not a serious attempt. The movement of the walking queue hesitated, to avoid the scuffle. Nikki Caine tutted in a superior way. The two shovers quickly abandoned their victim, called out 'Spastic' and ran on ahead. The lad who had been jostled took after them for retribution, his juvenile school bag slapping on his back, so loose were the straps.

'Tinks live there.' Galbraith nodded to the outpost of caravans in the wasteland up the small embankment to their left.

'What, your cousin?' Nikki spoke in a reasonable voice which you'd use in reply to a teacher or adult.

Simon laughed exaggeratedly.

'Nut,' was all Galbraith managed.

'Not like your peach?' She nodded. Simon obediently raised the fruit and bit into it. Without hesitation a stream of juice shot up his wrist and far in under the cuff of his white school shirt. With a full mouth of juice, Simon mumbled, 'Ugh,' and canted his head forward so Nikki giggled.

'Hurl it at the ducks, man,' Galbraith suggested.

'Leave the ducks alone,' she said.

'Hey, Crimmo. Let's go see our stupid bus anyways. Tell them all *we're* going back on a service bus just to piss off wee first years and that.'

Simon shook his head. 'I can't be bothered. Some spazzer might want to come with us. Gumbo or that and we'll be stuck up the town with him.'

'Oh. Are yous going up the town?'

'To be honest, Nikki, *I* was going to the garage to see if my old man was there and to get one of the lorries out to Tulloch, but I don't think any will be this late on. Want to come with me, up the garage?'

'Aye. I says I would.' She sounded dubious since Galbraith wasn't cooperating at all. Nikki Caine then asked, 'How many lorries does your dad have now then, Simon?'

Straight away Galbraith shouted out, 'Eight and two juggernauts.'

She nodded.

Galbraith snuck a look at her then launched his apple core out across the burn where it buried itself in the foxgloves of the further bank.

'That better not have been a wee duck's nest, Galbraith.'

Simon just shook his head, not knowing how to get rid of either Galbraith or the peach in his hand. He could feel the awful stickiness up his arm, beneath the shirtsleeve, reaching as far as his elbow.

They came to the bus park and high-school pupils of all years were running in various directions, peering up at windows, trying to identify their own particular village bus, then climbing aboard or moving onward to scrutinise the next vehicle. Excited confabulation and commerce involving sweeties or packets of crisps went on inside and spilled out and around the open exits of each bus. Even pupils from thirty-five miles distant – almost to the county line in Glen Lochy – used the Nine Mile House bus.

The Back Settlement bus was parked next to the one that went out to Donan – a village – but really just a big council estate with a shop and a primary school on the main road to Tulloch Ferry. There was another bus that headed north over the old ex-railway cantilever bridge at Tulloch, and a bus that headed south of the town to the disused slate quarries. There was another bus for town pupils on the Port's far side, at Townhead Bend and the Brae Estate, then towards the castle and the Sands. There was even one service bus which started its route to transport island kids to the boys' hostel, beyond the ferry terminal and down the Sound. Though most island pupils had received permission to return on the last ferries the night before.

Galbraith was looking for the Tulloch Ferry. 'Oh no, look, it's yon stupid old banger. Like a greenhouse thing with all the wee windows.'

For the last school day, the bus company had rostered the old 1959 Bedford, with it streamlined edges and chrome beading – sun windows above the driver and front exit. Simon could tell by Galbraith's voice he was a touch disappointed to be missing out. 'Well, why don't you go back on it then?' and he moved his eyes towards Nikki Caine, signalling his predicament.

Without pause for reflection, Galbraith replied, 'Naw. Let's go up the garage and see if your old man's there. Hoi, Nikki. Do you no ever use the Brae bus?'

'I don't use buses much and certainly not on bonny days.' She crisply added, 'And by walking, I pocket the bus money from off my folks.'

'Oh, right. Smart. Suppose you'll need it to add up to the price of a umbrella.'

She ignored him.

They had almost reached the back of the Tulloch Ferry bus. From the rear window, Big Davie of the fifth year pointed down first to Simon then to Nikki Caine and immediately inserted his forefinger repeatedly into an O-shape he had formed with his left hand.

Galbraith was in laughter and turned his grin. Nikki pretended not to see as they moved along the side. There were the usual knocks on the window glass above – rude gesticulations as they passed down.

Galbraith stepped up on the first two stairs of the front door and he shouted something into the entire bus. Whatever he said was largely ignored – as usual – but some of the first years down the front did wolf whistles.

Nikki Caine hesitated back a good bit and she looked around as

19

if to take stock of the entire bus park, across the blaise pitches, the cattle mart, and as far as the escarpment and television aerial half a mile south across the railway line. When Simon came opposite the bus door, he heard Galbraith calling, 'Crimmo says he's leaving the school, everyone.' Some unidentified first year called, 'Hooray.'

Doubtfully, Galbraith added, 'He's lying. Who's driving the bus the day then? Is it Michelin Man? Even he'll struggle to speed in this crate.'

'Hey, Galbraith. Any nudie books on you? Lend us one for the summer,' the younger Milligan had shouted.

Fat Gumbo was up on his feet, heaving down the aisle. Simon snorted, 'Galbraith, stay on or get off. We're away.'

Gumbo's belly came out from underneath the untucked shirt as he half ducked from the exit, hanging onto a handrail. 'Crimmo, that Forthy was here looking for you.'

'Eh?'

Galbraith snapped his head straight round and looked at Simon.

'Yon Forthy, man. From the town. He was here looking for you. There's a rumour goed round you're fighting him. You're no, are you? He's fucking dead hard.'

Big Davie had now come all the way down from up the back of the bus, so Galbraith was forced to step down from the bottom step. Davie put his head round. 'Are you fighting, young Crimmo? Are you fighting that Forthy?'

'Nut. No ways. I'm no fighting anyone. That's impossible.'

'Forth was here looking for you, my man. He come on the bus and everything. Oh, Crimmo, what have you went and done? Tut tut.' Davie called over to Nikki Caine. 'Hoi. You. Love. You're no goin with Forthy, are you? What's in your bag? Flunkeys?'

Galbraith laughed.

Nikki Caine had turned away, still pretending to look far over towards the steep and wooded hill with the town's television aerial behind its flat, tree-lined summit. She deigned to glance back briefly at Big Davie − as if to record his face for future reference − then she moved her head and tutted loudly. Simon looked at her but she continued pretending to stare away. Big Davie was gone, up into the bus.

'Fight, fight fight fight,' first-year boys chanted from the front.

Galbraith said, 'Fuck sake, man. Forthy. Why should he be looking for you? He's a mental fucking hardcase, man. He's hard as anything. Hard as anything, man. Got twelve of the lash off of the Rector and he didna blink. He fought a lad from Glasgow who wasnie even in school and he fucking burst him. Are you shitin it? Are you shitin it? I would be. Hey.' He turned and walked towards Nikki. 'Can I have another apple, if you please?'

'Suppose so. Thought you didn't like fruit.'

Galbraith stepped to Nikki Caine and rooted in the paper bag, selecting an apple, then immediately crunched his teeth into it while still close to her. She held her face aside with a sour look.

Simon announced to nobody, 'I'm nothing to do with Forthy. I've never spoke to the guy.'

'Well, he's looking for you, man.'

'I know, Galbraith.'

'Maybe he's goan kill ya?'

'Fuck sake, man. Thanks.'

Simon stepped over to Nikki. 'Sorry about all that.'

Nikki Caine still smiled. Simon realised that the bitten peach remained in his hand. To try to look unconcerned he put it to his mouth. He placed the opened fruit section against his lips and it felt stingy. He dropped his hand. 'Let's cut up our garage right now.'

Nikki Caine wrinkled her nose. 'That Forth is in remedial. He was in my registration class in second year and brought in a sick note from his mum and it was written on a piece of old newspaper. He's what my dad calls a borstal boy.'

'I know. Come on.' He liked saying it, since it sounded as if they were together in some official way, but he could feel Nikki studying his face for signs of weakness. They only made it a few steps away before Galbraith ran after them.

'Wait on us.'

They were just at the front of the hostel bus when Bobby Forth emerged from around its rear end. Right in their path. Forth made a most minute movement of his small head in acknowledgement – but no more – and the two dark eyes moved to Nikki Caine then returned straight back to Simon. Forth walked right up to them.

'Aye,' Forth grunted. He was not even wearing a single token of school uniform. He was in bother boots, high-waisted and flared brown dress trousers with sharp creases, and zipped right up, he had on that black jean jacket with tartan lining.

'Aye,' Simon yelped. Both he and Nikki had halted, since their way ahead was blocked by Forth.

Forth's quick eyes darted at the peach in Simon's hand. Forth's forehead was somehow tanned and dead smooth but Simon noted deep little blackheads embedded within it. A tiny crease appeared on that brow. Forth said, 'Are yous two goin together then?' The tone sounded oddly impressed.

Nikki Caine said nothing.

'Eh, nut,' went Simon.

'Oh, right,' Forth replied, strangely passive. 'Been looking for you.'

'Have you?'

'I was wanting a wee a word. With you.'

Simon nodded swiftly.

'You're Simon Crimmons. Old man has all the lorries, eh? Drives a big white Jag.'

'Eh. Aye. It's second-hand.'

'Was just wondering. With it being summer holidays and that. Any work going with him the now?'

'Oh,' went Simon. His voice lightened. 'Eh, I don't know really.'

'Aww, right.' But now Forth sounded as if he'd been slighted. He didn't make to move.

'I mean, there might be. Do you want me to sort of ask for you?'

Forth looked down. 'Aye, on you go then.' He used an encouraging register.

Simon nodded. 'I will then. Aye.'

'All right then.' Forth nodded. There was no talking. Suddenly Simon said, 'We're going up there the now. Do you want to see if the old man's up the garage? Or the foreman and that?'

'Yous're going up there right now, up that lorry place?'

'Aye.'

Forth sniffed, looked at Nikki Caine then back to Simon. 'Okay then. I'll get yous up there.' Very quickly, Forth nodded at Nikki. 'You used to be in my registration class years back, didn't ya, doll?'

22

'Yes. In second year.'

'Recognised you. Your hair's gone all long now.'

Nikki Caine did not respond in any way.

'What's that?'

'Peaches and apples.'

'Eh?'

'Peaches and apples.'

He smiled. 'Are yous away home to make fucking jam together?' He laughed shortly.

Galbraith couldn't help snorting his distinctive animal sound behind them.

Forth twisted his body slightly, so he peered past Nikki Caine's shoulder. 'I know you.'

Galbraith fell very still and silent.

'You're Galbraith.'

'Aye.'

'You're from the Tulloch Ferry as well.'

'Aye.'

'Snobsville,' Forth stated. But then he suddenly seemed to reassess his purpose and mellowed. 'I saw you. Smoking up the huts there that time. Up by the blaise.'

Galbraith remained unspeaking.

Forth backed up his statement effortlessly. 'I was walking past with Troy Potter from the caravans. It was fucking pishing down.'

'It's always pishing down.'

Forth narrowed his eyes just a fraction, but it was enough.

Galbraith quickly added, 'Oh aye. I mind now.'

'It's no pishing down the day though, is it, smart-arse? It's like a scorcher. It's roasting, man. Good weather for the fishing, if you've rod and line. Or out on the boats for the real fishing. Got any smokes on you the now then?'

'Eh? Aye.'

Nikki Caine turned round and gave Galbraith a look.

'Goan give us one then, pal?'

'Aye. Aye. No here though, case a bussy or that sees.'

'Might tell your mummy, might he?' Suddenly Forth bent his head aside and he spat. He did it with a sharp tut – somehow ejecting a spit of saliva through his front teeth with a push from the tongue. Forth's huge spittle hit the side of the double tyres on the bus's back wheel and it dribbled down.

Simon could not believe a boy would do that so uncaringly right in front of a girl as fanciable as Nikki Caine. It seemed to indicate some great triumph over the male quest. Or some utter, hard-won indifference which was strangely chaste.

'Come on then.' They followed his stooped walk and Forth immediately added, 'Fucking brilliant that the school's finished, eh?'

Nobody responded.

Forth demanded, 'Eh?'

'Aye,' went Galbraith.

'Yes,' went Nikki Caine.

'Aye,' went Simon.

Forth stared at Nikki Caine whom he correctly suspected of excess studiousness. 'Good riddance to bad rubbish,' he stated. 'They won't be getting me back in there. Fucking loada old shite.'

Nikki's voice seemed to have gone a bit high but with both hands she thrust out the bag of fruit towards Forth. 'Want some?'

'No thanks, doll. I'm no a monkey in a zoo. You keep the silage for your boyfriends.'

As they moved up the lane, back behind them, they all heard the chain reaction of school buses starting up their engines. A nostalgic, forlorn sound of familiarity and safety.

Forth walked a measured distance ahead, as if he did not wish to be seen with them, yet at the same time he was required not to draw too far ahead and effect a complete disassociation. Forth quickly bent his head aside and spat again, into the weeds at the side of the road. Finally Simon gave up and dropped the once-bitten peach into that verge as well. Nikki noticed but said nothing.

As they walked on up the roadway with the orange-coloured blaise of the football pitches on either side of them, there was an oppressed silence. Absolutely no conversation. They walked ahead as if alone, looking at the ground.

They were almost at the trades cash and carry when Forth stopped and called back, 'How about that smoke then, Galbraith?'

'Ah don't want his old man to see me smoking.' He nodded at Simon.

'I'm no asking you to join me in one.'

'Eh?'

'Just give us one. You don't have to have one as well. Do ya?'

'Oh. Right then.' Galbraith looked both ways up and down the long roadway. A car approached and Galbraith painfully waited until it passed then he fished into his interior blazer pocket and quickly took out a pack of Embassy Regal blues. He opened the top of the packet, closely watched by Simon and Nikki. There were eight cigarettes there.

Forth had walked back up to them and he took a single cigarette from Galbraith's fingers then immediately placed it in behind his left ear and covered it with his hair which was really long. Mockingly, Forth turned his head aside, folded back the hair from his right ear and displayed another cigarette already safely concealed there. He gave a grin.

Galbraith quickly put the cigarette packet back in his blazer. Forth now walked beside them. Before the hump of the railway bridge they turned left, off the metalled road and onto the short muddied entry drive to the open security gates of the garage compound and workshop shed. They could all see a faded red-and-cream six-tonner: CRIMMONS HAULAGE and the office telephone number stencilled professionally onto its side.

'So you goan tell your old man I'm a good worker then?' Forth chuckled cynically after he had said it.

Simon got away with just smiling.

'So what would I be doing then?' Forth demanded – he stepped round a puddle and stopped dead.

'Eh?'

'What would I be doing? Warehousing and all that; loading the wagons? I fancy a shot horsing around on your forklift.'

'Aye. That kinda thing. We don't get so much goods coming in here for storage any more. It's mostly contracts and straight deliveries, to sort of the same places. We've a run coming up from Granton Harbour twice a week.'

'Granton? Where's that when it's at home?'

'The docks in Edinburgh,' Galbraith told him. Galbraith and Simon had once done the run down and back together in the lorry cab with Willie the driver and the trip formed a great landmark for them. They had glimpsed Edinburgh Castle in a mythical distance above a huge city.

'Edinburgh. For fuck sake,' Forth said obscurely. He shook his head and looked troubled. Now he wore that mocking smile but it was eerily directed at Nikki Caine. 'Watch the telly much, do yah, doll?'

'Not much.'

'*Watch With Mother*, she likes,' Galbraith suggested.

Nikki Caine said nothing but turned a sour face on Galbraith.

Forth laughed appreciatively; quick to join forces with any cruelty, whatever its source. 'Do you go to the flicks then, doll? Like a night at the picture house? Up the back row?' He let out a whine.

'Nut.'

There was an uncomfortable silence. Then Forth hissed a spit into a puddle where the white swirl floated buoyantly and he ordered, 'Come on,' as if they had delayed him.

Forth led them walking into the yard across the turning area of spread two-inch chips. Billy Strachan the foreman came bounding out the Portakabin and raised his arm. He called, 'Here comes this week's five-aside team,' into the open door of the office but then his gaze clearly rested on Forth, who strode confidently towards him. Strachan stood still as Forth stopped in front of him.

'Aye,' went Forth.

Strachan – in his oily boiler suit – nodded the once.

Simon was a few steps behind and he came up beside Forth. 'Eh, this is—' He realised he couldn't remember Forth's Christian name.

'Bobby,' Forth sneered.

'He's wondering about work.'

'Work?'

Simon said, 'Aye.' He coughed. 'Is Dad round?'

'He's just away ten minutes ago.'

Forth nodded encouragingly at how things were going. He said, 'Aye. Was wondering if yous had any work going about here?'

'What's your experience?'

'Ah. Graft.' He held up his right arm and used his other hand to feel the biceps. 'I'm wanting on the fishing boats but I'm too young yet. So they keep saying.'

'Go in there and leave your details, son.' Strachan nodded at the Portakabin.

'Details?'

'Aye. Your details.'

'What's details?'

'Details. Name and address. Experience. Other employers.'

For the first time, Forth looked his age. He peered cautiously at the Portakabin door. 'Aww. Right.' Forth walked directly to the door and stepped inside without knocking on the side of the cabin, as was etiquette.

Strachan looked back at the three of them. 'That's school done for another year then?'

'Aye.'

'Magic, eh? I used to walk three mile to school but I used to bloody run it home.'

They all laughed. Simon went, 'Is there a wagon out Tulloch this afternoon?'

'Wullie might be taking the Leyland out Nine Mile House with a water tank but that'll no be before −' he looked at his watch − 'back of five. Was yous looking for a hurl?'

'Aye, but it's no bother. We'll get the bus or train from up the town.'

'That's a waste of good pocket money, when you could be getting a hurl.'

Simon glanced at the Portakabin door. 'Nah. It's no bother. Thanks, Billy.'

'Okay then, kiddies. Enjoy the holidays. We'll be seeing you here but, Simon. Won't we?'

'Oh aye.'

'Right yous are then.' Strachan walked away towards the maintenance workshop.

Simon turned. 'C'mon. And quick.' He flicked his head towards the gates and began running.

Galbraith fell in immediately behind but turned to Nikki and said, 'C'mon, C'mon. Horse it.'

She understood and, tucking the bag of fruit in against her chest, she also started to run.

The three of them raced across the scattering stone chips of the turning place, the sound of their feet changing on the muddied drive, dodging puddles as they swerved. Both boys turned to look at the girl running behind – keeping up – the scarf flapped right round and her hair swung from one side to the other.

At the metalled road they turned left and Z-bended on the single-track bridge up over and across the railway line. The sound of Simon's shoes slapped along the narrow road which ran parallel to the railway, where the rail tracks dropped down lower into the stone cutting then beneath the signal gantry and final bridge into the seaside terminus of the Port.

The road they were on led along the bottom of steep woods – the huge and wooded embankment of the television aerial hill to their left was too steep ever to have been built upon. At the second lamp post, Simon stopped running. Galbraith was ruddy-faced, following up. Nikki Caine was not that far behind but when she noted they had halted, she broke off into a fast walk and the lengths of her hair suddenly fell away out of sight, back behind her blazer.

Simon was breathing heavy but he said to Galbraith, 'Will we tell her?'

Galbraith leaned forwards, his palms spread on his thighs and he pecht, 'Fuck sake, man. I'm gasping here.'

'Will we tell her?' Simon nodded to the woods up the steep hill beside them.

'Oh, Crimmo. What if she goes and tells? Town boys and that.'

Simon lowered his voice. 'We could go up there. She might come, so's to get out of Forth's road.'

Nikki had almost caught up with them.

'Aye, all right then, but get her to swear on her bloody life.'

'Aye.'

Nikki Caine walked up to them and she laughed. 'He'll go mental. Did you hear it? "Doll, doll, doll." Thinks he's Elvis Presley; a right he-man. Aw my God, just imagine having to kiss the likes of him.' She lifted her shoulders as if her spine tingled. 'You would just all sick up.' She looked at Simon. 'I think you were dead brave. You don't want him working for your father. He'd just pinch and pinch.'

'Nikki, if we told you something will you promise not to go and clipe?'

She changed expression. 'What?'

'We're going to show you something. A secret but you've no to tell another soul. Especially no boys.'

She frowned but then her voice became lighter. 'What? What is it?'

'C'mon.' Simon looked both ways for any traffic, turned so the railway line was to his back then he launched himself across the narrow road at the steep verge, up a low grassy bank into where the treeline began.

'Where are you going?'

'Shush. Don't shout. Forth'll just be coming.'

'Eh?'

Galbraith clambered up into the verge weeds below Simon and called, 'C'mon. Don't be a feart scaredy.'

'In up there?'

'Aye.'

'What? To hide from Forth? He'll probably go back down the blaise into town.'

From the edge of the trees, Simon spoke down to her. 'He won't. He'll look all across the blaise and see in a jiffy we're no there and he'll know fine we's come up this way. I'm telling you, we need to scarper. Make ourselves scarce.'

'Up in there? I can't. There's stinging nettles and brambles and all stuff. Bracken has got ticks in it. I've got −' she looked down; her school kilt was worn quite above her knees − 'bare legs. I'll be scratched to bits. And my shoes.'

'You'll be grand. Galbraith'll give you his breeks.'

Nikki Caine suddenly laughed.

Galbraith turned on Simon, actually serious. 'No I'll no.'

Simon and Nikki Caine laughed.

'C'mon. We've something to show you.'

'Galbraith in his Y-fronts. No thanks.'

Galbraith took on a brasser.

'Come on, Nikki. Forth'll be coming. Please.' Simon held out his hand. Nikki Caine looked both ways up and down the road. 'What if a car comes and folk see me going up in there with yous two. It'll be all round the town. I was, y'know? Up woods with yous. And what if we meet the Prowler.'

Galbraith went, 'Ach, the Prowler isnie real. Only primary kids believe in the Prowler.'

She frowned. 'He's been seen. Up the Woods by the Witches.'

'This is no the Woods. It's just a brae.'

Nobody spoke then Nikki tutted and went, 'Och,' and stepped towards the verge. Awful slowly, she picked her way into the initial weeds; turning her leg sideways she got her wee-heeled shoe in for a grip then climbed up one step, trying to balance.

Galbraith swung his sports bag round and says, 'Here, slowcoach. Give us yon.'

Nikki Caine stood and reached up with the fruit to Galbraith who unzipped his school bag and roughly shoved the brown paper in through the zip so you heard the topmost fruit tumbling out loosely within.

Now Nikki Caine was a bit more mobile she let herself lean over, both her hands going into the short undergrowth for support. Her long blonde hair fell forward again but she more easily pulled herself to the next level, so her face was at Galbraith's knees. Simon turned and disappeared in among the flouncy wigs of silver-stemmed birch twigs. When she looked up, Simon had completely vanished behind the leaves. Galbraith reach out his hand to her. 'Here.'

'Get lost, Galbraith,' she told him savagely, but at the same time she balanced on the bank, unknotted her scarf and threw one end up to him while holding the other with both hands. Galbraith grabbed the scarf and went, 'Heave-ho,' bracing his stance and pulling. Nikki's legs stepped quickly up the bank with the momentum.

Galbraith turned and led her through the saplings.

By the time Nikki Caine had made it up through the initial thinner tree trunks on the level ground, Simon and Galbraith stood still at the very bottom of the steep slope, looking upward as if trying to solve a logical problem.

It was a very extreme gradient above them, with small rock faces of moss barring some possible ascent routes. The banking was completely wooded – younger birches, then, as you looked upwards, great and older sycamores and huge beeches, some hundreds of years mature and the wide summer spread of the leaf canopy above them. The acoustics had suddenly closed in intimately about them.

'Where are we going?' she whispered.

'Up there.'

'Yous're mental. I can't climb that.'

'I'll pull you up on your scarf. I just pulled her up with her scarf, Crimmo. Like mountaineers.'

'Forth might spy us out down here. We need to hide – get on up high there, and besides, something we want to show you, at the top.'

'Is it badgers? Foxes? Foxes bite, Simon. Is it baby hedgehogs? They've got all fleas. Mr Garrison in Biology says.'

Galbraith breathed out. 'Dinna be daft.'

Simon led the way upward, showing how to move, weaving to the right and to the left – not straight ahead – getting footholds in root declinations, leaning forward letting your hands get grips when you needed to almost crawl.

Nikki Caine tutted loudly in a way which was becoming familiar to them but she followed behind Galbraith.

The three of them climbed slowly in silence until Simon got onto a slightly flat area in behind a huge beech. He waited there, put a hand down and got Galbraith's arm to haul him up. When Nikki Caine was beneath him he put out his arm. He did not take her hand though she herself suggested this to him, by daintily trembling her fingers up and down. He shoved his hand past her fingers and took hold of her arm on the blazer sleeve just below her elbow. He felt how thin and delicate her arm seemed, and after three goes to seize her firmly, he suddenly pulled her up to their level. She dropped her head, breathing in front of them. They stood here, gasping with a combination of exertion and excitement.

'Where are we *bloody* going to?' she asked and used her fingers to move hair back behind her ears.

Simon smiled upward. 'There's something there.'

She looked at them both suspiciously. 'See, if yous are jesting me or trying something on, I'll tell my dad, I will.'

'We're no trying anything on. Just wait and see.'

'I'll wait and see but –'

'Uh. Shut it.' Galbraith held up his hand so they followed his gaze, staring back down the sector of slope they had already covered. Through the chromatic shifting of leaves, the branches layering at differing levels because of the degree of ascent, they could still make out hazy areas of the grey road surface. Showing between the green leaves, slowly moved a patch of black. A dark figure crossed there.

'Shush. Told you so,' Simon whispered, looking at Nikki.

Forth was moving along that road beneath them – his already familiar figure and the black shoulders of his jean jacket briefly visible as he slouched across a bare space between the larger leaves of a sycamore and the smaller leaves of a birch. He was smoking. Galbraith flattened himself against the tree trunk and Nikki suddenly stooped down, so her knees pointed upward and the skirt showed a lot of her lower thighs. But all their eyes were trained downward. They remained like that without moving or talking for a long time, hearing each other's breathing slow down and soon fall silent. They heard the light breeze move the leaves high above them. Still Nikki Caine crouched – as she must when she had a pee, Simon imagined.

Then this hushed arcadia was disturbed by some strange rumble so they all frowned and looked at each other. A metallic screech. Soon, well below them and beyond the road, they saw the bright-blue-painted roof of a diesel locomotive appear under the bridge which they had crossed. They could hear the engine and exhaust slit idling, the low whoosh of the radiator fan which – through intervals in the leaves – they witnessed revolving in its wide circular grille. Grey tank wagons followed, one after another, each the same shape with glossily soiled, oily flanks repeating themselves.

'A goods,' Galbraith whispered knowledgeably.

Simon nodded. The screeching sounds of the heavy wagons diminished, growing deeper in along the stone cutting, finally becoming inaudible as the train slowed further and went away under the signals and road bridge then into the spread of the station terminus and goods sidings by the pier which distributed the train's sounds out across the bay.

Simon whispered, 'Come on.'

Without complaint now, Nikki Caine followed them upward. She noticed that Galbraith had the golden roundel of a drawing pin lodged in his shoe heel.

They climbed through the layered humus of the previous winter, grabbing out for tree trunks and branches to assist. Twice more, Galbraith hauled Nikki upward on her scarf. 'It's like Mount Everest.

I'm fucking Sherpa Tenzing. He couldn't of done it without him,' Galbraith called.

'Shush.'

Simon began to lead them across the banking rather than up it, to control their direction. Galbraith and Simon both continuously peered higher, seeking for somewhere specific. Just before they had angled back into the climb, Nikki Caine lost her footing and she fell flat in front of herself with a masculine grunt. The slope was so steep she did not actually fall far forward but they had heard the breath come out of her. Galbraith moved down to her gallantly, sending loose a rush of old leaves and twigs. She just lay there, her fists dug into the sloping ground around her.

'Are you all right?'

'Just great. Thanks.'

Galbraith held out his hand and this time she took it. He assisted her to stand upright then he said, 'You go up first. Then if you fall, I can stop you sliding all the bloody way back.'

'Aye. Okay then.' She brushed herself down. 'But you keep your eyes to yourself.'

Simon couldn't reach the scene below so he just nodded and pointed upward.

As they all climbed higher, Simon moved deliberately slow, so Nikki Caine caught him up. With a flat palm on a tree trunk, he reached down. This time he took the girl's hand and she allowed him to pull her up and beside him.

'You lead,' he said.

'Nut.'

'I'll tell you what way to go.'

'No ways.' She sounded angry, then privately whispered, 'Galbraith can see right up my skirt.'

Galbraith heard her though. 'No I can't,' his voice protested from where he was paused further down the brae.

'Is this much further? Look at my hands.' She shoved them up. There were little tracks of wet mud which gathered on her palm lines in a sort of pattern. 'And my shoes. They're my big sister's. She'll kill yous if she ever finds out.'

Simon and Galbraith exchanged a meaningful glance.

'We can clean them.'

'Aye – how?'

'We've got everything. Go on.'

She sighed but draped her scarf round her neck, flicking her hair up over it, leaning a bit as she moved to wipe at her soiled knees. Then she moved onward. When Simon looked down, Galbraith nodded and smiled.

Sure enough, as they climbed higher still, Simon could sometimes see a good bit up Nikki Caine's skirt. Just the back of an upper leg white as a seagull, the muscles and tendons drawn out, long and agile, as she scrambled. But then as she breached the last gradient onto the level, she went too far forward and came the shadowy cast of her pale underwear up beneath. Simon felt his stomach react. When the swift view ended he turned, but Galbraith was concentrating furiously, glaring angrily at the ground before him, his arms out and fingers in clods of grass, tugging himself up.

Simon came onto the level where Nikki stood. There was something different about the terrain there; just beyond one of the largest trees, the ground had been scuffled bare to the polished roots then, beyond the tree, the slope fell away steeply, layered thick with fallen brown leaves. It was so steep there it would have been impossible to descend without tumbling down. Nikki held onto a tree branch, 'Oh God, what a height. This is just scary now, Simon.'

'It's okay. Just go in past this tree a wee bit.'

She shook her head and carefully moved round the trunk. Suddenly she spotted the path. 'Oh.' She took two steps ahead onto it.

Immediately to the girl's left, a very thick four-inch tow rope hung from one of the powerful and sturdy boughs of the ancient beech above them. The rope dangled down vertically alongside the trunk; the deeply fissured bark of the tree was patched in matted green moss. At the end of the rope a horizontal iron bar had been inserted through it and lashed secure with thinner coloured cords of synthetic twine.

Breathing deep, Simon said, 'It's Galbraith and me's swing. We built it. You go right out there on it. Feels like you're flying through space. We used one of my old man's tow ropes from the lorries, though I think he nicked them off the pier one night.' He pointed above. 'I climbed up there and right out to saw off the end bit and all the wee-er branches, to loop the noose in. If I'd fallen, I'd have been dead for sure, I'm telling you. Eh, Galbraith?'

Galbraith was leaning on the trunk next to him. Not looking at them, just taking in and then exhaling huge breaths. 'Aye. He would of for sure, man. He'd have split his head open down there. He got the rope up though; nerves of steel, Crimmo, yah bass, I'll say that. It's strong as fuck our swing and the best anywhere going.'

Nikki Caine nodded thoughtfully – in an unusually masculine acknowledgement of the achievements here.

'C'mon.'

They followed Simon along the worn pathway on the level which was blissfully easy-going after the ascent. They had to duck right down under a screen of some overreaching branches at the end of the path.

Nikki Caine stooped, one hand on her skull to stop her fine hair from snagging on thorn-bush twigs, then she stood up straight.

Before her was a large level rock – naturally part of the escarpment but projecting outward – the moss worn off the top. The first thing she noted was the charming domestic detail of furniture: two chairs and a table. One seat was of the fold-out picnic variety, but the other was a wooden dining chair. And the tabletop itself was strewn with small puddles of bright rainwater, twigs and leaves. The table was square wood with shaped legs, though the varnish had long peeled and fallen away from much of it.

One area of the rock was sheltered by a large green tarpaulin, the upper half of which had been lashed to the trees above and it descended at an angle for the rain to run off. The lower section was tethered and stretched taut to some birch saplings which sprouted from the very lip of the rock edge itself.

To the right was a natural, low-roofed cave which went in only a short distance before the stone ceiling canted steeply down. The girl bent over slightly to look inward – you could see twisted tree roots had grown down through cracks in the stone from above and the roots had multiplied upon themselves in solid whirls and knots whereby the trunks above gained their solid purchase. Lots of poly bags were stored in there, weighed down by small stones. Now Nikki Caine stepped to the drop

35

and very cautiously stretched her upper body forward to peer over the edge of the great rock. 'Oh my God. The height, Simon.'

Formally, Simon said, 'Nikki, welcome to Meditation Rock. Our headquarters.'

She laughed and smiled and shook her head all at once. 'My God. You two really are crazy but this is kind of brilliant.'

'Meditation's when you sort of sit and think about stuff. I read it in a book about a guy in the Himalayas pondering the impossibles.'

She looked at him, sizing him up.

'Me and Crimmo are going climbing in the Himalayas one day. Aren't we's? Do you know Hillary and Tenzing conquered Mount Everest, Nikki? Donkey's ago. Twenty-nine thousand feet. That's fucking millions higher than this.'

Nikki Caine ignored him and murmured, 'You've got good vocabulary in English on you, Simon. Mrs Peters said so.' She meandered around. 'Oh gosh, though, yous two. Look at all this. Yous are strange ones.' But she was smiling.

'It's fucking magic up here, eh?' Galbraith, because of the restricted space, had to remain at the edge of the flat rock area, observing them. 'Don't tell anyone, but a few times we've jinked off the school and come up here.'

Nikki opened her mouth wide and looked at Simon. 'Have yous?'

'Just once, Galbraith.'

'Twice.'

'We just got off PE early that time, man, that wasn't proper jinking.'

'Aye, but one time, Nikki, when we were building all this, we went deliberate late to registration then we jinked out separate to come here and work on everything. We rendezvoused. How about that for fucking vocabulary? We was lucky we didn't get caught.'

'Smoking and jinking; yous are as bad as Forth.'

Simon tipped up the wooden chair and used his palm to brush the seat clear of twigs and damp leaves. 'Please, do take a seat.' He said it in a mock-polite voice.

Nikki smiled nervously. 'Is this rock fixed proper? Could it no just fall off?'

'Only if Galbraith farts one of his massive rifters.'

They all laughed.

Nikki Caine crossed to the other side of the table but using the inner route, away from the rock's edge, and there she did indeed sit down.

Galbraith flopped into the picnic seat but then he immediately leapt up again. 'Och, it's soaking. Oh, my breeks, man.' When he turned to study the picnic seat he had a glossy wet patch on the bum of his black trousers and the other two laughed.

'He always does that,' Simon said. 'Every time.'

Galbraith tipped the picnic chair forward but his trousers had absorbed all of the rainwater.

Simon ducked into the cave and he removed one of the poly carrier bags from Low's supermarket, unknotting the top. 'Want some juice, Nikki?'

'It's Garvie's American Cream Soda,' Galbraith specified. He sat back down with a troubled face. As he did so, Simon noted the seated girl immediately using the side of her hand to karate-chop the fabric of her skirt between her thighs and she shut her bare legs tightly then looked out through the leaves. 'You can see right to the castle way past the cathedral,' she pointed.

'Aye. You see it all from up here. We're gonna get a telescope, to spy in bedrooms, aren't we, Crimmo?'

Sharply, Nikki Caine huffed, 'Yous pair of randy so-and sos.'

'You were meant to be getting it for Christmas, Galbraith.'

'Aye, well, I didn't, did ah? We can't all have dads that have got big huge houses, Crimmons.' Galbraith watched Nikki Caine as she looked out towards the view. 'You can't tell anyone, Caine. This is our secret. Just the threes of us. You're the only other person else ever who's knowed. No other boys know. We've never telt.'

'Aye. I won't tell. But don't yous tell anyone I come up here with just the two of yous. Right? It would be all round town.'

'Galbraith, this has been opened. Thought we left one full bottle?' Simon hoisted the bottle of cream soda.

'Oh aye. Right enough. Last time we were up. I was fucking gasping, man, so I had a wee sip.'

'Fuck sake, Galbraith. It's half empty. It'll have gone all flat now.

You're aye gobbling everything that's took up here for yourself and we went halfers on this.'

'Well, there's fucking half left for you.'

Simon twisted the top and, sure enough, there was no report of carbonation. He thrust the bottle out to Nikki. 'Sorry. It's a bit gone flat and we've no cups.'

'No thanks. I'll just get my breath back.'

'Here.' Galbraith reached out a hand and Simon gave the bottle over to him. Galbraith took long and continued gulps from the bottle then slapped his lips aside. 'That's no bad at all.' He handed it back.

Simon took a swig and immediately moved his mouth away from the bottle. 'Yeauch. That's just flat as a pancake.'

'You can taste it just fine.'

'Och, that is minging. Bogging.'

Nikki Caine said, 'Good. I'm no drinking out a bottle after yous two have spat your slobbers in it.'

Simon felt childishly stung by that.

Nikki Caine sat idly, hands folded in her lap, looking out over the view between the leaves, ducking and adjusting her head a little, in relation to the slow swaying of the branches, to catch the differing panoramas of the town that were now revealed below and across from her.

She could not quite see the railway terminus and pier of the ferry terminal because of the angle, but she had a clear vantage across most of the Port: its differing roofs and its jumbled spires placed awkwardly on the hills and ramparts. She could see the walls of the never-completed Hydropathic & Sanitorium Hotel and the cable-car house, on the top of the long escarpment above the south of town – its overgrowth and whin bushes. And further round, on past the roofless, rounded and empty Victorian amphitheatre, were the massed villas and below was the glazed band of top bricks on the distillery chimney. Beyond the esplanade, the view gave over to the pine trees behind the Complex and the King's Way as far as the chimneys of the council tenements behind. 'Wow-weeoww. The town looks all different from way up here. You can see the roofs of my bit.' She pointed, excited at the Brae Estate roofs.

The water of the town bay, sparking on the brightness, showed like an excited energy through the very edges of the further trees. The emerald green of Shelter Island could be identified if you settled your eye on one spot before moving your gaze onward.

'This is pretty amazing,' Nikki whispered, seemingly to herself.

Galbraith pointed to the table. 'Know how we got the table up?'

'How?'

'A long rope. We did it in wintertime and that; then there's not so much brambles and stuff to catch on it. Carried it up from Crimmo's garage, chucked a rope over the branch of the big swing tree and Crimmo hauled while I climbed with it, shoving and making sure it didn't get caught.'

'You didn't do much shoving, Galbraith. I was pissing sweat.'

Galbraith went on. 'We don't come up much in winter and that. I mean, there's the weather and stuff, so we have to take the roof there down, in case the gales just rip it off; but mainly cause with there being no camouflage – leaves and that – we don't want it to get seen by town boys. Eh, Crimmo? If we got spotted by town boys they'd all come up in a huge gang. Maybe fifty of the bampots. They'd fucking wreck the place. Cut down the swing. They'd probably chuck us off the cliff if it was psychos like Forth. Kill us, man; they'd be so angry us village boys had a den in their place. Cause that's what this is: it's a den; a secret hut! I mean, we'd hold them off as long as we could. Chuck stuff down on the gadges. We've got the ammunition store over there if we're attacked. Logs and old branches and that. Not to kill them; just scare the bastards. They'd soon retreat if we sent a big mossy log rolling down that hill. Like in the film? Eh, Crimmo? Fucking *Hannibal Brooks*. Brilliant film. This is our place and we're protecting it. That's why you cannie ever, ever tell anyone. If you've a brother or that.'

'God sake. Shut up, Galbraith. I've got no brothers, thank God, if they're anything like you. I'm no telling anyone about your daft hut.'

'You've a big sister. I know that all right.'

'Aye, so? What?'

'Do you swear on your life no to tell about this place.' Galbraith leaned forward, quite seriously.

'Aye. I said.'

Galbraith thought for a moment. 'And once town boys found

out they'd no take long to suss that they can just come at us from behind, up the road to the television aerial.'

Nikki Caine frowned. 'Eh?'

'Just up there is the top. It's easy to get here from up the road to the aerial.'

In an incredulous, outraged voice she asked, 'Yous made me climb up all that and we could of walked round a back way?'

Galbraith paused. 'Aye. But. We was escaping from Forth and that. We got caught once coming up with the chair you're on, by the sort of workmen doing something to the aerial, and they fair sent us scampering, man. But you can spy if anyone's about and leave back down that way. You won't need to go all down the cliff again. We'll take you down the back road by the aerial, Nikki.'

'Oh, thanks a lot. Now you go and tell me.'

In a weak voice, Galbraith asked, 'You get STV up the Brae, don't you?'

'Course.'

'We don't.'

'You don't?'

'Nut. Not out in the villages. We only get BBC1. Unless you live up on the hill, Crimmo, eh?'

'That's right.'

'You don't get STV out in your village?' She looked both wry and pitiful. 'That's just rubbishy.'

'Aye. Only higher-up houses on hills get it in our village. Don't they, eh?'

'Away up and give the television aerial a good kick then, Galbraith,' Simon said.

Nikki Caine laughed quite loudly.

Galbraith had a sour look. 'It means we miss all them horror films. Draculas and that. They're always on STV at nights, aren't they? The horrors; the Draculas?' Galbraith mused to himself, shaking his head. 'I'd love to have seen some of them Draculas.' He coughed, then he said, 'What flavour crisps you got there?'

'Cheese and Onion, Salt and Vinegar and Plain,' Simon stated.

'Give us Cheese and Onion. Plain, man. Why is Plain? Why is there Plain potato crisps. It's a waste of time. Plain. No point.'

'Ready Salted they're called. Not plain,' Nikki sighed. 'How can you eat with those hands, Galbraith? That's minky. I'll need a bath after all this. It's like cross-country in bloody PE is this.'

Simon, standing at the wee cave mouth, tossed the crisps over to Galbraith.

'I've got this cloth thing here too, Nikki. You can wipe your hands a bit and clean off your shoes.'

'Oh, thanks, Simon. That would be good.'

Simon fished among other sealed poly bags but he ground his teeth as he came upon the well-thumbed *Forum* magazine Galbraith had lifted out of Menzies. He turned slightly aside to conceal it. He found the yellow polishing cloth intended for the fabled telescope. He chucked the cloth across to Nikki and she began to wipe her hands. She even leaned and spat a little, repeatedly, on her fingertips, then smeared it into her bare knees, trying to get the mud off with the cloth. She was leaning forward so her face was out of sight of them both as she moved on to cleaning round the sides of her black leather shoes with the buckle and small heel, folding her legs upward.

Galbraith crunched away on his crisps and winked at Simon. 'I wiped my arsehole on that cloth after a big shite.'

Her voice went wearily, 'Aye, Galbraith.'

'What about that Forth, eh?' Galbraith looked around.

Nikki's voice came from under the table. 'Aye. What a grot. What a grotty, grotty guy. He's dangerous. They say he was caught with a knife on him once.' She raised her head up, the face slightly flushed. 'You should tell your dad, Simon. He'll pinch stuff. He's a pincher.'

'Aye. I don't think there's jobs going anyways. Course I'm going to be working there; if I want. I'm going to learn to drive lorries. Get my HGV.'

Galbraith guffawed. 'You've gotta get your driving licence first, wee Crimmo. You cannie do that till you're seventeen and you're just a wee bairn yet. Nikki?'

'Shut up, Galbraith.'

'Do you know that Crimmo's still fifteen, till August?'

She looked up at Simon, actually interested.

'He's a wee bairn. We're sixteen, man. We can get married. But you can't, Crimmo. We can get mairrit. Can't we, Nikki?'

'Not to each other, Galbraith. That's for sure.'

Galbraith went on. 'Forth is mental. He's one of the hardest in the town. Big Davie told me that. Aye. Did you see Forth trying to be asking you to the pictures, Nikki? Were you thinking of going with him?'

'Och, just get lost.'

'Jimmy Lamming is the hardest in this town,' Simon said.

'Aye, but he's twenty-one or something. I reckon Forth could give him a run for his money. That would be some fight, man. Last ages. Did you see him mooch a fag off me and he already had one? Sleekit bastard.' Galbraith dropped his voice and even looked around. 'He's a tink. Right, I'm going for a swing. Coming?'

'Nah.'

'Eh? What? Are you just goan sit here? I'm goan on the swing, man.'

'On you go.'

'Aye, on you go.'

'Don't fall off,' said Simon.

'I don't mind if you do,' Nikki smiled.

Galbraith stood and slouched away under the twigs. Simon looked at Nikki and she shook her head then said, 'He's a pain.'

'Aye. Worse than my wee brother.'

'What do you hang round with him all the time for then?'

'We only "hang around" on the swing.'

She smiled. 'Ha ha. What age is your wee brother now?'

'Nine or something. Worse luck.' Simon wiped at the picnic seat and sat down.

On the other side of the foliage they both heard the creak of the rope which increased in rhythm then remained at a steady rate. Just beyond it, if you listened, you could hear the clanking of that train, moving down at the railway terminus.

'You can see him swinging like a monkey; the dafty,' Nikki Caine tutted.

There was a silence. Simon – suddenly alone with a girl at last – didn't know what to say. 'Sorry about that Forth.'

'It's not your fault.'

'Aye, but I was thinking. I should just have gave him the office telephone number and sent him packing. I went and forgot.' He shrugged.

'Oh aye.'

'Ach well.'

Nikki looked out to the view and uttered the words, 'I'll need to be going soon.'

He nodded. 'Eh, Nikki?'

'Aye?' she said quickly.

'Nothing.'

'What? What?'

'Nothing.'

She asked, 'Are you really leaving school?'

'Dunno.'

'What O grades did you do again?'

'English, maths, geography, history and biology.'

'That's loads.'

'But you're doing six.'

'Yes.'

'And you'll get As and Bs.'

'You might. In English you will.'

'Oh naw. I want to work with the old man anyway.'

'Simon?'

'Aye?'

'How come you never went to End-of-Year Dance?'

He shrugged his shoulders.

'I was sort of. Looking for you.'

'Ah.' Simon turned his head.

'What is it?' Nikki whispered, the voice afraid-sounding.

Simon canted round in the seat. 'Galbraith's stopped swinging.'

'Oh. Already?'

'Oh, nut,' he said cheerily. 'He's started again.' He paused. 'Look.'

'Aye?'

Simon announced, 'Maybe I'll see you during the summer?' He found himself pause and he quickly added, 'I'll come in the Scotch Wool Hosiery when you're working?'

'Don't.' She must have seen how his face changed. She added blankly, 'Just my auntie is always there. She's dead strict.'

'Oh. Aye. Right enough. Well. I don't know then. Yes I do. I'll write you a letter.'

She made an amused, exhaling sound. 'A letter?'

'Aye. "Nikki Caine. The Scotch Wool Hosiery. Dear Nikki. How are all the balls of wool?"'

She laughed.

Simon said, 'Aye, well.'

'I'm sure we'll see each other round the town and that,' she stated realistically.

It was the immoderate beginning of things not being enough for Simon. 'Aye.'

She looked down at her legs. 'Do you think other people can see it?' She bent over and rubbed at them; there were tinted veins of yellowness in the shallow patterns of skin on her bare knees.

'Naw, naw. Say you got a bit of suntan on your knees. Great knees, Nikki,' he caught himself stating.

She laughed. 'Oh thanks,' frowned but then chuckled.

He could feel blood pumping in at the back of his throat. 'Nikki, would you like to go out one night? Or afternoon? Or morning?'

She looked at him, not smiling, 'Aye, okay then.'

'Aye?'

'Aye, if you want.'

He smiled. 'Oh, right. Aye, okay then. Eh. How'll I see you?'

She shook her head sternly. 'Simon. Do you not have a telephone and the telephone book out in the villages as well as no proper telly? Just phone us. We're in the book. We're the only Caines on Brae Drive.' She laughed. 'You villagey boys.'

'Aww. Right. You mean just telephone?'

'Aye!'

'What if I get your old man? I mean your dad.'

'Leave a message.'

'Leave a message?'

It suddenly struck him that boys must often telephone Nikki Caine. 'Right. I'll telephone.'

'Okay then.' She spoke with a patient tolerance.

'I'll phone,' he repeated aloud but it was only to himself.

Suddenly they both heard Galbraith crashing back along the path towards them.

'That was brill. Hey, fancy a smoke, Crimmo?'

'You weren't long on the swing.'

44

'Rope's still sodden wet.'

'Do *you* smoke, Simon?' Nikki Caine narrowed her eyes.

'Naw.'

'He does so.'

'Take the odd wee puff but I don't like it. You cough like hell.'

'You don't do it proper, man.' Galbraith took out the packet of cigarettes and a box of Swan Vesta matches which he shook. The other two watched him place a cigarette loosely in his mouth and open the box of matches. 'One night we was up here so late we had candles burning, didn't we, Crimmo?' His voice was softened by keeping the cigarette in his lips.

Nikki stated, 'You can get chucked out school if you're caught carrying cigarettes.'

'We're not in school. Or haven't you noticed? Want one?'

'Me? Nah,' Nikki shrugged.

'Are you scared? Again?'

'I'm not scared. It's a dirty habit.'

'That's where you're wrong. Gets germs out you. It stops you getting colds.'

'That's just rubbish. Mr Garrison in Biology says it kills you.'

Galbraith shook his head solemnly and sighed. 'That poor Mr Garrison. He knows nothing.'

Simon laughed and, oddly, Nikki spluttered out and shook her head. 'God sake, Galbraith, you're a dummy.'

'Have a puff?'

'Nut.'

'Just a wee puff.'

'Nut.'

'Will one wee puff kill you? No. Or I'd of been deid yonks ago.'

'Smoke more then, Galbraith.'

Simon laughed.

Galbraith tried to light a match twice and eventually on the third attempt it erupted and he lit his cigarette. He showed off, standing stiffly, taking a big drag and blowing out smoke.

Simon said, 'Galbraith, I dare you to smoke while going on the swing.'

'Aye,' said Nikki. 'That way we might kill you off two ways at the same time.'

Galbraith said, 'Och, there's no need to be so nasty after me helping you up that hill.'

Nikki Caine did seem a bit chastened and she gazed out at the view. She mumbled, 'Look. We're even above the seagulls.' Then she said, 'Go on. Give us a quick wee puff then.'

Simon turned his head, amazed, as Nikki stood and reached across the table. Galbraith passed her his lit cigarette. 'Thought you says it was just a dirty habit. Do you have other dirty habits, Nikki?'

'F-off. And I'm not smoking one with your gobbers on it. Give us a new one.'

'Oh.' Galbraith did not appreciate this development but he had to go along with his challenge, so he sacrificed another cigarette from the packet and passed it to her with the matches.

They watched as Nikki Caine put the cigarette in her small lips and fiddled with the matches. Her match struck first go and she gave Galbraith a triumphant look then raised the flame to the cigarette tip. She shook the match out, placed it daintily on the table, then removed the cigarette with one of her mud-streaked hands and blew smoke out her lips. She studied the cigarette burning. It did not look like the first time Nikki Caine had smoked. 'Big deal,' she said.

When Simon had noted her place the spent match, in a straight line on the table before her, he had mused that her bedroom must be very tidy.

'You've got to inhale, Nikki. Kill the germs. Kill the Germans. The mighty *Wermacht*.' Galbraith made a strident military salute, associated with the Second World War.

'What are you on about, Galbraith?'

Boldly, Simon said, 'Give us a drag,' and he stood up, relinquishing the picnic seat which Galbraith immediately dodged down into.

Simon crossed and crouched beside the girl.

Nikki Caine had adjusted her pose to undertake the smoking. She had leaned back in the chair and crossed one leg over the other, her head held far backwards so the hair returned to life again, moving and languishing down her blazer in all different and golden ways. She took another drag and held smoke within her mouth then slowly passed smoke outward, round her small teeth, and she didn't cough. Simon crouched right there close to an actual bare leg as she rested an arm on the chair. Carefully, the girl's fingers passed the cigarette down to Simon. He moved his hands quicker, taking a rapid drag then blowing out. He passed the cigarette straight back up to her and she received it into her hand. She met Simon's gaze as she very slowly placed the Regal back into her lips. They saw her cheeks change shape as she sucked in and then slowly blew out a long line of grey smoke puckering her mouth. One, two, three perfect smoke rings came out.

Galbraith frowned, outraged. 'Have you never smoked before?'

'Nut. But I watch my sister doing it.' She was still looking down at Simon beside her and she said to his face, 'I have to be going now.'

There was a silence.

Galbraith asked, 'Now? How come? We only just got here.'

'Just do.'

'We've only been out the school an hour, man. Hey, Crimmo. Isn't there a train to Tulloch Ferry round about half five? Let's get the train home for a change, man.'

'The train? It costs more than the bus. Forty-five pence or something.'

'Aye, but it'd be good.'

In a quiet voice, Simon said, 'What do you feel like doing, Nikki?'

'Mum's at work but I need to be home five-ish.'

'That's hours. It seems later than it is cause we's've got off early.'

'I'll get yous up the town a bit if yous are going now. But down the aerial way, no down that bloody cliff.'

'Aye. Okay then,' Simon said quickly.

'What about all your fruits things?' Galbraith leaned over and grabbed his Adidas school bag up into his lap.

'Och, yous can keep them if yous want.'

'Oh. So are they all mine now?'

Nikki shrugged. 'What did you bring a school bag in today for, Galbraith? For nicking more dirty magazines out the shop, was it? It's last day at school; there was no way we were going to do any work.'

Galbraith had started to go all red but shouted, 'Well, you should be glad I brought it to carry all your fruit things.' He reached in and took out a peach. He pondered it a moment, turning it in his hand before his face. 'Yous'd get the skitters if you ate all these.'

'Galbraith,' she said.

Galbraith immediately tossed the peach over the edge of the cliff. Nikki took in a swift breath but they all listened and heard the dainty swish as it slashed through some leaves then the soft plump as it hit far below.

Simon laughed. Galbraith took out an apple and he stepped up to the edge and threw it out further. The fruit curved then sped down through the leaves and burst onto the slope far below; a scattering of leaves were rustled up. Nikki laughed and she stubbed out her cigarette carefully on the tabletop. Suddenly she stood, bent over and reached into Galbraith's bag and took two fruits out. She passed one to Simon. 'See who can get them furthest.'

The three of them stood on the cliff edge, casting out one fruit after another into the sunny sky, laughing as Mrs Robb's apples and peaches raced out and arched down through the canopies, bursting and rolling invisible below, throwing out more and more quicker and quicker in a barrage, the three of them fumbling together into the bag to seize the prizes until there were none left and the woods fell silent again.

The two lads stood on the railway platform of the unmanned station at Tulloch Ferry and watched as the passenger-train coaches slowly gained some speed past them. At the back, the guard, who had pretended to pierce Galbraith's earlobe with his ticket punch back at the barrier in the Port station, stood in an open door which swung inwards. He smiled and raised a hand. Galbraith pulled back his hair and tugged out his ear towards the man as he swished by.

They watched the back of the train. A red lamp lit even in daytime hung at the rear. They observed the train passing by the oil depot then down the descent towards the level crossing until its blue-and-cream coaches were gone from sight on the distant curve.

Tulloch Ferry station was up the back of the village hotel, beside the oil depot. The old dead island platform for the closed branch was stranded opposite, with the track lifted on either side, the iron lattice footbridge dismantled; the platform was overgrown, its glazed earthenware plant pots lost among summer foxgloves and filled with weeds.

On the running platform was the main station building, boarded-up ticket office and the waiting rooms which once had coal fires burning every morning when Simon was a small boy; the long thin glass panes of the canopy were stained brown and falling out, so rain would often flood down from the roof onto the platform and flow off the edging. There were no lights, and approaching the platform in black night, locals wishing to board or meeting people off the train frequently carried electric torches. You would see several, moving on the platform like weak signals of alarm. A poster time-table and bold black-and-white bill informed passengers it was another unmanned station and that tickets were to be purchased from the guard aboard the train.

They moved beneath the broken, rust-stained glass of the canopy and out, walking side by side from the decayed station building and on across the turning place before going down the side path by the metal fence.

'What're you doing tomorrow then?' Galbraith asked.

'I dunno. We've a whole summer, eh?'

'Is it okay if I come round?'

'Eh? Aye. If you want, aye. Well, maybe I'll be going in to town. Come the day after tomorrow?'

'Eh, aye, okay then.'

They were walking out from beneath the trees where they had caught the school bus from that morning. In front of the hotel, the paddocks and walls of Tulloch Villa were just across the road.

'Right. See ya, Crimmo. Ya bass.'

'Aye, see you.'

Galbraith hitched up his empty sports bag and was making away, along the main-road pavement, past the old petrol-pump shed. He was heading down the road for the turn on the far side of the hotel paddock, where the single-track road would take him up to the small estate of council houses on the back moor.

'Hey, Galbraith?'

'Aye?

'If something's doing, come round the morrow though. If the boys are going up the river or something?'

Galbraith raised a comradely arm in salute.

★ ★ ★

The ash-bucket men had emptied the bin and it sat on the pavement by the gate, its rubbery lid carelessly sitting on top. Simon lifted the corrugated-metal bin and held it up before him by both handles yet not allowing it to contact his school uniform. He walked down the tarmac, the two front lawns divided by the drive and herbaceous shrubs. The lawn verges were primly cut by Simon's mum.

Tulloch Villa sat on the loch side of the main road: a large, two-storey, Victorian dwelling with hardly a whisper of Gothic; its tall granite walls were pecked with mica, there were bevelled sandstone lintels and a carved heraldic shield on the porch exterior wall, there to chisel in the construction year of 1881. Yet it was never engraved and remained blank.

Above the windows of Simon's bedroom was a recessed roundel and then the stone soffits climbed steeply on either side of the roof's double pitch where, at the very top, the finial stonework decoratively formed into a vaguely Celtic clover shape – often wishfully mistaken for a Christian cross.

Along the sea loch shore were the large gardens. Eight-foot-high stone walls circled the boundaries of the paddocks, outbuildings and kitchen garden. Tall Japanese privet hedges divided off the actual loch shore and then the gardens' further inner sanctuaries. The tarmac drive encircled the main house and the hedged-in drying green.

To the rear of the property, a great sycamore tree stood halfway down the steep banking of lawn, stuttering the wide, sparky sea loch. Across the moss bogs of the far shore, the distant Ben itself was a dappled screen, visible through the coriaceous leaves.

As Simon carried the bin he looked up at his bedroom. Each sash window was about two inches open. His mum would've done that when she made the bed. The Jaguar was parked just along from the kitchen door and his mum's blue MG could be seen down in the garage where the double sliding doors were pulled half over. He put the ash bucket to the side of the steps.

His mum was wearing her Scholl's at the Aga, fiddling with the pressure-cooker weight.

In a robotic Dalek voice, Simon said, 'The-great-one-has-returned.'

'He has, has he? Where were you this time?'

His voice became normal. 'Me and Andy Galbraith got the half five train.' He walked up behind his mum and placed both his hands on her shoulders and he leaned to kiss her on her cheek.

'All done for another year then?'

'Thank God.'

'Wishing your life away.'

'Not my life. Just wishing school away. I'll be leaving.'

'No more of this or I'll get cross now.' She had on her worried voice. Simon's mum made a virtue of fretfulness – she considered it a real flaw in others who did not worry quite enough for her liking.

He took his hands off his mother's shoulders and spun round on the coloured tiles of the kitchen floor.

'Don't. You'll mark the floor. Your dad's in the garden.'

'Where's Jeff?'

'Upstairs, bored without you and pestering your dad.'

'Wee idiot.'

'Si.'

He halted at the directory underneath the telephone which was fixed onto the kitchen wall. He rifled through pages, making straight for the Cs.

'So what're you going to dedicate yourself to this summer? Basic housework?'

'I was thinking more a motorbike.'

'No way, mister. Tuck in your shirt. Och Si, it needs the Bendix.'

'Just a tiny wee fifty cc. You can't go fast on it, Mum.'

'Talk to your father.' She reached up to the cupboards. 'Now then.'

Caine K.M., 44 Brae Drive . . . 5598

Simon put down the phone directory and strode through the house in a lively gait. He passed through the living room to the corridor then put his head in the big blue room and saw one of his long-playing records leaning against the polished wood of the Dynatron music centre. He turned and shouted up the stairs: 'Jeff! Don't be touching my bloody records.'

'I was just looking at the pictures,' a small boy's voice immediately called. Simon knew from the acoustic that Jeff was sat on the very top stair.

'I'll break your fingers if you scratch one.' But the moment Simon said it, he realised how half-hearted it sounded, because his mood was so happy.

From all the way through in the kitchen, the pressure cooker had started to hiss but his mother still reprimanded, 'Si! No being wicked to Jeff.'

Meekly, his wee brother appeared at the blue-room doorway. ''Cause you've finished school can I play "Fire Brigade"?'

'What?'

'Can I play your "Fire Brigade" single? It's my favourite of them all.'

'I bet you've played it anyway today, while I was out.'

'Haven't.'

Suddenly Simon launched himself and his wee brother flinched badly, pulled his elbows up to protect his face, but Simon shoved his hands under Jeff's oxters and tickled him repeatedly all up and down both his sides. Wee Jeff screamed with laughter, bent back and wriggled as Simon cradled him then put his hands in under Jeff's arms and lifted him up to his own face level, disguising what was a hug as something else. 'Pah. You're getting really heavy.' He put his wee brother back down again.

'Can I then?'

'Aye. Away up to my bedroom and get it but don't be touching other stuff in there. The Move are brilliant. You know what the song's about, Jeff?'

'What?'

'It's about a classy girl burning down her school. You should listen to the words.'

'Okay.'

'That's my school burned down far as I'm concerned.'

'Has it? Honest?'

'Naw. I'm just joking. But I'm not going back again. Off you go upstairs and get the record but play it down here or you'll break my stylus. I'm just out to see Dad a wee minute then I'll come play with you.'

Simon walked back along the corridor and he turned the key in the outside door. The steps led down onto the drive and lawn on the loch side of the house. He looked around, walking towards the sycamore. He passed the hydrangeas with their vivid, medicinal scent.

His father had the big wheelbarrow at the end of the privet hedge in the bottom paddock. The barrow was full of small branches and twigs. His dad was wearing that ratty old overcoat with a greasy waterproof topping which was peeling off across large sections of the garment.

Simon gave a quick, World War II American-style salute with a loose hand.

His father looked at him and nodded, announced out loud, 'Here's His Lordship. That's you done with school this year then, Professor?'

'Yup.'

'See you've come dressed to help.'

'Are you wanting a hand right enough?'

His father chuckled and shook his head.

'Do you know a family called Forth, in the town?'

His father lifted up the rake; he lay it on the top of the debris in the barrow.

Simon said, 'They're kind of a gadgie lot. One's in my year; Bobby. He's a hard nut with a good build.'

'Was he bothering you?'

'He was asking about work the day.'

'He was, was he? There's no work.'

'Oh, right. I took him up the garage.'

'You took him up the garage? What did you do that for?'

'He just kinda followed me up there. Couldn't get rid of him.'

'You just watch who you're taking round there.'

'I know. I do, Dad.'

'I don't mind Andy and the fat laddie, but don't be taking every tearaway in school there. Next, some daft wee bugger'll be going underneath the back of a reversing wagon and I'll be up in court.'

'Billy saw him and I think just kinda asked him to leave his details, but I don't think the boy can hardly write his name.'

His father shook his head and looked down the paddock for

anything he'd missed. 'Last year was a good year for us. Even I was surprised. The bloody taxman was rubbing his hands but with the price of diesel and everything this'll be a quiet summer, son.'

'Will there no be new lorries this year?'

'There will not.'

'That's crap.'

'Don't use that language.'

'I was really wondering about leaving the school.'

'What's the point in leaving? You can't do anything with me until you're eighteen. You get some paper to your name, laddie, then we'll see.'

'I want to leave.'

'I know you do. But you won't.'

'You can apprentice me to Billy, in the shop? Mechanic.'

'You're welcome in the shop.'

'Aye, but no just for summer.'

'"Not."'

'Not just for summer. That's like playing. I mean for real. A real apprenticeship.'

'You go back to school for another year and you can get on the lorries when you're older.'

Simon looked around and tutted. 'Can I get a wee motorbike for my birthday then?'

'Give over, laddie.'

'Och, you always just say that. It would be daft waiting till Christmas, with ice on the roads.'

His father looked straight at him with a sort of admiration. 'God's strewth. You're a fly one. You stick to your books. Your face is always in some book anyway. You wouldn't think you'd want to leave any school.'

'That's books. Books isn't school.'

'Me and your mother had to leave school at fourteen.'

'I'm nearly sixteen.'

'We'll say no more about it today.'

'Och, Dad. Just a wee fifty cc. Please?'

'Take this barrow up to the midden but don't be getting your blazer torn on the thorns.'

'Och, Dad.'

'Anything happening at the garage?'

Simon paused for a moment then replied, 'Nothing. Willie was meant to be going out Nine Mile. Out *to* Nine Mile.'

'He did. I saw the wagon go by an hour ago. Did you not come out with him?'

'No. I came back on the train just now with Andy Galbraith.'

'The train?'

'Aye.' Simon felt in under the sleeve of his school shirt. It was sticky from the juice of Nikki's peach. He fitted himself in between the two handles and he lifted the big barrow – despite the bulk of twigs, it was very light and he began to wheel it ahead, along the sides of the tall hedge.

Behind him, his father shook his head and said, 'The bloody train. Giving money to the competition and then asking me for a job. You're a fly one right enough.'

Wednesday 4 April 1973

Each man's right hand was stained black with glossy wet muck. Elliot the Englishman had been wiping so hard at his own fingers using a hanky that he almost drew off his signet ring. He put the muddied handkerchief away and then extended his bizarrely large golfing umbrella.

Standing beside the Englishman at the far end of the long gravel pathway were the two Ians – big Ian Mhor and Wee Ian – alongside Lawless. Erchie Hannan was there too. All of them watched John Penalty's slow approach.

'Penalty's leg is no looking very good at all.'

'Eh?'

The noise as the rain hit the wide umbrella and the fine gravel around them made it difficult to hear.

'He's saying, John's leg's no looking good.'

'He'll be next at this rate.'

'Don't go saying that.'

'We're all thinking it.' Hannan wore a black mac gone all shiny; his clean hand moved his wet hair up into a conglomeration of spikes and loosed drops dribbled down over his eyebrows. He blinked then held out his other dirty hand into the rain. 'Saturated but it doesn't clean this off, does it?'

The Englishman said nothing.

The two Ians wore matching Harris tweed flat caps which seemed to absorb the rain without reaction, though the men's shoulders hunched as the large spots came down.

Hannan smiled at the Englishman. 'Now's the time for you to be thinking about your bloody wet and dry people.'

'Just so, Mr Hannan. It's a fact. There are the wet people and dry people in Scotland, and all you west coasters are dry people. It seems to bounce off you.'

Lawless didn't look at him. 'I've never telt you, Elliot. But here's the secret to keeping dry. I walk up to the engine *inside* the fucking carriages when it's raining. Ya don't need to be a genius, ya Sassenach diddy.'

'Oh.'

The other men all laughed.

'But you arrive on the engine dry even on the midnight freight, when we're way out in that yard.'

'He crawls underneath the wagons. Blind drunk out of a lock-in at the County.'

'We've heard your theory, Elliot. It goes well with our theory. That all Englishmen are daft. Mind him, boys, Percy Thrower here, stopping the midnight mail yon night in the cutting up the Tulloch Bank just so's he'd could lean out with his bloody secateurs and snip off yon bramble branch that was bothering him so much. A train driver coming to his shift with a pair o bloody secateurs.'

'English secateurs in Scotland's green garden. You'll be kept busy, man.'

The others all chuckled.

'Can you no tell yet us west coasters get born with a wee layer of wax on us – like a duck?'

'That's just all your Brylcreem, Lawless.'

'Fuck off.'

'The Jerry Lee Lewis look.'

'The wife likes it.'

'The wife gives you shampoo for Christmas but you keep fucking drinking it, ya cunt.'

'Despite your waterproofing, are you sure you don't want to share this? One of you?'

'That's the kind of brolly they issue at Toton Depot, is it?' Hannan licked his tongue around his wet lips.

Big Ian smiled. 'Red Hannan thinks the umbrella is a sort of bourgeois conspiracy.'

There was laughter.

Lawless nodded. And out came the hip flask. With the top still screwed tight, he mimed tipping a little bit onto his balding scalp and using the other hand to massage it in.

'That explains why he's baaldy,' said Wee Ian.

Hannan said, 'Explains why he's still *got* some fucking hair.'

John Penalty was still slowly coming up that pathway towards them – alone – cigarette in the corner of his mouth despite the rain, and true enough, the gammy hip was making him fairly roll to the left that morning. Penalty's right hand was also black with muck which they could tell he had not tried to wipe away in his distress; lumps still clung between his short fingers. They'd all witnessed how long Penalty had taken, stooping to the earth and getting himself back up again to drop the handful of wet muck – with a slap – down on his co-driver's coffin.

Lawless offered the flask across to the Englishman, who frowned. 'We're backshift.'

'Aye. Too right we're backshift. And it's eleven on a pishing-down morn.'

Hannan announced, 'By now, Legless Lawless is banging the door of the County desperate for opening time.'

'It's been known for fucking closing time when the train's late in on a backshift.' Lawless quickly screwed off the top and offered the flask.

Hannan took the flask and spun round to take a swig, facing away from the congregated crowd up by the graveside.

'Watch yourself. Lincoln's just over there.' The Englishman nodded towards the Area Manager, then he stepped forward and up the path towards old John Penalty where he turned, sheltering Penalty under the big umbrella without a word – the brolly at arm's length so he himself was left mostly exposed to the rain. Penalty just nodded to the Englishman as they moved together, back towards the other drivers. Penalty wore full uniform: official issue suit, waistcoat and the hat with the zigzagging British Rail insignia in gold and purple backing – showing his length of service.

'Got the full uniform on the day, John?' Wee Ian often stated the obvious.

Penalty called back from underneath the held brolly, 'Old Peter might be down there but he wouldn't have recognised me out of it.'

'What about your famous doms nights?'

Hannan interrupted, 'Is the goods shunted?'

Lawless shook his head. 'Naw–is–it–fuck. The Tory was up here like a shot. They said the coal yard is greeting already. They just put it all in the fence road. The tanks too. They'll be shunting it in the fucking dark at this rate.'

John Penalty reached them at last and he looked directly at Hannan. 'Aye aye. Another vote gone at our branch meetings.' Penalty was upset but they all had to smile at the tough quip. Penalty patted at his big stomach in the black waistcoat and looked at Wee Ian. 'Ian, we wore our uniforms to our doms nights as well.'

They all laughed.

'Some turnout.'

'Aye. From down the whole road. Even signalmen.'

'It's a nice gesture.'

Ian Mhor laughed. 'They must have left the wives in charge of the signal boxes.'

'The railway'll run like fucking clockwork now, boys.'

'The windows'll be washed on every box.'

'They'll have ironed curtains hung on them by now,' Wee Ian said.

As well as the rain hitting the earth, now came the sound of the large funeral party crunching its hesitating way back up the gravel pathways as everyone retreated from the graveside.

The entire railway had split into its groups: the six guards in theirs and the signalmen from town and all down the line were clustered in consultations. The clerks from the station and all the conciliation grades had formed gangs too. The many spare shifts had all donned uniforms in their guilty leisure.

Umbrellas were popping up which had been ignored by the graveside. There were staff from the Back Settlement, one man each from Nine Mile House and the Fort Junction. Even the family from Ardencaple passing loop had sent an ambassador from the box. Then civilian figures from the town itself – who almost outnumbered the fifty or so railway persons – even Donaldson the butcher, who one of the drivers moonlighted for. Then there were dead Peter's two sons and a good show of other aged, retired railway.

'Some turnout right enough,' Lawless said.

Five more drivers approached: Jonty with his driver, Shoutin' Darroch followed by Coll, Hannan's own driver. Toshack was coming and Duncan 'The Tory' was a bit behind. They had all taken the next pathway up, through the chequerboard of graves, walking stooped in the rain.

'Aye. Sad, John, eh?' called Jonty.

'Aye.'

As usual, Shoutin' Darroch said absolutely nothing. It was known Jonty got a lot of reading done on the engines – even if it was mainly nudie mags.

'Come along. Let's get in the cars and down that house.'

'Aye but, boys, boys.' John Penalty held up his muddied hand, still sheltered by the Englishman's brolly. 'Get our hands washed off of this shite so Bunty and the wee grandkids arnie seeing it.'

'Toshack has all oily rags and stuff in his car.'

There was no talking.

'Fucking sad,' said Toshack.

'It is. Aye, Tosh.'

'That's the end of an era that,' Lawless announced. 'Nineteen fucking twenty-two Peter joined the railway. Cleaning out boilers and fireboxes.'

Among the men, nobody said a thing.

'Nineteen twenty-two,' Penalty repeated.

'Some retirement.'

'Aye, the same story. Four month to go. Didn't taste a pint of his retirement money.'

Every man nodded without hesitation.

The others were thinking it, but Penalty alone had the authority to state, 'He did taste plenty of the wage though.'

The others chuckled softly.

'Want a nip yourself, John?' Lawless tipped his head back questioningly.

'I've gone and took all ma fucking wee coloured Smarties, haven't ah? Ach, on you go then.'

Lawless side-palmed the flask and Penalty took it up in his muddied hand. They watched him swallow two full gulps and then pass the flask back with a sour noise. 'That's powerful stuff.'

The Tory walked along the path towards them, his brogues crushing the gravel. He gave a look at the flask.

'Aye.'

'Aye.'

The Tory stood beside Toshack. He took his glasses off and tried to wipe the rain from the lenses with his clean fingertips. 'If it weren't for the circumstances, this would be like a good Hogmanay, boys. It's no often the lot of us are all thegether at one time.'

Hannan announced, 'We're just no seeing enough of each other, eh, boys? Unless it was a strike call, Duncan? Eh?' he taunted. 'It's going to come soon enough. For the ASLEF at least.'

There was no response until the Tory replied, 'We'd better get down the house. Lincoln was saying we should go with you in his car and that'll give you a bit more room, John?'

'Are yous coming to the house? I thought you'd that goods to shunt?' Hannan asked.

'Oh aye.' The Tory looked at his watch. 'Oh aye. Popping in to pay our respects.'

'That fucking ferry'll be late in anyway. Day like this. Could be you'll find yourselves twenty minutes down leaving.'

The Tory shrugged and looked up into the sky. 'It's more rain than wind. We should have started that twelve twenty-five engine up before we left. The coaches will be cold.'

'Aye but ya cannie risk leaving the heating on. What is it?'

'Eh?'

'What machine is yon?'

'Sixty-two. Is it, Tosh?' The Tory looked at Toshack. 'What machine's yon we've got?'

'Aye, sixty-two. That one's all right. Fucking boiler in fifty-seven is no fit to be unattended. The Vital bloody Spark that one is. Even down the bothy for twenty minutes and I'm on tenterhooks. The fucking coil pressure is blowing off every minute. Put it in the book twice but Glasgow done fuck all.'

'Can you no fix it yourself?'

'Naw. Needing dismantled.'

Big Ian said, 'Look at the railway bodies here. That station must be fucking empty.'

'Did the last cunt out switch the lights off?'

'Folk'll be thinking that's the railway closed down, at long fucking last. An end to its agonies and put out its misery.'

'Aye. They'll be stealing the fittings.'

'They've closed the ticket office right enough.'

'Never?'

'Oh aye.'

'Another crash in profits. There must be at least six people and a donkey wanting out the villages on a day like this.'

'Isobel the Ticket just closed the window.'

'Here's President Lincoln.'

Lincoln and McGarry the station master came up, grinning grimly against the rain. They both had blackened right hands but they didn't want to put them into the pockets of their good-quality overcoats. Lincoln's spectacles were steamed up too.

Nobody said a thing and John Penalty went, 'Isobel closed the ticket office, eh, James?'

Lincoln shrugged. 'Quite right too. It's only for half an hour.' With his clean hand he awkwardly removed and squinted at his railway pocket watch on its chain.

They all began to walk towards the main gates.

The six guards had come up behind the drivers, each with blackened hand. Hannan pointed. 'Young Colin, that can't be you, can it, caught doing the shunting without your gloves on?'

'More like he's been busy wiping his arse while a train he's on is due to leave.'

They all laughed.

'I hear you havnie shunted the goods yet? There's a surprise.'

Young Colin just smiled.

Penalty shouted behind, to the guards, 'Boys, mind. Clean your hands before goan up this house. There's wee grandkids there as well as Bunty. No fucking queuing up to wash your mitts in their scullery sink, for fuck's sake.'

Allan Kinloch the guard said, 'I telt yous we's should of all brought our coupling gloves to do the ashes-to-ashes with in this weather. Peter would've understood. A real railway send-off.'

Hannan shouted, 'No way young Colin'll have his gloves with him. He keeps them under his pillow at night so he dreams of the railway and he's went and forgot them.'

Men chuckled.

Penalty claimed, 'Nah. With gloves on, we'd have upset poor Peter, looking down on us; he'd be supposin we were keen to get back to our work, and we all ken that's no the case.'

They all laughed. Even Lincoln.

'John?' Lincoln stepped up behind Penalty. 'Want to go down with us? It's just, it's a bigger car.'

The Tory, McGarry and Lincoln were all looking at Penalty.

'Nah, you're all right there, James. Thanks all the same; I'll go back with these bloody monkeys.'

Lincoln nodded and stepped away.

The Englishman took the brolly from covering Penalty and walked to another car. The others all moved to the same cars they'd taken up from the town. Hannan, Coll and Penalty crossed the car park with Toshack to his old Ford Cortina.

As they opened the unlocked doors, the others stood and briefly surveyed across the road – mainly to give Penalty time to painfully lower himself in. The pedestrians continued to come out of the cemetery, the family and railwaymen were distinguished from the townsfolk by each having the black hand of peat muck from the graveside – with that hint of whisky contained deep within the earth's scent.

The car windows and windscreen were steamed up as Toshack turned the key and they all wiped at the glass with tissues or even greasy rags, then each man used the wet clods of tissue and cloth to clean up their dirty hands as best they could.

Spanners and tools clunked down in the footwells of both the front and rear passenger seats in Toshack's car as their feet touched them.

They watched through the moving windscreen wipers as the Tory got in the front of Lincoln's new Cortina Mark III. McGarry got in the back. There was still a space – even two spaces – in the rear.

'"It's a bigger car,"' Hannan quoted, and the men laughed.

'Fucking . . . I used to drive a Zephyr before this.'

'You're gone down in the world now, Tosh.'

'Tosh musta cannibalised the Zephyr, boys. Half of those fucking North British engines musta been kept running with Tosh's Ford Zephyr parts holding them together. An NBL-Ford hybrid.'

'More like the fucking Zephyr was running on railway parts.'

They all laughed.

Toshack started to get in gear but Hannan said, 'Hold on. I want to see who else gets in Lincoln's car.'

Toshack just chuckled. 'Och, come on, the wee Kremlin, and give us a break. They're no ganging up on ya.'

'Young Colin will get in.'

'Nay, he has his own car now.'

'So he does. Already, at his fucking age. I don't know. I couldn't get anything all the years I was a fireman and now a fucking guard a few year on the line can drive a car. How do the young ones afford it nowadays?'

'The hire purchase. Another ten year and the people are no going to need any fucking railway. They'll all be driving cars to Glasgow for the Christmas shop.'

'Aww, who else? It's the councillors.'

They watched the two councillors duck over, one using a newspaper to shelter his head; they stooped and got into the back seat of Lincoln's Cortina.

'Who did they come up with?'

'Took Tommy's taxi on the council's penny, nae doubt.'

Hannan said, 'Fuck sake, boys, do yous know nothing? Councillors sleep in the cemetery at nights. They have a whole coffin each.'

'Look at the signalmen go. It's like a fucking rally.'

The cars of the signalmen from down the line all turned to the right, then headed along the bushes by the main road, past the railings of the cemetery, away from the town and towards Tulloch Ferry and the south-east.

'Who's in our box the now then? Is it empty? If Glasgow found out, Lincoln would get shot.'

Toshack told them, 'Walker the Walker and his dug'll've volunteered. Walker hates funerals. Could answer anything on the phone and Glasgow wouldnie know he wasnie a qualified signalman. Knows the *Signalling Rule Book*. Walker could run a better box than fucking Musty – instead of track walking. Just as well he didn't come up or the dug woulda cocked its leg into the grave.'

'The fucking dug could run the signal box better than Musty.'

They chuckled.

'The dug could run the whole railway better.'

★   ★   ★

Toshack had the headlights switched on and he drove them round the road curves, under those old elms which dropped painterly blots of water onto the windscreen. Then the roof beams of the new school construction and the wet slates of the Brae Estate were down at the bottom of the steep slope below them.

Hannan banged the worn, red dashboard top and stated with mock excitement, 'So this is the great relief vehicle, boys. Tosh the driver comes to British Rail's rescue again. Saves the day with his trusty toolbox. Eh? Even in the snow Lincoln has you down that fucking road, fixing bollixed locomotives that should be done on railway time, no your own.'

'Fucking Brezhnev.' Toshack clucked his tongue. 'I've saved *you*, ya cunt, off the Nine Mile Bank in a foot of snow. Came over the fucking fields to you, up to ma balls in drift. Your passengers were freezing up back. So were my balls.'

'I couldn't give a fuck, Tosh. All I needed was a six-foot blonde to keep me warm in the engine room.'

'Allan Kinloch would have had her wrapped up in mailbags in the brake van.'

'Long as the cab heating is working, I'm okay, boys. I'd of stayed there all week, long as it's my wage I'm collecting.'

'Aye, Tosh,' Coll sounded up. 'Hannan would only call you out and over the moors if the cab heater broke down. Or his fucking coffee flask sprung a leak.'

They all laughed. Hannan too.

In the back, Penalty's foot shifted a spanner on the floor of the car, which touched another – the sound signalling the relative size of each tool. 'Coll? Mind in our day if we had a leaking boiler on the wee tank engines we'd sling in some porridge oats to plug it, eh?'

'Away?' Hannan laughed.

'Right enough.'

Coll nodded. 'Aye that's true. On the branch-line tanks.'

'I'm telling yous,' Penalty stressed, 'get a leak, the water's jetting out under pressure at the rivet joins, tip a bag of some porridge oats into the boiler and they'll go straight to the hole and plug it up good; that bran water'll do till you get it welded proper.'

'What were yous doing with porridge oats on a footplate?' Hannan was a diesel man.

'Porridge! Make our fucking breakfast on winter morns from the hot tap, man. Bit of boiling water with milk over your oats and you got a good plate up there. Bit of a metallic taste, mind.' He chuckled at the memory.

The main road turned a right-hand bend and they braked on the sharper hairpin high on the King's Way. When the dripping rock cutting drew back, it revealed the north end of their perpendicular little town below. It was a curious meeting of flat bay water with precipitous cliffs, ridged with the expectant facades of Victorian villas; the honeycombing back lanes climbed in terraced curves to the circular Victorian folly and a small council estate stood at a stubborn angle down the short valley. Directly beneath them, through the rain, were the bright-puddled hard courts of the shabby tennis club and, beyond, the proposed municipal swimming-pool plot. If you turned your head, the roofs of the Complex, with white smoke coming from almost every chimney pot, were there. The distant television aerial had its top nipped off by a low slag of cloud.

Toshack turned the car left at the Knoll then another right at the bottom. Then left to where the widow's council flat was, in a small block with just two front closes.

'You'll no get parked in here the day.' John Penalty's voice was angry in the back seat.

'Naw. Yous get out and I'll go find a parking place.'

'Away and fuck, man. You don't need to be worrying about me.'

'I'm no, I'm no. It's pishing down. Get in there, yous.'

The other three men got up out the car – Penalty slowly – and they made their way along the concrete path of the communal front drying green to the main door where they sheltered beneath the porch lip. Some sodden tea towels were hung in the rain from wooden clothes pegs on the drying lines. Tosh's car drove off in the rain but immediately another vehicle pulled in – saw there was no parking – and then geared on up the small crescent.

Peter and Bunty Tait lived on the second floor which wasn't easy for Penalty's leg. Hannan said, 'I tell you now, I meant what I says about Tosh. Know what I heard the other day? Lincoln had the

66

new Cortina parked out by 4, bonnet up, and sure enough, Tosh had his heid in the engine footering at something.'

'Aye. Lincoln'll have him up his house soon, fitting central heating when Tosh's on spare.'

Coll said, 'Probably get him to take a good steam boiler out one of the fucking engines and fit that to the radiators in his big hoose. Glasgow'll be fucking scratching their heads about where their boilers are going to.'

'Better no use fifty-seven then or whatever one it is with the banjaxed boiler. Tosh loves each and every one of those engines, man. It's no healthy. He must sleep with his fucking spanners.'

Hannan and Penalty chuckled together, stood at the bottom of the stairwell by the ash buckets, lighting cigarettes. John Penalty was slicing the rain spots off the sleeves of his railway blazer with the blade of his hand; Hannan ascended one step at a time above Penalty, looking back down as the old fellow grabbed onto the banister fixed to the wall and slid his hand up it before each pull.

Hannan went on. 'I'm serious though, John. Station like ours out at the end of a hundred-mile line should have a permanent mechanical engineer. If four of us can be sat on our arse on spare, they can afford an engineer on standby. We all have to be a bit handier than the Glasgow boys. They fucking call in an engineer to change a cab light bulb. Up here we can be five hours from help. I accept we all have to be handy but Tosh goes too far; out his bed three on a morn, driving down the road in all weathers on his own private time. Never mind the union, he's no railway insured for one. What if he got killed in the car? For fucking goods trains. Goods! No just passenger.'

'Aye, but.' Penalty had reached the halfway landing on the stairway, with its window. He paused against the extreme pain that the coloured little pills couldn't fully quash and he looked out through the glass at the heavy downpour. He was short of breath but he'd still relit his rolly and it was puffing away in at the side of his mouth. Close up, Hannan noticed Penalty hadn't shaved that morning. They could already hear the chattering voices in the bustling scullery and parlour above them from through the front door which had been left wide open onto the communal stairwell.

Hannan continued. 'I accept we have to be flexible. It's one of the privileges of working a bonny road like ours. But there's an argument Tosh is doing too much, that he's wiping out a man's possible full-time job here.'

Coll stood at the top of the stairs waiting for them, but he'd been hidden around the red-painted curvature of the wall. Now his voice pronounced, 'Aye, Hannan. Save it for your fucking conference. Away and telephone Jack Jones about your issues. Today of all days.'

Hannan said, 'That's a national issue, boys. No yours nor mine. It's bigger than all of us.' He turned and walked on up ahead of Penalty.

Hannan and Coll paused, one before the other, to wipe their feet on the doormat before they entered into the wee corridor with its red carpet and its pictures hung along the walls – twee paintings of islands and rocks: many seagulls were a-flight.

Already there was a mix of townsfolk and relatives in the small council apartment. The good-looking daughter-in-law was sticking to the scullery. Coll and Hannan nodded to everyone but were given an unspoken priority as people moved aside to let them through and across the front room.

A fire was burning in the tiled fireplace behind the hearth, the mesh fireguard up. Bunty was right there, one arm holding aside the net curtains as she peered out. She turned round anxiously, as if taken by surprise. 'Oh, here's Coll! Here's Coll and Mr Hannan. I knew I heard a car.'

'John's just coming up the stair the now,' said Coll, crossing to Bunty Tait and he put his arms around the small woman. 'I'm awful, awful sorry, Bunty. The boys are all just scunnered.'

'I couldn't face it, Coll. And this weather's atrocious.'

'That doesn't matter, love. You were best out it. Lincoln made a good wee talk about Peter. Beautiful really, and a good few laughs.'

'Some turnout, Bunty,' said Hannan, and he too leaned in and briefly hugged the small old woman.

'Aye, Hannan. Thanks for everything you're doing.' Bunty turned to a random figure from the town and announced, 'Mr Hannan's keeping a weather eye on the pension situation for me.' Then she turned back to the railwaymen. 'There's sandwiches and beer and drams, boys. There's a whole bottle of Dimple there. Peter won't be needing it now. He liked a dram in the' evening.' She paused but then became reanimated. 'And there's a soup. Will yous have a soup, boys? There's a hot soup on for you all in the scullery with Fiona.'

'Don't you worry. Folk'll be pouring in. You worry about yourself, Bunty, we're all fine.'

'Aye, there's a soup.'

More firmly, Coll said, 'Dinna fret. Here comes John. Away and see John.'

Penalty was taking a long time and then Hannan realised he would be outside the front door, finishing or fixing a cigarette. Bunty nodded quickly and she stepped up the corridor.

Hannan and Coll looked around the room and nodded.

'Sad day,' said a fellow by the name of Gemmell who worked in Red Star parcels, but he'd been off on the sick for months: some suspect back complaint with an infinitely extending doctor's line.

'Aye,' Coll said curtly.

Gemmell nodded his head a vulpine fraction and Hannan followed its indication. He saw a round table laden with upright cans of Tennent's and Tartan Special beer.

'Oh-John-oh-John-oh-John,' they heard Bunty up the corridor. They could tell old Penalty and the woman were embracing.

Hannan coughed and, despite Gemmell, stepped ahead, picked up a beer can, got his finger in the ring pull and, trying not to spill the liquid as the pull jerked back, he tore it free. The side of the beer displayed a semi-naked young woman in a crochet bikini. She had a suntan and an extremist smile but her complexion was striped red by some imperfection in the colour printing of the can. Hannan placed the little ring pull and metallic nib in his coat pocket then took a sip of the beer. He occupied a free space in the corner near the windows, standing beside a little table with a lace cloth and an ivy plant upon it.

'There's a hot soup, John, take a hot soup.'

'Don't you be worrying about a hot soup.'

'I'm so sorry, I couldn't thole it. I'll take more flowers up later with my boys. Thought I could, then at the last minute, no.' She exhaled the last word with a weariness.

'Nay bother. It was a wonderful turnout and you were right for you and the wee ones no to come.'

Penalty limped into the room after Bunty. He nodded at Hannan with the beer can. 'There's Red Hannan, first off from the starting line.'

'Will you take a hot soup, John?' said the daughter-in-law quietly from the scullery door.

'I will not, Fiona. I'll take a hot dram though.'

Bunty actually chuckled. 'There's a full bottle of Peter's Dimple on the table there. Here. Someone pour a Dimple for John Penalty. Take a seat, John. Give a seat to John, someone.'

'I'll stand just fine for a few years yet. Don't you worry about me.'

'Oh, here's more boys. Here's Toshack.'

'Aye-Bunty-terrible-sorry.' Tosh quickly stepped into the room. He crossed directly to the fireplace, and aiming his cigarette butt behind the guard, he darted it in and walked back a distance to stand beside Penalty.

Some more townsfolk arrived, then the two Ians who took their caps off. When the Englishman entered from the corridor, Hannan immediately called across the room, 'Elliot! Your bowl is on the floor in the scullery there, don't make a mess.' The Englishman, as well as others, laughed. But when the Englishman had procured a saucerless cup of tea from the daughter-in law, he criss-crossed and stood right next to Hannan. Both men fell into an immediate and serious discussion about the stalled progress of construction on the new primary school, up the Brae Estate.

Now Lincoln and McGarry entered. The Area Manager did not embrace Bunty Tait but he put a hand out and touched her arm. 'I'm very, very sorry, Mrs Tait,' he said. 'And I can only stay a moment too, I'm afraid, before I need to be back at the station.'

'I'm all right, Mr Lincoln,' she nodded. 'I appreciate you coming and I'm very sorry I couldn't go to the graveside.'

'Oh, I understand.'

'In the old days the women never used to go up the graveside, but I know things have changed. I just couldn't face it. I'm told you said some lovely words and I'm grateful.'

'It's nothing at all. It's an honour,' the man said.

Wee Ian called to Bunty, quite delighted, 'The whole station closed for him, Bunty.'

She nodded and smiled. 'Will you take a hot soup, Mr Lincoln, and there's ham pieces?'

'No, no. I'm fine thank you.'

McGarry the station master said nothing but he leaned in and embraced Bunty. They'd known each other decades – from the days when there was a vibrant railway club, and over the course of many a Hogmanay. Even from the days when McGarry was a station porter. Bunty said to McGarry, 'Will you take a dram, Philip?'

'No thank you, Bunty.'

'And will you take a dram yourself, Mr Lincoln?'

To everyone's surprise Lincoln accepted straight away. Presumably out of politeness.

Standing next to the table of beer, Gemmell seemed to have appointed himself the role of unofficial barman and he poured out a fairly stiff one for the Area Manager. Bunty herself was taking a drink: a glass from a bottle of India Pale Ale.

McGarry immediately said, 'Oh well, maybe I'll join James and have an ever so wee one, please.' McGarry stepped straight to Gemmell and asked, 'And how are things at the doctor's?'

'Still the same. Still the same,' Gemmell repeated triumphantly. You had to give it to him on the brass-neck front, and as Gemmell handed them over, one glass was ridiculously more generous than the other – the one intended for McGarry was no more than what Lawless called a Wee Young Nun's Pee. Hannan was waiting for Lincoln to ask for a dash of water but all credit to him he did not.

Lawless himself now squeezed through the corridor which had filled up. He nodded to everyone and moved past John Penalty. Lawless observed the whisky glass in Lincoln's hand and also noted the ranks of full beer cans upon the table. He was in fearful dilemma. Lawless turned aside. 'I'm so sorry, Bunty,' and he put out his hand and shook hers, almost looking in another direction.

'Is Duncan here?' she asked.

'Aye, he's just coming the now.' Lawless stood a moment longer – helpless – then turned to Allan Kinloch the guard and in low voice asked, 'Is the toilet just there? Must dash for a wee tinkle.'

The Englishman looked at Hannan and Hannan met his gaze.

In a voice submerged in the hubble, the Englishman said, 'Looks like I shall be doing the drive down tonight. He's taught himself to wake up exactly two hundred yards before each station. Quite remarkable.'

Hannan laughed and nodded.

The Tory came quietly in.

Bunty said, 'Oh, Duncan, thanks for coming.'

'Aye, Bunty. Ever so sorry. And I'm afraid me and Toshack and Allan have to fly; we're down on the twelve twenty-five.'

'Oh, are you on the twelve twenty-five?'

'Aye. We'll just stay a wee minute.'

Toshack put his back against the wallpaper and lifted his match to a cigarette. Even though others were smoking he politely nudged his head at his cigarette. 'Is it okay, Bunty?'

'Smoke away, everyone. Peter stopped but I never did.'

Penalty also nodded and immediately took his tin of Golden Virginia from the side jacket pocket and began rolling another. Penalty had long ago perfected doing a rolly using just his right hand, so he could keep the left on the vacuum brake handle.

The whole railway in its multitude seemed to be filing in and milling round; the volume of talk was rising in the tight confines of the apartment. Jonty came in and paid his respects; even Shoutin' Darroch – a driver canny of his own shadow – was seen to turn aside and exchange two whispered words with Bunty.

The Stronach with his bloody accordion appeared and he stashed the box in a corner.

Lawless was back from powdering his nose. He moved – agile and nervous around the alcohol, attacking the ham pieces, and then he soon had a plate of soup on the go as well.

Penalty called across to Bunty Tait, 'Christ, Bunty, it's stowed-out; the railway's a fair frightening sight when you gather it all together.'

People laughed.

'Here! Stronach's brought his box,' a voice said, tinged with shock.

Bunty spoke up immediately. 'Oh, I asked him to, everybody. I don't want it to be all sad. Tears at a wake and laughter at a wedding, but a box is good for both we used to say. Eh?'

Hannan shouted, 'Not for Mr and Mrs Lawless; there were tears from the faither-in-law yon wedding day.'

A huge peal of laughter went up and Lawless himself nodded with a mouth full of ham sandwich, eyes sparking.

'Hannan, you're terrible,' Bunty went on. 'Let's have some music in a wee while. The young ones always want the records on but I'm no one for these records.'

The Stronach had a dram and nodded his head, the end of that stiff beard punching at his sternum. 'Aye. The records. *That's* the thing with the young ones these days.'

Suddenly Lincoln held up his whisky glass and immediately the room fell silent, the last voices to die out were right up the corridor.

Lincoln said, 'Peter Tait.'

'Peter Tait,' the room, corridor and scullery answered. Those with alcoholic drinks raised them and those without nodded.

Lincoln took a fair old gargle from the glass. Then with a second, moments later, drained it.

The babble slowly rose again. The Tory had been standing with his hands in his pockets but now he shuffled over to Bunty to say something. She nodded and the Tory turned to look at Toshack and Allan Kinloch. They both nodded too and began moving to the corridor.

'We might as well go too, Mrs Tait,' Lincoln announced.

Toshack called out, 'Right, we're all away down on this bloody train, Bunty.'

'Come up when yous're back in at half four,' Bunty called. 'They'll still be bodies here. We'll be fair dancing by then.'

'Oh, I'm very sure of that,' said Toshack.

The Tory was about to depart but he pushed his spectacles up his nose and turned. He looked around the assembled train drivers, addressing them en masse in a craven tone. 'Will someone get that goods shunted for us?'

Penalty nodded.

'I'll get it shunted myself,' Hannan moaned. 'I've nothing better to do with my life.'

'Tut-tut, Hannan. That's your own time, no railway time,' Coll smiled.

The Tory nodded once then moved up the corridor. Allan Kinloch, Toshack, McGarry and Lincoln all followed, squeezing past people in the corridor.

There was a perceptible change in the atmosphere with the managers gone. Of course, within fifteen seconds, Lawless put his soup down and lifted a can of beer. He held it politely for another fifteen seconds, studying the girl on the side, then cracked the can open.

After a short time there was a commotion and three wee kids came down the corridor, their heads turned quietly in wonderment at this unprecedented gathering of adults in their granny's house. The wee girl went straight through the scullery to her mum but the two boys, one about ten and another younger, stood in the centre of the room while efficiently surveying all the talking people. They paid especially close attention to the figure of the Stronach, with all the SNP tin badges pinned to his dirty shirt.

Bunty was standing next to the guard Breck and she told him, 'That's the little ones down from up the stair. Up at Elsie's all morn. They don't really understand at that age, do they?'

The eldest lad was standing before John Penalty and he turned to the old man. The child looked shy but suddenly spoke. 'You played dominoes with Grandad all the time.'

'That's right,' Penalty nodded.

'You're Steam Train John.'

'Call me anything if it isn't bad, son.'

'Do you drive a steam train?'

'Naw. They're all gone away up to the big scrapyard in the sky and I'm no far behind them.'

'How fast does a train go, mister?'

'Not very fast.'

'Do you do a hundred?'

'Noooh. Trains don't go a hundred up in these doldrums. Unless Mr Hannan over there has found his coffee flask is empty. Then he's a speed merchant.'

The wee boy turned to look at Hannan then laughed at him. Hannan stuck out his tongue and the child laughed again. The wee boy turned back to John Penalty and pressed ahead with his interrogation. 'Can you no even do a hundred in your train? That's useless.'

Bunty said, 'Don't be cheeky now, Stevie, or you'll get a clip. Stop bothering Mr Penalty or he won't let you a hurl on his train one day when you're bigger.'

'He's no bothering me. These other fellows are bothering me. Been bothering me thirty year now some of them, but not you, wee man.'

'I want a hurl on a steam train,' the wee guy announced. 'With all smoke.'

'You're all out of luck there, laddie. Only these daft diesels now.' Coll leaned down a bit to the kiddie. 'Steam Train John used to drive the fast trains though; and he was a fireman too. Do you know what a fireman is?'

'Aye. Course. He puts in all the coal with a shovel.'

'That's right. John here drove the LMS express trains to Penrith and Carlisle down in England from Glasgow and back. Now they went very fast.'

The child looked at John Penalty, expectant for some major response. Penalty blew out cigarette smoke. 'Aye. Pulled out Carlisle twenty-five late and got in to Glasgow Central ten minutes early. That was my record when I was driving. I stoked for much better men than me though.'

'Get your breeks off, John, and show the wee laddie,' Coll laughed.

'Nay nay, man, I'd need another dram and I don't want to scare the children. And impress the women.'

The railway guys in the room all laughed; so did Bunty and Fiona, who'd seen the show before.

'Away. You're among friends. Get them down, Penalty, and show the laddie.'

Hannan shouted, 'He's worried his long johns might have holes.'

The drivers laughed.

The wee boy turned round, said out loud, savouring the phrase, 'Long johns!' and he laughed as well.

'Away you go. These are brand new from Caird's.' All the same, Penalty pulled up his waistcoat and cautiously checked the elastic of his underpants. 'Oh aye. These are grand ones.'

Hannan laughed.

The railway weren't shocked but the townspeople looked on with dismay as John Penalty balanced his cigarette in the corner of his mouth and undid the buttons on his trousers.

'Get the box going, Stronach. Do the cancan striptease.'

Everyone laughed.

Hannan shouted to the daughter-in-law, 'Fiona, away in the scullery now and cover your eyes.'

Big Ian said, 'You'll give the wee fellow nightmares.'

'Are you joking? With the Stronach in the same room? We all know the mothers tell their kids to be well behaved, or the Stronach'll come and get them.'

There was laughter – including the Stronach's own.

'This'll give the young lassies the good dreams,' Penalty said and he laughed. 'So you want to know about steam trains, son.' Penalty slowly dropped the black trousers so the waist slipped down more on his left leg, showing the bare thigh and calf beneath his baggy underpants.

Lawless called, 'Watch out the Minister doesn't walk in on us now, folks.'

Everyone laughed.

'He'll be straight back out that door thinking we have very queer parties.'

Bunty laughed and so did the two wee boys, clearly thinking this was quite tremendous stuff.

Penalty's left leg, which troubled him, was very skinny and very pale, with the odd blotch of fierce-looking thread veins. The real problem was within his left hip they said he took all the coloured pills for. They all knew the hip was disintegrating fast and that he probably wouldn't make retirement. But there was something else on the thigh that they all could see and the room fell silent in respect of it.

'Oh my goodness,' said Gemmell.

Some townsfolk and even railway leaned forward and shifted position the better to see it – the child smiled with that macabre gleefulness of young boys, but the much younger child's mouth slowly fell wider open.

Penalty said, 'In them days Glasgow crew'd pick up the train at Penrith. Train goes back over two summits: Shap and the Beattock – fair brutal climbs for a steam engine, so I'd start stoking the firebox at a standstill in the station and I didn't stop shovelling till Carstairs. Hours of stoking in that heat non-stop. Your driver would tip a bucket of water over your heid every now and again, even in winter. That's why I've got these big bushy eyebrows like Denis

Healey. They got burned right off and grew back in mighty queer.' He looked down at the wee boy and brushed his own left eyebrow into action with a busy finger.

The wee kid looked round the room with a cautious delight.

'I had muscles on me so I could lift you over my heid with one hand.'

The nipper held still at this.

'They've all gone now, mind, so don't ask me to. So me and my driver, Teddy Monk, Old Monckton, were out to break the records. Teddy was above every speed limit and I was stoking like to make Hell itself. Not a signal against us. Snow on the ground all the way up and it could get cold on a footplate – ice in the drookin bucket – but I had the firebox wide open like a blast furnace, watching the pressure gauge, making sure she didn't drop a single pound. Over the Shap sixteen minutes up and the Beattock even better and I keep stoking. We're at Rutherglen and I start to feel mighty weary but we'd broken all the time records for the run – there was gonna be a good few pints for us that night in the railway club. Two mile before the Glasgow Central I hit the floor of the footplate like a sack of tatties.'

Donaldson the butcher was in the corner with his shiny roaring face. 'What happened?' he asked, frowning at the leg.

'I woke up in the Victoria hospital. Monk had stopped the train at Polmadie. Almost at the bloody station and I was ambulanced off the footplate on a stretcher. Monk got her into the Central an hour and a bloody half late cause of me or we'd have had the record. Last thing I'd says was just to keep going cause we had clear signals but the silly bugger went and stopped.'

The railwaymen all laughed.

'I'd just got my first wee railway flat in town. Those days the London Midland Scotland had flats for firemen. I had the house keys in my dungaree pockets here.' He tapped his thigh. 'Though the dungarees were fireproofed the house keys had melted in the heat and the hot metal run all down my leg and just opened it up like a fish belly.'

Everyone in the room looked at the marble meandering of scar which rivered from Penalty's thigh, curving round below the kneecap, moving vertically down his shin and presumably pooling onto the foot; the rough scars of staples at intervals still showing how the mess of the burn had been clamped shut in surgery. As if some dreadful stinging monster from the deep had lashed up a tentacle onto him and held fast.

John Penalty pulled his breeks up but with some difficulty and got the button fastened.

'Bloody hell,' said Donaldson the butcher, and he held up the missing tip of his middle finger. 'Doesn't really compete, does it?'

Penalty just smiled in a grisly way and puffed away at his cigarette.

'Did it hurt?' the wee boy whispered.

'Didn't know a thing, son. Near a month in the hospital on full pay. Luxury. And a wee nurse from Troon. I mind her still.'

That was it for the child. He moved in and stood at Penalty's side for a long time – proud to be associated with the great hero.

'God, I need a dram after that,' said Lawless and his mitts went on to the whisky bottle before Gemmell could interfere.

'You need a dram after *Songs of Praise*.'

'Aye, how about some music to cheer us up?' said Bunty.

'Sing "The Dark Island", Fiona. She's as good as Moira Anderson.'

The daughter-in-law went, 'Och no,' in a voice shy since school.

'"An t-Eilean Muileach", the Stronach,' someone called.

Hannan shouted, 'Not "Farewell to Whisky", with Mr Lawless present.'

Everyone laughed.

'You need the fiddle for Neil Gow,' the Stronach scoffed.

Then Big Ian called, 'Tell them another, John.'

'Aye. Tell them the Queen,' Wee Ian's squeaky voice said. 'We don't have to see your underpants for that one.'

Folk laughed again.

'Nay more stories. You know fine I'll go all day.'

'Och, come away. Tell them all the Queen. That was you and Peter himself, man. You got to tell them about you and Peter.'

'Aye, tell me that one,' Donaldson the butcher shouted.

'The wee fellow'll no understand all that stuff,' Penalty shrugged.

'Tell them the Queen,' the Stronach nodded. 'It's about my favourite story in the history of the world.'

Some railwaymen laughed, and in the pause which followed, the miraculous occurred. Shoutin' Darroch leaned against the wallpaper by the scullery next to the daughter-in-law who stood in the doorway with her own daughter at her knees. Darroch said in a very quiet voice, 'Tell me the Queen one again, John.'

All eyes went to Darroch and he lowered his face.

Penalty said, 'Och, anything for our spokesman Mr Darroch then. Bunty'll tell yous that Peter and I leaned towards the Communist spectrum in politics.'

Some folk chuckled.

'Bunty'll tell yous as well, Peter — like myself — wasn't a big man for the monarchy.'

'Wooof. That's saying something,' Bunty nodded. 'That telly got switched off in here at three sharp every Christmas Day.'

'Aye. He hated the monarchy fierce. He was like Willie Hamilton there. Hated them. Years back the Queen come up here. Some of yous remember it well.'

Gemmell told them sharply, 'Aye. She come up to open the Hydro barrier in the Pass for yon bloody toff-thing, Bultitude.'

'That's right. She come up on the Royal Train from Edinburgh on the old Callander line. Television cameras in the station and everything. And some of us driver boys then — I won't mention any names —'

'The Tory,' Hannan blurted.

Railwaymen laughed.

'Exactly. Certain wee fellows were dying to drive that bloody waste-of-money train. Area Manager in those days was Dewar. Mind wee Weedy Dewar?' Penalty looked around and some townspeople nodded. 'Dewar gathers all the drivers in the station bothy and there's such a fuss about favouritism that Weedy makes all us drivers and firemen draw bloody matchsticks to see who has the great honour. And guess who draws the short matches to bring the Queen's train up? Me and Peter.'

There was more laughing.

'It was a set-up, I reckon. We say we don't care and we want to give the shift away but Weedy Dewar is no having it. Insists it's a rostered duty you can't refuse. And I actually think he and the Tory took a wee pleasure that it's me and Peter have to drive the bloody thing.'

More folk chuckled.

'So off Peter and I go, down in a light diesel to Callander to pick the Royal Train up. She was a steam engine and you could of ate your tea off the footplate on yon. They'd put a wooden bucket of flowers on the footplate with us. Peter chucked it into the firebox in a jiffy, bloody bucket, water, flowers and all. And you should of seen the puss of Peter's face. Card-carrying Communist reduced to driving Her Majesty up through her hills and glens. I thought I wouldn't need to stoke the engine, just sticking Peter's fuming head into the firebox would have created enough steam.'

More folk laughed.

'This Royal Train carry-on was non-stop to the town here on a strict working timetable, cause though she seems to have all the leisure in the world, our Majesty aye seems to be in a hurry to get places. So we take the train up toward Glenoglehead with Peter driving as jerky as he can, but we get pulled by a signal on the platform at Balquhidder, station master screaming blue bloody murder at the box to get our train moving again. In them days steam engines carried a head code on the front. Four paraffin lamps hung up in different patterns to tell you what priority the train has. Royal Train head code was a full four lamps in each position, three along the bottom and one on the top, like a T upside down. So we're stood there on the platform and I amble up the front of the train with a cloth, looking as if I'm dusting, but I take two lamps off and quickly carry them back to the footplate. We get the off signal and we're away.'

Hannan said, 'Tell them what you changed the head code to though, John.'

'I'd changed it to just two lamps, one at the bottom in the middle and one on the right.'

'What's that mean?' a townsperson asked.

'Fish Train.'

Everybody started to laugh.

'Aye. Bloody Fish Train or Perishables. And Peter was saying right enough – her and the Duke of Edinburgh up the back there are about as perishable as it gets.'

Everyone was laughing now.

'So we're horsing through the land, waving at the signalmen. Course it means nothing to ordinary folk to see this Fish Train designation on the Royal Train. You had all the staff in full uniform and wee schoolkids out on the station platforms of every village, waving Union Jacks; organised by the Conservative and Unionist for a packet of toffees. All stood there to attention like bloody wee Mussolinis.' Penalty himself started to laugh at the memory and lit another cigarette he'd been rolling in one hand. 'But the station-platform staff, the signalmen, the P-way boys, platers, gangers – all the railway folk we pass is doubled up laughing.

'It was all going grand until top of the Tulloch Bank. Planned to make a wee unofficial stop there at the summit crossing, and I would climb down and change the lamps back and nobody in the town would be any the wiser. But as we made the top of the bank, guess who is stood beside the track with some delegation of the Masonic Lodge? Morrison: the worst Big White Chief Inspector, up from Glasgow for the day in a bloody frock coat. Peter and I look at each other and know straight away we're buggered for our jobs. Bad enough no carrying the correct head codes on any train, but on a Royal, showing Fish Train. We just keep over the top, look back and see Morrison horsing for the summit box to get on the telephone to Dewar down here in the station.

'Now those steam engines had no way out onto the ledge above the wheels but I was still fairly spry then. Peter is bawling at me no to even think about it but I tie both the lamps to my dungarees belt, slide forward the engine canopy, climb up on the back of the coal and jump for my life onto the cab roof. I make it too. Peter's trying to keep the train slow along the bank and it's a whole lot of curves there; I'm getting down on the ledge above the wheels and the pistons and I almost went over the edge but there was the handrail. So I make my way along to the front of the bloody engine. Might not seem much, but stuck on the front of a steam engine even at thirty mile an hour is nae fun. Going along the side of that hill there – with the town way below me – it was like I was seeing through the eyes of a seagull flying over our town, I used to dream about it sometimes – but I hooked those two lamps back. Made my way along the handrail on the bloody cliff side. Jesus, I could've fallen straight in through the roof to the bar of the Lodge Hotel there. Pulled myself back up top across the cab roof. That was the tricky bit; I didn't want to end up stuck to the side of a bridge. Never moved so fast in my life and I swung back down onto the footplate.

'Course the inspector had phoned ahead to the station, screaming how we'd gone through the summit with Fish Train head code on – how it was an affront to Queen and country and we should be shot. But Peter pulls her into the station steady as you like. You should have seen Weedy Dewar's face. Even shook his heid like he wasn't seeing right, but there was the four Royal Train lamps up front. He knew fine no man was crazy enough to jump a cab and get down the front on a moving train. But I bloody done it.'

The railwaymen all laughed.

'Oh aye. Those boys never figured it out and me and Peter were over drinking our pints in the County before yon woman was off her own train. She wasn't getting to shake my hand. I use it to wipe my arse anyway.'

The railway and townspeople all laughed again.

'Gone days,' old John Penalty called out, shaking his head. 'Aye, all long-gone days and long-gone men.' And he limped across to the fireplace as people moved aside for him. He had three rolly butts resting in the leather palm of his right hand which he had just let die there as if it was an ashtray – a time-served fireman's hard hands which felt no burn – and he dropped those dead butts in behind the fireguard, feeling the passive heat of the flames on his face – a weak echo of those far-off days.

Monday 18 June 1973

The sun was high and it was dazzling if you lifted your warmed scalp. The heat melted the sighted distance low down into slow and pendulous shiftings. In that liquid-like fumigation, eight horses and their erect riders were still walking slowly along that old drove track, across the countryside, as if proceeding through delusion to some impossible place.

Maybe a quarter-mile behind, the four lads still stubbornly followed on foot. Flies were circling and they frequently waved them off – wary they were biting clegs.

They had been ghosting the pony trek since they picked it up at the single-track road, leaving the council houses behind them on the old back moor. The final rider – definitely a younger female figure – had occasionally turned round to look rearward over her shoulder, across the cantle of her saddle as if something inexplicable – even horrific – followed.

Wee Jeff again lifted up his plastic Winchester rifle that once made a sound but was now broken – he aimed past Big Davie and, imitating recoil, pretended to shoot that final rider.

Galbraith said, 'If we went over the bank there then we would cut them off. Spy down on them.'

Wee Jeff said, 'Aye. Cut them off like Apaches and cavalry. Ambush them.'

The older boys ignored him.

'There's woods there and we could sort of make noises down,' Galbraith suggested.

Big Davie sighed and turned to wee Jeff; Davie dipped his face low but the question was addressed through the side of his mouth to Simon, as if addressing an interpreter. 'What'll we do now, boys? It's a scorcher. We could be way up the dam. The lassies are definitely going up. I want to see Ann Trotter's arse in that swimming costume again.'

Galbraith yelled, 'Trotter's has a big pimple on it. Oink-oink,' and he ran from side to side as if playing tig.

Simon shrugged and looked down at Jeff. 'Are you tired, Jeff? If you start greeting to go home I'll break your fingers.'

'Look,' Galbraith pointed. 'One's done a big huge plop.'

They all moved forward and surrounded the fresh, olive-coloured horse turd. They studied it.

'Flies lay their eggs in that. Minky things.'

Galbraith carried a flat stone over and each boy scattered for safety. Galbraith launched the stone from a distance and he himself retreated backwards, his feet reversing rapidly. As the stone hit the horse dropping, wet discs were thrown outward which landed as adhesive medallions upon the dusted track.

'Minging, man.'

They stood, idly observing the shattered dropping, then they looked to the horse line drawing distant as if there were some awkward conundrum connecting the two phenomena. Even at that distance they could see the mounted figures also waving flies away with sudden arm movements.

Wee Jeff said, 'We could just go up the wee reservoir then? There's tadpoles in it to catch.'

'How brilliant.' Galbraith's voice was extremely deadpan.

Big Davie stated, 'It was your idea to come trekking all the way up here for nothing, son. We'll chuck you in the reservoir.'

'Don't. He'll start greeting,' said Simon.

'I will not.'

But Simon was looking away after the line of pony-trekkers, squinting against the sun.

Galbraith said, 'I tell yous, if you cross that wee bank then they have to pass back in front of it. The track swings all the way round behind here.'

'C'mon.' Big Davie led the way.

They had been at this for all their short lives – a youth spent under weathered skies in open and uninhabited lands, traversing the verdure according to whim and urge. They had hillcraft, an instinct for foot and handholds – the surety of branches or the slipperiness of river rocks underfoot.

With a martial purpose, the lads scattered and moved quick and easy up the embankment which was spiked in young birches. Jeff was left struggling to keep up, getting twigs slashed back in his face, but the older boys didn't wait for him. Over the top it was more heavily wooded with tree cover.

Galbraith called out as usual, 'We's should have took something to drink. I'm gasping, man.'

'We'll find a stream,' wee Jeff called from behind – always keen on any orienteering project.

From the small, heavily wooded far-slope side, as Galbraith had rightly promised, the yellow ruts of the track did pass by down beneath them. It was cooler in among the jittery light of the trees and the boys spooked out the panicked flight of a few angered thrushes, eyes barely following these flushed birds.

The three older boys sat – the better to conceal themselves – and waited. Wee Jeff took time to catch up, pushing noisily through the leaves with the plastic gun slung tight across his back on a bit of tied string. When Jeff arrived he started getting his gun off his back and making noises as he pretended to load it.

'Jeff. Shut it,' said Simon. 'I never should of took you.'

Big Davie told them, 'Here. They're coming. Shut it.'

Slowly the line of horses approached down the track below their position, the tack and links of bridles clinking.

The first rider was recognisable as prim, tall Margaret Forbes – the buck-toothed woman who ran the hotel stables back in their village. The next rider and the ones after exuded pure tourist credentials: cameras on straps, waterproof overcoats tied at the waist, small backpacks; even the hyperbole of water canteens which Galbraith eyed. And each of these figures wore black riding hats secured beneath the chin, the tops incandescently silver in the sun out there.

Big Davie had a recognised and admired skill in the spontaneous raising of impressive burps from his stomach – often into the faces of schoolgirls upon their bus. This talent was now exercised to the full by his letting go a swinish and elongated repeater from deep within his guts.

The other boys burst out laughing. Galbraith did a Red Indian woo-woo-woo, patting his flattened fingers repeatedly onto his pursed lips. Simon joined in with a gibbering jungle gibbon sound. Jeff made the guttural report of every gunshot as he sniped each passing horseperson through the leaves. To their disappointment, there was no reaction from the riders below.

Now Big Davie was pretending to beat bongo drums, shaking his long hair enthusiastically, and he repeated, 'We eat English, we eat English, we eat English, taste very good, taste very good.'

Simon laughed out loud for the first time in days. Though the boys rose up onto their hunkers, ready to make a swift escape back across the wooded ridge behind them, not even a horse tossed its head in reaction to this facetious racket from the woods.

The last rider now passed. She had no riding helmet. Her head was not bare though, for she wore a floppy sun hat over loose jet-black hair with natural waves; a neckerchief circled the long and narrow tube of her pale neck like a choker and she had on a T-shirt and jodhpurs, and shining black riding boots came up her calves.

None of the boys had seen this figure so close up, since the trek had already appeared far ahead of them when they first followed. This girl's physical appearance silenced each one of the older boys. The only sound was Jeff's final spitting as he shot the young girl.

The older boys recognised the girl as being firmly anchored in their own age group; the small breast shapes showing through the T-shirt, the long bare arms to the idly held reins, the legs taut on stirrups against the tawny horse flank.

The female rider passed on in silence with a small turn of the head towards them and something was said among the riders which passed along. A dismissive, mature laugh came from further down the line.

Simon quickly said in a low voice to Davie, 'Who the fuck is she?'

Davie leaned slightly forward so he could see Galbraith and both of them exchanged an indecipherable look but with flavours of mockery.

Galbraith said, 'I know who that one is okay. Do you no know nothing round here, Crimmo? Sometimes it's like you've never even lived here. The way you never used to come to the youth club Christmas.'

Simon looked between them both, frowning. 'Who is she? What year's she in?'

Big Davie said, 'She's fucking nuts, man. *That* was yon Bultitude lass. The Bultitudes from the Back Settlement? Rich as kings, man.'

'Who? What age is she?'

Davie shook his head and shrugged. 'Seventeen? Put it this way: she doesnie keep her seat long at the dances. If she'd went to any. Awww, Crimmo son. Now now. You just stick to wee Nikki the Flasher.'

The others all laughed – even Jeff.

'Fuck off, Davie.'

'Gonna make me?'

Simon went silent.

Davie said patiently, 'That's the daughter: Varie Bultitude. Fucking spunk-dripper on a set of legs, man. I'd shag her bedroom floor.'

Galbraith whispered, 'They say she only goes with sort of older guys. Like men.'

Simon had turned and grimaced slightly towards Jeff on account of Davie's language.

Big Davie saw the look and went, 'Oh aye. Sorry. She doesn't go our school, Crimmo. Goes to boarding schools and that in fucking England that the parents pay for.'

'Boarding schools?' This idea was fabulously outlandish to Simon. He had never thought that there could be girls of his own age group operating unseen in his territory because the necessity of their schooling was conducted in some far place. He immediately felt cheated.

'They've got the big house, Broken Moan, and all the lands out at the Back Settlement.'

'Oh, that huge castle thing you see in the trees by the Pass?'

Big Davie shrugged. 'Aye. Mind, she did go up to the primary at the Back Settlement for a couple of year when she was just little and wee. Spoiled. She went up on the Nine Mile bus and it'd stop for her at the end of their massive long driveway. So the father built this wee sentry box for her there – you can still see it from the road in among brambles – for her to keep out the rain waiting for her bus in the mornings. The inside of it is all painted on the walls. Really good Minnie Mouses and Donald Ducks and all that. Envy of the playground that shelter was, I'll tell you.'

Simon turned from Galbraith to Davie and back. 'But she looked like a total ride now; the best screw I've ever seen round here in my life.'

Davie stared down at the ground a moment and he blew out breath. 'A bit on the fucking scrawny side, mind. I'd feed her up good and then she could gobble me proper. Ooops. A bonny-looking lass though and no two ways about it. Her old man's yon Commander thing.'

'Commander? What, he's in the army or something?'

'Wow!' went wee Jeff.

'Naw, naw, it's a sort of thing.'

'A thing?'

'A posh thing. Gives out school prizes and opens Highland shows at the gatherings and that. Like some kinda clan chief shite.'

'Oh, right. And she goes away to some boarding school?'

'Aye. Her and the brother. She's a big brother – a right weirdo too, gallivanting around. Called –' he elongated the name out, imitating a posh accent – 'Alexander. He's got really, really long hair and he wears this poofy coat like kind of an old soldier's coat. A soldier of olden times, I mean.'

'I've never even heard of them.' Simon said it in a quiet voice and he shook his head in amazement.

'Do you no know about Broken Moan, Crimmo? What's there?' Davie's voice spoke very quietly now.

'What's there?'

'The glass graves.'

Jeff paid closer attention.

'Glass graves?'

'The graveyard there is for their family. Their graves are all made of glass, man. You can look right in on top of them. No coffins. Dead bodies laying right in there so you can see them.'

'You're jesting me?'

Wee Jeff said, in a voice already afraid, 'You can look at the dead people?'

'Crimmo, everyone round here knows that. It's like I say, some-times you know nothing, man.'

Suddenly a heavy stillness seemed to be among them in their dell where they crouched together. Some appalling conjunction of images was occurring: the girl with her pale-clothed legs, and below a mildewed window reflecting the sky, worn yellow teeth grinned up.

'Patrick Sinclair from the Back Settlement seen them graves.'

'Aye, that's right; he told us.'

'How?'

'Sneaked in their grounds one night with Totsy and an electric torch. They were trying to spy her through a window in her scud. Pat's hard as fuck – Totsy too – does karate, man – says even he was shiteing himself petrified with the fright at what he saw.'

Galbraith went, 'My old man says they've the big house and tons of lands and that but nay actual money. They eat boiled eggs for their tea; one of the cleaners told him they like lettuce and stuff.'

'Salad?' asked Simon. The word heavy with ultimate dread.

'Aye, like salad shite that foreigners eat.'

Davie said in a low, oddly respectful voice, 'That's shite. They're rich, man. Look at the size of that house. My granny used to say there was one window for every day of the year in that house. Three hundred and sixty-five windows and you could look out a new one every day. Imagine that. And just to send someone to them boarding schools it's millions, man. My cousin Jim cut the woods for the Bultitudes when I was little.'

The boys now turned to Davie.

'That wife of Bultitude – that one's mother – she's died now. It was in the paper. She and her brother lived up there with them in the big house. Room enough, I suppose. That one's uncle he would've been. But he was queer in the heid as well, like all of them are. Took himself up into the woods one night with a golden chair and he hung himself from a tree. Now the big bedroom in Broken Moan faces the wood, so the Lady – that one's mother – is driven crazy by seeing these woods where her brother went and hung himself. So do yous know what she went and done?'

'What?'

'Had the whole wood chopped right down, every single tree of it; then she had diggers up to turn over the roots, so if you look today you just see open hill, but that used to be a wood there. And in one whole side of the house so you couldnie look towards that hill she had put in all them windows with all colours like in the church.'

'Stained glass?'

'Aye. Then the mother died too. Of a broke heart they say. Made it even more windy at Broken Moan with nae trees to the west.'

Simon said softly, 'So she's got no mother? Her mum died?'

'Aye. And I suppose her mum and uncle are lying in the glass graves too. It's sick, man.'

'And Bultitude drowned all them people in the sunken village, don't forget.'

Davie shook his head impatiently. 'Galbraith, dinna talk pure shite. He didn't drown folk.'

'Aye he did.'

'He did not. Flooded Badan village right enough so they could build the hydro scheme. The Bultitudes owned the village land so all the folk were moved up to the Jericho Road houses at the Back Settlement and the water came flooding in like a tidal wave theys say.'

'Aye, but I heard there was all wee boys locked in houses and they were all drowned.'

'Simon,' went Jeff's voice.

'Shut up, Galbraith. You're scaring my brother.'

'It's truth. Best he hears it. All the wee boys. Locked in their bedrooms. Forgot, by the last lorry that was leaving. Water came higher and higher up to their mouths.' Galbraith let out a real loud scream.

Jeff's head jerked back once and he blinked. Simon was startled and another bothered thrush took off further along through the woods.

Galbraith roared in laughter.

'Fuck sake, Galbraith.'

Davie laughed, shot out a hand to Jeff's shoulder. 'Don't shat yourself. He's just joking, wee man.'

'That's a cursed family.' Galbraith twisted his lip.

Simon turned his head quickly back to Galbraith. 'What do you mean, cursed?'

'Cursed. My old man says it. Stuck in that haunted house of theirs, all dying off one by one till there'll be none. They devil-worship, man. She was seen dancing naked under the moon.'

There was a long silence.

'Imagine her. Varie Bultitude, dancing naked for the devil? You still would though – given half a chance, eh?'

'What?'

'Go in for a fucking ride of her. Even if the devil was stood right there beside you.'

Simon looked from Galbraith to Davie.

'Aye,' went Galbraith, 'I'd do anything for a sniff of that. Who wouldn't?'

The horse trek had drawn too far ahead across the rolling moor backs and though Simon looked repeatedly he could not distinguish that final rider. The boys walked on down the track towards the Black Lochs then took the fork away north across the moorlands.

Peewees ground-nesting out in the moor cotton arose and circled before settling back down after the boys had made the passage past them, as if the diminutive human party crossing that heath gave out some violent vortex – a whirlwind – and the birds like brittle leaves were lifted, thrown high into the air then finally settled back down again in their wake.

The four boys came to a derelict crofter's cottage, corrugated roof festered into orange holes as if attacked by acid; large-leafed nettles and ground dockens filled the shell's interior. Sprouting strands of hugely long, scarlet-thorned brambles – like bent fishing rods with a heavy catch on – seeking outwards from the emptied window spaces. Bottomless pails and rolls of rusted wire lay all around the exterior ground. The cottage had probably been fully occupied until the 1950s then used as a wire store when the fields down towards the railway were fenced.

Galbraith put his head gingerly in the door space, calling out, 'Are you in there, Ann Trotter? Is this not your new house?'

'Do you think the Prowler lives in there?' asked wee Jeff.

Galbraith shook his head wearily. 'The Prowler. The Prowler. There is no such thing as a Prowler, Jeff.'

The three other boys were creeping around the walls of the ruined cottage examining pieces of debris. Then they were headed down towards Black Lochs Tunnel, but before it reached there, to avoid the necessity for embanking and support on the steep descent down the moorside, the track turned almost half a meandering mile to the right, ascending before its left haul back round again, using the natural contours in the ground.

Simon was staring along the rutted track. 'You know, this would be brilliant for scrambling. If I had a scrambling bike I'd be up here every day, man.'

'Crimmo's dreaming of getting his motorbike offof his old man,' Davie said to Galbraith and he sighed.

As if Simon wasn't there, Galbraith looked at Davie. 'It's no bikes he's dreaming about. He's fucking in love.'

'Fuck off, Galbraith.'

'You are too. Nikki Caine, Nikki Caine, all-through-your-fucking-brain.'

Davie laughed and looked at Simon. He frowned. 'You got anywhere with her yet?'

'Eh?'

'Have you got anywhere with that wee blondie yet? Snogged it; got the finger in?'

Simon tutted. 'Eh. Nut.'

'You never even snogged her yet?' Galbraith snorted.

'Nut.' Cornered, Simon said, 'I'm going out with her one night though.'

'Is he fuck,' said Galbraith.

'You wait and see.'

Davie looked down at the ground. 'You have to do better than that, Crimmo boy. Thing about a night out with a lassie in that town, man, apart from the back row of the Phoenix, there's nae winching space.'

'No what?'

'Winching space. There's nowhere for a snog and good feel off of a girl in that entire town, apart from stood up Jacob's Ladder by the benches. When I went up there with Maureen Laing before the End-of-Year dance there was a fucking queue of couples waiting for a snog on the benches there. It was pishing down rain as well. Maureen had those heel shoes on – randy-looking as anything. But she was getting well cheesed off. We were up and down that stairway three times. Know where we ended up together?'

'Where?'

'Sheltering underneath the kids' slide by the tower. I mean, standing underneath it out the rain best you could. A slide only gives you this much shelter.' Davie had took off his shirt and tied its arms round his waist; he held out his arms before his bare chest indicating around two feet of space. 'We had to stand side by side in between the snogs.'

'Did you get the finger in?' Galbraith shouted.

'Galbraith.' Simon nodded to Jeff who was listening closely. 'Jeff, away on down the road. We're just coming.'

'Why?'

'We're talking big boys' stuff. Do as I say and away down there and see if you can find us a stream for a drink out of.'

Jeff tutted and he walked on down the track, though he hesitated a few times, looking backwards.

'Go on,' called Simon, waving his hand to indicate further ahead then he turned to the two boys. 'Quit talking about shagging and everything in front of him. He'll go and tell ma mum.'

'So did you get the finger in?' Galbraith persevered.

Davie sighed. 'Nut.'

'Ha ha ha.'

'I thought I'd save it for after the dance. We'd a half-bottle vodka I'd bought out of Low's. I was drooked, man, mainly cause, to show off, I'd went down the slide for her in that rain.'

Galbraith laughed, impressed.

'She'd brought a coat at least and she was holding it over her head so that even when I was snogging her under the slide, boys, she didn't put her arms round me. She had this bloody coat held up over her hairdo to save it while I was kissing her.'

'Ha ha ha.' Galbraith twirled round.

'Halfway through the dance she goes, I've to go outside a minute. She started spewing up at the side of the gym hall. I swear she had three gubs of the voddy and no more, so I says to her, Can I feel your bum then? – she goes, Aye, but only through my dress. So she's bent over boaking up and I'm just standing behind feeling her arse with both hands as if I was searching for the fucking house keys in there.'

Simon and Galbraith laughed loudly.

'What'd it feel like?' Galbraith enquired in an urgent way.

Davie shrugged. 'A lassie's arse? Soft. But rain was trickling down my neck. It was a night out with Raquel Squelch no Raquel Welch, I'm telling you this. A car, boys. Yous need a car for the lassies.'

Galbraith scoffed. 'You want a fucking motorbike; a shitey wee fifty cc an all.'

'So what, Galbraith? I'll be all over the shop while you're arsing around up here.'

Galbraith turned sharply. 'Davie, have you ever put the finger up?'

'Course. Wee English piece, Alice, who was up here on her summer holidays. Down by the war memorial in broad daylight, man.'

'Crap.'

'You asked. It's for me to know and you to wonder, Galbraith.'

Galbraith was frustrated with the uninformative silence that followed.

'What's it like?'

'Nice.'

'Just sort of leave it in there?'

'You move it.'

'Fuck sake!' Galbraith gulped in excitement.

Simon turned. Jeff was still not at a satisfactory distance. 'Jeff, go away or I'll break your fingers,' Simon shouted.

Big Davie said, 'Jeff is no going to be like that Marko Morrell cunt; no going to be much of a guitarist when he gets big with you breaking his fingers every ten minutes, Crimmo.'

'Come on,' said Simon.

Jeff stood by the burn at the bottom and the boys all got down, lying flat upon the earth to lower their faces close to the running water's surface.

'If there's a deid sheep somewhere upstream we's could die,' claimed Galbraith.

'That's crap,' said Davie.

Galbraith added, 'A biting adder could get us then. They kill ya, man. Watch for them on rocks on days like this.'

The stream water was running and it was very clear; showing down in it were the furry, silt-covered rocks, vegetation fronds moving in slow leans – first this way and then that. A small pool was in at the far edge where legged flies and spindle beetles floated, seemingly helplessly, upon the elastic surface of those eddies.

They each used a single hand to cup cold water to their mouths in fast rhythmic movements. None of them talked as they drank. Davie cupped his hands together and brought up water which he poured in at the back of his long hair and splashed onto his face, but the other two lads did not imitate him. Davie looked like a pirate.

'Let's go up the river and watch the girls,' Galbraith said.

'Aye.'

They crossed the hill with the Black Lochs railway tunnel. When they stood above the tunnel's westerly mouth and looked down on the perfectly straight railway track below, they could smell the tar rising off the coated wooden sleepers. The track occasionally croaked and tinkled softly like a spent matchstick in that heat.

When they got back to the village shop almost an hour later, Simon said, 'Ach, you guys go on up the river. I'll be up in a wee minute. I'm just going back up the house for a new T-shirt, this one's boufing.'

'I'll come too.'

'Nut, Jeff. Go with the boys.'

'Or he'll break your fingers.'

'Will yous just take him up the river? Watch him at the edge?'

'Okay, man. See you there.'

He watched the three of them walk, heads down on the bridle path, towards the river where the dam pool was half a mile up. He waited till he heard the echoing crash of the swing gate, meaning they were out from under the high-roofed railway bridge. Simon made straight for the only phone box in the village further round towards the church. He hauled open the heavy door with both hands.

As the dial rotated backwards with that ratcheting sound, the earpiece was jumping in his hand with sheer nervousness. The ringtone sounded three times before it was quickly snatched up. 'Double five nine eight, who do we appreciate?' her young voice said.

The pips were coming, Simon pushed in the two-pence piece and said, 'At last.'

'Who's that?'

'Simon. Simon Crimmons.'

'Who?'

'Oh. Is Nikki there?'

'Did you think I was her?' There was solid loud laugh. 'I'm her big sister. Who's this?'

'Eh, I'm a friend of your wee sister's. She's asked me to telephone.'

'Did she now? You're the latest, are you?'

Simon was quiet on his end of the phone.

'What phone box are you in? Are you round the corner or something?'

'Tulloch Ferry.'

'She's seeking far afield; she must be getting desperate.'

'Maybe you could say I phoned?'

'I'll forget your name. I need a face to put to a name.'

'Simon.'

'Simon?'

'Simon Crimmons.'

'Simon Crimmons? Yes. But I'll forget.'

'Say from Tulloch.'

'I'll forget that too.'

Simon chuckled and suddenly said, 'I was going to ask her out.'

'Oh, you're quite sweet.'

'Where do you think I should ask her to go? What does she like?'

'Mmmm, good question. Why don't you take her to the flicks on Friday and buy her some sweeties?'

'This is Monday.'

'In a terrible hurry, are we?'

'Aye. All right then. I'll take her to the pictures.'

'It's a deal. I quite like you. So far.'

There was mutual silence.

'Quarter past six outside the Phoenix on Friday then.' The girl's voice said it as if the date was with her and Simon felt sudden concern about who he had made the date with. 'Bye.'

The phone went dead. Incredible.

Simon turned to leave the telephone box and pushed the heavy door, but suddenly he stopped and turned back.

He picked up the telephone directory and began to leaf through the pages, but the paper felt dry and swollen and then the smell reached his nostrils. Urine. Someone had dropped the directory on the floor and peed on it long ago. Simon let go of the pages and it fell back onto the supporting ledge. But then his curiosity led him and he gritted his teeth and thumbed through to the Bs.

Bultitude Andrew, Comm., Broken Moan,
The Back Settlement . . . 369

He placed another two-pence piece in the slot and dialled.

'Broken Moan House?' an elderly, Scottish female voice stated, the pips went and Simon shoved the coin in. Though he knew she was still out on that pony trek he said, 'Is Varie there please?'

'No. Who is this please?'

'Is Alexander there?'

'Who shall I say is calling please?'

'A friend.'

'Without a name? Those friends speak to his father first.'

Simon hesitated. 'Edward.'

'Edward?' There was a sound of a pot or something clanking close to the woman.

'Yes.'

'One minute then please.' There was the sound of the receiver being placed down on a hard surface then more noises in the background. It sounded like a kitchen. He could hear the talking woman had moved some distance from the phone; the more faint voice clearly said, 'A friend of Master Alexander.'

Simon repeated the word 'master' to himself in a mocking tone and silently moved his lips to the word. Then he made a thoughtless mistake. He waited for the sound of steps returning towards their telephone but there was a soft click and a young voice – very posh and English – aggressively said, 'Edward who?'

Simon realised there was more than one telephone in that big house which he should have anticipated – they had two themselves in Tulloch Villa. Alexander Bultitude had just picked up an extension.

The pause had been too long and again that voice said with more aggression, 'Yeah?'

Simon banged the phone down on the cradle.

Friday 22 June 1973

He had got a lift into town off Willie – all the way up to the garages – aboard the old Albion Reiver which was returning from a run. Willie was going back down on a night run to Granton Harbour, so Simon could return to the village on the same lorry later that night.

Simon walked across the railway bridge then along the road beneath the wooded slope. He did not glance up even once to the swing and their den above.

He crossed the high bridge and turned left beside the view window of the telephone headquarters, looking in at the switch mechanisms. Then he stepped onward, but at the corner down to the post office – suddenly – something completely new occurred. Simon looked in the window of the Labour Exchange – as usual intrigued by the adult realm within – and he stepped backwards to the double doors and entered in through them to the office.

There was a woman behind a desk and displays of small coloured cards on blackboard-like frames. Simon nodded to the woman and stepped up to these cards, studying their odd and often indecipherable telegraphese. He frowned; most jobs seemed to involve employment in hotels. One in the Bank of Scotland.

'Can I help you at all?' the lady called across – just like in a shop.

'Just looking thanks.' Simon coughed.

'If you're interested in anything bring the card over.' She spoke in a friendly manner.

'Oh, right.'

He spent some more time studying these cards and selected one. It was a job up at the hospital. This would be the hospital where the girl he'd spoken to on the phone, Karen, Nikki Caine's

99

big sister, worked. There was also a position as a marshal on the railway pier for the ferry company. It was an appealing notion, supervising the loading and unloading of vehicles onto and off the island car ferries, swinging them out dangerously, slung in their nets on the davits like a great haul of silverfish.

He took the two cards over to the woman.

'Take a seat please.'

The involvement seemed more than he'd expected but he sat down and looked around, mainly at the informative posters on the walls behind the woman.

'I'll need details from you.'

'Aye.' He was proud to be able to produce these easily and efficiently in a manner Bobby Forth could not. The woman took his name, his parents' address and their telephone number.

'Oh. Does your family have the lorry company?'

'Yes.' He said it defensively.

She glanced at him in that usual way. As if he was a runaway or something. Then she asked for his national insurance number.

'My what?'

'Your national insurance number.'

'I don't have that.'

'Never mind; we can deal with that when they interview you.'

She was not judging him and Simon felt puffed with pride that he would be taken so seriously as to be interviewed for employment just by handing in these cards.

'Date of birth?'

He recited it.

But now the woman frowned. 'You're not sixteen yet?'

'No. August.'

'Oh, but I'm afraid you couldn't be considered for these until you turn sixteen.'

'Oh.'

'Yes. I'm sorry about that.' She was putting down her pen. 'Look, it says here. Sixteen plus.' She turned one of the cards round and used her thumbnail to indicate a number. She seemed very disappointed though. 'Have you thought about part-time work? In the supermarket?'

'Nah. Och, I'll just leave it then.'

But the woman was not obstructive. 'Well, look. You never know.' Simon nodded.

'Why don't we apply anyway? Perhaps they won't find anyone first time round and by the time they do a second bout of interviews you could well have had your birthday? It's soon, isn't it?' She smiled – she seemed quite excited by his impending sixteenth as well.

'Aye, that's great then, aye.' He went to slide back his chair and stood.

'Will I copy out these details for you?'

'Ah, nah.'

'Well, all right. But I'll put all your details into the applications myself and hand them in. They are just standard details. If you sign at the bottom there please.'

He wrote his name on two forms the way he wrote it at the top of his school essays. 'Aye, thanks then, bye.'

He idled down the road and past the door to the County Hotel. He made the usual foray up beyond Boots the Chemist looking in the windows at the brightly coloured display bottles. He checked if they had renewed the window display of knives in the tackle shop – which they had not.

He headed for John Menzies before it closed – to check on the latest motorcycle magazines. In one magazine there was a feature on new Yamahas. He considered buying the magazine but then he'd have to carry it rolled up in the back pocket of his jeans.

He moved through and beyond the stairway to the books section. Abruptly he stopped walking with the shock of what he saw. Simon stared in a greedy and too obvious way then quickly turned aside pretending to look at random, uninteresting book covers. He was sure it could be no one else. He began to physically shake and had to grip his fingers – this trembling hand was helpless, beyond his control, it came from somewhere within him. He did not feel responsible for the feeling in any way. Simon moved further up the bookshelves. Then a little further. He glanced out the side of his eyes, studying which book the figure was considering. He coughed slightly then Simon turned and said, 'Have you read that? Book.'

The other young man turned extremely slowly. He was wearing actual dark sunglasses. Inside Menzies! Just for a moment Simon believed this guy was going to reach up and slide the sunglasses down his small nose, uncovering his eyes. It was a manoeuvre Simon had witnessed in films or television programmes, invariably set in the United States of America where people wore sunglasses.

But the other young man did not do this. He allowed the round, flat, black and intimidating lenses to cant towards Simon's face. There was silence. Simon said, 'I've read it.'

And when he spoke the voice was absolutely and tremendously English and equally posh – as if it travelled through toffee. Simon recognised it immediately. 'First prize to you.' In a rush the young man in the sunglasses placed the book back onto the shelves – as if to make an escape. But instead he hesitated, raised his hand to his smooth chin, and with two fingers began rubbing there, considering Simon – then he looked around. They were alone in the books section. 'You're not a plain-clothes floorwalker in mufti, connected with the security of these premises?'

'Eh. Nut.' Simon just laughed. He wasn't to be put off.

The other young man turned his face slightly back to the book on the shelves then round further towards Simon and in an odd movement, as if slapping it into obedience, he patted round the side of his long coat so it quickly followed him. He told Simon, 'Strange things are happening to me recently; and this warm weather.'

'I like your brilliant coat.'

Now he smiled. 'Honest words, honestly spoken.'

The coat was magnificent. As Big Davie had claimed, it was a military coat, but Simon had imagined some drab green garment. However, this was knee-length in a shade of powder blue with brass buttons and golden, braided workings all down the front.

'It's like Hendrix.'

'Thank you. I wear it at great risk from the mountain men of these here parts. You worship Jimi, and all his works?'

'I've four albums. Just got *War Heroes*. Who wouldn't worship Jimi?'

The boy in the powder-blue overcoat lowered his voice and leaned forward though he was not as tall as Simon. 'All these country squares.'

'I'm going for a walk,' Simon announced and he coughed.

'You end up doing that round here but it's no good, you end up back where you started. I've tried up in those lanes round that coliseum thing.'

'I'll show you where the *Grenadier* boat sank. If you like.'

Weirdly the head popped up in interest. 'A vessel sank? I love a foundering.'

'I'll show you.'

The boy in the long blue coat actually followed. But he refused to follow at the same pace and Simon had to pause twice, crossing the floor of Menzies, just to let the strange figure catch up with him.

Alexander Bultitude walked with a louping gait, moving his head from side to side as if trying to hear some constant sound. Every single customer in that shop, and the two ladies behind the cash till, paused or even turned round from the magazine shelves to observe the boy's passage across the floor towards the old wooden revolving doors. Alexander gave them all a bow as he exited.

Outside, people on the pavement stared at that self-conscious, countercultural attire – daring even for a large city. Simon was proud to be seen walking with such a very unearthly figure.

But this initial walk was to be very brief. Simon had moved up the pavement only a few steps and, in moments, Alexander crossed the road alone and over there he leaned upon the silver-painted railings, gazing out across the waters of the bay to Shelter Island and the boatyard there. Simon had to turn back and cross the road – looking both ways – to stand beside him again.

Alexander acknowledged Simon's presence by saying, 'The view is second-rate. This whole town is a glorified chandler's yard. Are you affiliated with the police in any way?'

'No. Why?'

'Until you interrupted without proper introduction, I thought of nicking one of their books.'

'Did you?' Simon chuckled. 'My mate nicks nudie mags out of there.'

'Really?' Then the tone changed. 'But they must be stocked next to the till so that is actually quite impressive. The most nerve-racking area to lift from. I've stolen two copies of *The Thief's Journal*. One in French. In Nice. Have you read it?'

'What is it? A magazine for robbers?'

Alexander laughed in a spiteful way. 'You haven't read *The Thief's Journal*? Your star is fading.'

'I'll read it if you lend us a copy.'

He jerked backwards and his very long hair flapped once on the rear of the coat. 'You'd need to steal it off me, my friend. Okay, I do admit I haven't quite finished it yet. I curl up with it nightly. It was written by a thief and it should always be stolen, never purchased. Always. Only the most faithless could stoop to pay for that novel.'

Simon nodded obediently.

'Look, young native. I slip these into the pages of their book stock. I go for the most dismal, woeful titles.'

From the coat pocket Alexander took a small length of folded card which was protecting the corners of some pieces of paper – almost the size of the cards in the Labour Exchange. Typed imperfectly on these bits of paper were various phrases:

WE ARE THE VIETCONG ARMY
AND WE HAVE YOUR HOME ADDRESS

THIS IS A BANNED PUBLICATION
CONTACT YOUR NEAREST POLICE STATION
IMMEDIATELY

EDWARD HEATH IS KGB
SEE PAGE 173

Simon laughed. 'You leave them in the pages of the books?'

'Uh, yeah.'

'That's completely brilliant.'

He nodded. 'It is, isn't it? I see myself as a Joe Orton figure. It's not defacing a book nor is it stealing. I don't really know what I could be charged with if I got caught. And I'm almost curious to learn. Have you read *An Enemy of the People*? Well, the majority is always wrong.' He took the bits of paper and folded them carefully back between the card, shoving it deep into the coat pocket. 'I'm sensitive to persecution in all its forms,' he explained.

Simon led him to the north pier and pointed across the sheet of water which separated it from the railway pier. 'My old man told me that years ago there was so many fishing boats tied up here you could walk across their decks from one pier to the other.'

Alexander Bultitude frowned out at the distance. 'But why *would* you? Were things really any better over there on that other pier?'

Simon laughed. 'My old man told me, so it must be true. The *Grenadier* was an old steamer boat that tied up here late one night. Went on fire and a wee fella was trapped downstairs. Stuck his head out the porthole and begged the policemen to shoot him. "My clothes are on fire, My clothes is on fire." They wouldn't shoot him and he burned alive with his head stuck out.'

Alexander drawled, 'The same way you boil a lobster, and it goes to show: you should always keep a gun handy just for when one of the locals starts to beg for it.' He lifted the sunglasses at last, standing near the edge of the pier, and he looked down into the waters. He had troubleless, dark brown eyes. 'The wreck isn't here.' He sighed. 'I've been beaten to it but it must have made a wonderful sight. Burning.'

'I guess it was took away.' Simon pointed off into the bay. 'But there's a wreck over in the boatyard there; you can see the mast sticking up.'

Alexander shook his head. 'I'm something of a scuba-diving enthusiast.'

'Wow. You're learning to be a frogman?'

'Yes. They teach us at my school on Friday afternoons. In a swimming pool. I don't relish climbing into this muck though.' He nodded down towards the bay water. 'I had more in mind the Tobermory galleon treasure. A lobster was seen over there crossing the road with a golden doubloon in its claw.'

'So are you from round here then?'

'That's not clear. I suppose you must go to the local high school?' He curled his lip.

'I hate it. Thinking of leaving.' Simon looked at his watch. He was eight minutes late for Nikki Caine. Loitering with a boy. Who would have thought?

'I'm going to steal more copies of *The Thief's Journal* – and send them all to Genet in Paris with an apologia.'

'Jenny? Who's she?'

He tutted. 'Genet. The guy who wrote it.'

'Oh, right.'

Simon looked at his watch again. 'Look, sorry, but I've got a date with a girl now.'

Alexander turned to him. 'A girl? What are you going to do with a girl in this place?' He looked around. 'Pushing her out to sea on a raft might be her only hope.'

'We're going to the pictures.'

'The pictures?' he whispered. 'Is there an actual art gallery here?'

'The Phoenix. The cinema.'

'Oh.'

Suddenly Simon sensed Alexander Bultitude felt abandoned so he added, 'Get me up the road if you want.'

'I'll walk with you, if you don't mind too much. I've never met a girl really.'

Simon laughed.

'It's true. I go to a school of just boys.' As they walked along the esplanade together they passed the frontages of the hotels and young Bultitude turned a suspicious eye on him. 'A bunch of Capuchin monks have me under their wing in a home for injured mountaineers at the foot of the Alps.'

Simon laughed.

'They do.'

'But you must have family here?'

Now the coat swished and the head turned. Simon was sure it was the word 'family' which caused the reaction. Yet the boy reported, quietly, 'I live with my father. And my little sister – who is a sort of girl – near the village named the Back Settlement. More like the Back Passage.'

Simon laughed.

'Hey. If you want to communicate, leave me a note in that book in the shop and I'll reply to you. I'm here for the summer. All of it. Every long hour.'

'I could telephone instead. What's your name?'

'Alexander. It's in the phone book under The Great.'

'I'm Simon Crimmons.'

'Simon of the Desert,' he murmured.

★   ★   ★

Nikki Caine was standing at the very top of the steps outside the Phoenix like a vision of every promise. Her face seemed different. Simon realised she had been dabbling in the sorcery of make-up – turquoise eyeshadow. She looked down at her watch in an exaggerated manner as she saw him approach, but then her plain expression altered as she noticed the lurching figure in the powder-blue coat and sunglasses – heedless of the gathering dusk – a-step with Simon's stride.

Alexander said, 'Is that your beloved? A sort of fisher-nymphette. My God, she's like a little ray of golden sunshine. How did you find her in this joint?'

But Simon had noticed something amiss with Nikki Caine. She wore flared jeans which showed skinny legs and those now-familiar buckled shoes – highly polished. However, she was wearing a jersey which came high up on her neck. Simon recalled Big Davie had told him once that a jersey was the regulation wear for girls on any first date to the pictures. A blouse was as good as an invitation for the wandering hand to try some unbuttoning. But a high-necked woolly jersey was the sure antidote and it stopped any love bites to the neck too. His spirits fell a little.

Nikki did not look at Simon; her eyes were fixed upon the figure of Alexander. It was a bit rude. Simon stepped up to her.

'Karen said quarter past on the dot, so you're late.' She stated it with that distancing tone she used on Galbraith, but even then Nikki didn't look at Simon – her eyes were set to his right and her voice faded away as Alexander mounted the steps, heading right towards them with his coat waving around his thin legs.

'Hiya, Nikki. This is Alexander. He's just going.'

Simon noticed her physically shift position and she moved her chin a fraction downward.

'I'm delighted to meet you.' Painfully, he seemed to mean it but ruined things by not removing the sunglasses and then by looking up in the sky as if an unusual aircraft was overhead. 'And I do hope you'll enjoy your evening's entertainment.'

Other than a fractional curdling on her brow Nikki Caine did not respond in any way.

Alexander turned to Simon. 'Write me through the clandestine pneumatic telegraph system we've agreed.'

'Aye, right. See you.' Simon said it a bit curtly and realised he'd changed tack. He had wanted to show off how physically attractive he believed Nikki Caine was, but now he was siding with Nikki, brushing Alexander off a touch more coldly than he should have. He wanted to be alone with the girl. And to add to the pathos, just before Alexander stepped away, two older lads over by the lobby cards turned to stare shamelessly and one said loudly to the other, 'Fuck sakes, man. It's Doctor Who.' Alexander must have heard but he continued meandering onward up the road, crossing opposite the optician's on the other side. Simon felt a tug in his heart.

Nikki turned straight to Simon. 'Who the f-ing hell was that? Is he cracked? What was he wearing?' She turned again and watched after the figure of Alexander Bultitude going away up the road.

'Sorry I'm late.'

'Yes, well. I've already been asked in twice. By boys.'

'I'm sorry.'

'Who was that freak?'

'Oh, Alexander? He's completely mad.'

'He looks it.'

'He doesn't like this town much.'

She turned round. 'He should leave then. Sounds English. And another thing. This's a war film.'

'Aye.' Simon looked up at the hand-painted banner above the doors: *The Battle of Britain*.

'I don't like war films.'

One of the charming features of the Phoenix Cinema was that although the seating layout was stalls only, with no gallery or balcony – and no difference in the discomfort of the seats – the management had devised an enterprising policy of charging more for the back half of the seat rows than the front, forcing adults and aspirant lovers to pay more in order to escape the bellowing, rabble-rousing youth positioned up front. Nikki insisted on the cheap seats and Simon paid.

Nikki mellowed when Simon bought an entire box of Maltesers at the sweet counter. 'Take the plastic wrapper off now,' he advised. 'If you try to in the dark the box can go flying and your Maltesers roll round all night and everyone kicks them. You get a game of floor billiards thrown in for free.'

She had frowned at first but then she smiled at this.

In the dark he had to blink and let her choose the seats, sensing this was the female's prerogative. She went for the left side close to the front and she moved along an empty row until she had her shoulder against the side wall so no one else could sit next to her but Simon. He found the privacy of her seating choice encouraging.

They folded down their seats and sat, both instantly placing their knees up on the back of the seat in front, imitating the supposedly casual manner of the town's youth. He held the opened box of chocolates in his hand and kept it there as she picked from them very rapidly, chewing quickly as she stared up at the screen. He studied her features in the light which came from the adverts. Angled whiteness was falling down from the screen. Towards the rear of the cinema many individual cigarette-smoke trails slowly rose in tall trembling threads, forming into coiling assemblages close to the ceiling as they passed through the projector's blue beams.

After the adverts and the trailers – all of which were for forth-coming war films – Simon leaned over towards where he judged her ear might have been under the hair and he whispered, 'Maybe the first film won't be a war film?'

The first feature began. *The Battle of the Bulge.*

Nikki Caine sighed out loud. 'Battles, battles, battles. It's not going to be about diets, is it?'

It seemed – in their town at least – there was little profit to be made from the more pacifistic themes of cinema. When each German tank finally began to explode, hearty cheers came in response from the outcrops of youth clustered among the ranks of seat backs to the front.

Very soon, Nikki Caine was bored with the film's narrative of ongoing destruction. She looked around to try and identify the cheering parties more than she watched the screen. She sat up straight. A few moments later Simon copied and he sat up as well.

He decided to time his approach, counting to one hundred with his hand on the armrest, but then try for where? For her hand or for her thigh? He plumped for the hands; always the hands. But after counting another hundred he decided to extend his deadline to five hundred. Then he became worried Nikki could sense him counting. When he got to five hundred he leaned over and said, 'I'm going to the bogs.'

In the men's toilets it was cold. He stood inside a locked cubicle, breathing and shaking his head while listening to his heart thump. This girl stuff was hard work. He washed his hands free of chocolate traces. There was only cold water. He dried his hands on the crap towel thing then rubbed them on the arse of his jeans. Then he went back into the darkened cinema, squinting to find her blonde head up against the wall. When he was sat beside her he counted to one hundred and put his left hand straight across and laid it on hers. Another German tank blew up. She had her hands bunched together in her lap and he was amazed how she quite easily unfurled them and gave him the fingers of her right hand which he held uncertainly. She also leaned towards him and whispered harshly, 'Your hand's freezing.' He was beginning to note it was always a positive then a negative with her.

Nikki Caine looked around her. The yellow curtains bearing the image of the huge blue bird emerging from the red flames were closing in an unsteady motion and the lights came up for the interval. But they still held hands even in the light. Then the next feature started once everyone was back from the sweetie counter. They both looked at each other and laughed when the credit for *Michael Caine* came up.

'Is that your dad?' Simon whispered.

She smiled, the mouth slightly open and the white teeth showing but coloured by the screen. 'If only.'

An hour into this film she started to shift from one side of her bottom to the other though she accommodated their held hands to each move. 'This film's boring,' she whispered.

'Want to go?'

'Aye. C'mon.'

Simon didn't want to leave and he thought the film was magnificent and rich with attractive details but he'd felt her lose interest as soon as all the chocolates were finished. She'd eaten almost the whole box.

Outside it was close to dark but the sky was still luminescent with an audacious northern energy; he smiled at her and she smiled back. He said, 'Want more sweets?'

'No thanks. I'm on a diet.'

'Want to go for a walk?'

'I *am* going for a walk.'

'Where?'

'Home.'

'Oh, right.'

'I've got to be getting back, Dad says. You can get us up the short cut if you want. It's spooky at night. Those big old trees creak.'

'Aye. Sure.'

They began walking side by side. Simon took her hand again. Though they were walking up quite a busy bit of road beyond the optician's with the odd passing car – and even the late bus – Nikki did not seem to mind being seen holding hands with him in public. An official announcement – so to speak.

'How do you know that weird guy then?'

'Alexander? Ach, I've just met him really. Know who he is?'

'No.'

'He's Alexander Bultitude.' Simon said it grandly.

She scrunched up her nose. 'Who?'

He repeated the name. 'They live in that big huge house at the Pass.'

'What a spasticky name. Isn't that something on maps in geography?'

'That's longitude.'

'I've never heard of them. Dad might.'

Simon stopped walking and he let go of her hand. He put both his hands on her upper arms. The jersey was very woolly – almost itchy. 'Nikki, I'm really glad you don't know him cause that's what I said and my pals all went on and on at me for not knowing who the Bultitudes were.'

She frowned and they resumed walking. But again she took his hand. 'You and me must lead sheltered lives then. He looks like a singer from *Top of the Pops*.'

'Aye.'

'But he isn't.'

'He's at a boarding school.'

'Oh, right. Like way, way away?'

'Aye. They're like away posh rich.'

'Oh, right.'

They were passing the old lodge house and taking the short cut. This was just a path up a heavily wooded hill – but a wide way which years of usage by the residents of the Brae Estate had worn down so the old tree roots protruded upwards, sometimes seven or eight inches with their bark worn smooth by footfalls. It was difficult in the gloom. Street light from below faded and the lamps from the escarpment above only scudded down a weakened glow. Simon wondered if he should grab and kiss her before they came back into light but he did not dare.

The short cut came out on the top of the cul-de-sac crescent but it was still a long walk through the pebble-dash estate streets to the dead end on the far side – almost at the new primary school which was slowly being built.

When they got as far as Brae Drive, Simon was sure Nikki was walking slower and waiting for him to make some move or other but he wasn't sure how to go about it. He was also becoming anxious about the time and sneaked a look at his watch by glancing down to where they were holding hands. If he missed Willie's lorry he'd probably get hell for phoning his mum or dad to come fetch him in the car.

'This is where I live,' she announced. He could see the steep bank of scrub at the back of the council block. He knew of a path there, up to the main road at the top.

They went in the main door of her close, number 44, but she pulled him insistently by the hand past the bottom of the stairs, beyond an apartment door and a series of under-stair lock-ups. Big Davie's phrase, Winching Place, now came to Simon's mind. He wondered who she had been there with before. He had to admit there was a perfect logic to this location though. This was the route through to the back drying green. No mums or kids would be going out there in the dark and also the place was concealed by the corner from anyone ascending or descending the main stairway. He could hear a television though, from through the door of the nearest ground-floor flat.

Nikki Caine backed herself inward, taking him with her by both of his hands – she placed her own back against the plaster wall which was painted a dark gloss burgundy.

'Nikki,' he said but his throat had dried.

'What?' She whispered it in an impatient manner that instructed him to speak quietly.

He too lowered his voice. 'You know how folks say: I want to get to know you better? Well, that's how I feel. I want to get to know you better.'

'That's sweet,' she whispered quickly, looking downward at their feet.

'I don't know much about you.'

She turned her face up to him. 'There's nothing to know.' She shrugged and said slowly, 'You see it all.'

For some reason he was shot through with a sadness at that statement. 'I want to know you more.'

'Start here then.' She kissed up and he pressed his mouth down with her hands in his hair. Her already attractive mouth was further blessed by the taste of Maltesers and he could smell a clean scent in her hair. He'd never kissed a girl before but he'd read about how to – on the mouth – and he put his tongue slowly in past her small teeth and so did she, upward into his own mouth. He realised she was breathing heavily through her nose. Weirdly, her little mechanical tongue movements brought to mind that mixer machine his mum used on Christmas Days, going round and round.

They kissed for long minutes, her compressed against the wall by his weight, their heads twisting together in conjunction and reaction, first this way and then that way. He felt himself go hard very quick so he had to lean his lower torso away from her slightly so she wouldn't feel it, threatening and demanding in against her there.

The pushing got altogether more frantic and now Simon squeezed the palms of his hands in behind her buttocks and she came forward off the wall to permit this. Her bum was shaped, hard, and he was surprised that she allowed him to continue. As she let him push back in on her, his knuckles were crushed between the cold stone wall and the back pockets of her jeans until he could not move his hands. But sometimes, she slightly lifted one leg and hooked it round his calf assertively, so he could smooth his palm over the rounding shape then up and down over the back of her thigh. He risked pushing a little closer in so she could feel him against her. She didn't react, so then he withdrew his right hand and slid it round to right between her legs, on the seam of the denim. He rubbed, applying more pressure until she suddenly broke off kissing and made a panicked, breathing intake, then she hissed through her nose as she stretched back up to kiss him again. The wonderful sensation was of her becoming excited and slightly helpless. Suddenly her hand went to his wrist.

'Come and see Dad,' she quickly said.

The use of the word 'Dad', so soon after where his hand had been made him wince, but Nikki laughed and pulled him by the hand so he almost stumbled.

He wondered if he was to be allowed into the privacy of her bedroom to continue matters, but he whispered, 'Wait,' and he stood still. Their two arms were stretched out, joining them at the hands. She looked beautiful, with her legs all extended ready to step forward and her hair fallen to one side of her face. She looked like a wee film star, Simon thought, and a sudden, enormous emotion of dependence on her came into him.

'What?'

'Just wait a second more.' He smiled painfully.

She whispered, 'Is it? A hard-on? Have I gave you one?'

'Aye.'

She laughed, looking at him excitedly – into his eyes.

'All right yet?'

'You can't hurry these things.'

'You don't need to be all embarrassed.'

'I do in front of your dad.'

To his surprise, their flat was the ground-floor-door one with the noise of the television, so they had been just outside her home – where he realised she must have felt secure.

Nikki's father was in the living room watching that television they had heard outside. He had an armchair with a high back, so whenever he made to address Simon, the man had to bend

114

awkwardly to look round the chair and out through the living-room door to the corridor where they both stood side by side, not venturing in. That chair had a calico covering and creaked with each of his shiftings.

'Is that Nicola back with her friend?' he said, calling this out generally through the house before he turned round more. Creak.

In a voice almost a whisper, Nikki said, 'Dad, this's Simon.'

'Hello, son.'

'Hello, Mr Caine.'

'You're both nice and early home; unlike some. Thanks for seeing Nicola up the road.'

Simon presumed this was an instruction to immediately depart, but the father added, 'I see your dad's lorries round the town.'

So they knew fine who he was. 'Aye.'

'How many lorries is it your father has now?'

'Ten.'

'And was the picture house good?'

'Aye, thanks, Mr Caine.'

'It was war, Dad,' she said and she tutted.

'The flicks is the flicks, lassie; it's better than sat in that awful bedroom of yours.' The father paused, then said, 'If you want to wind her up, Simon, call her Nicola.'

'Nikki's my name.'

'No it's no. I've the birth certificate right here and I'll show it to Simon too.' He laughed. 'You were christened *Nicola* no Nikki.'

'Och, Dad.' She looked straight at Simon. 'My mum's at the cards club so he's picking on me.' Then suddenly she led Simon up a small dark corridor.

'Watch yourself!' the father called from the front room and there was a creak.

Sure enough, Nikki pushed open her bedroom door and Simon stepped in after her. He felt his anticipation regenerating.

The bedroom was very, very small. Smaller than Galbraith's and all the space to the left was taken up by a bunk bed hard against the wall. 'Hello.' On the upper mattress lay an attractive, bare-legged young woman with very blue eyeshadow. She was in a thigh-length skirt, no shoes on her feet, stretched out and filing at her fingernails very fast but looking over them directly at Simon. He instantly recognised her as the nurse sister. Karen Caine.

Nikki hardly glanced at the young woman. 'Don't be filing your nails above my bed. That's disgusting.'

'Hiya,' Simon replied casually, but he knew his surprise showed.

'I'll have my shoes back then thanks, madam. How was the pictures? Good?'

'Nut, they were war, but we had a laugh. I thought you'd be gone?' Nikki made a face with a secret meaning to her sister.

'Did you pay her in – Simon – cause she owes me forty pence?'

'Aye.'

'And he bought a big, big box of Maltesers,' Nikki added. 'We ate the lot.'

'You should've brought some back for me, ya wee besom.'

Nikki had stepped forward, close to the window. The curtains weren't drawn – even in the dark – so you could see across the drying green to the bulk of the back embankment. Simon noticed a small, white Formica table with a broken slice of mirror just balanced on it against the painted wall. Every available inch of the table was covered in bottles, tubs and lotions of girl make-up stuff.

'You'll need to take *me* out, Simon.'

'Och,' Nikki went.

The sister looked at Simon. 'It's like *The Liver Birds* in here, eh?' She quickly swung her bare legs round so he almost saw up the short skirt but she dropped down smoothly off the bunk; Simon had to flatten himself against the wall so Karen Caine could move past him towards Nikki and the table. The wall felt very shiny behind him and when he glanced, he saw it was one huge poster of David Cassidy. Or was that Cat Stevens? He was sliding against the man's face.

Nikki was taking off her shoes and her big sister was bending over, her arse bundled in the little black skirt and she was putting on the same pair of buckled shoes which Nikki had just shed.

'Och, they're all mud from the short cut,' Karen said.

'So? Thought you were going to wear the yellow ones anyways?'

'Mmm.' Karen angled herself in front of the uneven mirror. 'Now I look at it, I will.' The sister kicked off these shoes and the buckles tinkled. The other pair of shoes were very high heels, higher than any of Simon's mum's, so Karen suddenly rose in height as she angled her feet into them.

'So, Simon. I'm away out the night. Will you get us down the short cut?'

'He's only just got here, Karen.'

Simon said, 'I do kinda have to get going or I'll need to phone my dad to pick me up.'

Quickly Nikki said, 'Phone from here then. He could come get you here?'

Karen said, 'No way. Then I have to go all the way down the brae and round. Get us down the short cut or the Prowler might jump me.'

Nikki tutted. 'Karen, you use the short cut all the time on your own in the dark. Drunk.'

'Are you green with jealousness? Simon doesn't need to be feart of me. C'mon and kiss each other a wee goodbye then.'

Nikki tutted again and turned to Simon. 'God's sake, sorry about this. I thought she'd be gone.' Now she turned to her sister. 'You said you were gonna wear the yellows anyways so you just stayed to spy on us.'

'I changed my mind, didn't ah? They're both my shoes.' She tottled forwards on the heels and Simon noted there was no carpet. There was just painted lino on the floor.

Karen stated in a formal manner, 'I won't even make him climb out the window. I'll leave through the front door.' Then she added, 'Though I suppose you'll have him climbing in and out it aplenty soon enough.'

'Och.'

Simon had to flatten his back onto the shiny poster once more to let Karen pass him. She smelled of all perfume, moving out the bedroom and down the corridor. 'Kiss bye-bye then,' Karen called over her shoulder.

Nikki was sitting on the stool by the make-up table and shrugged as they looked at each other across that bedroom.

'I've got to go.'

'Go then,' Nikki said curtly.

He crossed over to her and she jumped up and kissed him on the lips.

'I'll phone,' he said. 'I promise.'

She whispered to him, 'After half three, any days,' and then with a mischievous look showing more interest than in the phone calls she said, 'How's she going to get down the short cut in those shoes?' She tutted and shook her head.

Simon stepped back into the corridor where Karen was talking with her father.

'Back by one,' the father said and the chair creaked.

'I'm nearly twenty and I'll be back when I want to be. Might go to Lynne's after eleven.'

'You still live here. Back at one. Or you wake wee Nicola up.'

'It's Saturday tomorrow.'

'Aye, she's at the shop though. And no climbing in that bloody window thinking your mother and I can't hear you. That window gets locked at nights. We're going to get robbed one day with yous two going in and out twenty to the dozen and leaving it unlocked.'

'Och, Dad.'

The father said, 'Look. Here's Simon. You're some boy, Simon. You arrive with one daughter and leave with the other. And I tell you, you're welcome to either of them.' He laughed. 'I'll leave you my collection of beer mats in ma will.' He jumped out a number of laughs which made the chair creak.

'Och, Dad,' Karen said – exactly the way Nikki did.

'Aye.' Simon shrugged awkwardly and felt himself redden up, but luckily it was quite dingy. 'I'll get Karen down the road. Thanks very much, Mr Caine.'

'See that? That's a polite boy, this one. You need to find one of them for a change.'

'Och, Dad.'

Mr Caine creaked in his seat. 'Watch out,' he called again and he cackled.

Everything about Karen Caine seemed fast to Simon – as if she were already late for her whole life. She walked fast, the heels clicking quickly on the pavements, and the shoes were so high that each step thrust her body forward so she moved in a busy, jerky way, and she talked fast, lifting her hands above her face quickly to touch at her hair, and when she lit a cigarette using a lighter, without offering one to Simon, she smoked quick – in angry puffs – snarling, 'I canna smoke in that house. Sometimes in wintertime it's too cold to open the window so I pretend to do the hoovering in our room, but I just sit, blow a few puffs of a good ciggy into the sucky-up bit. Here. Hold my coat.' She quickly slashed her folded-up, shiny raincoat towards him and he was to hold it as they continued. 'So are you going with my wee sister or what then?'

'Well, I'm hoping to see her again.'

'You will that. Did yous snog?'

'A gentleman never tells.'

'She'll tell me anyway. She tells me everything. You're a damn sight better that that Neil.'

Simon coughed.

She looked at him slyly. Her hair was fixed up with hairspray and it kind of wobbled with every step – and of course the breasts in the short top reacted in the expected manner as she moved under a particular street light which buzzed with a fierce current above them.

'Who's Neil?' he carefully said.

'I don't know, sweetheart. Wasn't as tall as you. And his daddy wasn't as rich.'

'We're not rich.'

She parped a mockery sound out of her lips. 'You're a rich kid. Box of Maltesers.' Then she pursed her lips. 'You're tall though, and pretty good-looking. Like in that way. Laddies from here don't look like you, much. You've good teeth too. Teeth are important.'

Simon had reddened once again but knew it couldn't be discerned in the street light. 'You work up the cottage hospital, eh?'

'Did Nicola tell you that?'

'I just heard it around. I applied for a job up the cottage hospital the day.'

'What?'

'Today. I applied for a job there.'

'What job?'

'Forget what it was called. To do with broken legs.'

She laughed. 'What are you on about? Never knew you were a doctor too. There's nae jobs going. I know everything happening up there.' Aggressively – should there be any doubt – she added, 'I'm tellin ya.'

'There is so. I was up the Labour Exchange the day.'

She laughed. 'What the hell are *you* needing a job for? You can go work with your faither any time.'

'Eventually. In bloody years.'

'I should think so too. Then the business'll be yours one day and you'll be dead-dead rich. I'd make the perfect wife if you weren't so young.' She shrieked a laugh at the storeyed flats around them. A car went by with its headlights on and she violently scrutinised it.

Simon sighed. People would never stop going on about his father's business. Often he wished he lived in a council house like everyone else. 'I was just thinking of getting a job till I'm eighteen. I can't drive the lorries till then.'

'You should stay in school then.'

'Aye, everyone says.'

'Well, I miss school and I never thought the day would come I'd say that. I bet my teachers didn't either. Hated it at the time but what a laugh we's had and now I'm on shifts; you couldn't imagine the times I'm out my bed at. Starting at five in the morn and all hours in the rain and wiping old folks' arses before the sleep's out my own eyes.'

Simon laughed.

'It's no funny.'

He stopped smiling. 'Where're you going the night then?'

'Where do you think? Meet some of the girls. The Modern Lounge, the Mantrap for the dancing; maybe the County. And I'm late.' She walked quicker.

They were turning left up the cul-de-sac crescent hill.

'You like Nicola then?'

He shrugged and looked at her shyly.

'Blood out a stone, you. Give us my coat back; I'm freezing now.' While she quickly walked with the clicking sounds of the shoes, she whipped the coat round and cracked it out in the air like a sheet which she was shaking the dust from. She shrugged the coat up her arms and shoulders – even the garment made a busy, quick noise. She coughed. Rapidly and repeatedly.

'I think she's lovely,' Simon said. 'Not just brilliant-looking. A nice person.'

'That's sweet. It runs in the family.' Sharply, and in an ominous way, Karen added, 'She's dead brainy though.'

'Aye, I know. We're in English together. She sits behind me.'

'Is it true you're just fifteen?' She laughed quickly.

'A gentleman doesn't say.'

'Och, you're a right one. With that height on you, you could get served.'

'What?'

'Served. In a public bar. I go to the lounge bars myself.'

'Could I?'

'Aye. In the County. Maybe no in the Modern Lounge.'

She suddenly stopped under a street light, unclipped her handbag and took out the cigarette packet. She paused, staring down at the open packet, her lips just moving. She was counting them.

'Can I have a drag?'

'Nut. You're too young.' She put the cigarette packet back without taking one out then clipped her handbag shut.

At the top of the short cut the council had inserted a series of concrete steps and railings and here Simon watched how Karen turned slightly sideways to descend – a hand out on the railing, lowering one high heel down before the other, as if repeatedly testing for the thickness of ice on a frozen loch. Her legs were bare and orange because of the new street lights.

But slowly the light faded as they both moved down into the darkness of the true short cut, among the trees below; the start of the unlit rough path was to the left. Karen Caine said, 'Going give us a piggyback then?'

'What?'

'Give us a piggyback or a fireman's lift. Cannie walk down the path in these shoes. I'd end up back in the hospital. Bend over.'

'I don't think that's a good idea.'

'Take me frontways then.'

He lowered himself down and she pirouetted round him. Now their faces were almost togther. She jumped up and he caught her, both his hands under her coat pressed hard into her buttocks – exactly as his hands had been placed on her younger sister, shortly before. Karen threw her arms round his neck and both her breasts came close to his face. The cleavage – what Big Davie, who spoke the Gaelic, memorably called Cluain Meala, the Vale of Honey – now directly before his nose. Her calves here folded low down on his back.

She laughed as he hiked her higher. 'You're quite strong. Don't drop me now, or I'll give you total hell.'

He was able to descend the first section of the pathway holding the young woman like this, his eyes sideways and constantly looking downward, stepping his feet cautiously over the exposed tree roots. Sometimes the hanging back of her overcoat obscured the path surface and it made it difficult for him to see as the fabric tapped against the back of his hands.

As they moved lower on the short cut, she leaned back, her hands clasped in the middle of his shoulders where her handbag bumped with their movements. The breasts moved away from his face as she relaxed in his lift. His hands remained fixed on the arse and he was aware of trying to make their placement there in some way neutral and functional.

Assisting him to descend, her head looked aside, trying to discern the root shapes on the blackness of the ground by their feet. 'Watch. There's a big one there,' she said, sounding tetchy.

It took him some time to make it all the way down, supporting the girl in this absurd manner – and his breathing was very laboured. He thought he could feel sweat breaking out under his shirt. He believed as they approached the bottom, returning into the street light from the King's Way, that Karen could have relinquished the lift and got down. But she did not.

'You've knackered me,' he hinted.

She laughed. 'Do you know what knackered means? It has a meaning; do you not know, little boy?'

'Nut,' he breathed out.

She laughed again and held her head back to do so. 'It's a medical term, so it is.'

'What's it mean?'

They were at the base of the short cut but she didn't move so he held her – clinging there.

'You'll need to ask,' she said. 'Nicola knows.'

He looked into her face.

'Are you going to put me down? Or. Not?'

There was a pause. Yet surely it was up to her? She only had to unfold her feet which were crossed lower now, over his own arse. His legs began to tremble and he was not sure if this was purely fatigue.

Suddenly Karen whipped her feet apart so they swung round and his hands moved quickly upwards on her buttocks, sliding higher to support her back. Her high-heeled shoes wobbled and settled firmly on the ground. The coat, wafting down, touched the back of Simon's hands and he felt her torso slide by, slim and hard, then the bump as his palms travelled over the lumpy knub of brassiere strap. He heard the plastic coat fall against the back of her bare legs. He hesitated, his hands on her shoulders an instant, then he dropped them. But her arms still gripped, the fingers folded at the back of his neck, the handbag resting against his shoulders.

She suddenly unclenched her bound fists and the handbag came swinging round but Karen still stood there – right close up – facing him. He was breathing out a bit. He felt her right hand move across through the small space between them and it went to her handbag which she clicked open, still keeping her eyes on his. He stood his ground but she'd lifted a gold cylinder out the bag and she used her other hand to cross and take the top of it off. She started to apply lipstick. Using him as a mirror. 'Dad doesn't let me put this colour on up the house, he thinks it's too tarty,' she stated quietly. He watched as the pointed end of the lipstick moved skilfully round her mouth. 'Is it on okay?'

Simon frowned and nodded, unsure. He could hear the tacky, sucking sound the lipstick made as she moved it round her mouth. She puckered her lips and he heard them adhere then softly tear apart; a single icicle thread of saliva stretched thin between the lips then vanished as she opened her mouth wide and moved her face even closer to him – she went more on tiptoe so the lips came to his eyes. 'So? Is it on right?'

'Looks great.'

'Does it now? Is it even? At the edges?' She puckered her lips once more making a putting sound.

'It looks it.'

Quietly, and the tone deadly serious, she said, 'I'll trust you. Mind, I'll be going straight to the Ladies' mirror in the Modern Lounge to check if you're right.'

'I hope I am.'

'Do ya? We'll see then, won't we?' She turned suddenly and walked on ahead.

Simon was about to say something to her – though he was not sure what. Then the reason he didn't finally speak was because up at the old lodge gate he saw the burgundy-and-cream lorry parked in the lay-by.

'Oh shit,' he said. 'That lorry's waited on me.' He looked at his watch. Twenty minutes late. He began running.

'That your dad's big lorry, is it?' she called.

'Aye. Got to get it.'

'See you then,' she called out, well behind him, her voice high, slightly startled, and the fast clicking of the heels on the tarmac commenced.

He turned, moving backwards, and raised his hand then put his head down and ran faster.

The lorry's engine was switched off and he reached up and opened the cab door. Willie was sat behind the wheel but he wasn't snoozing. 'Jeezo. Here you are at last, stranger. I was about giving up on you.'

'Thanks for waiting. I'm really sorry.' Simon pulled himself up.

Willie's eyes went beyond Simon, out the open cab door and up the way towards the short cut. Simon knew fine Willie spotted the young woman in the heels walking frantically – her handbag held out at arm's length for some reason.

Willie could even have witnessed the girl hoiked up on his chest – as if he was riding her or, at the very least, indulging in a very passionate farewell. Simon was not altogether ashamed. He turned for a last look at Karen Caine; her pale face was lifted to the tree branches with another cigarette alight. She was critically scanning the skies, the stars shuttered behind an injustice of cloud.

Sunday 12 August 1973

Under the high moon Simon whispered, 'There's no blood.'

'Do you hate me now?' Her eyes appeared far away in the darkness which made them impossible to read.

So. Daft Galbraith had not been wrong, Simon thought. He said, 'No.' Yet he felt jealousy assembling. He kept himself from sighing at the weight of it. 'Who'd you do it with?'

'Och.'

'Who?'

'Nobody you know. Think I'm slutty?'

'Nut. Ever done it with others?'

'Nut. Just once.'

There was a long silence.

'It's none of my business, Nikki,' Simon finally admitted.

She spoke in a very low voice. 'There was no blood with him either, cause one time I used a carrot with baby oil.'

'Good for your eyesight.'

She chuckled and touched his hair.

'What was it like? With the other guy. Not with the carrot.'

'Och. I amn't talking about that *now*.'

There was a pause. The leaves of the trees moved above them, their serrated edging brilliantly defined by the bold moon. 'Sorry.'

All the same, she answered, 'Bit crappy. Not like that. It was sort of crunchy.'

He nodded. 'Uh-huh.'

'You're an innocent,' she whispered beneath him.

'Wonder how long you'll think that?' he replied – with considerable foresight.

But she took it as a statement of intent and smiled. 'Let's do it again.' She lifted her pale face closer.

'I've only got two more of these.'

'Make them last then.'

'What's the real meaning of knackered?'

She said, 'Knackered? That's like right now. After you've been doing it. You're knackered.'

All her bareness and legs beneath him were stockinged and sheathed in goosebumps alone. She began again – like he had seen it written in the books and magazines – a sound at the back of her throat, then repeating, getting louder, like an obscure pain.

Her hard ear stud touched his bottom lip when he whispered, 'Am I hurting?'

'Nut. Opposite.' But her words were all long and strained.

He liked raising himself up, so her arms could not reach around his shoulders any more and they fell redundant to her sides – then he could see the full length of her in the moon glow; and him going within and out her slowly, then more rapidly – slightly unforgiving – then suddenly shallower. He soon discovered he could prolong variations till she called out and looked in his eyes, her fingertips distinct against his skull in among his hair. He wondered if the house far below the cliff edge heard her soft calls.

After they were both used, the contraceptives got flung over the edge of the cliff – to Nikki's amusement. She had asked, 'Can I maybe put your shirt on just for a bit?'

She stood and his checked shirt reached her lower thighs in the dark. As he lay there on the itchy blanket, she was tall and dominant above both him and that small night town beneath them – like one of those nude goddess statues, perched on buildings over city squares. Then she sat by his naked body and they kissed. 'Are you not freezing?'

'I'm too happy,' he told her. She pushed him back; the front of the shirt was not buttoned and he reached into it. After a long time she only whispered, 'Teeth?'

He shook his head, looking out at the irritating hysteria of the tiered town lights moving far beneath – showing differences and inconclusive patterns as the branches shifted out of time with Nikki's tiny movements. When those lights started to spin and turn inside his mind he looked down to her rocking head then after a while he touched her scalp gently away and she slid up to lay beside him and whispered in his ear, 'Think I'm a slut now?'

'No,' he smiled, putting his lips curiously to her mouth, and she returned the kiss aggressively. After a while she said nothing but crawled on her knees to the cave mouth, still in his checked shirt. He watched the two ghostly eggs and black crescent in her moonish rump. He heard the plastic bags rustle as she searched through them and the gritty scrape of the top being removed. She was drinking from that old cream soda bottle despite its vintage. She clambered back and kissed him again so he could taste the drink and he slid the shirt clear from her shoulders.

Later he discovered how he loved to lean on his elbow and watch her dressing: the practical details, the untamed movements of her small breasts before the bra captured them, the utter intimacy of her stepping into underwear as light as a leaf, which they'd both had to search for — these private necessities he had not considered before which now deepened a closeness they were immediately addicted to.

After he had dressed, in her old practical voice, Nikki asked, 'What about this?' The table and the chairs had been pushed right over to the far side of the rock to make space. In the near darkness she lifted a corner of the tartan picnic blanket.

'Just leave it. Chuck it in a bag in the cave and I'll collect it another time.'

'Or we will,' she said.

'Or we will,' he replied and smiled.

'Ouch,' she called, crossing the fence up above. They held hands moving down the darkened track, as if they strolled in daylight on the town's esplanade. It was so dark they could not see the aerial rising above them. He held his new motorbike helmet in his free hand.

'Oww,' she said when they climbed the No Entry gate.

He kneeled to take the lock chain off the Yamaha FS1-E which was parked down by the bungalows under the street lights. Then he stood and turned his back to her so Nikki could unzip the rucksack in a familiar movement and lift out his spare helmet which she then placed onto her own head. The helmet was too big for her and when she turned her head aside she had to hold the metal beneath the visor so the helmet turned with her. It bothered Simon since he was sure the helmet would come off in a spill – yet neither of them could afford a new helmet at that moment.

Nikki quickly climbed on behind him and went, 'Owwww,' and he let the bike freewheel with the engine off. Only at the choice of the left turn did Simon stop, turn on the headlight, kick the pedal and rev the engine alive.

As he drove down the lanes – cautious on the corners for cars – Nikki Caine put her arms around Simon, clasped as she pressed her chest against the deflated rucksack, laying her helmeted head sideways against his shoulders – secure but somehow utterly relaxed.

During that summer this was always how Nikki Caine travelled with him, pillion on the new motorbike – never watching where they were going, indifferent as to the sights through which they passed as they moved across those known lands. Simon loved this: the way she seemed to trust him.

Sometimes, in fair weather, Simon aimlessly drove them both for hours on epic, looping routes – out on the roads – the back roads – along the rarely used routes of their domain with the often-complaining engine, like a third moody companion under their groins.

The shape of her helmet rested between his shoulders, her arms round his chest or her hands clasped to his stomach – as if she were anaesthetised during their unplanned time along the ways. And when they finally returned to the town or reached the Sands or a riverside or twice out to Tulloch Villa to meet his parents, Nikki Caine would never mention the journey which had brought them to such-and-such a place – as if the journey were some unspoken pilgrimage which must be committed to memory but without reference.

Even this shortest journey on that night felt like the others. Through the town at twenty miles an hour, across the main square and up past Boots the Chemist and Menzies on the waterfront.

They passed figures from school and town whom they recognised but did not acknowledge; they drew by cars attempting to park.

They alone were speeding at a new velocity out of their childhood and into who knew what – in rebellion against the paralysis they once felt; they moved along the esplanade and past the lodge house at the bottom of the King's Way.

The bike struggled with their combined weights on the hairpin corner at the top of the King's Way and he had to turn the handlebar gear down to second with the bright headlights of an impatient car behind them before he indicated left and pulled in.

This lay-by, so insignificant in their previous lives, had now become their place of meeting. The need was less furtive and romantic than that the engine on the new bike struggled to take them both up the longer and steeper hill within the Brae Estate – as Simon had discovered on his birthday. Almost all Simon's comments on any future Nikki and he would share involved refer-ence to a more powerful, anticipated motorbike.

He rechained the bike while behind him she returned his spare helmet into his rucksack and they walked down together in the dark, hand in hand. She crossed the gate there, swinging each leg over rather than bothering to open the bolt, and she didn't exclaim about any discomfort.

At the top of the path which wound down below they could see the back of her ground-floor council flat on Brae Drive.

'Och, would you look at that?'

'What?'

'Karen's in. As per usual. And she'll be asking me all stuff. I'll go straight into the bath. See? The light's on in our bedroom. She's always in.' Nikki turned to him. 'She needs a boyfriend too.'

They both laughed.

He took her hand to lead her down the endarkened path on the steep scrub, then they stepped off it, through the grass where they could hop down the small brick drop into her drying green. They waited till they silently reached the back door to the close – almost next to her bedroom window – where they then kissed for a long time.

'Nikki?'

'Shush. Karen might hear. She'll probably be listened right now at the window.'

'I wish we could go to a hotel.'

'A hotel?' She spoke into his ear.

'A hotel or a guest house or bed and breakfast. So we could spend a night in a bed. This whole bloody town's full of hotels and we can't be anywhere.'

'I've never stayed in a hotel. Don't be daft. Mum and Dad would go mental if I stayed out all night.'

'All afternoon then. Think of a lie.'

'Can't in this town.'

'We'll go on the bike somewhere else then.'

'Your house is so big.' She pulled his body close in.

'But bloody wee Jeff's always sneaking about. We could go to a hotel a whole afternoon. Won't stay the night. Just pay and leave. It'd be warmer.'

'That's right enough but they'd know fine in a hotel what we were up to.' She made a sudden face.

'What?'

'Nothing. Just. I'm in bloody agony here.'

'I'm sorry.'

'Don't be. You've rode the life out me.' She whispered it in concentration, as if she wished Simon to remember the phrase. 'I've to go. Phone.' She held up her palm and he slapped it. 'Drive careful,' she hissed.

'Don't tell your folks you were on the bike,' was the last thing he said as he started walking off back up the dark hill. He looked down and saw Nikki knock on the glass of the bedroom window. The curtain moved aside. The glass canted out, carrying the round moon for a second, Nikki climbed in and pulled the flash of moon back closed behind her. The fabric fell into place and there was the curtained glow from within the sisters' bedroom but nothing changed again.

The road was quiet so he did 40, leaning a bit on the curves before opening up on the straights beyond Donan, the wind a weight against his chest which felt like the imprint of her absent grip on him. He obeyed the 30 sign at the hill before Tulloch Ferry, changing down the gears. As usual he took the loop through the village, hoping someone would see him but it was deserted in front of the closed village shop. Houses had their curtains still open and television screens showed – some black and white in the council houses, some colour in the villas.

At Tulloch Villa he rode round the house the long way – his arm extended in the air victoriously – but the living-room curtains facing the loch were drawn. He parked the bike in the garage and turned on the roof lights. With the rag he wiped down the side of the petrol tank and the chrome, but the exhaust was too hot to mop. Then he examined himself, making sure there were no leaves or twigs stuck on his clothing; he pulled a bit at his jeans. He wondered and smelled at himself standing there, then he switched the light out and was in dark.

His parents were in the living room and the television was switched off after close-down. Jeff was away to bed but still had his brown jar of sweet Virol on the table with a spoon handle stuck out.

There was a momentary hesitation then his father said, 'If I've told you once, I don't like you riding it in the dark, Si, and with the wee lassie on the back.'

'I'm sorry.'

'And don't be thinking you can use the back road. That's even more dangerous. You'll be in a ditch one night with a broken leg. If you keep riding at night, I'm going to take some tools and screw that bloody headlight right off. That'll jigger you proper, you wee bugger.'

Simon moved across the carpet and opened the door to go through to the corridor.

Up in his bedroom he used the chair he'd requisitioned from the kitchen to jam under the door handle so Jeff couldn't bother him. He pulled the curtains, switched on the record player and lifted the needle onto the long-playing record which already rested there, but he turned the volume right down cause his brother was sleeping. He took off his trainers and lay on the bed which his mother had made sometime earlier in the day.

He looked at the ceiling, listening to the music.

Thursday 23 August 1973

The railway station was busy compared to the last day of school in June when he had been there with Galbraith. There were gathered echoes accumulating like mixed radio transmissions beneath the glass canopy roof – quite a lot of tourists were about with luggage.

Simon held his motorbike helmet under his arm and looked around. To his left was the door to an office; in its obscuring, knobbled glass lurked a hint of sea green. A blue-and-white sign on the door: *Area Manager*. Simon stepped and knocked; waited and knocked once again, but there was no response.

Next door was *Parcels Office*, so Simon knocked at that. He really almost turned round and just walked, but he put his hand on the doorknob, opened the parcel-office door and stepped in – perhaps he just wanted to see a load of parcels with their air of eternal promise? A man at a counter of dark wood with a pencil behind his ear looked up – brown packages and boxes were stacked on shelves behind and around him.

'I'm sort of meant to see a guy called Area Manager.'

'Area Manager's his job. No his name. That's Mr Lincoln. Are you trying to get a bike on a train?' The man nodded sharply to the motorcycle helmet held under Simon's arm.

'Eh, nut. I've got a letter from him.'

The man just looked down at some papers. 'Try the Station Master's office, over by One.'

Simon passed the buffers at the bottom of Platform 1, close to the corrugated-metal end of one of three brown plywood railway vans, parked in under the wide glass canopy by the short goods platform. There was an open side in the station at the platform for lorry access. Against this northern side of the station building was a door which had a *Staff Only* sign and next to it was another: *Station Master*. This door was already swung inward to a short corridor so Simon carefully stepped along it across a rubber foot mat. There was a further office door with a glass window – more of that glass you could not see through clearly. Simon knocked twice and a blurred figure moved before the glass as the door opened.

'Aye?

'I'm meant to see *the* Area Manager.'

The man was elderly and squinted at Simon. 'Are you trying to get a motorbike on a train?'

Simon just took the letter out of the breast pocket of his bomber jacket and handed it over.

'Oh. Oh, right, aye. I'd forgot all about this. Well, well. Come in.' The elderly man chuckled but still looking down at the page as he pushed the door wider and Simon stepped inside the office.

It was only then Simon realised how old this railway station place was. The office – panelled in that darkly varnished wood – had a desk so large it must have been built into the structure. A fireplace had some crappy old oil painting of a speeding steam train hung above it; the hearth still contained old ashes – and the mantelpiece seemed horridly antique. There was something oppressively unpleasant about the station interior and Simon realised this was precisely because the architecture was so identical to the old building of his high school. Gloom and dark wood embossed with Victorian decor and hints of furniture-polish smells. It was like the Deputy Rector's office. The redundant, thin metal piping of an old gas-supply system was still visible down by the skirting, entombed by rough repaints; ancient gas lamp fitments, the glass shades stained yellow, were still on the wall but a bright fluorescent electric strip hung on the high ceiling above.

The Station Master was looking at Simon. 'What age are you, sonny?'

'Sixteen.'

'Is that right enough? You look much younger.' The Station Master nodded. 'Come along.'

Simon followed the Station Master out of the office, but they immediately turned right and entered in through that next door with the *Staff Only* sign.

This was a wide common room with two large open spaces and linoleum floors divided up by high walls of wooden lockers, but here the wooden wall panelling had been painted a garish lime green. A big stainless-steel water heater with a black plastic dispensing tap was screwed to one wall. On the floor under the tap was a bleached stain from years of drips. There was a communal table with many folded newspapers and teacups on it. Teaspoon handles emerged at angles from every cup. A curious electric heater had been fitted high on the wall above a boarded-up fireplace. This heater was almost at ceiling level where its convection had branded a careless and dark stain onto the panelled ceiling above.

On a long bench an old man sat behind the table reading a newspaper and he briefly looked up. He was wearing a full railway uniform but instead of a railway hat he wore a flat tweed cap – the type which old farmers and teuchters wore. He grunted as Simon and the Station Master entered then he dropped his eyes back to the paper.

'Seen James?' asked the Station Master.

The seated man pursed his lips and shook his head.

'This young fella's in for Peter's job.'

Now the man suddenly pushed the newspaper away from him and he studied Simon. A smile appeared at the side of his mouth. 'Will we's need to help him with his homework?'

Simon reddened. 'Nut,' he replied as if it was a serious question.

Both of the men chortled.

'You take a seat, laddie.' The Station Master indicated vaguely with his arm.

There were only two options. There was a rickety-looking dining chair over by the block of wooden lockers or there was that end of the long bench itself, behind the table and next to the seated man. It seemed presumptuous to sit beside the railwayman with the newspaper, so Simon felt he had to sit on the chair which was pulled out, almost into the centre of the floor. He sat down and placed his motorbike helmet on the lino in underneath the chair legs.

The Station Master turned and he departed through the outside door which swung shut and the man behind the table resumed reading the *Sun* – a newspaper which was never seen in Simon's house. Occasionally he glanced at Simon but said nothing.

Shortly afterwards the door opened and now another railwayman entered. Again he was an elderly guy. Nobody young seemed to work on this bloody railway, Simon thought. Then he realised he seemed to recognise this man from somewhere. This man nodded, 'Aye,' and he walked into the adjoining room. Simon could see a glass case at shoulder height along most of the wall there – with many documents pinned up inside – and the new character studied these, humming a tune to himself. He came back through. 'I'm swapping with Kellan for the backshift.'

'Are you?' the man said from behind his paper but it was not so much dismissive as very familiar. 'You wanting tea? The heater's been on since the night.'

The new figure looked at Simon and frowned, glanced down at Simon's helmet but ignored him and crossed to the table where he picked up a newspaper. Simon remembered. It was the train guard on the last day of school who had pretended to pierce Galbraith's ear with his ticket puncher.

The man behind the table said, 'Yesterday's.'

'Oh aye.'

'You can have this. In a wee minute.'

The latest man looked at Simon again. 'Are you putting a motor-bike on that train the night, son? You're here way too early. The coaches are no in yet.'

'Naw, naw.'

The man with the newspaper said, 'This is Head-Casey Jones. Junior. After Peter's job.'

The other guy really stared. 'You're joking?'

'He's doing trains for his next Scout badge.'

The guard guy laughed.

The door opened. Yet another fellow came in – another oldie.

'Aye aye.'

'Aye, Tosh.'

This one – Tosh – wore a full boiler suit and carried a pair of gardening gloves which he immediately tossed over onto a shelf. Simon noticed other dirty gloves rested there in an unsteady pile. This boiler-suited man glanced at Simon but he too moved to the next room and began removing his boiler suit; peeling it away and down, twisting and gyrating his body. Underneath he too now revealed a railway dress uniform – black blazer, black trousers.

The Station Master returned, accompanied by a man in normal clothes who was carrying two bulging shopping bags from Low's supermarket. This man was a bit younger than seemed normal – middle-aged. Seeing those carrier bags, Simon immediately wished he *had* applied for a job in the supermarket instead. This man moved quickly, looked directly at Simon and he burst out two or three harsh laughs. 'Oh man. Oh man, oh man.'

'What?' said the Tosh guy.

The man with the shopping bags said, 'No heard?'

'What?'

'This tiddler's in for Peter's job.'

The man holding his folded boiler suit stared at Simon and laughed. 'Ian says he's doing it for his Scout badge.'

The Station Master laughed and in a long, relaxed voice said, 'Och, ease off on him, boys.'

But the man who had got out of the boiler suit said good-humouredly, 'Good for you, son. Good on you for giving it a go.'

'Thanks,' Simon said. The men all seemed to surround him – studying him – so Simon had to turn his head from one side to the other, ready to parry any verbal attacks but helpless to do so. He knew his face was bright red.

The shopping bags' guy crossed to the bench and put his stuff on it then seemed to change his voice to a serious and more caring tone. 'You're out of luck, son. Job's gone. Rush back and you might catch *Watch With Mother.*'

One of them chuckled.

'No. No, Hannan,' the Station Master said. 'That fellow's gone and pulled out.'

The one called Hannan turned round.

All the other men seemed to change their attitude.

'Pulled out? Yous never had us told. Some Brummy fella?'

'Has he?'

'Did yous no hear? Come up here on his holidays in the summer – fancied a wee jaunt in our fucking neck of the woods so he put in an application for transfer. Know when that was?'

'When?'

'Nineteen sixty-seven.'

The men all laughed.

'Married with two bairns and a house. Lincoln phoned his depot the other week and the fellow withdrew the application.'

The one named Hannan said, 'Thank fuck. One Englishman too many on this railway already.'

The others laughed, but now they all turned and looked at Simon more closely.

'Who *are* you, son?' asked the man who'd got out of the boiler suit, and all the men waited for a reply.

'Simon.'

'Fucking Simple Simon. You've got the job, son,' the one named Hannan shouted and the men all laughed.

'The fizzog. Boy looks like he's gonna greet,' one of them stated, matter-of-factly.

This made Simon furious.

'So would you, if you'd fifty year payments till retirement.'

'That's no all, boys. There's another one appeared next door the now,' the Station Master announced.

'Och away!'

'No?'

'What age?'

'Looks about ages with this one here.'

'Oh fuck sake. We'll have emptied out the primary schools onto the railway at this rate. Bring it through; bring it through and we'll put a price on it for the mart.'

'Hold on now,' said the one called Hannan. 'If this Birmingham boy has pulled out then this wee kitten is the real thing. It's one or the other.'

'They're both tiddlers. The other yin too.'

'Doesnie matter. They've put in legit applications and it's to be taken seriously. The position is needing filling.'

'No it's no. With the spare shifts here, we can go one man down for years. Fuck sake man, we can go four men down.'

The one called Hannan said, stressing the points, 'The position's been advertised in the circular and it's needing filling, boys, and that's that.'

'Get the other yin in. Get them to clean the teacups at least.'

The Station Master laughed and he left.

The one named Hannan walked up to Simon's chair, bending down slightly to examine him. 'So you fancy yourself on the railway, son?'

'No really.'

They all began chuckling.

'No really! That's the right fucking attitude, young fella. You'll go far on the railway. Why'd you apply then?'

Simon shrugged. 'I thought it was a job at the hospital.'

The men all looked at each other.

'The hospital?'

'Thought it was a job up the hospital. Traction Trainee.'

'Aye? Traction Trainee. That's a train driver apprenticeship. Takes you eight year to qualify as a driver.'

Simon said, 'I thought that was a job at the hospital. Traction. Is that no what they call it when you've a broken leg up on a pulley thing? In traction. I thought it'd be up the hospital, training for that. Thought there'd be nurses and all.'

The complete laughter was general and it was very loud. The old men looked from one to the other, mouths open, complexions flushing as they laughed. Tears actually came into the one called Hannan's eyes.

'Oh, that is priceless.'

The door opened and the Station Master came back in followed by a smallish, wiry lad.

Simon had gone completely red but now his face halted, facing the door.

The one called Hannan quickly turned to the Station Master. 'Fucking listen to this. Tell us again, tell us again, son.'

But standing just behind the Station Master, his shoulders lifted in displeasure, was Bobby Forth. He too looked a little daunted as he peered around the collected old men in that Staff Only bothy. Of course Forth's eyes soon came to rest on Simon. Forth furrowed that smooth brow.

Simon felt he could only nod back. Forth looked very confused – as if he had been properly tricked for the first time in years.

'Tell us again, son; about the hospital.'

In the expectant silence Simon said, 'I thought this was a job up the hospital called Traction Trainee. I thought it was when you got a broke leg up on pulleys and it was all doing that.'

The Station Master laughed.

'He thought there was going to be nurses!' said Hannan, looking around.

'Plenty fucking walking wounded but nay nurses.'

'Isobel the Ticket will mop your brow, son.'

'Diesel Mary the cleaner might just be under fifty, son. We could get her in a nurse's uniform for you at Christmas nae bother. She'll show you the ropes.'

The old men whooped it up good and proper.

Hannan now turned to Forth, who had continued only to glare at Simon. 'And who do we have here then, as reinforcements?'

Forth found nothing amusing in all this scrutiny. He gave Hannan a look up and down and he said, 'I'm Bobby Forth. Who's asking?'

'Oh, ya beauty, this one's a biter,' someone muttered.

'Never you mind who's asking, son. So you're wanting on the railways too?'

Forth said nothing but took a different line of attack. He leaned slightly to the side and he butted his head in the air towards Simon. 'What are you doing here, Crimmons?'

'They know each other!'

'Aye, fucking right they do. From the Tufty Club. How to cross the road safely.'

The men all laughed again. Even Simon smiled, but Forth did not. He continued to study Simon who was isolated on his chair in the centre of the floor – as if he were under some sort of special consideration. Simon shrugged and replied, 'I'm just leaving now,' and he stood up.

A big soppy 'Awwww' came from several men.

'Hold your horses now, Evel Knievel. You just sit down on your erse.'

Simon sat back down.

Forth looked at the Station Master and he nodded. 'Is he up for this job too?'

'Aye, he is,' said Hannan defensively.

'What's he needing work for?' Forth asked.

This produced a reaction. The older men now looked between Forth and Simon.

Forth pointed. 'His old man's loaded. Owns all lorries and that. What's he needing a job on trains for?' Forth then looked away – as if his point had been made and all his arguments won. He stared at the water heater. Simon wondered if Forth was figuring out how to unscrew it from the wall and carry it away on his back, leaving a glistening slug trail behind him out of that tap.

The guy who had worn the boiler suit now turned to Simon. 'You related to that family; have all the red-and-white lorries?'

'Aye,' Simon said. 'Red and cream,' he corrected.

Someone omphed.

'What relation would that be then?'

Everyone in the bothy looked at Simon, except young Forth, who seemed to have lost interest and was now peering at the high corniced ceiling.

'Eh, Bertie Crimmons is my old man.'

Someone whistled.

'The son of the fellie who owns it all? Yorkshireman? Drives a big white Jag?' Red Hannan called out.

'Christ almighty. I've seen it all on this railway now; we're employing rich kids.'

A judgemental pause hung in the soft light which passed in through the opaque glass of the windows to the left. Simon helplessly noted how an unpainted board of wood had been affixed along the bottom of the windows, so that the leaning shoulders of men seated on the bench could not crack the lower panes. Ironically, at that moment the yellow flank of one of the National Carriers Limited lorries shifted backwards, reversing out in the goods yard.

Hannan studied Simon carefully but it was he who said, 'Your father was in the war, eh? A fellow up your garages there once says to us.'

Simon nodded. 'Aye.'

The men looked at one another, weighing any response as if something important counted on it, and Tosh – the boiler-suited one – looked at Hannan and simply said, 'War hero.'

'But there's a man who would dearly love to see this railway gone.'

Hannan shrugged and changed tack after the shock. 'Oh, is the laddie a fifth columnist now? Doesn't matter if his faither is King Farouk. The boy's still applied for the job, and if he wants it, he can only be dismissed on medical unsuitability.'

There was a pause.

The newspaper holder looked towards the boiler-suit guy and said, 'You'll need an extra engine on, just to pull the weight of this yin's wallet.'

The men laughed and Simon noted how Forth smiled to himself. Simon shrugged and stood up. 'Aye, well, like I say, I'm no bothered. Just asked for work up the Labour Exchange.' Simon looked at Forth. 'You can have the job, man. I didn't even know what job it was so. You take it, Forthy.'

Oddly, when he could have snatched victory, Forth nodded in solidarity – joining Simon in outrage. 'Aye. It was Labour Exchange put *me* up for this karey-on too. Nothing to do with me. Trains? I'm wanting on fishing boats, no fucking trains.'

'Ah Christ,' said the one with the newspaper. 'Now they're fighting over who *doesn't* want the job. Changed since my day.'

Hannan laughed. 'You might be on the fishing boats sooner than you think on this fucking railway, son. Ian there's got his own wee lobster boat.'

Forth looked straight at the guy with the flat cap and newspaper. 'Is that right enough?'

'Watch it or Ian'll press-gang you, son.'

Hannan pointed. 'Look. You. Sit down.'

Simon sat again.

'Do yous want the fucking job or don't yous? This is a good job for a young fella. Bad hours but good money and, eh, holidays.'

'Is it fuck.' The newspaper man – the one called Ian – shook his head. 'There's nae overtime up here. Too many of us. Young fellas want the overtime. Down in Glasgow the railways work on overtime, no here. We've had to invent our own overtime, whether it's the boat or the butchers or whatever.'

Both Forth and Simon had turned their gaze and looked at him.

'Good money if you're sixteen year old with nae binds and it's going straight in your pocket,' Hannan corrected.

'Straight o'er the bar of the County it'll go.'

'Can these wee ones even lift a buckeye or a screw coupling? Never mind a fucking pint.'

'Right enough. Look at them. Scrawny buggers needing fed.'

'The alleycat yin looks like he can.'

'Can they even lift a loose coupling? Look at the skinny arms on him. That's some weight in a loose coupling.'

In Simon's defence, Forth turned to the guy with the newspaper. But he addressed them all. 'None of yous exactly look like fucking professional football players.'

The men began laughing but it died off quite sharply and a more unwelcoming atmosphere was left behind in the silence.

'You just mind your language in front of me, son.'

'Yous lot all swear like troopers,' Forth pointed out, childishly but accurately.

'Three times your age, three times the swears, son, so you watch your fucking step talking back to me.'

Forth looked like he might tackle the one called Hannan. But he did not.

The men now gave their attention to Simon – perhaps curious if he too was going to rebel – but Simon was bending forward and quickly lifting up his motorcycle helmet which he dropped on his head as if hostilities were going to break out.

The men all laughed.

'Oh, this one is born railway.'

'He's a comic.'

'Sense of humour and a deep pocket.'

'Aye. Remember – Simon, is it? Mind, mine's a pint of heavy, a double whisky and a packet of crisps.'

'And a steak and chips with a bottle of brandy.'

The men laughed.

Simon removed the helmet and smiled at them, cradling it on his thighs.

The man who had climbed out of the boiler suit said, 'Hi. There's a loose coupling, bottom of 1 there by them vans.'

'Away and get it, Kinloch; see if theys can lift it.'

The guard guy who had come in to check the noticeboard departed the bothy, snatching up a pair of gloves from that shelf as he went.

'Fuck sake. It's no a weightlifting competition. Look at them. In two year with a few pints in them they'll both be hearty young brutes that can chuck any of us away over their heids.'

'Handy for getting Penalty up on an engine.'

Someone laughed.

'Jesus, aye, when did John Penalty last lift a fucking loose coupling on this railway, eh? His leg's been away with it two year now without him getting off an engine in the yard. He cannie. We've been covering the grumpy old bampot for years.'

'Fuck sake, but he's just an old fella, Hannan. You'll no be far behind him one day. These two things have got it all ahead of them.'

'Aye, but I'm making a point. You cannie be judging them. A laugh's a laugh but it's no a kangaroo court.'

The newspaper guy said, 'Have they fuck got it all ahead of them. There'll be no railway here in five year. Yous're giving the laddies a job where they're gonna have to up-and-down south in a couple of year to stay on the engines. This place'll be a fucking cardboard stall on the pier. We all know fine it's coming, boys, but we're never saying it. This railway's getting closed down. It's a totally daft job for young local laddies their age. It should be an internal railway transfer for an older, experienced man. Ask them if they want to live in Glasgae.'

'And what about their medicals?'

'Aye. Can you see?'

'Eh?'

'Eyesight. Can you see, lads, or yous won't clear your medicals?'

'I can see fine,' said Forth. 'Thanks for asking, Grandpa.'

'This cheeky wee cunt's on his way oot the door. Use helmet boy; Little Lord Fauntleroy there.'

Forth snorted.

'You wear glasses?'

Forth said, 'Glasses? You think I'm some kind of poof?'

The man ignored this. 'How about you?'

Simon stood up again as if he were in English class at school and he shook his head. 'I've never had my eyes tested since primary school.'

'When was that? A month ago?'

'Sit down, I telt you. We're no finished yet.'

Simon sat straight back down again.

'Here, here. Can yous see this between you?' The newspaper guy with the cap on held up his newspaper and he folded it out, displaying two interior pages.

The men all laughed.

'No the page three, for fuck's sake, Ian.'

Forth's mood seemed to have veered elsewhere as usual and even he laughed at this.

'They'll see her fine.'

'Who cannie see that pair of crackers? Blind young Colin could see them.'

'Hey, son. That's Diesel Mary the cleaner, but she's left her nurse's uniform at home.'

'I'll take the job then,' Simon said.

There was more laughter.

'Evel Knievel's sharp.'

The guy turned over the newspaper pages, smacked them out flat then held up two further spread pages – this time print head-lines and news photos. He pointed a finger down. 'What letter's this then?'

'Aye, aye. But get the lippy gibbon up next to this fellow, so's they're the same distance away.'

'The Snellen Eye Test man. You need to be ten foot away.'

'All right then.' The Station Master now told Simon to stand up while he reached out to take Forth by the shoulder, but Forth aggressively pulled himself away. It didn't put the Station Master off; as if he were a policeman and Forth a detainee, he simply shoved young Forth into a position shoulder to shoulder with Simon. 'Stand there, stand there, you cheeky wee bastard.'

Forth and Simon stood side by side. Simon presumed Forth would be furious with him personally, but when their eyes met, Forth raised his in an exasperated way and Simon nodded to him.

'What's that then?'

'"General Election by next year."'

'Nay, not the words, laddie. The letter.'

'It's a double U,' said Simon.

'You. This.'

'Pee,' said Forth angrily.

'Och, they can see fine.'

'What about that?' The finger pointed to another, smaller letter. 'Ehn.'

'Nut. It's an Ehm.'

'Helmet boy's right; it's an Ehm.'

Forth tutted.

The door opened. Walking stiffly, the man named Kinloch had re-entered the room. Both his arms were down in front of his groin and he held a thick and rusty three-link chain with both hands.

'Here we go. That's your loose coupling for shunting, boys. See if it takes both of yous to lift it.'

Kinloch put the chain down on the linoleum, the final link falling aside with a bump on the floor which they all felt through their feet.

'You sometimes use that for goods wagons, lads, so yous need to lift it well above your belly to get it coupled onto the hooks. Give them some gloves there. Wouldn't want their nail varnish to get spoiled.'

Gloves were tossed to the young boys. Forth put the gloves on, stepped forward, immediately bent and lifted the loose coupling. The linkages moved slowly but Forth got it up off the ground easy.

'Higher. Lift it to your chest, to the height the coupling hooks are.'

Forth lifted it up to his chest, leaning his spine back slightly, though his face coloured.

'Right, put it down careful and mind your feet.'

Forth dropped it a little too rapidly so its first link hit the ground with a loud thump.

'Dinnie wreck the place man.'

'You. Evel Knievel. Hoik it.'

Simon stepped to the loose coupling. The gloves were too big for him but using both his hands he got a grip. He lifted, holding it close to his body, and though his legs shook a little, it came up easy for him. The weight seemed lighter than Karen Caine's arse in his hands, that dark night on the short cut.

'Aye, he's got the height for it too.'

Simon lowered the chain and placed it gently back on the floor, letting the links fold onto each other.

'Right,' went Hannan and he clapped his hands together. 'Mechanics. What's a four-stroke engine, lads?'

Forth looked at him. 'A what?'

'A four-stroke engine.'

Forth looked baffled. 'It's got four strokes.'

The men all laughed

'You. What's a four-stroke engine?'

Simon looked around the men. 'The pistons move in a four-stroke motion in their cylinders. For compression and ignition and all that.'

'Woow. Not really correct but no bad.'

'Tosh's got a disciple.'

Tosh said to Simon, 'A diesel engine doesn't have spark plugs. How come, son?'

Simon frowned. 'Is it cause the piston heats the air inside the cylinder heads; you get ignition when the fuel's sprayed in?'

'Christ, Tosh, send this cunt to Eastfield sheds to mend the engines; he's wasted here.'

But then the door opened. James Lincoln came in. His eye immediately dropped to the loose coupling in the middle of the bothy floor. The men fell silent. Lincoln said, 'Are these the bodies in for the job?'

'Aye,' said the Station Master.

'What's going on here?'

'Nothing.'

'Just explaining. Railway stuff.'

Lincoln nodded to Simon and Forth. 'Sorry, boys. I'm Mr Lincoln. Area Manager. Come along here a wee minute.'

Simon lifted his helmet and he followed Forth. They both paused at the door to shed the dirty gloves and toss them onto the shelf. The railwaymen watched them go without comment. The boys pursued Lincoln out of the oppressive bothy and the three of them crossed the forecourt in the soft light, filtered down through the dirty panes of the glass roof above. Lincoln looked at them both and he frowned. As they walked towards the

146

pier-side entrance Lincoln asked, 'Are yous boys both over sixteen years of age? Yous don't look it.'

'Aye.'

'Yes, Mr Lincoln.'

Forth looked at Simon and sneered.

A bell rang and Lincoln turned, pointing across the buffers at the end of the bay platforms. The bell was hung on the wall above the Station Master's office door. Lincoln nodded towards it. 'That's the train belling from the Back Settlement. When it leaves there we get two bells from the signalman to tell us it's on its way to us. That's it nearly half an hour away.'

Simon nodded as if he was interested but Forth seemed unmoved by this knowledge.

'Do yous live at home, lads?'

'Aye,' Forth shrugged.

'Yes.'

'Yous know there's night shifts on this job?'

'Night shifts?'

'Midnight till five in the morn. Down on the goods at one in the morn and up with the mail train that arrives back in here at four. Is your mithers going to see eye to eye with yous coming and going to your work all hours of the day?'

Forth shrugged indifferently; his life was rich with all manner of nocturnal wanderings.

Lincoln went on, making it sound like a challenge. 'Another shift starts seven in the morn and another all week starts three in the afternoon. Yous won't be home till close to midnight. There'll be nae running around to picture houses, dances and stuff. Yous'll have to be in your beds a lot of nights when all your wee pals is out and about, playing.'

Forth screwed up his nose with offence.

Lincoln nodded to Simon's helmet. 'You got a motorbike then?'

'Aye.'

'Where do you live?'

'Tulloch Ferry.'

Lincoln shook his head. 'It's really better to live in the town for this job, son. So you're good and handy for us. Your bike takes you in and out okay, does it?'

'Aye. I go everywhere on it.'

Forth grumbled but amiably enough, 'You need to give us a backie.'

'Aye,' Simon went.

They had walked out of the high side entrance to the uncovered car-parking area alongside Platforms 3 and 4, just adjacent to the Seaman's Mission and the other pier buildings. Up past the railway-parking places were the four sidings of the goods yard with a small static oil tank for the fishing boat derv and the coaling staithe. The ice factory stood between the tracks of the rail yard and the far end of the pier for the island ferries. Forth and Simon were asked to get in the back seat of Lincoln's new Ford Cortina and he drove them up the town saying nothing. Simon looked across the bay to the green of the island which was bright in the sun.

'Where are we going to?' Forth asked, sounding a little daunted.

'Never you mind.'

'Nice car,' went Forth, looking around the vehicle interior in canny assessment.

They parked outside the Phoenix Cinema. Lincoln locked the car doors and led them both across the road like a schoolteacher. They entered the town's optician's. All three of them waited, seated on chairs in the lobby room among the display cases of spectacles. Simon felt embarrassed, as if he were with one of his parents as his chaperone.

The optician was a woman and when she showed a customer out Lincoln stood up. 'Railway,' the Area Manager announced and he winked in a friendly way at her. 'Find out if they can see past their noses.'

'Oh yes.' The optician laughed.

Simon volunteered to go first. In the dark of the test room the optician breathed on his face and she asked Simon if he was excited about becoming a train driver. She mentioned how much her toddler son liked trains. Simon said, 'Not really.'

'I thought it was every wee boy's dream,' the optician told him and Simon felt himself go red in the dark.

Outside, Simon sat down again while Forth went in with the optician for his test. Mr Lincoln didn't talk to Simon as they waited there together. He read last week's *Port Star* newspaper from the pile of magazines. Simon just sat, stooped forward, his hands clasped together and clutched between his knees, the motorcycle helmet on the carpet. Sometimes they could hear Forth's gruff voice grunting a response next door. When Forth came out with the optician holding her clipboard, Mr Lincoln said, 'Wait for me out there a minute, boys.'

Simon and Forth stepped outside and stood side by side on the pavement across from the cinema. Forth immediately took a cigarette from behind his ear underneath the hair then matches from his black jacket. He lit the cigarette and tossed the match into the gutter. 'What a bunch of old bastards back there, eh? Chancing their luck. It was like getting a talking-to by the polis in a fucking old people's home. Imagine working there, man! It would be like having twenty faithers, breathing down your neck at you about all stuff.' Forth paused for thought then dolefully added, 'I don't even have one faither, never mind a whole fucking team of them.'

'Aye.' Simon nodded cautiously.

Forth frowned. 'You plugging that wee bird of yours; the blonde thing? Wee ride you was hung about with?'

'Aye.'

'Are you? Good for you, man. There's nothing like a ride.' Then he bluntly added, 'There was no jobs at your faither's joint.'

'Aye. I'm sorry about that.'

'It's no your fault.' Forth shrugged reasonably and exhaled smoke. 'I don't see why you want this job.'

'Like I say, I thought it was up the hospital and there'd be nurses and that.'

Forth laughed harshly. 'You eedgit. And you're already plugging a wee screw, ya dirty fucker. Are you greedy or what?'

'Naw. Och. Aye. Suppose.'

'That's right. Who isn't? So one of them old fuckers has a lobster boat, eh? Who'd of thought? I'll need to look into that.'

'You should ask him for work. I think that one was called Ian.'

'Was he now?'

Mr Lincoln came out of the optician's and immediately looked at Forth smoking. There was a pause. Simon sensed Lincoln wanted Forth to stub out the cigarette on the ground, but the lad did not, he just looked back at Lincoln in that eternally insolent manner.

'Right. I took yous up here cause there's no point in sending yous to Glasgow on railway money if your eyesight is poor. The railway will pay for that test.'

'I should think so too,' Forth said sharply.

Lincoln looked at Simon. 'You're okay. Perfect eyesight.' He turned to Forth. 'You've perfect eyesight as well, son.'

'Course I have.'

'But know what?'

'What?' Forth frowned.

'You're that wee bit colour-blind, son.'

'What?'

'You've a touch of the colour blindness.'

'No I don't. How does yon biddy know that?' Forth glared at Lincoln. 'What's she on about?'

'That's one of them tests you did, son, on them coloured cards with numbers.'

'Oh.' Forth looked across to the cinema. 'But I can see colours everywhere just grand. That car over there's blue and that one's brown.'

'You wouldn't pass muster at a railway medical, sonny. Sorry. I mean, I can't stop you if you want to go down with this laddie on the train and take it in Glasgow; that's up to you. But I'm telling you now, you'll no pass any railway medical and you willnie get on the Diesel Traction course. There's nae colour blindness on a railway, son. Not for footplate. Even for guards. I'm sorry.'

'How?'

'You've to see the signals at night, son. Green and red. You cannie have even a wee hint of colour blindness. We'd all be shot if there was an accident and they found a colour-blind bugger driving the trains.'

'Oh, right.' Forth shrugged. 'I dinna give a fuck anyhow. A fish is silver. That's all I need to know. They're aye the same coloured fish round here and I know them all. Tim Mackay wants me on his prawn boat.' Using his middle finger Forth efficiently flicked his cigarette butt far out into the middle of the road before a car passed them.

'Mmmm. Do you want a lift back to the station?'

'No. I'm going this way. Right. Mind and give us a backie on your bike sometime.'

'Aye.'

Forth just walked away. Simon watched the boy stuff his hands into the front pockets of his jean jacket and go a distance up the road, but then Bobby Forth paused uncertainly, choosing which way to head. He spat quickly in the gutter while he chose then took the route on up the pavement towards the Gathering Halls – the same route Alexander Bultitude had taken that night, as if both boys had nowhere specific to go in this whole world.

Lincoln and Simon drove back down through the town. Mr Lincoln motored very slowly, looking cautiously over the steering wheel – maybe it was his eyesight: those thick glasses suggested he must have been a regular himself up at that optician's. Mr Lincoln said quietly, his fingers moving tenderly upon the shiny plastic of the steering wheel, 'Who was that lad?'

'Bobby Forth,' Simon replied.

'Oh, right. Isn't his family all a bit?'

Simon said nothing.

Mr Lincoln bit his lip negotiating the corner by the square. 'From up the Cona Estate?'

'Aye.'

Mr Lincoln nodded slowly. 'So, son. If you think you can make it in and back from Tulloch Ferry through the winters on a motorbike, you'll go on a wage and we'll get you down Glasgow for medical and Diesel Traction School for three week.' Suddenly Mr Lincoln triumph-antly added, 'Less! Cause *you* won't do the electric trains. We'll have you up on them engines in a fortnight.'

'I have to go all the way to a school in Glasgow?'

'Aye.'

'How will I do that?'

'The railway gives you the hostel accommodation and they teach you. Diesel mechanics, steam-heating boilers, signalling rules. It's mainly signalling rules. You pay attention to your signalling rules now, son, cause they'll test you on it good and proper and if you're no sharp on your signals, you're out. Understand?'

'Yes, Mr Lincoln.'

'You're no at school any more. No joking round this time. This is serious learning. Understand?'

'Yes, Mr Lincoln. Are you sort of saying, I've got a job?'

'Aye. What do you think of that?' Mr Lincoln smiled aside at him.

'Grand. Magic. Aye. Thanks.'

'You come in direct to me the morrow, no into that nest of a bothy with yon lot, and I'll explain to you all the pay and conditions and you'll sign some papers and we'll get you onto the Diesel Traction School straight away. Aye, Diesel Traction. That's the business. What's your name, son?'

'Simon Crimmons.'

'Crimmons the lorry people?'

'Aye,' Simon said weakly.

'Away. You're joking me?'

'Naw.'

'Is Albert Crimmons your faither?'

'Aye.'

'Never?'

'Aye.'

'Mind before I left here to Aberdeen he only had one lorry and look at him now. What's he going to be saying about you working on the railways?'

'Och, he'll be fine.'

'Well, you see and have a word with him first.'

Simon drove from the station and parked his motorbike up by the distillery at the bottom of Jacob's Ladder then he walked round into Menzies' newsagent. He moved through to the books section with his motorbike helmet under his arm. He checked neither the motorcycle magazines nor the record department that day. Instead he lifted *Narziss and Goldmund* by Herman Hesse down from the shelf. There was a handwritten note folded in on page 159. Simon looked both ways, sliding the note out into his hand then he put the book back on the shelf.

Thank you for mildly amusing missive. Especially the spelling. Heartening to communicate in this e-pissed-a-glory manner. Yes. Confinement among your bogs continues. Solzhenitsyn had it easy. Glad you have the transport mode of T.E. Lawrence rather than David Herbert who rode upon his own phallus. Meet me in the Marine Hotel cocktail bar for brandy on afternoon of your choosing. I am in love with the barmaid but require you to translate. You *must* hear the Pink Fairies album. Yes I do hold driver's licence but rendered worthless after the opera of getting it – Father will not insure his vehicle for me. His small-mindedness is appalling; thus I travel in a van strewn with severed antlers – Francis Bacon meets Edwin Landseer. The only alternative: intimately on my equestrian sister's horse, holding her tight across these terrifying wastes like something from a rained-off *High Noon*.

Your humble servant,

'Brandy' Alexander the Great

Outside, kneeling, Simon wrote his reply on the back of the same note, leaning on the seat of his motorcycle then he walked back to the bookshelves to return the note to the inside pages of the Penguin Modern Classics book.

Simon's father shouted, 'You must be joking me, laddie. I've never heard anything so utterly stupid in my entire life.'

Simon's mother said, 'Oh, he's not joking.'

'No, I'm not joking.'

His father said in the low and threatening voice, 'You've a whole life for making mistakes. Don't start with the biggest of your life at your age.'

'It's just a wee job.'

'No it's not. You're leaving your school. To work on a – on a bloody railway line. There's no future on a wee railway line here, son.' His father added, bewildered, 'There's just no money in it.'

'There's more than I was getting working on the lorries.'

His father's face was hurt as well as surprised. 'Exploiting you, was I?'

'I'll just do it till I'm eighteen, then come work with you.'

'Not under this roof.'

'I'll sleep in the garage then.'

Jeff laughed.

'Just be quiet, Jeff. Don't be silly. And don't you be cheeky too.' His father stared at Simon.

His mother chipped in, 'When do we ever ask things of you, Si? Your father and I have never asked a thing of you in your whole life. You've always got everything you wanted – a new motorbike all wrapped up was sitting there in the blue room for you. It could have stained the carpet – and now you go and threaten to do this to us.'

'Why is it so bad?'

His father wouldn't look him in the eye and stated it all frankly as if it were the simplest thing in the world. 'You'll never drive a Jaguar if you become a train driver, son.'

'I can drive a Jag round and round the house here any time I want.'

'Don't get cheeky. I'll soon rip off those pips you think you got on your shoulders. You take this job and you won't sit in that car again. You can go live somewhere else.'

His mother tried to arbitrate. 'Do you not want your trifle?'

'No.'

His father picked up his own plate but he put it back down again. 'I left school at fourteen. When I was eighteen years old I had to go fight in a bloody war. I didn't fight in a war so my son could go back to shift work, slogging on some railway.'

'Hitler wasn't in on the plot, Dad.'

'Watch your mouth, smart-arse.' He spoke in gasps of thought and anger. 'You don't run rings round me. Jesus Christ, son, you'd be earning what your grandfather did. Your mother and I running around left, right and centre working our fingers to the bone for you and Jeff. Listen. That railway's going to close down soon enough and good riddance to it. Look at the state of this bloody country. Unions are going to bring us to a standstill soon enough, and you want to start thinking about your future, boy, instead of buggering around with a silly carry-on. Bull. Wake up, boy, and get some gumption.' Now his father turned to his mother and as if Simon were not present he added, 'And he has that little lass and something starting up between them.'

'At least listen to your father a wee minute, Simon, and think about it.'

154

'I haven't even signed on for the job yet.'

'Well, don't.'

'I've to go see Mr Lincoln tomorrow.'

'Who's Mr Lincoln?'

'He's the Area Manager.'

'Is he now? Lincoln? Never heard of him.'

'He's dead decent, Dad.'

'I'm sure he is. Getting a clever boy like you in his bloody circus rather than some wee keelie. Some toughie. Jesus Christ almighty, son, I'd thought I taught you better. That railway is our bloody rival! If I could get the contracts for oil and coal and Boots the Chemist and all the haulage that comes up in the vans with those clowns. Jesus Christ. You're a haulier, boy.'

'Your language, Bertie, please.'

His father took a breath and lowered his voice. 'The railway *is* National Carriers Limited. How often have you and I sat here and laughed about NCL lorries? Now you want to go and work for your father's main rival.'

'But it's just, like a job. I can quit when I want. Working on trains'll be more interesting than working in Low's supermarket. I could be sort of your spy there.'

'I don't need a spy there. I know fine what's happening. People are sat on their arse and it's paid for by us taxpayers. That's a nationalised, state-owned, subsidised business. And they need someone to come along who's in government and kick them up their arse. They can truck stuff about and undercut me every single time. I see that NCL driver sleeping in his cab down the road. Willie used to drive for NCL, he'll tell you. There's money in the bank, son. You don't need to go out and work as if we're bloody poverty-stricken. Jesus Christ almighty.'

His father's voice had got louder and now he stood up and he reached round. Here came his totemic emblem which had been torn free on other occasions to make various points. His father felt into the back pocket of his slacks and from it pulled a pinked wad of twenties secured with a thick elastic band. He waved the wad in Simon's face so Simon blinked. 'Look at that, son. You see that? That's what it's all about; if I've told you once I've told you a thousand times.'

155

Simon looked down. His father banged the money on the cloth of the dinner table. Then again for emphasis.

'There you go, laddie. You have that. On a railway it'll take you six month to earn what I carry in my back pocket. You take it. It's the last penny you'll ever get out of me.'

'Don't want it.'

'You will though. You will when you're twenty and you will when you're thirty and you will when you're forty and you'll remember this day and say to yourself – my father was right.' He banged his hand down on the money which lay by the salt cellar. The heavy table jumped. 'That's all that matters, son. Sooner you realise it the better. Christ, just the feel of me sat on it in my back pocket cheers me up every day of my life. A job is a job, but you're going to bloody take it out my pocket anyway with this daft proposal, so you might as well help yourself.'

There was silence at the table.

'Okay then, I won't take the damn job.'

His father snatched the wad back up and put it round his back. 'Good. Now you're using your loaf.' He sat again and muttered, 'Never heard anything so ridiculous in all my life. You better watch it, son. I'm telling you. The very thought. You've got your wee motorbike. You're stuck in the biggest house in the village. Learn to live with it and grow up.'

Simon was close to tears. His mother looked at him and could tell.

Simon said, 'My school results were good. You went on at me to get good school results and I got them. Now it's do this and do that.'

His mother said, 'It's not do this and do that. It's be sensible.'

Tuesday 28 August 1973

Alexander Bultitude was seated at a round table in the small upstairs cocktail bar of the Marine Hotel on the town's esplanade. Simon ascended the carpeted staircase with his motorcycle helmet under his arm. Somewhere in the middle distance, a vacuum cleaner whined – as one always did, during mid-afternoon in a seafront hotel – and it seemed to be hoovering back and forth at the very far end of the empty dining room below.

Alexander was not wearing the famous powder-blue overcoat but there was no chance of missing him. He wore a sherbet-yellow shirt and was leaning forward in a long Afghan coat – the white wool collar and cuffs did not err to the side of cleanliness. The sunglasses were temporarily placed on the table with their arms extended alongside a brandy, as well as an identical but emptied snifter glass. Alexander turned his head towards Simon and drawled loudly, 'Here is the chargé d'affaires from my consulate.'

'The what?' Behind the small horseshoe-shaped bar was a young barmaid in a pale blouse. She had brown hair and sat scowling on a tall stool – her arms folded. She barely moved her head to note Simon's arrival, instead she stared straight towards Alexander. She had a round, pleasing face – red lipstick – but she was a little plumper than Simon envisioned and he thought he might recognise her younger self. A third- or fourth-year lass, from his first year at the high school?

'Why do yous want to come drink in here?' She shook her head in bafflement. 'Cause yous're in here, I'm missing my lunch. Nobody drinks here during days; just the odd old biddie after dinners. Young folk dinnie drink in a place like this.'

Alexander Bultitude smiled and patiently paused. 'It's delightful here – in your little bar – so you need to become accustomed to us. What nostrum would be to your pleasure?'

Simon said, 'A can of beer.'

'A can!' The barmaid giggled in high reaction. 'I don't sell cans.'

'A pint then?'

She immediately interrupted. 'I don't sell pints either. This is a *cocktail* bar. You'd be better served away in some grotty pub.'

Yet Simon felt the barmaid was more sympathetic to them than she was revealing and she finally helped him out by suggesting, 'Would you like beer in a bottle?'

'Aye, okay, then.'

'Ginger beer?'

He heard Alexander quickly snort behind him. Simon began to redden and presumed his number was up because of his age. He shook his head slowly, testing.

The barmaid finally said, 'Export, stout or lager?'

He didn't know what stout was. 'Lager.'

She sighed loudly and slid down off her stool,

Alexander held up a one-pound note in his raised arm, as if he were hailing a taxi on a busy city street. 'Use this to pay the young lady.'

She placed a red Watney's beer mat on top of the curved bar and then a glass with a short stem. She opened a brown bottle of Tennent's lager on a bottle-opener device fixed in below, so they heard the metal top drop and briefly bounce within an empty container.

The barmaid carelessly poured lager from the bottle, letting too much froth build up in the glass. She took the pound note and turned to the large mechanical till behind her. Simon glanced back at Alexander who winked. The barmaid had to use a thumb to force down the key on the till. Simon looked; her bum in the tight skirt was pretty nice but he preferred Nikki's. And Karen's. A loud bell rang and the mechanical cash drawer shot open. The barmaid turned round with the change but would not put it into Simon's palm – instead she placed it down on the bar top.

'Thanks.'

'All right then.' She slammed the till drawer shut in a final way then repositioned herself back up on the stool.

Simon bent over and put his helmet down on the carpet by Alexander's pointed shoes then slid the change out of his palm into Alexander's hand. 'You know it would be much easier to meet up if I could phone you.'

'That's something the board shall take into consideration.' Alexander lifted his drink.

The bar was high-sided and Simon found that only the barmaid's forehead, brown fringe and the arc of her ponytail were visible above the top – despite the high stool she sat on. So both she and Alexander were staring at nothing when they addressed each other – as if they were talking into the concealing grille of a confessional. Simon shuffled lower in the seat, to be completely invisible to the girl. She wasn't giving up though, and the fringe shook, the ponytail jumped and her voice repeated, genuinely distressed, 'I don't know why you come in here.'

Alexander told her, 'It's your personality, dear.'

'Don't call me a "dear". You're no my nan.'

'It is quiet here, no mountain men who don't approve of the way I dress. And speak. And look. And where I come from. All fairly fundamental matters to me.'

She giggled and the voice declared, 'You talk posh, dress like a hippy but you don't seem like one. You're like a disguised secret agent. Or something.'

Alexander smiled at Simon.

Her visible forehead rose up and now frowned. 'Aye. You could do with a haircut right enough. Longer than mine.' Suddenly the hair of her head ducked. A section of the bar top lifted at the other side and the girl was there, holding an empty brandy bottle. She closed down the bar top behind her.

Alexander put on his sunglasses and drawled, 'Don't you trust me to be left alone with that bottle?'

She crossed to the stairs where the wrought-iron gates of the cocktail bar were secured open. She paused, standing right before them both and laughed. 'Aye, that's right, pal. I'm taking it away from you for your own good.'

'When I need a top-up, I'll come to find you.'

'Will you now? You'll need to fair do some tap-tap-tapping with your white stick. Cause I'll be in the canteen for ma scran. Custard the day.'

'Really? I'm sure he has perfected it delightfully, but don't run away with the chef.'

'Get lost.' But she was smiling. There was a pause and then she held the bottle up. 'Isn't enough for a measure. I'm away to get another, just for you, so, drink slowly.' She looked at Simon and she added in a neutral voice, 'That's his fourth.'

Alexander lifted his drink. 'Bravo. The party has begun.'

'Don't yous dare go in behind *that* bar; either of yous.' She pointed specifically, as if there were two or three bars in the room. 'You'll be out of here like a shot.' She went carefully down the carpeted stairway into the lobby below, but she looked back up once, with an odd smile and shook her head. Both boys watched her descend.

'Come back soon!' Alexander whipped off his sunglasses and turned to Simon. 'I'm a bit blotto, cock. See that zip at the back of the skirt? I dream of that zip. That's the girl I wrote of. Hostile but irrepressible and what on earth is scran? Is it some kind of pork?'

'Food. In general.'

Alexander readjusted himself on his seat and raised his voice. 'Isn't it just wonderful in here of an afternoon? I love this bar. It's like being on a big ocean liner in the gay 1930s. Or were they the twenties? Anyway, it's art deco. Art *deco*. I'm setting sail on the seven seas and the barmaid can be the captain of my heart. Steer me through the rocks down in the Cyclades.' He lifted his brandy again.

Simon's beer tasted awful sour. 'I think she likes you,' he fibbed over the glass rim.

Alexander chuckled and shook his head.

Simon got the impression Alexander wasn't altogether serious about the barmaid.

'Look. I brought you along a couple of books and some albums.' He reached and lifted a plastic carrier bag with six or seven long-playing records and some paperbacks squeezed in alongside.

'Wow. Thanks.' Simon took the bag and immediately began removing the records and studying their front and rear covers one by one. The first record flourished out into a gatefold sleeve.

'*That* is brilliant. Wonderful cover. They are a real people's band.'

'Haven't heard of them.'

'Study the lyrics closely. They advocate the expansion of human consciousness through space travel. A worthy ideal.'

'I could have brought you some albums too.'

'No point. I'm off to school now and I'm not allowed record players in the dump; only cassettes. I phoned the Dean but they put me through to the music department. Which amused me.'

Simon frowned. 'You're away?'

'Off to quench my thirst for knowledge; and my father's thirst for A levels.' He lifted the brandy yet again and took several adult-like swallows. 'Plunge the albums into safe keeping until I'm back at Christmas and I'll get them off you.'

'Thanks. Christmas? That's ages.'

'Watch for a star in the east. You'll know I'm back.'

'That's a real shame.' Simon rested the records on his lap and looked at the boy. 'It'll be boring without you around.'

'Oh, shucks.'

Simon said, 'I got a job. A real one.'

'How terrible.'

'On the railways. Didn't even mean to get it.'

'Life is without meaning. On the railways? Punching tickets on the local boneshaker? My God, it's like Chairman Mao's Cultural Revolution. All the finest minds of our generation are ruined.'

Simon smiled. 'I'm going to be driving the trains.'

'Oh. Well, actually that does sound fun. *La Bête Humaine.*'

'My old man – my dad – is going mental at me. He might chuck me out.'

'What is it with fathers? Mine threatens the very same thing. Regularly.'

'He really might. Doesn't talk to me at teatime or nothing any more.'

'Teatime?'

'When we have our tea.'

'Oh, in Scotland by tea you mean dinner, don't you – not cups of tea?' He jerked his head towards the windows without actually looking. He seemed to equate the view with the construct of Scotland.

'I've to go down to Glasgow on Thursday for training. Two weeks in a dorm with all other lads. I hope they're okay with me. They'll all be from Glasgow and that.'

'Sounds like my school. We're the same, you and I. Training on the trains? This all sounds very involved. Very involved indeed. Be careful of becoming too *involved*. What about school?'

'I'm leaving it.'

'Crikey. Very Victorian but lucky for you. Wish I could. You are probably learning nothing in a state school anyway, because all your important learning in life – and your sense of honour – comes from books and albums. I've told my father this many times.'

'Aye, I agree with you.' As he had listened, nodding, Simon had removed the paperbacks: three Penguins. He turned each carefully from the front cover to the back, then repeated this action. *Devil in the Flesh*, Raymond Radiguet, Victor Serge's *The Case of Comrade Tulayev* then *Cat and Mouse*. In future years, just a glimpse of those spines on the bookshelves would remind them of that day – the slight drunkenness, the watery light from the bay reflected onto the polished wooden sides of that curved bar.

'That one by Serge is great when you're a bit fed up with all of Dostoevsky's bloody problems. Have you read Günter Grass?'

'No.'

'You need to.'

Alexander thrust his wool cuff aggressively – in the manner you would make a tough accusation across a room towards someone. 'Here is my little sister. She's long-jump champion of her whole school.'

Stepping up the stairs to the bar came the black-haired girl from the horse, pale face fiercely held on her brother. She had not smiled and seemed to rise up those stairs in her apparel – as if out of the darkest loch.

Alexander said, 'He's a Kraut.'

'Eh?'

'Günter Grass.'

The girl mounted the top stair beside them, crossing directly in front of their table. Simon could not help his head from rudely following her violent paleness – the white hand went through the hair. She wore a black lace dress with a man's old tweed jacket over it. But what you noticed most of all about the girl were the dilated eyes in that face, like two black pebbles suddenly caught and trapped in white snow.

She passed the next table in her heeled boots then kneeled on the armchair which faced her. She gazed out the small windowpanes onto the wide view across the bay, placing the white hands up on the windowsill and the lace dress lay a semi-transparent hem across the back of her pale thin calves.

Alexander refused to acknowledge his sister's presence. 'I was tremendously impressed by *Cat and Mouse* but Heinrich Balls just got the Nobel.'

The girl continued to stare out the window.

'Oh. Did he?' The black heart and chalky sweep of seagull excrement was on one glass pane close to her. Simon turned and looked at Alexander, nodding.

'Yes. You should make up your mind who you like best. Balls or Grass.'

The girl climbed backwards off the armchair. She stood and very meticulously looked around the cocktail bar from ceiling to carpet – as if she was searching for the vital clue in a treasure hunt.

Alexander said, 'Balls or Grass. Sounds like cricket.'

In two long steps the girl reached their table, lowered herself silently into the armchair next to Alexander and picked at the badly frayed cuff of the man's jacket – which was too big for her. Simon was not even sure she had noticed him. Her brother turned his face to her for only the briefest instant and then he looked back at Simon; Alexander's hand went out, took his brandy, tipped a dollop into the empty glass then slid the offering across the table towards the girl.

'*Cat and Mouse* was always the place to start with Grass. Should rattle your rooftops a bit.'

'Uh-huh.'

'These fellows are one million miles from Hesse though; not benign at all. I can quite assure you. And *Devil in the Flesh* is just heartbreaking. It's so sad. He died at twenty much like I will, probably.'

'Mmm.'

Alexander frowned, trying to retrieve a detail with great seriousness. 'Now what's that Heinrich Böll story where the sentry hears the cracking noises all through the night then in the morning discovers it's all the gold fillings, being removed with pliers?'

Simon shrugged.

Alexander went on. 'They tried to teach me German in that encampment beneath the Alps. But I put up pretty consistent resistance. That Gothic script is impossible to take seriously. I felt I was being made Teutonic, just looking at the page.'

The dark girl broke her silence; she exhaled, cold words falling off a wry tongue. 'Before you burned down the library.'

Her brother gave a sickly little smile. 'Little sister exaggerates. All I ever did was I once slightly set a small waste-paper basket alight in the library. The Floyd had a new album out and I just had to get sent back to England.'

The sister chuckled and looked down into her brandy glass, studying it as if there was a complex mechanical trap there.

'It's quite impossible to buy a Pink Floyd album in Switzerland. That's what I call neutrality.'

The girl looked up, chuckled again. She was gawky in those long, boyish movements and appeared to have no shape of breasts beneath the lace dress – but her eyes were wonderment: so dark Simon thought there might be something physically defective about them. It was difficult to tell if the girl was looking at you or into some zone slightly behind your shoulders.

It was clear there were going to be no formal introductions here. Simon casually said to Alexander, '*Meddle*?'

'Worth it, wasn't it? Everyone's mad about *Dark Side* just now, but I'm not so sure about its boogie-woogie tendencies and you need a quad hi-fi.'

Turning to Alexander she whispered, as if she were at a long dinner table, 'What boil did you lance to get this stuff?'

'It's the hotel brandy, dear.'

She had lifted the glass and she smelled it before lowering the rim back down from her small nostrils and squinted sideways across the cocktail bar. There were the weakest, flaky hints of freckles on her nose. Her skin was so white, wrinkles at the side of her smiling eyes appeared softly pencilled in; then they vanished like dust puffed away when her face opened up. 'This is a quaint little den for you.'

'I was just saying to Simon, it's like an ocean liner, dear.'

So this was where all the 'dears' originally came from. The only young female he ever addressed was the sister, so he thought the term appropriate for every girl.

'You could imagine us on an ocean liner, mid-Atlantic, with not a care in the world, heading for the Captain's table.' Alexander's voice changed into a flat and practical thing. 'Is Father at that agricultural suppliers? He spends hours down there chatting to a stupid man.'

'He's got so much horse feed in the back of the van, I'll need to sit on your knee again. He'll be in the fishing tackle place after four. How do you get a drink around here then?' She turned her head from left to right. 'Your ocean liner has the air of an abandoned ship.'

'She's gone to get me another bottle of brandy.'

Now the girl's voice changed as well, from defensive boredom to concern. A mix of Home Counties with the cushion of Scottish inflexions on the puffy edges of some words. 'Alex, be careful drinking in this town or you'll get bashed by someone.'

'Only had two glasses.' He looked at Simon. 'I drink filthy brandy because no one in our house ever touches it. Whisky is the common currency there. Even she drinks it.'

The girl smiled across at Simon and told him, 'He replaces flat Coca-Cola into the brandy bottles to fool our father.'

Simon noted how she behaved like a proud manager – chaperoning her eccentric music-hall act. There were little bells in her black scarves. She reclined and with bright voice said, 'There's Babycham, but I shall drink a small wee whisky.'

'You'll need to wait till Deirdre of the Sorrows comes back.'

Varie lifted her boots and legs off the carpet and curled herself into the armchair next to her brother. 'Remember that time we went into the awful pub around here?' Her voice hushed down and she embraced her own shoulders.

Alexander leaned towards Simon to lower his voice. 'We went into a public house at Easter and suffered abuse. Would not leave us alone and they made the vilest of comments. To her.'

'He called me a papist whore, rather than just a plain and straightforward whore.' She carefully moved a hand to her lips.

Alexander laughed, his face wide with admiration. He turned to Simon. 'Watch yourself, old cock. My sister's a bra-burning women's libber.' He cackled and spun on her. 'It was your little crucifix and that skirt you had then; that one was much too *short*, dear. You could have caught your death of cold. You were virtually *non intacta* when you sat down.'

She cawed out a rude laugh.

Then his quieter voice added, 'You are a papist.'

'That crucifix came more by way of Black Sabbath. Anyway, all those idle fishermen should have been fishing. Or too blind drunk to bother with us.'

Alexander lifted his thin knees, rocked back and forward, sniggering. 'He did call you "scary witch." Remember? – "You scary witch," he said. You are more of a scary witch than you are a Catholic. Or a whore.'

'Thank you, on both points, brother.' She leaned her head back and flicked her hair. It wasn't clear if she was addressing Simon. 'I read tarot.'

Alexander encouraged her. 'What was it you said again? To the bottom feeder?'

'I picked a random date, and pointed.' She pointed directly at Simon and she quoted in a low, solemn voice, '"On the sixteenth of October of this year – you die!"'

Alexander laughed. 'He was alarmed. That was then he called you scary witch.'

'He ought to have been scared. I am a creature of doom and have great power.' She told them, 'I'm the Green Manalishi with the two-pronged crown, just like the song. Just one little talisman dropped into his pocket and the fire demon would come for him.' She threw out her white arms in their lace webs towards Simon. 'Bow down, to the fire demon!'

Simon blinked, genuinely menaced. Long screw curls of her black hair and bits of the scarf dumped down across her face then she laughed. '*Night of the Demon*. Seen it?'

'Eh, nah; don't think so.'

'It's an old black and white on the telly some nights. It's funny, but dead, dead spooky too. I like all that.' Varie suddenly studied him. 'Do you come from here?'

'No. I'm from Tulloch Ferry.'

She turned to Alex. 'The next village. Where I do the pony-trekking.'

'I know. I do know, Varie. I've lived here all my life too,' and Alexander lifted and drained the last of his brandy. 'Give me some of that back, dear, why don't you?'

'No.' She grabbed her glass off the table and held it high in the air, out of his reach.

Simon coughed. 'We live opposite the hotel in Tulloch Ferry.'

She stared up at the glass of brandy in her fingers, 'I've worked at that hotel's stables this summer.'

'We live right there.' Simon carefully went on. 'Don't you work there any more?'

'Well, one more Saturday to go.' She studied the penny-bronze liquid held high in the glass as if she were a connoisseur.

Alexander said, 'I'm over a year older than my little sister but the clever thing is off before me to her university in weeks.'

'If you hadn't been thrown out of all your schools you would be going too.' She swirled the brandy around and around up in the suspended glass and she speculated on it.

'Father wanted her to go to the proper English ones like he did but now she's decimated her potential allowance by heading to misty old Edinburgh.'

She turned on her brother. 'I explained to you. It's like a sand quarry down south; not so much as an anthill for a hundred miles. England's just a dried-up glass of Andrew's Liver Salts. The oldest rocks in the world are right here under our very feet, on our doorstep, so Edinburgh makes perfect sense. I love the Scottish Highlands even though you hate it here. Why, I'm a Scottish Nationalist now.'

Alexander turned to Simon. 'She'll be studying Geology. It makes sense. She has a heart of stone.'

She returned the glass to the table but placed precariously, at the far edge so her brother couldn't reach it.

Alexander had become thoughtful. 'What I *do* like about Edinburgh though, as well as the festival, is the far superior chimpanzees' tea party at the zoo. We must go to that together when I visit you. You'll be lonely because you'll be the only girl on that course of study.'

'Good.'

'It will all be bearded rock chippers who sleep with their chisels.'

The girl turned to Simon and looked at him for a moment then asked in an urgent voice, 'Did you have to go to the high school here?'

Simon nodded slowly and claimed, 'I could have gone to university too but I've just left school.'

'Gosh. Have you?'

Simon tried to show off. 'My dad has a business. Ten lorries. And he's getting more. We have a big lorry business.'

'Oh.' Her voice gave just a minuscule of possible approval but no more. She frowned. 'But you're from here. How do you know my brother?'

Alexander said, 'We were brought together by Hermann Hesse.'

'By who?'

'A book drew us together. I call him Simon of the Desert. This place. It did for Unity Mitford and it'll do for me.'

'Oh, storybooks. Mister Fezziwig Fuzzywog Charles Dickens and all that.' She tutted.

'Oh, old stones and all that,' Alexander tutted, in mimicry and he turned to Simon. 'She has a hammer and chisel and rides her horse, clambering up the bens, chipping away at whole cliff faces. She could start an avalanche. And you – a scientist – with tarot cards wrapped in velvet.' Alexander glanced to Simon and shook his head with squeamishness, but suddenly he was cheery and he shot his long arm around his sister's tweed shoulders and drew her in close to him – which she easily permitted. Simon watched as she stretched over, rested her tolerant face on her brother's chest. Alexander said, 'Ouch. You've given me an electric shock, dear. It's remarkable. She's always electric. Now, next summer when the water is clear, my little student sister and I are planning to scuba-dive together. There's an actual sunken village close by where we live.'

Simon nodded. 'Oh aye. In the New Loch.'

'Correct. Old Badan. After the barrier was built it slowly disappeared under the water. Remember, you would see the weathervane from the top of the church in summer; but it fell off?'

'Aye.'

'Our grandmother's old house is under there so we're going to dive on the village when the waters are clear, swim right down through the houses, out the kitchen door and up the back hill together. Aren't we, dear? Across the seaweed gardens, over the lobster beds we shall glide, hand in hand back along the little main street with the fishes. Just like when we were young.'

Varie Bultitude giggled, her snow-white jaw moving against her brother's yellow shirt. 'It's our hidden paradise. We'll swim in and out the windows of the village shop where Mummy used to buy the paper packets of sweeties.'

'We'll put a letter full of pearls into the postbox on the corner, where we used to reach up and send our Christmas cards from.'

You could tell they had delivered this dialogue to troubled listeners before.

Varie told no one in particular, 'Then at Grandmama's, we'll kick our flippers on the stairway past that round bobble of wood at the bottom where Uncle hung his hat and we'll swim up into her old bedroom.'

Alexander said, 'I'm going to swim into the lounge of that little hotel; sit myself down with my air tank at the old wooden bar, lift a silted brandy glass and shuck a very fresh oyster or two.'

Varie laughed. 'Oh I'd so love to see you try that.' She was breathless already and with a single speck of white reflection embedded, her black eyes slid over to Simon. 'And we're going to find that slimy old weathervane from the top of the church steeple and haul it up to the dinghy on the end of a long rope.'

'We'll *salvage* it, dear. We'll have it polished up by Mrs Mac and then hung in my bedroom.'

'No, in my room, Alex. Please?'

'Simon of the Desert here can drive the dinghy. You'll wait faithfully up top for us and haul on the rope, won't you?'

Simon found it hard not to imagine the scene and was excited. 'Aye. Sure.'

'I'll prepare our house to receive you. There you are, my dear, a man who shares our vision. Two tugs means haul away, six tugs means Varie has peeled off her wetsuit and is swimming naked around the steeple top, so cover your eyes.'

'Shut it, Alex.' Varie reached for the brandy glass, took it to her lips and drained down the alcohol with a frown which formed a singular vertical and one horizontal line on her forehead – which then evaporated. Her voice changed and she spoke as if the three of them were all the oldest of friends. 'Look at us. I'm off to university. It's quite terrible. I wish we could just be kids again. I added them all up the other night and do you know that although

I'm seventeen, in ten thousand days I shall almost be forty years old? Ten thousand days. Daddy will have passed on and our family will be poverty-stricken. It's all disgusting.'

Alexander chuckled. 'Ditch your gee-gees and convert the daft stables into self-catering chalets. We'll get the anglers up all year round; we'll be tripping over pots of gold at the bottom of the stairway. I've told you and I've told Father mucho times.' He winked at Simon, 'Nice little earner,' but then his mind went elsewhere. 'Here now. How is that little bird of yours?' He turned to his sister. 'Simon has himself a bird, a real girlfriend. I've had the pleasure of meeting her. She's like a little drop of golden sun.'

Varie moved her smoky eyes. For the first time she appeared interested in Simon.

'She's furious against me leaving the school.' Simon addressed Varie directly. 'My old man, my father, is just going mental at me too. I think my father's going to chuck me out and the girlfriend's just going to chuck me.'

'Exciting,' Varie said in a deeper voice. 'What's your girlfriend's name?'

'Nikki.' It was all Simon volunteered.

'Oh, surely you both won't break up? She's a little doll.' Alexander turned anxiously between Simon and his sister.

Varie narrowed her eyes at Simon but said nothing for a long moment until she slurred, 'Are you going to work in your father's concern?'

'No.'

Alexander announced, 'Simon has joined the board of British Railways at a higher executive level. He's going to be a train driver. I'm quite jealous.'

Varie stated, 'How working class.'

Alexander stood up and slapped at his Afghan coat as if searching for a cigarette lighter. 'Well, I have to visit the lavatory now and it's all the way downstairs. Art deco too, so it will be an honour to micturate amongst splendour.'

'Alex. Please.'

With his hands in the deep overcoat pockets he descended the stairway to the lobby below.

Simon was left alone with Varie Bultitude in the hushed cocktail bar of the hotel. It was amazing. The Hoover sound had stopped at some point but he hadn't noticed. He blurted, 'Your brother's like a sort of genius. He's read everything.'

She laughed but half-heartedly, as if she had heard the words of some mediocre comedian's joke on a wireless behind her. She stood, crossed back to the windows, repositioning herself in the kneeling stance on the armchair to look out towards the island mountains and the far peninsulas.

Simon obediently pranced up and stood in the space next to her by the windows.

She turned and gave him a quick and threatening look then she faced out the window again. 'Our father is ridiculously protective about us and he doesn't like us doing anything *he* construes as dangerous. He won't let Alex drive, absolutely condemns me for riding my horse. Didn't want us to go out on those −' she said the words with a wondrous distaste − 'putt-putts,' and she pointed at the little motorised boats for hire. 'He went on and on that the life jackets wouldn't work. He doesn't like us trying to scuba-dive the loch either. It's all quite awful.'

'I know what you mean.'

She gave him that darting look once again. 'Do you know why?'

'Because all parents are like that?'

'No. It's because we are doomed. We are a doomed family.'

'How do you mean?'

'We're doomed. We have terrible bad luck. Fatal.' He saw the testing glance that she granted before the black eyes were given once again to the outside view.

'I'm sure you aren't.'

'But we are so. Our mother died from sudden illness; we were just young things. Her brother, Uncle Stephen, who lived with us, he died too, and it was all quite disgusting.'

Simon nodded, repositioned his body, and he looked down on the girl. She turned her face upwards. Simon thought his voice might fail with a sudden but real compassion. 'I'm really, really sorry. I didn't know all that,' he lied. 'That must have been awful.'

She snapped her head forward. 'Do you go to bed together then, you and your little ray of golden sun?' and now the glance she made towards him was swift and full of testing evil.

'Biblically speaking, but an actual bed is the issue.'

She laughed – a glassy titillation. 'I know what you mean. The backs of cars and sleeping bags on floors and rowing boats in the rain, but for a bed, oh God, my kingdom for a bed.'

They laughed like they were big shots and Simon shyly said, 'Yes. We meet up outside. I have a tartan picnic blanket my mother hasn't missed.'

'Very romantic. Bracing.'

He confided more. 'Aye. I'm hoping to wheedle her down to Glasgow when I'm there to do with my job. Get a warm hotel room. Some place like this.' He sniffed nervously.

Varie's teeth came free from behind the lips as she looked at him. Simon was expecting to be outmanoeuvred and mocked in some way, but as if it had never occurred to her, she said, 'A hotel? That is a good idea.'

Simon swallowed. He noticed he was short of breath though he was not physically exerting himself in any way. 'I've got it planned out,' he said and his voice grew more uncertain as he realised Nikki would not approve of these disclosures. 'In Glasgow I'd book the room from morning time; say my cousin or something was arriving at the airport. She'd come down on the early train. Then she could stay until past six in the evening. When the last reasonable train back here is . . .' His voice petered out.

Varie Bultitude nodded very slowly in obscure encouragement.

He leaned slightly towards her. 'Sometimes I wonder if I'm taking this job just to get that hotel room in Glasgow with her.'

'Mmm. Is she ever so pretty?' she almost whispered.

'I think so.'

'Then it will be worth it, won't it?' She pushed her nose close to the glass. 'You're very frank. The Scots are. And you, in particular, seem frank.'

He shrugged and saw the expression waiting so perhaps because of the glass of beer he had drunk he said, 'If I'm being frank then I hope lots of people tell you that you're dead beautiful-looking.' He coughed. 'You have amazing good looks.'

Her face went blank, but in contrast she replied, 'What a sweetheart thing to say. You're my absolute favourite friend of Alex now.'

'So you're going to be living in Edinburgh?'

She shrugged. 'Father will find me digs with some respectable old woman but I want a little room in a sort of big flat. They have flats by the hundred down there in Edinburgh, up winding stairways, you know? I've seen them. I've been drunk in Edinburgh and the pub was like a swimming pool with all tiles. It was rainy as if sheets of lace were draped on the steeples. Not like here. Imagine a flat with other girls? Kindred spirits. A kettle, Baby Belling and a big wardrobe with a mirror, and all slap-bang in the middle of Edinburgh. Imagine that compared to this dump.'

'That would be amazing,' Simon claimed – without any evidence.

But they had heard a sound so Varie turned her head on her shoulders. Alexander was coming back up the stairway singing a song to himself. Simon could think of nothing else to say except, 'Here's Alex back.'

She let out a priggish laugh. 'He's just a big silly-billy. Aren't you, brother?'

'I asked at reception for the lost barmaid.' He paused to get his breath. 'Told them it was like Flannan Isle up here.'

'*Your* friend is telling me all sorts of shocking secrets about his pretty girlfriend.'

Simon felt himself begin to colour straight away. He thought she was going to torment him but instead she jumped back off the chair, swirled round once like a dancer and put her hands against the bar. 'Yes. I want my wee whisky now,' and she glared at the bottles, at the ones on the glass shelves and at the three or four which hung inverted with their attached measuring spigots.

'Ah ha. The day is saved. Here come the fresh boxes of ammunition.'

All three of them looked down to the lobby. Simon noted how, with a predatory concentration, Varie Bultitude's dark eyes followed the barmaid crossing the carpet between the spread-out coffee tables below. The barmaid was carrying a bottle of brandy by its neck, slung down by her thigh. Halfway up the stairs the barmaid cheerily called, 'Ready for another, I suppose?' Only then did the barmaid notice the tall and pale girl looming against the bar counter in her dark clothes.

Simon had expected the barmaid to be cautious about this glamorous new addition but instead she asked, 'Varie? Varie? Haven't seen you in donkey's.'

Varie's face expressed nothing. She gave the barmaid eyes which were without generosity. 'I'm sorry?' She spoke quietly.

The barmaid lifted the top hatch of the bar and ducked under. 'Don't you mind us then?'

'Pardon me?'

'I'm Shona Innes. My hair was lighter them days. We was primary three and four together in the Back Settlement Primary.'

'Oh yes. Of course.' Varie said it in a dead manner.

'Then one day all of a sudden you were gone and went. Off to your schools – away – I suppose. Hardly ever saw you again. Saw you on your horse about a year ago going up on the river road.'

'Oh yes?'

'Aye. Look at you and all. You've gone and shot up.'

Varie gently told the barmaid, 'Well, I'm very sorry, for my whole life.'

There was a cruel silence. Varie managed to add, 'And how are you?'

'You see it all.' There was a fragile smile.

'I would like to tackle a whisky.'

Efficiently, in a suddenly more formal accent, the barmaid said, 'Yes. These are the better bottles, these old ones. Need a wee dust but they are the best.'

'Don't want those, thanks. I want that one.' Varie pointed abruptly.

'That? The Dimple?'

'Yes. I like the silly shape of the bottle.'

Simon stepped to the bar. He had a five-pound note and said, 'Let me pay for these.' He ordered another beer and for Alexander another brandy as well, from that new bottle.

The three of them resumed their seats at the small round table and the barmaid took her high perch once again upon the stool, her ponytail waving expectantly from side to side. But as they looked into each other's faces they recognised that the barmaid's return and her continued presence had changed things.

Varie made no effort at all to talk either to the former primary-school classmate, or to Simon or Alexander. She seemed to sulk only because she had been recognised. She took the silence out on her glass of whisky which she busily devoured in innumerable, tiny medicinal sips – like a bird drinking at a puddle – then after a final tip of the glass she put it down conclusively on the table and looked away.

Simon and Alexander leaned together carefully, Alexander murmuring in a cautioning manner for some time, warning Simon that while the last album by The Free was completely brilliant, Santana had 'gone all strange' on their new album. Simon was nodding at this.

Varie lost patience with such boyishness and said, 'Well. Getting close to four. I suppose we should be going.'

Simon included himself and the two young men nodded obediently and rushed their drinks before they stood up. Simon secured the helmet in his left hand along with the plastic bag of records.

'Well, I shall see you anon then, I suppose.' Alexander nodded to the barmaid and he coughed.

'Aye, right then. Good to see you again, Varie.' The barmaid spoke uncertainly.

Varie pushed her cheeks up a fraction into what might have been a dubious smile.

The three of them descended the stairway down from the cocktail bar then turned left through the hotel porch. Outside, side by side, they squinted against the flannel of cloud above and felt the connecting conspiracy of alcohol.

In seconds the sunglasses were snatched from Alexander's pocket and whipped up onto his face. 'Gosh. That brandy. I feel like I've been stabbed by a swordstick with a sharp, poisoned end. You know, dear, you might have been a little nicer to her up there. I wasn't to know you'd been up at the village with her. She's sweet – if a bit stern.'

'She's a pudding, Alex, and you can do much better if you just want free love.'

'Eat a meal, you waif. Start with some Juicy Fruit.' He produced a yellow, metallic packet of chewing gum and she took one stick and carefully unwrapped it. Alexander offered some gum to Simon. 'If you would like to be introduced to our father you must have one of these so he can't smell drink on our breath.'

On the corner the three of them each dipped their heads and spat their chewing gum into the spring hatch of a public bin marked

Litter Please, because Alexander and Varie were not allowed to chew gum either.

Andrew Bultitude – the Commander of the Pass by Appointment of Her Majesty – stood on the pavement by the tackle shop beside a parked van. He was squinting up at seagulls in the sky and eating a fresh cream cake. He was shorter in stature than Simon had imagined and wearing a padded anorak with the white stuffing showing at a torn elbow. The van was a full-sized blue Ford Transit with the back seats removed; double tyres on the rear axle. Andrew Bultitude looked like a schoolmaster ferrying canoeists about. As they drew close – still looking in the sky – the man announced, 'I was a touch peckish.'

'You have cream, all around your mouth.' Varie reached fingers to her father's lips. Of course, her hand was the same colour as the cream itself. The man's sudden, blinking eyes were brown; wrinkles streaked back from them, lost in the short grey hair at his temples.

Alexander said, 'Father? This is my . . . local friend, Simon Crimmons.'

'And how do you do?' Alexander's father hurriedly glanced at Simon, making it sound like a genuine question. Then he nodded at his son's Afghan overcoat. 'So, the animal skin after all. If you'd fallen out of those life rafts you'd have drowned, you idiot.'

'They wouldn't allow us out in the putt-putts. We just meandered.' Varie lowered her chin and gave Simon a smirk and he smiled back at her. 'After all, this town is the world capital of aimless meandering.'

Mr Bultitude said, 'If you have to possess the vice of dressing like that, Alex, do it wandering around the privacy of our grounds, not just anywhere. I have business to conduct in this town.' Now the eyes returned to Simon. 'You don't parade around like that. Bike enthusiast, are we?'

Varie hardly looked down at the motorcycle helmet while she abstractly licked at her fingers, glancing in through the van's side windows at the ranks of hundredweight sacks in there – it seemed to Simon that she might be implicated in offloading them.

'Yes, Mr Bultitude.' Simon had not verbalised their family surname before and he feared that the strange word might drop like a glass

among them. But the family's fame appeared to be carelessly accepted
– no one reacted.

'Not a Triumph then?'

'Naw. No. Wish it was.'

Andrew Bultitude's laugh was incisive and businesslike. 'Fine
bikes, fine British bikes.'

'Aye. They're brilliant. Mine's just a wee Yamaha, I'm afraid.'

'I used to ride the Triumph Thunderbird myself.'

'Wow. I mean, that is a real classic bike.'

He nodded. 'A good one, yes. Had it in storage for years but I
gave it away. To a chap.' Bultitude scanned his children with his
brown eyes. 'This was when I was down in Sussex more. I mean,
the climate up in these parts for a bike. Well. You need your scuba
masks.' He tilted his head at Alexander and Varie.

Simon laughed. Bultitude was holding his gaze on Simon's hair
which grew down over the ears but not much further despite his efforts
with his mum. The man made a nod towards Alexander. 'You can't
talk him into getting his bloody hair cut to a sane length, can you?'

Simon chuckled. 'I don't think so,' and he glanced carefully to
Alexander.

'And do you really have to wear those silly American sunglasses?
What is it you're afraid of being dazzled by, Alex – is it the bloody
truth, suddenly staring you in the face?'

Simon was surprised at the undisguised and harsh tone. He
presumed Andrew Bultitude was about to laugh to soften the
comment but instead the man coughed and said, 'Crimmons?'

Simon jumped.

'Your family isn't in haulage? Operating out of here?'

He nodded rapidly. 'Yes we are. That's my dad's business.' Simon
noticed that Alexander and Varie showed interest.

Bultitude dropped his voice. 'I've heard that your father is a
decorated Battleaxe.'

Simon frowned. 'Sorry?'

'Your father's war service. He was an NCO decorated twice for
Italy. He was in the Seventy-Eighth. It was in the local newspaper
here once when they were on about him buying new lorries.'

Simon said, 'Oh aye. Aye, in the army. I don't really know about
all the numbers and that.'

Bultitude chuckled. 'All the numbers and that. You should ask your father.'

'Doesn't really seem to like talking about it.'

The man nodded cautiously. 'I see. You'd do well to remember the Seventy-Eighth under Arbuthnot. Lot of good men there. I was in Italy myself as a young fellow.'

'Don't start, Father,' Varie whispered.

Bultitude smiled at his daughter. 'Watch them, young Mr Crimmons.' He chuckled. 'I've raised the west coast conscientious objectors. Listen to them and we'd be speaking German.'

Alexander tutted sharply. 'I almost did at that school you sent me to.'

'Russian then.' Bultitude opened the passenger door of the van then he shut it. 'That door isn't closing properly,' he told Simon as if he were a qualified mechanic before turning to Alexander and Varie. 'So don't fall out, Pinky and Perky.' He opened the door once again and turned to Simon. 'You won't be wanting a lift if you have your motorbike?'

'No thank you. That's kind but my bike's parked up there.'

'Just as well, there's hardly room, I'm afraid.'

Varie suddenly said, 'You drive a motorbike? Just anywhere?' She frowned, as if Simon carried a motorbike helmet around with him only for show.

'Yes.'

Mr Bultitude said, 'All aboard then.'

Alexander climbed in the Transit first then Varie ducked and moved up, her long arm planted on her brother's thigh to hold her steady while Simon had the best view of her legs so far. She faced front and sat down in her brother's lap as he exhaled air and yelped. They both turned towards Simon and laughed at their predicament.

Alexander closed the squeaky door softly and wound down the window two inches to speak out of the space. 'Until Christmas. Peace on earth.'

Simon nodded.

Varie smiled rather privately at Simon and quietly said, 'It was nice to meet you,' making it sound very final. Mr Bultitude slammed the door on his side and the van juddered as the engine started.

Simon looked directly at the girl who looked back at him. The van pulled forward and up to the right turn with its indicators going. As it drew ahead, Alex had made a mocking, severe military salute, his hand at the side of his head among the black lengths of his sister's hair.

Simon watched the van circle the traffic island and he waved.

He drove home on his motorbike; the music albums and paperbacks in the plastic bag hung from the handlebars and would suddenly jerk in the slipstreams like a spinnaker.

He used the single-track back road which went across the golf course, under the railway and then off, ribboning onward over naked moors and between the foothills. The clouds were lit white at the top but were a dirty grey across their long base as they soared eastward, nudging their blocks of shadow along ahead of them over the dappled earth. It was mainly bracken and farmland back there – slightly wilder scarp arose higher up with skull-shaped rock croppings.

Simon stopped at the knoll of Barrancalltunn, which in the old texts is named the Golden Hill. Here he kicked down his bike stand then peed in behind the beautiful roadside elm there. At his feet, the transformed beer frothed greenly among the ribs of roots and his feelings were covetous and they were melancholy.

Tuesday 8 January 1974

The alarm clock was ringing. Green, glow-in-the-dark clock hands showed. The noise was switched off by Simon's finger depressing down a bent nub of metal at the top. Often that alarm clock rang so vigorously it vibrated across the surface of the bedside chair, fell to the carpet and continued with a muted thudding, reminiscent of that track always double-clicking beneath his feet in open country.

He had left notes in the bookshop but heard nothing back from the Bultitude siblings and this lay a sadness over his whole Christmas.

Simon pulled the blankets and bedspread aside and he sat up. The paperback he'd been reading when he fell asleep – *Principles of Geology* – slid aside quickly off the bedspread and his bare foot stepped onto the book, bending over the cover; he tutted at himself.

His bedroom was darkened and cold; his railway uniform was thrown across the back of the big armchair. He washed his face in warm water and when he brushed at the bedroom sink, the cold tap water was so very cold his teeth ached from it.

His white shirt heated on the cast-iron radiator, arms splayed out in cruciform. The central heating had just come on and was banging and creaking through the cold piping down below. His father had refused to adjust the time clock by even a half-hour to accommodate any of his changing shifts.

When Simon held the curtains aside to peer out to the far-off dawn, leaky stars still trembled and he was sure he could see a crust of frost on the tops of the walls and on the lawn around the cherry tree's black branches. There was no traffic on the main road through the silent village. By the lawn below, the brown husk skulls of withered azalea heads tossed once to the right in a sudden glut of frozen breeze.

He dressed, then last of all picked up the peaked cap with the gold arrow British Rail insignia. He didn't even need to bring the hat home, but wee Jeff loved to wear it round the house, playing – making train noises up and down the corridor.

As Simon stepped from his bedroom he noticed how wee Jeff's door was still a few inches ajar – how he liked to sleep at nights. Another two hours till he'd be up for the new term at school. Simon tiptoed on past.

Downstairs in the darkened front living room he was surprised to see the sharp fluorescent light under the kitchen door; English voices could be heard coming from the radio. His father was in front of the Aga with his boiler-suit back to him and there was a fine smell of bacon grilling.

'Oho. Here's the common working man.' His father turned round briefly. 'Not on the three-day-week yet; or were yous always on it?'

Simon yawned. 'You going in the day?'

'Aye. Leyland is needing stripped. Thought you were on the late shift?'

'That was yesterday. I'm rest-day relief, different shift every day. Out on the morning train, back on the goods.'

'You wanting a bacon piece?'

'Aye then, please.'

'Tea in the pot.'

Simon swung open the overhead cupboards to get a cup then served himself with milk as he sat at the American-style bar. His father twisted his head round again. 'Every time I see you now, I think it's the school uniform you're in and you're either late for school,' he flipped a piece of bacon, 'or up hellish early. Listen.' He stabbed the fish slice at the old brown radio. 'Gormley'll have that Barbour clown finished. The country's going to be shut down in a week.'

'Mmm.'

'What do you mean, mmm? It's all your pals causing it. They got you in the Communist Party yet, you daft bugger?' He laughed.

'Nut, Dad.'

His father shook his head. 'Six in the morning. You're going to make yourself ill at this rate, boy. Be fed up with this carry-on inside a year. School's not like leaving the Boy Scouts and then wanting back in them again. You'll not be getting back into the school. Want me to slice it for you with the sharp knife?'

'Aye, please.'

His father leaned across the plate and cut through the white bread and crispy fat of the sandwich diagonally, with a slow and sawing motion. 'How's your wee Nikki?'

'The same. All worked up over the head of her school stuff.'

'Aye. Shame. I bloody wish you were. Well, I'll give you a bit of advice, lad.'

'What now?'

'When she's out of the hospital. Always slip one on.'

'Dad, God's sake.' He shook his head and looked down at the bacon piece. The white bread had gone grey and almost transparent where the dripping showed through.

'So are you going on strike with the miners?'

'Give over.'

'Some of you are on strike now.' His father chuckled. 'It's on the wireless right there.'

Simon chewed. 'Not really up here. How come you're going in so early? They can strip down the Leyland themselves.'

'A new boy's started.'

'Eh?' Simon stopped chewing and looked up.

'I've a new boy starting in the shop. He was a machinist. So he says.'

'Who?'

'Some Glasgow keelie. What?'

'Well, why didn't you give me that job? Then I might no be sat here in a railway uniform. Who's this guy?'

'He's a trained machinist; a mechanic to trade. I didn't want you to leave the school for me any more than any place else. But you went and did all the same, so.'

'Och. Leave off.'

'Son, I'm not always niggling at you every day to annoy you.'

'I know. Just lay off on me. I'm bringing in more money than any boy my age.'

'Aye. And do you ever stop to think who pays your wage for you, Simon? It's me. And all the other bloody taxpayers. Do you

182

actually know the rate of tax I'm paying, son? Jesus. At least I'm getting a wee rebate through you. For the baked beans bill. A few years and all your wee school pals that stayed on are going to be earning more than you. Decent jobs in heated offices. Not crawling around in raw shit under a train.'

Simon sighed. 'That only happened once to another guy. Not me. To Rudolf the red-nosed guard. Passenger flushed a toilet when he was down coupling up. I never shouldn't have ever went and told you.'

He laughed slowly. 'Well, don't get high-falutin just cause you've got greasy hands and you're moving the fiddler's elbow on that bonny lass. You're still just a child to your mother and me. Me and your mother . . .' He shook his head and bit into his sandwich. 'You and Jeff are the whole world to us, son. The whole world. You know we'd do anything for the both of yous. I just feel I've let you down.'

'I'll be seventeen this year. You haven't let me down. So lay off us.'

His father listened to the radio for a bit and then started nodding towards it and looking at Simon. He went on. 'You're going to end up dead on that icy road as well. Buying you that bloody motorbike was the biggest mistake I ever made in my life. I'll drive you in today.'

'Nah, I need to go up and see Nikki after work.'

'When's that afternoon train get in; four-ish, is it?'

'Four twenty-six.'

'You sound like a bloody shop steward already.' He let out a grunt. 'Can drive you home then? Leave the bike up at the yard?'

'Naw. Thanks but I'll caw canny on the roads.'

'Don't come home on that back road. It'll be treacherous.' He turned round to look at the battery clock on the wall. 'Let me go first. You follow. *Don't* try and overtake me either, ya wee bugger.'

When his father started up his car, the 8-track stereo briefly sounded out the incongruous and glamorous melancholy of Herb Alpert's 'Tijuana Taxi' before the heavy door was slammed shut. Simon followed the white Jaguar on his Yamaha through the coldened darkness. He tried to keep his own front wheel on the wide, twenty-inch left-tyre tracks coming out from beneath the low car; bobbles of smoke footered around each of its twin exhausts. The motorbike's single headlight wobbled left and right on the yellow back number plate. The fastest they ever went was forty with the fields on either side an encrusted mix of frost or accumulated hailstones.

The council gritters had sanded the King's Way and Simon heard salt ticking on his mudguards as he braked and followed his father's crawl down the hill. Sometimes it was hard not to let his imagination lapse back into the childishness of several years before, pretending he was an armed bike escort to some grand dignitary in a motorcade.

The roads were empty and he followed his father's car on down into the town square where they circled the small gardens – the Christmas tree was still lit up, its armful of rough-painted household bulbs weakly lit, and one heavy branch hoisted up in the winds and shivered. Simon raised a gloved hand while his father lifted his within his car as a lonesome signal. The Jaguar indicated left, on up towards the post office and railway bridge by the signal box, away to his garages, while Simon took the next left round to the railway station.

He chained his motorbike to the lamp post over by 4. Across the railway pier buildings, on the quayside wharfs, the huge flank of the morning ferry was tied up – generators humming. The lozenge-shaped windows of the passenger deck were illuminated. It was like a theatrical backdrop to an opera set, some massive scene which would swing away and move out into the bay come eight o'clock.

Under the canopy, Simon crossed the station concourse, lit by milky fluorescent strips hung on the glass roof. He opened the *Staff Only* bothy door. Nobody was inside but the water heater gurgled as usual.

He opened his top locker, lifting down the metal-cased British Rail issue torch which he was very fond of. By revolving the small coloured shutter over the bulb, the torch beam could be converted from normal to green, red or amber.

On the table he placed his blackened gloves then his rolled-up coupling jacket – a long, dark blue overgarment. He dropped his leather motorcycle gloves inside his helmet and hoisted it up into the locker space. Nikki's new helmet which had come through the catalogue too late for Christmas was stored at the rear there, still wrapped in shiny paper.

Allan Kinloch arrived in through the door behind him, eating an eggy roll from the station buffet in a sedulous way, as if he thought it poisoned. He spoke through his chews. 'How goes it, Young Fella? Heard?'

'What now?'

'ASLEF carry-on, pretending to be out; they've refused to pay them if they don't drive.'

'Right enough?'

'Aye. Quite fucking right. No workee no monee, as they say in Chinese. They told Hannan last night and he went batty of course, so he's no in the day.'

'Eh?'

'Hannan. You're no on with Hannan the day.'

'I can't drive on my own.'

'They've a special treat in store for you, son. Guess who they've got fresh out his bed for you.'

'Who? The Tory? Darroch?'

Kinloch laughed. 'Who do you think? Mr Happy hisself. John Penalty.'

'Oh no. You're joking? He hates me.'

'That's cause you replaced his best old pal. Face on ye. Are you gonna greet? I knew you'd love it, laddie, so I did.'

'What? He's coming in the now?'

'Aye. McGarry's away up the house in his own car to fetch him down. Some mood Penalty's going to be in; he'll be crabbit as anything cause the spare won't come out, and you'll have him all to yourself up front. An audience with the Pope,' Kinloch chuckled and re-bit the roll. He crossed to the corner. Three dirty tail lamps were lined up on the floor there. Kinloch lowered an arm, lifted and shoogled each lamp by its handle, one by one, testing how much paraffin was in each. 'You know you have to wipe Penalty's arsehole too, cause he cannie reach round there?'

Simon looked sharply at him.

'Only joking you, son.'

'He can't get about on that leg, eh? He shouldn't really be working.'

'Fuck sake, lad. Never let Peg Leg Penalty hear you say that, cause he's just trying to make it to retirement. Like the rest of us are – before this railway goes arse over tit. You're in an old folks' home on wheels in this joint, son. Is there nae bloody tea bags?' Kinloch was shuffling his hands around in the communal locker.

'Don't know. I'm away up.'

Simon left the staff bothy. Without his motorbike helmet on, breath now showed from his mouth as he squeezed between the wooden barrier and the railing, onto Platform 2. He walked up alongside the utterly silent passenger coaches of the train – their interiors still dark.

After the third coach, the glass station canopy ended but above him no light of dawn showed anywhere. At the platform top, the two shaded lamp posts almost lit the surfaces, so he used his thumb to switch on his torch.

When he came adjacent to it, the silent engine was 27037. Again; he'd had her for backshift on Monday but now she faced the other way with the quiet cab end topmost. The blue flanks of the locomotive were dirtily engrained with brake-block dust, adhered over time by the rain. At the top of the engine he pushed down the smooth handle and shoved in the driving cab door. It resisted, scraping on the warped cabin floor, so Simon lifted his left leg and kicked. You could see where the dirt had been slid away off the blue metal door by other boots kicking at it there. He stepped higher into the cab darkness and that now familiar smell: slightly sweet diesel mixed with a hint of masculine body odour – and tobacco. He forced the door shut behind him and pushed down the light switch on its abutment – but the lights did not work.

'The Young Fella!'

'Jesus.' Simon whipped the torch round. Its circular disc of creamy illumination fell upon Erchie Hannan, sat in the secondman's swivel chair, leaning back with a smile on his face. The man squinted slightly against the light. Simon took a breath. 'You nearly made me crap myself. I tell you, we should lock up these coaches and engines at night.'

The older man laughed. 'Who'd steal this scrap? Ach – thirty-seven's no so bad. She still fair canters on the hills.' He remained leaned back in the chair.

Simon smiled. 'Allan said you weren't coming in the day.'

'I'm not.'

'Here you are.'

'I came to see you, son. Thought you'd come up to start her.'

'Look. There's something up with the battery.' Simon clicked the cab light switch up and down a few times for emphasis.

'I took out the lighting fuse.'

'What did you do that for?'

'Call it sabotage.'

Simon stood, frowning, alone with this older man in the silent engine. The locomotives were so noisy and dramatic, their unnatural silence when shut down always seemed exaggerated to him.

Hannan laughed. 'Only joking you. Nothing against a good bit of industrial sabotage but I didn't want nosy Musty up the box seeing me and you having our wee chat. In fact, technically, I'm illegal on these premises right now.'

'How do you mean?'

'Do you no understand what's went on, son?'

'Well, yous lot are striking and we aren't.'

'Too right we're striking, and so should you be. ASLEF are refusing to drive and the board are refusing to pay on the days we won't come out.'

'So they're not paying you a penny if you won't work?'

'That's right. The shape of things to fucking come.' Hannan leaned forward and since the torch was the only illumination in the driving cab, Simon felt obliged to move the beam to follow his face. The projecting, colour-coded metal pipes containing the insulated electric wires and pressure tubes to light switches and boxes ran like a diagram all over the back cab wall. They cast smeary shadow upwards.

'I don't really understand.'

'This could be it, son. If we'd all only stick thegether we could be rid of this government in months.'

'Right enough? Edward Heath's?'

'Aye. If workers stick thegether.'

Simon lowered his voice. 'Sorry. I just. Lincoln gave us the form and I just signed.'

'Fucking right he did. NUR's a soft union, son; that's why him and McGarry wanted you in it. NUR're in management's pocket. Thought I had you telt good to join the actual train drivers' union?'

'Aye, sorry. I didn't really understand.'

'I know you didn't. You're NUR now, but a footplate man can change unions whenever he wants to. You could say you wanted to change over right now. And no drive this train.'

'What?'

'I'm saying you could go tell them right now you're minded to be heading over to my union and you're no driving any fucking train. Don't tell them you saw me up here. Just that you want to come out in solidarity with the boys and you're changing over union. You do know what solidarity means, don't you, or is that a word your faither wouldn't allow in the big house?'

'It's nothing to do with my father.'

'Yes it is. And all his sort.' He had said it quite aggressively then studied Simon. 'Did you ask your father what I was saying?'

'Aye, I did.'

'What did you say to him?'

'I asked him if he was Tory.'

'And what did he say back?'

'He said: I'm no Tory, but I'm no not Tory.'

'What?'

'I'm no Tory but I'm no not Tory.'

Hannan lifted his hand and ran it through his hair. 'Jesus. That's a smart answer. But he's nae fucking socialist. You have to admit that in yon big house of yours with a bloody Rolls.'

'It's a Jaguar. Second-hand. I can't help it, Hannan. I mean, I can't help what job my folks went and did and made a bit of money from. They work hard.'

'But he's making cash off the back of the working man, son. Surplus value, like I've taught you. That's you young ones down to a tee these days; yous let your fucking hair grow down your backs and think that's rebellion enough. Growing your hair and listening to the fucking Beatles is no going to change the working man's lot.'

'I don't really like the Beatles. I'm more into heavy rock.'

'Shut up. Away back and tell McGarry you're no going out.'

There was a silence. They both looked at each other in the shadowy cab.

Simon told him, 'Philip is bringing John Penalty in instead of you.'

'Is he?'

This seemed to be news to him.

'Aye. He's way up in his car now to fetch him down. The spare won't come out cause of their sly jobs.'

'Good. Cause the doddery old Scottish Nationalist so-and-so cannie drive the fucking goods on his own with that leg of his.'

'That's right enough. Ahab himself.'

'Eh?' Hannan looked down, he tapped two John Players out of his pack then handed one to Simon. Hannan lit the match flame, showing a vibrating and bulky shadow of his head up on the curved cab ceiling as he lifted the flame to Simon. 'Don't call McGarry Philip. Call him McGarry, cause he's a sneaky old cunt and nae friend of yours.' He lit his own cigarette and tossed the match down. 'Hear you've still been coming out all hours?'

'What?'

'For learning this road. I hear you've been coming in on your days off, down and back on every bloody engine, playing up and down the country on the timetable like yous was some sort of wee fucking train enthusiast.'

'Nut. No every one. Phil – I mean McGarry – says it would be good for us learning the road.'

'Good for ye? Tell you what's good: doing your allotted bloody hours is what's good for you and all us, no up and down on every train that just takes your fancy.'

'I'm only learning the road. I'm no driving.'

'What you're learning is how to let them wrap you round their finger. You just work the hours you're rostered for and learn the road in them. You'll be like Tosh next, jumping to every beck and call. Hearing me? Time and three-quarters on a Sunday engineering train and you worked yon for nothing.'

'Aye. Suppose.'

Hannan paused. 'You suppose? You could fair bring this railway to a halt the morning, boy. You'd be our wee hero. Just refuse to go out. They cannie do a thing and I'd protect you all the way.'

Simon said nothing. He inhaled but quickly blew out; stood with the cigarette in his fingers until he sighed, 'I'm not sure.'

'What are you no sure about? Are you chicken?' Hannan leaned back and blew out smoke.

'Well, I mean, what's the point?'

'The point? The fucking point is writ there on your wee NUM badge. Workers of the World Unite. That's the fucking point, yah daft big cunt; you're wore the answer on your lapel.'

Simon spoke quickly. 'Look. If I don't drive this train all that'll happen is John Penalty will get in a worser mood with me than he's already in. Then the Glasgow men'll bring the goods all the way up here instead of us crossing them at Nine Mile House. So this train will go down anyways with the Glasgow boys on it. I mean what's the point in all that, to get a train running forty late? They'll make up lost time when they get to the fast running before Glasgow and you and me'll lose a day's pay. Hardly going to bring British Rail to their knees.'

'It'll shake up the geese in the back there. Yon pimpleheid from the Highlands and Islands Development Board is meant to be down in first class the day, Isobel the Ticket telt us. The pepper'll be going up his arsehole, sat here for half an hour. Strategy, son. And dinnie get sharp-mouthed with me, scabby. It's the principle.'

But Simon continued. 'And we're rest-day relief. Tomorrow and the next's covering the spare – so we're no working anyways, since the spare's a scam. Courtesy of Lincoln. Then we're rest day ourselves. So are you going on strike and no getting paid for days you don't work on anyways? Just seems a bit daft to my mind.' He put the cigarette back in his lips to show he had finished talking.

Hannan gave him a long stare. 'Calling me daft? Striking isn't skiving. It's a duty. I'm here the day.'

'Too right. You're out your bed in uniform sharp enough like the rest of us.'

Hannan sighed. 'I'm no getting lectured *to* by you of all people, Oor Wullie. Point is, you'd have showed Lincoln and McGarry you can make up your own wee mind. That you're no to be pushed around.'

'They don't push me around. They treat me fine.'

'Management, son. All the same pudding race. It's the bigger picture here now, what's happening through the country. We're united. No just this sex-starved, rain-drenched wee place. England and everywhere. Just cause we're stuck way up here doesn't make us irrelevant. It's the labour struggle, son, and there's going to be winners and losers so don't be letting us down.' He lowered the voice. 'We could be on the verge of a fucking revolution, son, and you need to get on the right side.'

'What do you mean?'

'You just watch the news on the goggle box and mark my words. You have your convictions. That's the word you used the other day.'

'Aye. Some.'

'You're a smart laddie. I see you with those books in your pockets and they're no just storybooks. What is it they're called?'

'Günter Grass.'

'What the fuck's that one about then? Laying lawns? What are your convictions?'

'This and that.'

'What? Pulling a lassie's wee miniskirt off?'

'Naw. War. I'm against war. It's shite. And nuclear war.'

'And what're you doing about all that, son?'

'Eh? Well, I keep meaning to join CND.'

'We're affiliated with the CND at our branch.'

'You mean, when you say branch, all three of yous?' There was no edge of cynicism to Simon's tone but the brute statement seemed like a clear put-down.

They both looked at each other. Hannan quietly said, 'I think you're going to have to team up with the Tory as your driver from now on, son.'

Simon talked as he would when his wee brother was aggrieved. 'Och, come on. I says to you I'm interested to be involved in the union but I'm just on the job a few month and I don't want to start swinging swords.'

Suddenly Hannan lost patience. 'Get that fucking light out my eyes. Away back in there and put them fuses in.'

Simon stepped to open the engine-room door but Hannan snapped, 'Put your coupling jacket over your uniform. Maybe you're the type can afford the Perth dry-cleaner's bill, but most working folk can't.'

Simon put down his torch by the power handle on the corner of the driving console, dropped the cigarette on the greasy cab floor and stubbed it out using the toe of his brogue as if thoroughly killing a wasp. He unfolded the overcoat and patiently pulled it on then fastened the buttons all down the front with the British Rail insignia stamped on each of them.

Hannan was shaking his head. 'You're some fucking generation, you lot, right enough.'

Simon took the torch and opened the engine-room door with its adhesive warning sticker on the dirty glass, insisting that ear protection be worn when the engine was running; but Simon had never been given any earmuffs and the men just didn't seem to bother. He went in through, past the train heating boiler, and he opened the second door. Beyond the bulk of the heat exchanger and the long tube of the intercooler was the Sulzer engine itself – stretched down the middle of the tight spacing, with two narrow metal walkways on either side. The torch showed the occasional smears of Glaswegian mechanics' dirty hands on the duck-egg-green paintwork.

Simon turned round to the fuse box inside the main control cubicle. The 5 amp with a *Cab Lights* caption and the 15 amp *Engine Room, Boiler Room and Cubicle Lights* had been visibly eased out, so he shoved them both fully home again. The engine room lit around him then he shuffled sideways down the walkway next to the main generator. The battery isolating switch was against the side of the bulkhead here, so he took hold of the plastic knob and pushed it to *On*.

As he walked back, Hannan was standing but still hadn't put the cab lights on through there.

'You just turn on that Battery Isolating Switch?'

'Aye.' Simon stepped back into the cab and pulled the engine-room door closed behind him; the vibration echoed hollowly through the quiet locomotive.

'So that's your mind made up, is it? You're going to start up this engine and go on down the road?'

'Why don't you ask Penalty as well? Why just put me on the spot?'

Hannan laughed coldly and he narrowed his voice down to a nastier thing. 'Thanks a bundle. Some hero you. Well, when you try to get your fortnight holidays so's your wee bird and you can both go off riding each other in Torremolinos – and McGarry's no giving you those right dates – don't fucking come greeting to me. Get out of my fucking road.' He jerked open the cab door onto the utter darkness of the railway pier side. He turned round. 'That other young boy would've been better in this job than you. He'd have understood responsibilities to his class.' Hannan stepped forward into the black, so that he was completely gone. The door slammed hard shut behind him with a breeze of air.

Simon put up his hand and clicked the switch. The roof cab lights illuminated – their malarial-tinged glow came from the accumulated nicotine on the plastic covers of the bulbs. He aggressively pushed the master handle from the metallic *Off* tag – riveted to the enamel desk – to *Engine Only* and behind the drive pumps started to moan within the engine room.

Simon stood still, breathing and thinking, the compressor and the pumps running to let the oil pressure build. At one point he muttered, 'For fuck sake,' under his breath then his finger pushed the rubber-covered *Engine Start* button. The locomotive rolled slightly from side to side on its suspension as the pistons punched up, the exhaust spat three or four very noisy coughs of black smoke, then the whole clockwork ticking, pressurised hissing and mass of interactions began as the locomotive came noisily to life.

After he'd got the steam-heating boiler going and outside put the platform water hose into the boiler water tank which was underneath the locomotive, he walked back down that same dark pier-side platform, glancing across at the ferry.

Kinloch had gone through the coaches and switched on the lights in each; a few passengers were already aboard, choosing seats. Simon didn't look into the first-class compartments.

He passed through steam clouds now coming from the train heating, the frothing edges evaporating rapidly in the cold. Steam hissed from some areas beneath carriages. Where the coaches were linked, more white vapour leaked and blew from the bags running the train length. A steady jet was escaping in a sharp blow from the final bag which was twisted back and chained secure on the end of the rear coach. So much steam was coming out that the noise was filling the whole area under the station canopy. Simon stood still and squinted at the cock but the lever was fully closed in the vertical position. These cocks always leaked on a shorter train with the pressure. He checked the red paraffin tail lamp was hooked on and lit.

Simon halted outside the bothy door, took a breath, then opened it and stepped in. He went, 'Aye.'

Old John Penalty was sat behind the long table with a cup of tea and he was rolling a cigarette. He didn't look up. He had his reading glasses on the tip of his nose so the spectacles were supported more by the arms behind his ears than by his nose. In fact, when he spoke, the spectacles tilted up off the nose and remained levitated above it. Penalty had six brightly coloured pills lined up before him. His lips moved as he lifted three to his tongue, took a swig of tea, took three more then another gulp from the cup. He put down the cup, looked at Simon then mumbled, 'Still playing about on the railway then?'

Simon said, 'I've started the engine up and that's the heating on.'

Penalty said nothing for a moment but ran his tongue along the adhesive edge of the cigarette paper. 'You wanting a kiss on the cheek?'

Simon just stood still then looked down at his digital watch and squeezed the side button to illuminate it.

'That's a fancy watch.'

'It's a digital. Got it for Christmas.'

'Did you now? Where's your best pal Hannan?'

'Uh. Allan says he's no in the day.'

'And do you have any idea why that is?'

'Nut.'

The voice became stern rather than indifferent. 'Well, I'll tell you why. It's cause he's playing the fucking fool again. Joe Gormley himself. At your age you're impressionable. Well, don't be impressed by *him*.'

'Eh, John?' Simon coughed. 'Think the heating's all right; it's fair hissing out the back bag on the last coach?'

Penalty lit his cigarette. He announced, 'The flint in my lighter's nearly up. What machine's that?'

'Thirty-seven.'

'Eh?'

'Two seven oh thirty-seven.'

The spectacles jumped up and he actually shouted, 'The old number, no the fucking new one.' He spoke more calmly. 'I only know these things by their old numbers. McGarry's wrote a sheet in there showing the conversions; away and read it. Why'd they go change all the engine numbers? More Mickey Mouse ideas on a Mickey Mouse fucking railway.' He shook his head and chuckled to himself.

But Simon stood his ground. 'Think she used to be eighty-nine.'

'Is the boiler on the top end?'

'Aye.'

'Away up and keep an eye on it then. What'd you come down here for? So we can watch you play with your wee willie? And another thing.'

'Aye?'

'Musty won't know I'm on the now, not the Red Hannan, so he won't bother bringing the tablet down to the engine. Away up the box and fetch it.'

Simon looked at his watch again.

'Go on. And don't fall onto your daft arse on the track or I'll fucking run you over.'

Simon was about to open the door when Penalty shouted, 'Hoi, son.' He'd softened his tone a good measure. 'You get more trouble off of a steam-heating boiler than anything else on this railway.'

'Aye.'

'Driving the train's a doddle; it's the boilers, eh?'

'Aye.'

'And your drivers too, eh, son?' Penalty wrinkled the edges of his eyes into what might have been taken as a smile.

'Aye.'

'Read your *Type Manual* on the boilers, son, that's what it's for. It's a bible. I know it's a hassle tending the fuckers. You'll see when summer comes along that it's a relief to get shot of the heating for a bit, but you don't get two-man operation in the cities. Heating and the token system. That's why there's twelve bloody loco-men and only six guards, way up here on the edge of the fucking world. We're the Dirty Dozen us, eh? And you're one of them.'

Simon nodded.

'Jesus's twelve disciples, eh? That's us bastards all right, and the railway's our church.'

'Aye,' and Simon chuckled.

'Away up the box now and get the tablet off that man for us, lad.'

Simon nodded. 'Righto.'

'Hoi, son.'

Simon turned again.

'If we're the twelve disciples, then who's going to end up being fucking Judas?' Penalty winked, let the spectacles sink to the nose and started making up another cigarette, the baccy tin squarely placed in front of him.

Simon walked quickly back up along the train on 2 and there were more passengers getting aboard. He nodded back through the window at someone in second class who had nodded to him – but he didn't know who the person was. Social respect at last.

Clear of the station roof, he flicked his fingers before his face – it was minute drizzle, floating and bumping upon the frozen air. Up ahead the boiler wasn't blowing off any excess from the roof.

It was spitting raindrops when he reached the locomotive, the roof exhaust punching repetitively, the fans whining behind the side radiator grilles, expelling their warm air. A gust of wind coming over from the pier caught a lariat of exhaust smoke that twisted down suddenly off the roof and across his face; he felt its powdery warmth and sweet smell, blinked.

He shoved the resistant cab door, checking that the signalling token tablet in its leather pouch hadn't already been placed in there by the signalman. Simon picked up his torch off the driver's desk and jumped back down, pulling the door behind. That door didn't swing all the way onto its latch and it stuck upon that uneven floor, leaving an eight-inch gap. He left it.

Simon hunched his shoulders. The home signal at the platform end was up, showing an oval of green glass in front of the electric lamp at the top, giving the road as clear ahead.

He slouched down the ramp, making his way onto the actual railway track in front of the train; he moved along it, into rain and dark.

Two hundred feet up the track curve, towards the signal box, the three adjacent tracks turned left and vanished in unison beneath the road bridge into the complete blackness of the cutting. The terminus signal box was a long upright brick building with windows for its full length – like an artist's studio – tucked in by the bridge. Simon could make out the movements of Musty's white shirt and red braces through the slim wooden panes, highlighted against the coloured ranks of the lever frame and token block machines. Coal smoke drifted from the stove's metallic chimney on the slated roof and he could smell it in the cold morning air.

Simon flicked the torchlight this way and that across the rails and through the raindrops to light his way. Suddenly his left brogue skidded out on a greasy wooden sleeper and he cursed aloud. Rain was on his face but he'd stupidly left his hat on the driving console back in the engine. The figure of Musty inside the signal box became still, doubtless regarding Simon's swaying torchlight approaching up the rail track. Suddenly Musty hurried around inside the box.

Simon stepped down off the rails beside the small, elevated wooden pulpit with its handrail from where the signalmen would stand to pass the token loop up to the departing engine crew, or to hook one with a curved arm as the trains arrived in. Simon had to step carefully across the mechanical rods which changed the points – some running back to the station and others on up, into the invisibility of the cutting beneath the bridge. He raised his feet over the flywheels and the lifted wires of the signal cables. At the back of the token platform, he used the official pathway of cross-laid sleepers to step over the pier running track.

'Who's that? What's wrong?' Musty had come to the door of the box and was calling down from the platform at the top of the wooden stairway. So as not to dazzle himself, he hadn't switched on that exterior lamp which could shine down there.

'Simon. New secondman.'

'Oh. The Young Fella. What's the matter, sonny?'

'Nothing. Old John Penalty's on and I've come to get the tablet.'

'Aww, I thought the signals was set wrong or something jammed. I was staring away at the panel having a fit.'

'Nah, everything's grand. Just, you know, John doesn't like to reach down to get the token.'

'I thought it was you with Hannan on the rest-day relief?'

'Hannan's no in. To do with this ASLEF thing.'

Musty shouted, 'Oh, now is that right enough? No in, is he no? Why's that?'

Simon looked down at his digital watch, hooking his torch on a left finger so he could push the button to illuminate its red face. 'Ah. It's actually time any minute now.'

'Aye aye, son, got it here. Nae hurry on this railway, boy. You're no stood outside King's Cross at rush hour now, are you, so don't kid yourself you are.'

Simon squinted up into the rain; Musty had the token looped over his shoulder. He was holding back inside the porch so he didn't have to emerge across the guttering into the rain. The man unfolded the token and held it down over the banister; he wobbled the loop end impatiently, as if teasing a cat with it. Simon stepped in underneath, stumbling a little, holding up his arms; the signalman dropped the token and Simon caught the leather-bound ring, letting the weight of the brass tablet within its leather pouch swing round and bounce once against his thigh, then he hoisted the loop over his own shoulder.

Musty sang, '*Merry Christmas, everybody*. Don't say Santa wasn't good to you.'

'Aye. Thanks.' Simon had already turned and called this without looking back over his shoulder, picking his way carefully across the track again.

Once across the signal wires and point rods, he stepped rapidly down the main track of 2, frowning. He could see amoeba shapes of water droplets clung to the face of his torch were being projected forward, cast down onto the flat, wet sleepers at his feet. He almost spat the rain away from his lips. Why had he left his bloody hat back in the cab?

The horn on the engine loudly sounded twice, up ahead of him, and its first tone made Simon jump. He cursed, squinted, looking down the full length of train – the dark engine at the top. He hurried ahead.

The cab lights were still on, showing the yellowish interior – the small central window gauzy with dirt, the route indicator lit behind its roller screens but set to the meaningless configuration of IB00. The coach windows were lit all down along the lengths in a pattern and through the clouds of steam he could see the green torch Allan Kinloch would be hoisting above his head from the guard's door on the BG at the very rear. Simon looked towards the engine and spoke out aloud, 'Hold your fucking horses, King Lear.'

He climbed up the ramp onto the platform and could see Penalty's head stuck out of the driver's cab window, turned, looking backwards, his hat on and the regular puff of smoke – or was it just cold breath? The driver's windscreen wiper was chugging left then right, with an unreasonable interval of hesitation. Simon trotted the last fifty feet up to the engine. Penalty's disembodied head rotated to observe Simon's approach, the reading glasses still on the end of the nose. Out the window, Penalty called, 'What do the clocks say? You're making this train late, golden boy.' He jerked his head rearward. 'Always check the back lamp on your way up. Dinnie trust a guard.'

'Did.' Simon shoved in the closed cab door roughly and pulled himself up on the handrails. His torch banged on the superstructure. He shut the door behind him with his weight, leaned over in front of Penalty and hung the wet tablet casing and loop over the AWS disc abutment in front of the power handle. 'That's you.' Simon crossed to sit in the secondman's seat – where Hannan had sat earlier. He switched off his torch, placing it in behind the handbrake wheel. His hat had been tossed onto the wheel and he slapped it onto his wet hair.

But now Penalty grumbled, 'Here. This yin's your fucking chair to get your teeth pulled in. You're the body driving down, no me. I drive the goods back.' Penalty swung round. He was so short a man his feet did not reach the floor and he gingerly slid off the edge of the driver's swivel seat. 'You left the fucking door open too and rain's gone and come in. Look how slippy the floor is and we've nae a fucking newspaper between us. Do you no read a newspaper, just the fucking *Beano*? I could go right skiteing on that.'

'Oh, right, sorry.'

They swapped places. Even though Simon's coupling jacket was wet he could tell he wasn't going to get time to remove it. He sat in the driver's seat and immediately stuck his head out the open window, looking rearward, back down the train length, squinting through the steam plumes, ensuring all the coach doors appeared closed and flush against the sides. There was no green light. 'Fuck.' Then he could hear Penalty's voice droning something inside the cab behind him. Simon withdrew his head back in. 'Eh, John. There's no green light from Kinloch any more.'

Penalty was looking towards him, puffing smoke.

Simon repeated, 'There's no green light from Allan. Should I just go?'

'No. You're forgetting something.'

'Eh?'

'You're forgetting something important. You're an airheid, son. There's more air in yon wee heid of yours than in the brake cylinders. What's on your mind? Riding wee lassies or working on the railways?'

'What?'

'You tell me, smart-arse. What have you forgot?'

'Eh? We've got the token and home signal. There's no green light from Kinloch?'

'Not that.'

'What then?'

'You've still got the fucking water hose out there stuck in the side of the boiler tank.'

Simon looked at him, quite incredulous. 'Could you no have taken it out yourself?'

Penalty exploded. He screamed at Simon louder than anybody had shouted at him since Mr Gilmour in Modern Studies. 'I'm no some fucking servant in your big house. I'm your fucking driver so show me some respect. It's no my job to deal with a fucking hose, you're the fucking fireman. If I was no here, you'd be off up that cutting, dragging that hose behind you, ripping it out the mains, or worse: getting some poor cunt's legs caught up in it and pulling them from here to kingdom come. Stupid wee bastard.'

Simon sprang up. Tears punched into his eyes, yet Penalty was quite right. The running water hose had totally gone from Simon's flighty mind. He yanked the cab door open behind Penalty and jumped down onto the dark platform in the rain. He crossed to the wooden frame box, angrily twisting the tap repeatedly until it hissed off. The hose end rested in the brass feeder spout above the sixteen-hundred-gallon water tank slung underneath the locomotive. He heaved the hose out with two hands and flung it violently back across the platform, clear of the train. A rag of water vomited from the hose end, whipping across Simon's lower trouser legs and brogues. 'Fuck.' Then he realised he'd left the cab door open, again, right beside Penalty. Simon climbed back in the cab and slammed the door.

In temperate voice, Penalty told him, 'Felt a bit of a draught there.'

Simon jumped back into the driver's swivel seat and consulted his watch: 07:44. Four down. He looked out and back along the train. Still no green light, so he reached to the horn valve lever under the console and a powerful note of air thumped below the cab floor – his fingers were wet upon the small lever and its bobble. The green torchlight appeared once again through the steam at the far end of the train, waving impatiently. Simon heard Kinloch's guard's whistle – the old standard BR issue Glasgow Thunderer rattling its mighty pea.

Simon sounded back two quick notes on the horn, pushed and held his foot down on the deadman's pedal, shoved the master handle into *Forward* then moved the power handle to *On*. When he pulled his head in, Penalty was stood right next to him with his short fingers on the console to support himself; he'd switched off the cab lights to kill any reflection on the windscreen glass. The train creaked forward along the runnel between the two platforms and Simon looked out the window, backwards along the train once again, as he'd been taught; he advanced the power handle to the next notch, bringing his head back in with the noise rising behind them in the engine room.

In a louder voice, Penalty said, 'Watch your amps.' He tapped his grizzled fingernail at the glass of the glowing gauge with the green, yellow and red colour bands. 'Let the amps needle go up, keep it off the red, then the second it hesitates, add on another notch. That's the way. Aye, that's the way. Notch her up good. Ignore your Wheel Slip warning light – you'll learn to feel wheels slip and no trust the orange light.'

The ammeter had gone steady on the yellow so Simon notched up to around half power; he raised an automatic but invisible hand in return greeting for Musty's wave from inside the illuminated signal-box interior as they passed.

Penalty shouted, 'Just open it up all the way now, son.'

Simon pulled slowly backwards until the little indicator knob of enamel at the base of the power handle came to a stop at *Full On* and he rested his hand loosely on top of the black-enamelled throttle in imitation of the stance the older drivers maintained. He could feel the profound vibration of the whole engine trembling up through that handle under his resting arm. It always amazed Simon – his hand that he knew so well was causing all this 320-ton enormity to move. Beneath the road bridge, the noise of the exhaust hitting the undersides as they moved into the blackness of the cutting was very loud. Still looking straight ahead, Simon took his left hand off the vacuum-brake handle and slid up the window next to his shoulder.

'You check that signal on the gantry above?'

'Aye. She was off.'

'Good lad. Check your signals, even though you're going under them every day, don't get lazy.'

Simon told him, 'First day I drove up here, Hannan says to open the power full and I thought the train would just shoot away, doing ninety mile an hour up the hill. Huh.' He pointed to the stencilled sign between the two sitting positions, under the small central windscreen: *Maximum Speed 90 mph*.

To steady himself, Penalty now had the fingers of both hands placed on the console beside Simon, as if he were demonstrating piano chords, and he nodded then even chuckled in recognition of the naivety. 'You'll no ever be doing ninety on this shitey wee line with these gradients. That's for down in the big cities, fast running on level double track. Know what I mean?'

'Aye.'

'You'll get no speed here till you've climbed to the summit, then at Kellan's house you'll be coming down off the roof, as we say. Can you see, boy? It's fair fucking battering down now.'

'Eh?' It was very loud in the cab.

'Can you see the road all right? We could do with some fucking headlights like the Inverness shed fit. So many level crossings up that way they give them headlights on they two sixes. Driven nights before, aye?'

'Oh aye. Backshift. It's no too bad.'

'It's the glare coming off the bloody dash, eh?'

'Aye. Brutal.'

Penalty gently touched the round dimmer switch on the console with the bent tips of his fingers. 'That okay for you?'

'Aye. Thanks.'

'It'll be light in a half-hour anyway.' He nodded above – to the ceiling or to God. Cautiously, turning his back, putting his arm out to steady himself, Penalty crossed back to the secondman's position and, with difficulty, raised himself up on the seat there.

Now the shining tops of the track slowly unfurled towards Simon out of the morning darkness – a night salient of moonsilver track. The driver's position was to the left, the secondman's to the right, so the track approached each man at a slight angle. Simon dropped his eye to the speedometer. Twenty-eight. If he'd managed the acceleration more skilfully with five coaches on he'd have thirty-two before the top bridge by his father's garage.

The left rail was immediately below him like a thread of light, continually promising something far ahead; the wooden sleepers in their thousands flicked beneath. Future track under his scrutiny turned left or right in long curves or reached straight into invisibility, yet always coming closer and then eaten up and immediately dismissed underneath him. Walls of rock cuttings, tree branches and bridges rushed out of the dark towards Simon then vanished, flashing by his left cheek as he concentrated ahead, squinting, as if permanently puzzled, and focusing upon some furthest, almost mythical point which was always just escaping.

Engine hammering, the train climbed defiantly, the town lights now out below them on the left. Beyond the Cona Estate they went along the side of the hill, climbing above the darkened golf course.

'Does your foot get stiff, held down on the deadman's all the time?' Penalty suddenly shouted across.

'A bit, aye,' Simon yelled, but not taking his eyes from the darkness ahead.

'You'll get used to it, boy. Be second nature to you soon. Have your foot bent down like this in your sleep – the way waiters wake up with their hand, holding their tray.' Penalty stopped sharing the vague view out of his own windscreen in front and his head dropped forward.

Simon smiled at his comment and he could sense Penalty was making up another cigarette. Still not looking across but staring straight ahead, Simon shouted, 'I thought they were just joking at Traction School. When they called it deadman's pedal. Is it seven seconds after you take your foot off that the brakes come on?'

'Aye. Seven seconds, power cuts out and your brakes come full on. Same as the fuse on a grenade. Don't try and test it though. Sometimes they arnie accurate. Keep your foot pressed on the deadman's pedal through life and you won't go wrong, son. Keeps fucking drivers awake too in case we nod off. Christ knows enough when you're working with Shouting Darroch there's a chance of slipping into the land of nod as far as that cunt's conversation goes. Know what they've got in Australia on the Great Nullarbor Plain?'

'What?'

'A railway track with a straight section of three hundred and twenty-eight mile. Longest bit of straight track in the world. Imagine that. You'd be dying to hit a kangaroo after an hour or two of that. Deadman's pedal puts the brakes on if a driver falls asleep. You'll see some Glasgae boys up here jam them down; lazy bastards. Use a bit of cardboard, or even a screw bolt from the track. One boy had the deadman's jammed down once and it sprang free. On went the brakes at seventy mile an hour.' He chuckled. 'A Rangers–Celtic game was on. First time in history the lot of them were all hugging one another as they went flying from one end of the fucking train to the other.'

Simon laughed. 'Has a deadman's pedal ever saved a train? Has a driver dropped dead driving?'

'Fuck, aye. Happens all the time round the world. If I konk out on ye, mind, just roll me out the door and down the embankment and you carry on. McGarry wouldnie be wanting the train running late. Mind, shut the door behind me so's you don't get a draught.'

Simon laughed.

In a shout but a differing voice, Penalty advised, 'Watch your water hoses, son. If you drag it, could get fankled up in someone's legs. Happened in Dundee once. Driver forgot a shed lad had put a hose in his blind side and he ran the engine forward. Shed boy tried to grab it but it looped and tightened on his fucking leg cause the hose was snagged under the engine. Off the loco went up the line dragging the fellow behind – screaming blue murder. Driver was only going up the main shunt signal but that was a hundred yards. Then he reversed. By this time the boy on the end of the hose was unconscious. Probably deid. You'd hope so, cause the engine went straight over him and took his head off.'

The train wound the curves at full power, the throttle handle not being moved under Simon's hand – the auto regulator making small micro-adjustments to the amps as the steep gradient slightly reduced – or then increased – but never peaking twenty-eight miles an hour. The flanges spangled sound out of the curved checkrails as they crossed the railway bridge over the single-track back road. Simon glanced left, remembering that strange night down there with Nikki, on the motorbike; November past.

On the summit, beyond Kellan's house – the old signal box with the disused point levers still ranged along the viewing windows inside his actual living room – the rain stopped all of a sudden. There was a sluggishness to the last slow water blots on the windscreen – the rain endeavouring to become sleet. Simon and Penalty each stretched a hand forward to halt their hissing wipers – as if they had sudden revelations and were making urgent moves to chess pieces on a board.

They gathered speed on the tip of the downward bank, crossing small bridges of cattle creeps under the line because of the field severance on these owned acres of in-bye lands. Trackside hawthorn trees were twisted with a permanent lean to the east, away from the prevailing winter gales. Out to the mighty west, the dawn lay in the sea and the star fields were above with a goodly ration of that heavenly moon. Simon slowly shoved the power handle forward to *Off*, charging into the darknesses.

★   ★   ★

At Tulloch Ferry Simon opened his window and looked out onto the platform. He'd stopped perfectly – even beautifully. 'Oh fuck.' Simon's hat fell straight off his head. He'd forgotten he had it on. The hat fell down onto the dark platform then sprung once, away from the engine, and it settled somewhere out in the dark of the unlit platform.

Simon slapped the master to *Engine Only*, killing the deadman's, then stood.

'What's wrong with ye now?'

'Bloody hat fell off.'

Simon opened the stiff door with a grunt and he jumped down onto the platform of his home village. He bent straight over, snatched his hat from the platform, flicked it once – in case muck was on it – then he climbed back up into the warm black cab.

At first in the near dark he thought John Penalty was crying. His wrinkled face was further creased, like a smooth sheet of drawing paper screwed up in your hand then spread out flat again. Penalty was actually laughing, his shoulders jumped. 'Oh son. Oh son. I'll get Lincoln to get you in an extra supply of hats.'

'What's so funny?'

'Och, sorry. But that was priceless.'

Simon laughed out loud too. He looked at Penalty and suddenly tossed his own hat over at him.

'Hoi, you wee bugger.' Penalty grabbed it in two hands. 'I'll take good care of it,' and the old man pretended to balance Simon's hat in a silly way up on top of his own.

Six miles on at the Back Settlement it was getting light and the summit of the Creach was ringed in low cloud. Davey the station master was stood on the platform to pass them the new token and take the one they had. Penalty had limped over to the cab door behind Simon and tugged down the window with a grunt.

Davey looked up at them both. 'Goods is meeting yous at Nine Mile; she's cleared the junction quarter an hour back so's yous'll beat her there. Hope you're learning something off the new blood, John?'

Penalty blew out smoke. 'Oh, I'm fucking learning something right enough. We need a wee elastic chin strap to keep the cunt's hat on his daft big heid.' Both young Simon and old Penalty chuckled on their folded arms, just staring down at Davey.

Simon yawned. Over the lively, frantic turning of the engine lodged behind him, a dawn bird was sounding far out in the trees beyond the platform – the insistent weep of a robin redbreast.

Davey was staring back up the train. 'Right. That's yous then.'

'See you anon – in a half-hour,' Penalty nodded.

'Aye. I've a bleezin fire in the office. Get yourselves in for a warm-up and tea if yous're wanting.'

Penalty said, 'Ach, we're down so we'll probably just go straight through the day, Davey.'

'Is he a speed merchant, John? Try and keep her under a hundred mile an hour now, Young Fella.' Davey shook his finger in warning.

Kinloch was using the green flag in the rising daylight. The exhaust responded instantly up on the roof behind them while the whole train slowly moved ahead and as the platform ramp fell away, Penalty spat down his cigarette butt to the trackside then almost instantaneously slammed up the cab-door window. The old man crossed back to his seat at the other side but gritted his teeth when he heaved himself up on it. Simon took his head in and shoved closed his own window, looking ahead. Penalty nodded to the new token on the AWS.

'Gie us that over here a mo.'

Still staring ahead, Simon held out the token loop so Penalty could reach and take it from his own seat. Penalty placed it on the desk before him and started undoing the first of the two buckles on the leather pouch.

They cleared the stone bridge, crossed the hollow-sounding metal over the river and on down the two curves of the embankments with the sweeping flanks of the misty Creach straight ahead. Simon shut off the power and the pneumatics hissed in the contact switch box underneath.

'Do fifty but down to thirty-five for the horseshoe at the bottom, after the viaduct.'

Simon nodded. He knew that.

Penalty folded back the leather flap of the pouch to reveal the low brass sheen of the token, each key-shaped block unique to the release mechanism of the next station, so no two trains could ever enter the same section. He slid it out with his short fingers and put the flat golden nugget down on his desk. Penalty turned his attention to the pouch, twisting back the leather tongue. 'Look at that.' With the lid folded backwards he held out the exposed tannery flesh of the interior. It had thick black writing upon it.

Simon squinted across. 'What's it say?'

'*Saor Alba*. Know what that is?'

'Nut.'

'*Saor Alba*. "Free Scotland" in the Gaelic. The signalmen burn this stuff on with red-hot pokers from their stoves in the box, to pass the night shifts. Some of them are beautiful. Real craftsman-ship. Did you no see about it in the circulars?'

'Nah. Hardly read the circulars.'

'Threaten of dismissal if they're caught. Are you a Nat, son?'

'Eh?'

'Are you Scottish Nat? You for Home Rule?'

The political ideologies were coming hard and fast this morning. Simon smiled. 'I'm no a Nat and I'm no not a Nat.'

'No think Scotland should be a free country, son?'

'Depends what you mean by free.'

'A free Scotland with a parliament. A fucking socialist Scotland. A republic with nae fucking royal family.'

'No English? My own father's a Yorkshireman.'

'Is he now? It's nothing to do with the English. It's to do with ourselves and our own country, that was took away by fucking rich boys and Tories.'

Simon grunted.

Penalty softened the tone again. 'Well, it takes all sorts to make up the world. Suppose there have to be a few Tories tossed in as well.' He gave a grisly smile. 'But one's enough on this fucking railway. It interferes with smooth running.'

'I'm not a Tory.'

'You need and use your heid. Look at this Concorde karey-on that's coming. The money wasted so a few rich bastards can fly around the world a wee bit quicker. If the fucking money going to be squandered on yon was used on these railways we'd have the finest rail system in the bloody world for everyone.'

'Aye.' Simon looked across and saw, beside the wrought-iron

gates of the driveway, the little waiting hut for Varie Bultitude built by the estate carpenter when she was a wee lassie.

They crossed on the river viaduct. Even on some nights looking down, the furious toss and buck of white froth on the bouldered bed beneath showed if the sluices up at Bultitude's Barrier were half or full open. Velvet blackness down there meant the sluices were closed.

Penalty lifted the leather to his nose. 'Smell that. That's recent. Yon cunt Davey's done this in the night, the cheeky bugger.'

Simon said thoughtfully, 'I'm more a hippy, I suppose.'

'Aye. I can see that by your bloody lassie's hair. Could do with a good trim.'

'Will there only be short hair in the free Scotland?'

Penalty looked across at him but smiled. 'Away you go, ya cheeky bugger. Know what's that yonder?'

'Eh?'

'The big house?'

Cautiously, Simon called, 'What?'

Broken Moan was behind the mounds of roddies, blackened evergreens, monkey puzzle and copper beech, across those riverside paddocks.

'That's the Bultitudes' place there. Fucking massive. These lands is all their estate for centuries. Ever heard of Tom Johnston? You can read his entry on the Bultitudes in his book, *Our Scots 'Noble' Families.* Between the Bentincks and the Hopes. If I'm no mistaken.'

'Noble what?'

'*Our Scots 'Noble' Families.* You're aye reading your wee books. You should go away and read that one.'

'What is it?'

'All the aristocratic families of Scotland and what a load of thieves and rascals they all was. Johnston was a good socialist. Once.'

'Are the Bultitudes in the book?' Simon was amazed.

'Fucking right. Andrew Bultitude is Commander of the Pass.'

'Aye?'

'Was Bultitude took this whole dam system to the Secretary of State himself. Mad bugger flooded the whole glen for the money. Nineteen sixty, this was. Water level rose and rose slowly over a few month until Badan village went underneath.'

'Aye. I'm too young to mind, but I've heard all this.'

'It's true. That used to be land down there and a village. Everybody had been evicted by then – normal folk up to the Jericho Road council houses at the Back Settlement, where Davey there lives.' Penalty jabbed a thumb backwards over his shoulder. 'Davey the box was Badan. But I'll tell you this, Bultitude's mother refused to leave. The water level slowly rose over the fortnight but the old bat wouldn't flit.'

'Bultitude flooded out his own mother?'

'Oh aye. Big old manse house. All her best furniture – some of it from Napoleon's times – manhandled to the top floor as that water come up – stair by stair. They even says she'd a bloody manservant in a diving suit with one of them big brass helmets, swimming down to fetch her favourite copper saucepans from out the kitchens.'

'Never?'

'Oh aye.' Penalty laughed. 'They say the same old crow took to her bed on a raft made of oil drums, floating up closer and closer to the ceiling each night. She was seasick too. Had newspapermen rowed out there in a boat interviewing her, calling through a top-floor window. Eventually her bed and the floating furniture was all lifted up, pushed right against the cornices so she clambered higher into the attic and out the skylight, winched off the roof by a bloody rescue helicopter. Her servant was seen swimming off in the diving suit, chasing a velvet armchair.'

'You're jesting me?' Simon glanced across.

'Nae way, son, that family's crazy; bad blood in blue veins. Just you mind, every jewel shining on the Queen's crown shines for each family like them. That Bultitude still needs a man to bring him down a peg or two.'

Simon nodded slowly in the darkened engine cab. They had left behind the castellated gables and roofs, the low outbuildings and rigid formations of evergreens. Simon kept his eyes right ahead on the powder-grey track, processing out towards him as they entered the Pass. The sides of the gulley looked like two clamps, just about to complete their closure.

Thursday 15 November 1973

Since the luxuries of the centrally heated hotel room, Simon and Nikki's frustrations had steadily increased back home. In Glasgow they had moved back and forth between the crumpled twin beds through the greedy hours. In their pauses they heard the distant female voice of the announcement tannoy, vibrating through their walls, echoing from the wide concourse of the huge railway station – while they paused so still and so close.

They both felt pity for those excluded travellers, herded by the insistent voice and denied their intimacies. As the long day in the room passed, the tannoy woman's tones had cautiously become like the voice of a familiar friend – even an encouraging participant.

They had dozed together on those two beds, Nikki's bare thighs enlivened by outrageous sprays of auburn freckles, sealed beneath the dried membrane of his latest ejaculate from when he bothered to pull out. She fell into sleep easily, even with a touch of narcolepsy. It was strange to see her so vigorous then suddenly her eyes would close into untroubled sleep. Nikki's sleeping breath occasionally wheezed since they'd smoked a pack of ten cigarettes together. Her little wheezes often made Simon hold his own breath as he confused them with possible voices of sinister import in adjacent bedrooms. He had watched with a dilution of love as a twisted blonde length folded back, lying close to her lips. The sleeping girl's breath trembled her own blonde hair like the weed searching uselessly in the river of his village.

In the middle of their varied sessions they took a hot bath together in the huge old tub, frothing it absurdly with shampoo, and in that game of young lovers they reached, moulding shapes and snow mounds of foam onto each other's hair, their faces flushed under the pale meringues.

After Glasgow hotel rooms, the den up by the television aerial had become useless to them that winter. Early one evening – Nikki was in school uniform again – they had taken the motorbike up the back way and parked by the bungalows, climbed the gate together without talking and crossed the shoulder of the hill below the television aerial, holding hands through the darkness.

Down on the huge lip of rock, indecisive frenzies of rain came crashing down through the leafless branches and the clouds were too dark to judge when the next burst might come. They both frowned upward as if to some controlling god, judging their extent of sin.

The tarpaulin gave only a small strap of sheltered rock, while the wind carried droplets in underneath. They kissed standing, hopeless but chuckling at the inconvenience of the world around them.

The sea wind repeatedly flappered Nikki's school skirt upward, showing paleness high on her legs and she became alarmed as Simon did his winter duty. Out of the cave he took the sharp knife, stolen from his mum's kitchen drawer, and as Nikki crouched at the mouth, he cut away the tarpaulin ropes, struggling for control of it as she yelled – wary that a gust would pull him over the edge. He bundled the tarp into the cave for storage.

Chaste, they had clambered back up through the rain then over the fence and beneath the aerial again. They were so sodden her hair had turned dark and they didn't even bother to sweep the droplets from the motorbike saddle as they swung their legs over. When Simon left her in the back drying green by her bedroom window, Nikki had whispered memorably in his ear, 'My fanny's wetter than if something had actually happened,' and they both had to draw apart to stem their laughter.

But sometimes Simon frowned at his girlfriend's lively concupiscence. It occurred to him that the physical things – which Nikki appeared to be ticking off, like arithmetical exercises in her neat school jotter – could actually mean more to her than to him. Like successful exams, passed in her race for maturity. Her taciturn way and her gruff physicality left long silences and sometimes made their relations seem like a comradeship of extended pauses between grasping in awkward locations where their bodies became a testing ground. Sometimes he thought they should just legitimise everything with an engagement to be married.

And other times not. The first night of her new term she had discussed calling a halt because she accepted he was serious about the railway and not returning back to school with her. Yet in the dark back green outside her window just two hours later, her hand slowly drew her underwear down to the backs of her knees from in beneath the skirt, the fabric faintly luminescent in the occasional swinging headlight cast from the main road of the escarpment above, her contours vivid and defined to his touch by goosebumps.

Simon was fumbling with the little packet from the machine in the men's public toilets.

She whispered, 'Don't bother. I'm safe again.' Her palms went against the council house walls, only three feet from her bedroom window – though they heard her sister in there, listening to Radio Caroline. Nikki lowered one hand to bite her own finger and choke back giggles for the long minutes.

And another phrase of Nikki's from that Glasgow railway station hotel. Nosing around inside, Nikki had inadvertently allowed the large old wardrobe door to swing wide open, so for a spell on the right-hand bed the mirror on the door reflected them having sex. She paid very close attention to it, turning her head awkwardly again and again to view themselves, and she told him, 'We just look like the washing going round and round in Mum's new machine.' A curious enough statement but it was the 'just' which troubled Simon's sensitivities. He was surprised at his sudden insecurities but he also wondered if they might be grudges he was accumulating to assist him in one day betraying her.

It rained so much they had christened the motorbike the Yellow Submarine and together would sing the song on it while they grinned at the pelting drops. Nikki was pressed hard against his back, arms round him, under the open skies, ranging along the old back roads, seeking again for sheltered winching spots in the hostile land – treetops moving against the half-moon deployed above. Although the sky was mostly clear occasional raindrops still fell from it.

He had turned the motorbike round at the Golden Hill. There was an abandoned cottage on the roadside which they had never closely examined together, but it was useless for their needs – hopelessly clotted with brown brambles inside, and roofless besides. The hay barn up on the farm there was padlocked.

He accelerated them back up the hill, her plastered to his back and arms around him with consistent strength. They took the right on the single track up above the golf course.

Simon and Nikki passed down and underneath the narrow railway bridge there. A tight right-hander in the single-track road, with no oncoming headlights. Simon leaned the bike into acceleration, keeping to the centre to avoid the gravel at the edges. He felt Nikki draw in her denim right knee instinctively – the speed was good, true and exciting in the darkness with the sure throw of headlight before them as they went. Then he saw it – only for an instant.

A black demon was briefly caught in some appalling secret action in the middle of the road and no passing place. It seemed as tall as them, wetly black with actual wings.

Simon jerked the handlebars, put his right leg out, and he felt the appalling and slight contact as the beast impacted his foot and lower leg. The bike was almost in the left verging but he squeezed the brakes and eased right, steady, wisely, but then the road turned. The five-inch verge was only soft soil, but heavily wet from earlier rain. It shoved the front wheel hard on impact. He used all his strength to heave the other way but they mounted and the handlebars were suddenly pulled away from his fingers.

Nikki was still clinging to him and it was together they both separated from the bike saddle and moved off through nothingness, then Nikki's arms were torn so surely from him – gone in such an instant – he was sure that the untethered demon had swept in on them from behind and snatched her.

What he saw through his visor was only the headlight beam of the motorbike go up vertically in the night sky behind them, like one of those World War II searchlights his mother had operated on the Lincolnshire flatlands. The bar of light shuddered in the sky then it fell with a horizontal snap, lighting the grey tar up ahead. Through the privilege of this brief illumination, Nikki's helmet was seen skidding along, upside down then spinning to a stop, while he was briefly scraping on the back of his jacket along the tarmac.

Suddenly he had stopped and there was complete silence. The bike's engine had died. He stood up and hauled his helmet off, dropping it. He squinted into the night for both the thing and for Nikki, then he crouched in an aggressive position, lifting his fists, ridiculously ready to fight.

The fallen bike was only about thirty feet behind, the headlight now aimed down into the small ditch at the roadside and it lit the grass there a brilliant and emerald green. Ten feet ahead a dark shape lifted from the verge ditch and he adjusted his feet to face it then saw the pale swing of her hair.

'Nikki.' His voice was meant to be an urgent whisper but came out high and cracked, alarming to himself. He was on her in seconds. 'Are you all right?'

She said, 'Fuck it.' A word she had never used – except in the Glasgow hotel.

'Jesus, don't move. Did you see it?'

The girl giggled and now she was up on her knees, looking down her front.

He kneeled and took her face in his hands. 'Are you all right?'

She was gazing directly at him. 'Oh no. Your bike,' she said.

'Your helmet's come off. Are you sure you're okay?'

'Think so. Aye. These are my best jeans though.'

Now his head snapped up the road and he whispered, 'Did you see it?'

'What?'

It was a dumb question. As always she was travelling with her head sideways against his back, watching nothing though he knew she foolishly trusted him.

'You didn't see what I saw?'

'What?'

'There's something out here. I almost hit it.'

'What?'

'I don't know. A fucking animal or something?'

Now she sounded afraid and looked around. 'Animal?'

'Stand up. Can you stand? I'm sorry.'

'I'm okay. Aye. I'm all. Mucky.' She stood but he saw her put a fist up close to her eyes and examine it.

'Stay here.' Simon stepped slowly back up towards the motorbike, a shadowed yellow piece of its body showing. He went close to the bike but completely ignored it and its fate.

He looked down at his leg which had touched the demon. Sure enough there was a dark patch of blood where its poisoned talons had slashed him. He limped on the leg and spotted more fresh blood shining on the toe of his boot.

Into his mind came an image of Varie Bultitude in her huge and haunted house, bent over a single candle, murmuring, and he knew what she was doing – she was calling forth one of her demons to come and get Nikki Caine. That was why she was asking for Nikki's name and she must have pulled a long and slithering golden hair from his jacket when he wasn't aware, to cast her sure curse. The bitch. A demon to climb on top of little Nikki, tumbled as she was in the ditch, and to tear at her clothes and do things to her there.

Something moved in the verge to his left and Simon jumped back, squinting at the dark. Then it moved towards him, scuffling, and he could feel its coiled-up, potential power. He said, 'Oh, Jesus.'

'What is it, Simon?'

He turned and strode back to the bike. His limp was gone. He looked down on the bike. In blinkered headlight he saw the wet glisten on his leg was not blood.

'Simon, what is that?'

'It's okay. Come take a look.' He leaned over the bike and lifted it. The far side was doddled with mud, grass clots stuck on the rubbered footrest and there was a small dent on the fuel tank, but he couldn't see any major damage apart from the fitted mirror which was badly bent round and now underneath the handlebar. He grunted the bike down from the verging and turned the whole contraption round so the headlight shone back up the single-track road. He kicked down the bike stand at the side of the tarmac.

Nikki was walking towards him, not limping, just moving slowly with her head down. He studied her, waiting for something catastrophic to happen. For her to seize part of her anatomy and scream or for her just to crumple to the ground with internal bleeding. But she did not.

He said, 'Jesus. What a fright. Come and look why I lost it.' He took her hand and they walked back up the road together and in the light they could see it clearly. A huge and mature black swan was cowered against wet ferns at the road edge. It showed some white feathering round towards its flanks and flicky tail but it was strangely black and shining.

'Oh. Oh, a poor swanie. Have we hit it and near killed it?' She immediately sounded near tears.

'Naw. I missed it.'

She said, 'That swan is New Zealand. Did you know that? The black ones all come from New Zealand.'

'It's not. That's a white swan, look. It's oil. It's all covered in horrible oil or something.'

The swan was watching them from its hydraulic neck top. It again tried to lift a wing and they could see how it was matted in oil at the front yet pure and white at the back – the same perfect white as the shampoo suds they had piled onto each other's hair in the Glasgow hotel.

She whispered, 'Don't go close; a swan can break your arm with just wings.'

'That's a myth. What do you think we should do?'

'Do you know Lorrie McCallum?'

'Who?'

She tutted. 'She's in my year. One of the most popular girls in school and her dad's the SSPCA animal man thing. The house is always full of wee kittens and puppies. Just adorable. She even had a snake in there once.'

The bike engine fired up fine as he kicked down the pedal. He was worried for the steering but it seemed true and Nikki in her retrieved helmet climbed back on again. At the bottom by the sawmill – built from the very logs it chopped – Simon suddenly braked and halted. He pointed his arm out far into the dark.

The greens of the golf course came right up to the old road fence. A small rivulet gurgled under the road here and twisted across the green where dainty little bridges crossed for golfers to step over. Simon edged the handlebars round to cant the headlight beam across the fairway. Sat in a defensive bundle was another swan. Much whiter than the other but they could see its underside was blackened.

Lorrie McCallum's bungalow sat in the lee of the hill below the King's Way. The van with the SSPCA lettering on the side was parked at the kerb. Simon and Nikki each held a helmet under their arm and went through the garden gate which they secured behind them with the special fold-over catch. They could immediately hear dogs barking from the pen at the rear of the building, over the mossy roof tiles. The King's Way road was a cliff above this place. A bus passed there and they saw its lighted-up windows. Obviously the family used the dogs as a signal, since the blurred figure of an adult immediately appeared behind the moulded leaf shapes on the glass door, before Simon and Nikki even reached the end of the front path to ring the doorbell. The door opened and there was a man in a shirt, eating porridge or cereal from a bowl, and he used his foot to hold the door wide as he leaned against the standard. 'Hey now,' he said chewing. 'Wee bitty late to be calling on Lorrie, is it not?'

Nikki did the talking. 'Sorry, Mr McCallum. It's Nikki Caine.'

'Oh aye, Nikki. Hello there. How's your dad?'

'He's fine thanks.'

In moments Lorrie herself appeared already in girly pyjamas. She was at the far end of the corridor and called in a mystified way, 'Nikki? Hi.'

Nikki said, 'Eh, Mr McCallum. There's swans, two swans up the back road at the golf course all covered in oil stuff or something.'

Mr McCallum paused and to free one hand he put the spoon into the bowl and he left it there. 'Oh, not again. That's yon sawmill. Had the male in here before. They're spilling bloody horrible sump oil into that stream. The swans come down from the lake at the estate house.'

Simon said, 'That's pollution. They should be fined.'

'Aye, son. Are they saturated in it?'

Simon nodded. 'Aye. One's sat on the road and one's out on the golf course but they're both manky with it.'

Mr McCallum nodded. 'Right. Okay, kids, thanks for telling us. I'll get myself up there the now and bring them in or it poisons them quick trying to clean it off. Hell of a job.'

'What is it?' Lorrie had come to the front door. She was quite pretty – Simon remembered her face. He glanced down at her bare feet and could hear a television far inside; he tried to identify the programme then realised that this high on the hill it could be mysterious STV itself.

Her father turned to Lorrie. 'That's the swans from the estate loch all covered in oil again.'

Simon said, 'We're on a bike, I can show you where they are if you want to follow.'

'Naw, naw. I'll find them okay, son. No like they'll fly away now. And thanks for coming to tell us; that's good of yous.'

Lorrie McCallum looked at Nikki then back to Simon. Her eyes noted their helmets. 'Out there on the bike, were you, Nikki?' She said it in an incriminatory manner. Her eyes dropped mercilessly to the mudded knees on Nikki's jeans.

Nikki nodded. It didn't matter anymore; word was all round school that they rode the country together at all hours.

Simon drove them up to the stopping place at the top of the King's Way, then they descended the back path together, again hopping down into the rear drying green.

At their usual kissing place in the dark, he whispered, 'Sure you're all right?'

'Aye. But,' she sniggered, 'I'll have to take my jeans off at the door in case Karen or the folks see the knees.'

'Aye. They'll go mental if they find you come off the bike.'

'I don't know how I'll get them washed. I'll hide them and do them in the bath after school tomorrow.'

'Look, you might have some aches and bruises in the morning. If you've got pains or that you really need to go to the doctor and tell him.'

'Don't be a dafty. I'm all right. It was soft grass. You know swans mate for life? I read that.'

They looked at each other.

'Mental, eh, we could have been killed,' she said.

'We were lucky there.'

She said, 'I love you.'

He said, 'Aye. I love you too.'

They kissed, but despite his sincere concern he could not stop himself thinking of Varie Bultitude and seeing her face in his mind.

Saturday 1 September 1973

On the following Saturday after he had met Varie in the cocktail bar, Simon Crimmons appeared upon the square of the hotel stable yard at Tulloch Ferry.

The ponies and riders had returned almost silently across the hotel paddocks, and you heard creaking of leather, but as their hooves came into the rucked tarmac of the square, horseshoes began to click and scrape on the surface.

Simon felt horribly obvious standing there. The two wee stable girls had been glancing at him for twenty minutes.

The tourists began dismounting and three ponies shoved in, flank against flank, to drink from the old bathtub which formed a slime of green after the stables had closed down for winter.

He watched as Varie Bultitude arrived last, sitting high on her grey horse; she wore a white, long-sleeved cheesecloth shirt with embroidered flowers across the front pockets and she had on a black safety helmet. As her horse came to a halt, she instantly fell on the far side in a smooth, practised movement, sliding her front down the beast's flank. Simon noted, looking under the belly of the horse, a messy smear of diluted mud on one of the girl's tall black riding boots and the polished leather almost reached her knees. She walked forward from behind the horse, spotted Simon and stood still as he nodded to her.

Simon had expected annoyance or discomfort on her part but Varie surprised him by smiling – as if she wasn't at all surprised to find him there. Wee Fiona, Louise Sangster's little sister, who was horse-crazy and worked all hours as a stable girl, took the hanging reins from Varie's fingers. The little girl looked up admiringly at the tall young woman, then she turned a quick gap-toothed scowl on Simon.

Varie strode across, pulling her hat away from her head. Her long hair was fixed at the back of her neck in some elaborate manner. 'Hello there.'

'I came to see you,' he dumbly stated.

She smiled again, but amused, the head slightly askew, the black eyes. For a horrific moment, Simon believed Varie might have completely forgotten exactly who he was. Simon said, 'How's Alex?' hoping the question would act as a memory aid. She didn't respond so he nodded to the left. 'I live right here.'

Varie turned and looked down the slope where Tulloch Villa was generally hidden by the walls and holly tree, except for the roofs of the kitchen and utility-room extension. She kept staring towards the house. 'Do you? Right there in that big house?'

'Yup.'

'You could spy on me.'

'I wish I had.'

'Oh yes. I forgot. What am I? Am I beautiful-looking, was it?' She turned away from him. 'Have you come to try out our horses then?' She reached back grimacing, pulling things from her hair which squirmed in her palms – Simon looked down and saw they were elastic bands, big fat ones. Pushing her arms in against her chest, she squeezed those bands down into a tight pocket on the front of the jodhpurs. She shook her hair aggressively. There was a tiny, single disc of mud on one pale cheek.

Simon nodded towards a horse. 'What end is the front and what's the back?'

She laughed. 'I forgot, you ride your motorbike.'

'So how is Alex?'

'Away to start his new school. I wouldn't worry about him. He'll be back soon enough and you'll have a friend.'

'How come?'

She laughed. 'We all know he'll get thrown out again. He is a complete loon, that brother of mine.' As if enlivened by talk of her brother, she cheered up. 'So how are you?'

'I'm grand, aye, thanks.'

She quickly asked, 'Been to Glasgow yet?' then more quietly, 'To the hotel?' She dropped her chin in a demanding way.

'Not yet.'

'And your girlfriend? That little ray of golden sunshine?'

'In town. I'm maybe seeing her tonight.'

'Are you now?'

'Aye. Well, maybe. Look. Wondered if you wanted to sort of come down the house for a Coca-Cola or lemonade or that?'

'To your house?'

'It's just there.'

She looked down the small slope again. 'Are your parents at home?'

'Dad's at work. Mum's around and my stupid little brother's there.'

She frowned. 'Don't be beastly. How do you know if I might not prefer to meet your little brother rather than you? What age is he?'

'Ten.'

'Oh. That *is* too young.' She made a squeaky noise then suddenly admitted, 'I'm very thirsty and a cold lemonade would be lovely thank you very much. This is my last day here you know. Thank God.'

'Aye. You said the other day in the bar.'

'Did I?'

'Aye. Get your horse feed back okay?'

'I'm sorry?'

'The horse feed you had in the van. Did you get it all back okay?'

'Is that what passes for conversation in Tulloch Ferry?'

'Well,' he coughed, 'I'll wait for you here then.'

She stared at him and shrugged. 'Let's go.'

'Oh. Right.'

She crossed to the old flat-tyred car from the 1950s, which always sat in the stables hay shelter, and she placed her hat upon its dented roof. The corrugated iron of that shelter leaked and both car headlights had filled up with enough slimy water for a goldfish to live in each lamp.

He nodded as she fell in step right beside him. She seemed even taller that day. They walked side by side in silence, but as the drive and the frontage of Tulloch Villa came into view she told him, 'Gosh, what a lovely house. And what a great location. You stand right on the loch.'

'Aye.' He hadn't really thought about it before. His mum and dad had lived in this big house on the loch by the time he was born. Simon and Varie both looked left and right then crossed the main road together.

'Blimey. Where's your bedroom then?'

'That's it up there. Those two windows.'

'You have a veranda!'

'What?'

'A veranda. A balcony.'

'It's not a *real* balcony. You have to climb out the window and bang your head. Good for sunbathing though.' He gave her a cheeky look.

'I thought you might have the view of the loch at least.'

He sounded annoyed. 'My wee brother's room does.'

'Oh well, he was very clever. He got the better room.' She laughed loudly.

Simon glanced at her. They were striding past the cherry tree and the herbaceous plants and into the drive's curve which took them beyond the front porch to the kitchen door – the back door – as his family called it. He knew his mother was working behind through the gate in the high stone walls of the huge vegetable garden but they had passed by.

He asked, 'How's your father?'

'Busy thanks.' She said it in a sharp, officious way, as if Simon were seeking a private consultation with the man.

Despite all the new sights around her, he noted how Varie continually looked him in the face. She was not shy of eye contact and seemed to ignore her surroundings. He said, 'How was your pony trek?'

'Oh. Silly. You get horseflies when you have to amble along at that snail's pace and can't canter. And those old tourists ask me daft things.'

'Like what?'

'About Rob Roy McGregor and Bonny Prince Charlie. How would I know all those answers? They don't ask about igneous rock formation, that's for certain.'

He laughed. They turned by the hedge and up to the back door.

On the top of the steps Varie stopped dead. 'Shall I remove my boots?'

'Ach. Nah, well. Let's see.' He stood behind her and, like a horse being examined, she quickly lifted back one boot then the other from the knee, so he could examine the grips of the soles. He looked at her trim bum as well though. 'Ach, they're kind of okay.'

'Perhaps I should remove them? I could dirty a carpet.' She leaned against the door jamb and lifted each boot high, tugging quite hard and then dropping them as they pulled free. She wasn't wearing socks and, most remarkably, her toenails were painted a bright red – like a woman's fingernails. Simon noted a thread of elastic led from the bottom of the jodhpurs and wrapped round under each foot to keep them taut. Varie used a finger to hook each loop backwards to hang loose at the ankle. They went on in through the door.

'Of course, we're related to them,' she said.

'Who?'

'Bonny Prince Charlie and Rob Roy McGregor.'

Simon frowned. 'How can you be related to them both?'

'We are!'

'But they're two completely different families. From different times and that.'

She stood still in the kitchen. Challenged on a detail, she now looked away from him. 'Gosh. What a lovely new kitchen. It's all modern. I like your coloured tiles, they're nice and cool on my feet. I wish we had a modern kitchen like this; ours is a dismal old heap. You'd think we cooked for an army and all the pots are *enormous*. Hundreds of them that take an age to boil.'

Simon nodded. 'See in the sink there? It's a waste disposal crusher in the plug. You can put potato peelings in it and click the switch and it all just mashes them away to nothingness. It's meant to even do chicken bones. I'm always saying I'll put Jeff's hand in and switch it on.'

She patted over to the stainless-steel sink and peered in cautiously then returned. The black eyes went onto Simon. 'Are they different families? It's something my father always claims.'

'I don't see how the Royal Stuarts and the McGregors were ever related.'

Varie considered him. 'You are a terrible book reader, like Alex, aren't you?'

'I read a bit, aye.'

'That's why you love each other so.'

Simon's face coloured. 'We don't love each other.'

She smiled. 'I hate history but I like big history. Geology is big history in millions of years, not just silly little hundreds. You should try to read Lyell's *Principles of Geology*. It's like an adventure.'

'Aye, I will for sure.' He mentally noted the title. He turned and opened the tall white fridge door, keeping his back to her to let his colour cool. 'We have lemonade, Lucozade and Coca-Cola.'

'Gosh, all that? Lucozade?'

'Aye; it's a great colour and gives you zest.'

'Does it really? I'll certainly take some, please.' She giggled oddly.

'I'll open a new bottle cause it's bogging when it's flat.'

'What-ing?'

'Bogging.'

'The things you say.'

He took out the yellowy-orange bottle and began stripping the noisy plastic cellophane which shrouded it. Suddenly they heard an odd human sound from the living room next door.

'That's Jeff playing with his toy cars.'

'Oh, funny. Can I meet him?'

'Sure.'

She leaned back and she put her small arse against the American bar. 'So where shall you be going tonight then with Nikki?' Varie said the final word slowly.

'Go all around on my bike, if it isn't raining.'

She exhaled. 'That can't happen too often then.'

'Oh, we cover the miles okay.' He poured the fizzy drink, three-quarter-filling two of the tall, flower-print glasses.

Varie shrugged and said, 'She must think you're quite dishy,' and she looked aside sadly at the Aga.

Simon shut the fridge, handed her a glass, then led the way.

In the living room, Jeff was lying on his tummy on the floor with his legs canted up at his knees. He had a complex network of roadways laid out across the whole carpet as far as the dining table, using granite chips of building gravel to mark their edges. Gravel their mother had sieved clean under the kitchen-sink tap making sure one didn't fall into the waste disposal. Jeff had Dinky and Matchbox cars, tractors and lorries loaded with the chips, positioned all along the curves and straights. He had his Mamod Steam Tractor there that he'd got the last Christmas – though it was ridiculously out of scale to the other vehicles. Simon sniffed the air to make sure he hadn't lit the tractor's meths burner and he actually smiled affectionately. Several of the toy cars had been passed down from his own childhood to Jeff.

'This is Varie. Say hello politely, Jeff.'

'Well, hello there,' said Varie in a bright voice like a primary-school teacher.

Jeff turned his head and immediately fell shy at this stranger. He quietly said, 'Hello.'

'Varie does the pony-trekking up the hotel. She rides on a horse and she's a boss.'

Jeff studied the young woman from down there and looked a little afraid.

'My. What a great town you've built.'

'It's roadworks,' Jeff corrected.

Simon flicked his head. 'Mmm. Come on,' and they both had to tiptoe across the room, holding their full glasses of Lucozade, avoiding stepping on the gravel chips or the toy cars. Jeff's eyes followed, rigid on Varie's toes.

'Where are you going?' Jeff asked.

'Nowhere. Just mind your own business.'

'Is Varie your girlfriend now? She's no socks on.'

She yelped a laugh.

'Don't be cheeky and daft, Jeff, or I won't let you polish the motorbike.'

'Can I have a Lucozade too?'

'Don't drop the bottle again.'

'He's delightful,' she said as they closed the door behind them.

'Matter of opinion.'

She laughed. 'He looks like you, all shrunken down like the Incredible Shrinking Man.'

They walked beyond the toy cupboard, along the corridor.

Simon opened the door to the long room which stretched from the bay windows at the front of the house to those facing over the loch. There was a large white marble fireplace and G-plan furniture, coffee tables which slid into each other and a wheat-coloured sofa. 'This is the blue room – cause of the carpet.'

'What a lovely long room,' Varie said curtly.

'Mainly just use it at Christmas or for visitors – so my dad's forever turning off the radiators in wintertime. Mum calls it "once-in-a-blue-room".'

'Ha,' Varie laughed. 'That is witty.'

'My dad's always trying to save money. Mum says he's the only person who switches off a light every time he comes *into* a room. We could listen to records in here or, up in my room.'

'Oh, let's go to your bedroom. I want to see it.'

They climbed the stairs. At the halfway turn, Simon stopped and nodded to the view from the window seat. She immediately sat down and sipped from the Lucozade.

He smiled at her and he sat down as far along from her as possible. 'This is called a lovers' seat.'

She looked directly at him. 'I know. We have two, but one's next to a draughty window – the lovers would die of pneumonia. And the other has had stained glass put in front of it to block out the view.'

Simon nodded but of course said nothing.

'So you can only open the little windows in summertime and Father says not to ever, in case the glass falls out or the hinges snap. Your view is so much lovelier.' She stared out and suddenly sighed in a puzzled way. 'Your parents seem quite well-to-do.'

'Och, this place was a bit of a dump when they bought it. They done it all up and that.' Simon sniffed and he lifted his finger quickly to rub at his left eye.

'I'd much prefer to live here,' she whispered to herself. 'There are things to see. There's nothing to *see* out my bedroom window but the treetops and the big Pass thing behind. Do boats go by here?' She nodded.

'It's not the Suez Canal or anything. Some go up to the wee quarry.'

'I could sit here all day but I want to see your bedroom.'

'C'mon.' They went quickly up the rest of the stairs. 'This is mine and this is Jeff's.'

She now ignored his bedroom and instead looked into Jeff's but she politely hesitated at the door. Jeff's wee desk had been pulled over in front of his windows. Bottles of Quink, Gloy and Copydex glue sat on it with clear tubes of coloured glitter.

'Oh my goodness. Imagine waking up to that view.'

Simon stood almost next to her. He'd never considered the merits of the view. Jeff's bed was made, the stripy flannel sheets turned down and *Topper* comics lay rumpled on it, some of their loose and coloured pages showing. He led her away. 'This is my den of iniquity.'

To his surprise, Varie walked right in past him and made directly for the armchair. She plonked down in it and sighed again, looking at him. 'To be honest, my ass is a bit sore from the ride.'

He laughed but it was a disguise. She'd used the word 'ass', which he thought classy and internationally sexy.

She snapped her head from one side to the other. 'Your windows face the road,' she told him. Then her head went the other way to his record collection and hi-fi on the white table. She asked, 'What do you like best then, singles or albums?'

'Albums.' He closed the bedroom door behind him then he took the light chair and jammed it in under the door handle. You could see how the door's paintwork had been scored beneath the handle by this practice.

'Oh my. You're shutting me up in here with you, Si. I might get excited.'

He grinned, noting how she'd said 'Si', as those close to him did. 'The locks are all blocked with paint and I have to keep Jeff away or he'll just pester the life out of us. Wait a minute and see; he'll be up nosing.'

'You've got a lot of albums.' Then she added, 'But not nearly as many as Alex.'

'Aye. Even some of those are his ones.'

'And you've a sink to wash in, like I have in my bedroom.'

'Aye. It saved messing around in a bathroom when I was off to school in the mornings and Dad and Jeff were up too.'

'I splash water on my carpet in the mornings,' said Varie, 'and it's damp to the touch of my toes that night.'

He smiled in recognition. 'Me too.'

229

She wiggled her toes. 'I'll test under your sink in a minute.'

He noted the undersides of her long toes were shiny. 'What do you want to hear then?'

Now she placed her glass on the shelf by the sink and dived down, kneeling, ignoring the long rack of singles but flicking through his albums.

He said, 'I've all Pink Floyd there except *Dark Side*. Lent it to my pal Galbraith and I've no got it back yet. Typical.'

She replied, 'I don't know if I like them.'

She softly moved his albums past her tapping fingers while he sat watching her, leaning forward on the very edge of his bed. He glanced at her sharp bum but then retrained his gaze on the fingers and album covers because she kept turning round and looking at him. She must have been aware: the bum in jodhpur things. What a tawny doe she is, Simon thought.

Her fingers flicked beyond annoyingly good albums.

'So that's you away to Edinburgh then,' he suddenly insisted, putting a sadness into the statement.

'Yes. What on earth?' She swiftly hoisted out a music album into the air and held it high on display above her richly black hair. She sat her bum back down on the carpet, her legs crossed, her toes clenching and unclenching. As he looked closer, Simon was not altogether sure that her feet were particularly clean.

'Och, that's pretty rubbishy.'

Varie stared fiercely at the cover which was a photograph of robed figures worshipping at dawn, their silhouettes showing through the gaps in Stonehenge.

He said, 'Side two is no so bad but the first side is just awful.'

Varie opened out the centrefold cover of the record and studied the inner psychedelic illustrations of sacred hearts, eyes in pyramids, bursting stars, Egyptian gods galore. 'But what a great cover. Will you put it on?'

'If you want but it's crappy.' He stood and crossed, taking the record in its paper sleeve from her. 'Side two though, not side one.'

She laughed. 'Now I really want to hear side one.'

'Huh.' He set the record going, side two, then he sat back down on the end of his bed while Varie resettled in the armchair with her glass, taking the record cover with her.

She dropped her head. 'But don't you hear what this fellow's singing about?' She consulted the cover. 'He's singing about magic. Black and white magic and stuff.'

'Aye.'

'Are you not interested in that?'

'What?'

'Magic. I find it fascinating stuff. I read about all that as well as geology. Not just Carlos Castaneda; other things.'

'Do you?'

'Of course. Tarot and spells. It's all great. Wouldn't you ever try that?'

'What?'

'Magic. Making a big complicated spell.'

'What do you mean?'

'You can make spells to try to come into contact with beings.'

'Beings? I don't believe in all that.'

'How do you know if you've never tried?'

'Tried what?'

'Make a circle. Call the spirits down and they'll surround you but they can't get in.'

Simon couldn't help letting out a rattled look.

'You might be able to see them. You've to beware of invoking a demon.'

'Have you done it?' He smiled, but frowned as well.

She looked lower at the record cover. 'No. But I'd like to try. Someone said to me never to mess with that stuff.' She glanced up quick with the eyes. 'So of course I immediately wanted to mess with it. But I need someone to do it with and everyone is far too afraid. People can be terribly cowardly. They say they don't believe in it yet they won't do it. It's just a bit of fun, is it not? I find it really exciting, I want to satisfy all my curiosities.'

Simon stared at her.

She smiled at him.

Simon said, 'I'd do it with you.'

Quietly, so he could hardly hear over the music, she shrugged and said, 'You're probably not the correct person.'

'Yes I am. Why wouldn't I be?'

'Look, right now. A little demon moving the door handle.'

Simon quickly twisted his head. The wooden door handle was turning this way and then that.

'Och.' Simon shouted, 'Get lost, Jeff. Scram!'

Varie sneered. 'He just wants to look in and see what we might be doing.'

He met her eyes and stood up. 'He is a demon. You're right enough there.'

She laughed.

Simon took away the chair and jerked the door open. 'What?'

Wee Jeff stood in the doorway and his mouth moved unheard because the music was quite loud. Simon stepped over to the hi-fi and twisted the chrome volume switch down a bit.

'Do you have any swords?' Jeff said from the door. He was looking at Varie.

'I'm sorry, my pet?'

'Do you have swords? Do you ride on your horses with a sword like a cavalry?'

'Jeff, don't be stupid. You know she doesn't.'

She laughed. 'No, pet. We're not the cavalry. My father has swords though. Hung up on the walls.'

'Wow-wee-oww,' Jeff called. He remained at the doorway.

Varie looked at Simon. 'One belonged to Rob Roy and one to the Bonnie Prince.' Simon and Varie laughed loudly. She turned back to Jeff. 'Maybe you'll see them one day?'

'That would be brilliant. What record is that?'

Varie held up the record cover for the child to see, but Simon had crossed back to the door. 'Goodbye, Jeffrey.' He closed the door firmly. Jeff tried to shove it inward then he kicked the door once, hard, from the other side.

'Jeff, I'll tell Mum.' Simon fixed the chair back in beneath the handle. 'Little bastard. I'll break your fingers.'

'Oh, but he's so sweet.'

Simon turned to look at her. 'Can we sacrifice him?'

She shrieked with laughter. 'All right then.'

He spoke to the door. 'Hear this, Jeff? I'll give you bloody swords, okay?'

She laughed again. Simon looked at her and she smiled. He

moved over and turned the volume back up. 'If you like this record you can have it for keeps.'

'Can I really?'

'Aye. If you like it so much.'

'Why thank you very much. I'm not mad about music but the cover's very beautiful. I might fix it up on my wall in Edinburgh. That should cause scandal. I love scandal. Did you go to that concert?' She pointed aggressively to The Who concert poster, above the head of his bed.

'Ah, nah. Wish I had. Never been to a gig.'

'A what?'

'You don't call them concerts. You call them gigs. I'm going to start going cause I get free travel to Glasgow on the railway. And to Edinburgh.'

'I'll be going to concerts in Edinburgh, I would suppose,' she stated.

'You're dead lucky then. I'll come and visit you.'

But she only shrugged. He already felt furiously provincial and angry; Edinburgh seemed her domain and it appeared very impertinent of him just to mention the place. He cleared his throat. 'Pete Townshend's a genius, a really thoughtful guy with a great band. It's a real poster, it's no a reproduction.'

'"Pinball Wizard"?' She raised her eyebrows to test if she was correct.

'Aye. Wizards again. I haven't bought the new album though. It's hard to get up here.' He frowned at the spinning record and said, 'This guy is an idiot. It's worser than I remember.'

She laughed. Suddenly she stood and crossed to his windows looking outward up the driveway and gates at the main road and across to the new wing of the hotel. A tourist bus swooshed by in the direction of town. Then she glanced to the left. 'Look. Your gardener's working in your grounds.'

Simon said quietly, 'That'll be my mum.'

'Oh dear. I am sorry. I'm so very sorry.' She spoke as if she had mortally insulted him.

Simon stepped up beside her. 'She works away there all hours. We get great fresh veg in summer. She sells the veg and strawberries and stuff to the hotel over the road and to ones in town as well. She grew up on a farm and can't stop growing stuff.'

233

Varie laughed again but looking ahead. She studied the working figure, the grey hair loose, stooped over in an old anorak with a pitchfork stuck in the soil beside her. In a low voice Varie said, 'Your mother appears quite on the elderly side.'

Simon shrugged but he was offended in some way.

Varie glanced at him and frowned then she turned to the other window beside the sink, that same demanding expression on her face with that small nose. 'And do your grounds extend all the way over there?' The voice was not free of an estate agent's spirit.

Simon stood up close to her again, enjoying the proximity. 'Aye. That's our top paddock, right over to the far hedge.'

'Oh, please. Put side one on.'

'Och, it's absolute rubbishy.' However, Simon stepped across and turned the record over. He set the needle on the shining vinyl, the threads of run-in drawing the stylus across. They heard scratches and lazy clicks before the music.

Varie sat back down in the armchair and Simon put his buttocks on the very edge of his bed – almost in danger of sliding off – and he stooped his body well forward because leaning back on the bed to any degree could be interpreted as inviting her to join him there.

She had turned her head away from him and held the long side of her neck still – the tendon was emphasised like a spoon handle just emerging from the surface of cream. She tapped her bare foot to the faintly annoying music, looking at his books without comment until she stated, 'Not enough science.' Yet she turned back to him and then talked again for a very long time about magic rituals – about affecting the material laws with the immaterial and how just one example of it could alter your whole outlook. One thing he could remember her saying was that rock strata were: 'Almost monotonous. Everything I read about in geology shows hard and fast rules that haven't changed in millions of years. Imagine one thing shifted. Imagine an anomaly in the fossil record.'

Simon tried to divert the conversation onto his own ground and said, 'Have you tried to read Karl Marx?'

'God, no.' She frowned as if it were pornography.

She talked about the language of angels and Dr John Dee. Finally her laughing lips moved quickly, talking in obscurity about a ritual involving a feather, a candle and the breaths that came from your lips which carried magical power. 'You use a secret word that only I know,' she told him. 'You both do it inside a consecrated circle.' She paused and added, 'Naked. For purity.'

He felt his stomach hup towards his ribs at this suggestion. 'Sounds brilliant.' His mouth was utterly dry so he reached and sipped from his drink.

The music had finished. He knew side one to be twenty-eight minutes bloody long. That had been the length of her lecture. The silence which followed the music and the mechanical yawn and click of the record arm swinging back was very heavy.

'Don't you think,' he said, 'some of them results of it all might just be the power of suggestion? If you suggest something strong enough you might believe it.'

'Depends what the results are,' she whispered. Then she nodded. 'Do you ever do anything with Nikki in there?'

He turned round swiftly, foolishly looking at his bed, and he felt himself colouring again. 'No,' he croaked.

'Oh. So tonight then you'll both just zoom around and around on your motorbike thing together, like the Diddy Men? Big thrills.'

'Yeah.' Then he smiled. 'We find places to do stuff.'

'Do you?' She smiled heartily and she actually sighed. She leaned aside, reached an arm, taking one of his paperbacks from the shelf: *The Penguin Book of English Folk Songs*. She said quietly, 'May I tear just a tiny little bit of paper from this?'

Simon shrugged but secretly was upset. Albert Lloyd was to do with that book and he was a Marxist hero.

'Look, I'll use this back page here, where you never will read. It's nothing,' she told him. With the book in her fingers she tore a little strip of paper from the rearmost page then she let the book drop onto the carpet, holding the thin paper sliver up to her pale lips. 'Come here.'

He immediately moved forward and slid over the carpet on the knees of his jeans. She leaned, so her face was just above him. 'Come up a little bit.'

He rose up onto his knees. His face was right next to hers – the closest he'd ever been to her. So close he could see his face reflected in her eyes. Eyes that were like two cups of coffee before you put the milk in. She placed the piece of paper between their mouths. 'Pegasus,' she said. 'That's the name of my horse,' and the little piece of paper buffeted with the 'P' and he felt her breath on his own mouth. She smelled of Lucozade. 'You repeat it now.'

'Pegasus,' he said.

'Not so strong. Don't exaggerate. Pegasus.'

'Pegasus.' The paper leaned fractionally towards her lips.

'The paper is the feather,' she insisted and scowled.

'Pegasus.' He felt his legs trembling.

She looked straight at him. Their mouths were separated by two inches. He touched his head forward in a nod.

'But that isn't the secret word.'

'Uh, no. Yeah.'

She whispered in a harsh way, 'And now you'd get a communication, mentally, from an entity or maybe a demon would come marauding about.'

He lifted a finger to touch the tiny disc of mud on her white cheek, whispering, 'Eh, you have a tiny bit of muck there.' As his fingers touched the white skin there was an audible soft snap and a pull-feeling at his fingertip. He snatched his hand back. 'Wow.'

'Ha, I'm electric. I'm always like that. You should feel me when I get off the escalators in the House of Fraser in Edinburgh; you get a right shock off me. You can kiss me if you wish to, but if you do I shall cast a terrible curse on you for always.'

He tried a rotten line on her. 'You already have.'

He believed she'd have kissed him knowingly but Varie pushed down her face on him quite greedily and her tongue went straight in with an amateur skill. Oddly, he thought, she kissed like a boy should. He heard traffic passing by up at the gate. Their tongues began to slide over each other like tightly crossed fingers – hers was small and hard; different from Nikki's. He couldn't stop the wonder if their actual fannies would be casually comparable; then he felt his fingers into her hair. He opened his eyes and saw hers were tightly closed so he shut his likewise, dropped his fingers, lightly touching the skin around her neck – so soft and smooth it felt wet. Her hair was surprisingly heavy, like a bedcover, and she pulled his neck up harder, her head held the same way all the time. She didn't shift position – almost in a lazy way – then suddenly she leaned fully back in the armchair to pull her mouth free from his and she gasped air – she'd been holding her breath and not breathing through her nose like Nikki did.

His hands whipped away from behind her neck but he used this as an excuse to drop them possessively onto her upper thighs and he left them resting there as he stared up at her. Her jodhpurs were so tight and thin he could feel the swirled shape of those elastic bands within her pocket.

'You taste of Lucozade,' she stated.

'So do you.'

'What?' she asked.

'Nothing. No, everything.'

'Everything?' She giggled then she suddenly threw the little strip of paper in the air and both their heads moved to watch it flutter to the carpet. She asked, 'So, do you hate yourself now?'

'Eh, no.'

'Tut-tut. You are a naughty one but a good kisser and the demonstration has finished. Don't tell.'

'I won't if you don't.'

He felt silly on his knees before her, with his hands on her thighs, so he raised them, then he slid back across the carpet away from her and leaned against the end of his bed, knees pulled up to his chest. It was an erection of course. He sniffed and reached a finger to his eye.

She looked at him and frowned. 'What's that?'

'What?'

'That, on your face. There's something there on your face.'

He didn't want to stand up but his finger went to his cheek and touched there. Twisting himself sideways he stood and crossed to the tallboy mirror. As he did, he took a breath and it whistled in a wheeze but he hadn't been smoking. He had a red splotch on his cheek then, as he lifted his chin, he saw his neck was a mass of blisters, like blobs of fat floating on a stew. 'Jesus. What's this?' Round his watch strap and on the other wrist too, the skin was bangled with lifted lumps of white blister and his nose was pouring a smooth mucus. His heart thumped and he swallowed. He believed her magic might be real. 'What have you went and done to me?'

'I haven't done anything, you daft thing.' She stood to cross over beside him. 'Are you all right?'

'Look at my neck.' He held his head back.

She took breath in round those little teeth then said in a humorous voice, 'Oh goodness, I have put a hex on you.'

'Have you? Oh, come on, my breathing's gone all wonky.' His voice was panicked.

'Si, those are welts. You're allergic to horses.'

'What?'

'I've seen that before in people. Allergy to horsehair; to the oils in the hair.'

'You're joking.'

'I'm certainly not.'

'It's not funny. Listen. I'm all wheezy and my nose is streaming.'

'Oh God.' She shook her head and laughed. 'Look, I'm just covered in horsehair. I nearly always am.' She brushed her hand down the white shirt to the thigh of her jodhpurs. The materials were white, but he now saw the grey horsehairs layered all over her like thin needles. Varie stated, 'We can only ever see each other if I take off all my clothes.'

'That sounds a grand arrangement. On you go now and we'll do your magic ritual while we're at it.'

She gave a high cry. 'Oh no, mister. You're funny. You make everything so Scottishly prosaic.' She stared at him.

'I do know what prosaic means.' He sniffed.

'I've taken off my boots and that's as far as it goes. Today.'

'Christ, look at me. It's so bloody itchy.' He pushed out his jaw and studied himself in the mirror.

'Don't scratch. You need to put calomine lotion on it and just lie still. I'll go.' She herself went about lifting the record off the stereo and putting it in the paper sleeve then into the colourful cover. 'I have to get my pay from Margaret Forbes and then I take the train home. I should be getting paid more. I've been taking out most treks on my own.'

'You go home on the train? I could drive you on my bike.' He sniffed and reached his bare arm across his nose and wiped. A stream of clear mucus smeared down the blond hairs on his bare arm.

She laughed at him but then she looked down. 'I think I would like to try a jaunt on your motorbike. One day. But with me covered in horsehair it would kill you. Oh, this is just so funny.'

He took the chair away from his bedroom door and led her down the stairs, sniffing, while she swung the album cover cheerily back and forth at the end of her arm. She kept glancing at him and laughing as he sniffed. He let her out the front door so they wouldn't need to pass Jeff through the house. In her bare feet he followed her across the tarmac driveway; walking on that surface she tiptoed slowly and gingerly with her arms and the record out as if she crossed hot cinders. He followed round to the back door where her abandoned riding boots lay on top of the steps. He observed her as she sat down there and pulled each boot on. 'When will I see you next?' he asked, following her a short way up the drive.

'Don't know. Christmas, I would suppose, when I'm back from university.'

'Right then, bye.' He sniffed and wiped his arm across his top lip, watching her walk up the driveway to the pavement as he stood. She turned once at the main road and lifted the album high in an obscure semaphore.

He ran upstairs and washed his face in cold water then lay on the bed grinding his teeth, wheezing and trying not to scratch.

Sunday 3 February 1974

Out of curiosity on a Sunday, Simon had stuck his head into
the County Hotel public bar, which stood as part of the old
travelling salesman's inn, along the side of the railway station. As
usual the railway was well represented. The frequenters were all
out of uniform; Walker the track walker was at the corner table
with his black Labrador underneath, its coat slick and happy eyes
blinking.

Lawless and Rudolf were up on bar stools, but leaning at the
far end of the bar, Hannan stood – talking to a guy in smeared
yellow waterproofs and wellies from off of the fishing boats.

Simon bit his lip, tried to duck back out, but too late. Lawless
shouted, 'It's the fucking Young Fella! He's found British Rail
Headquarters at last. Come on in out the rain, son.' He pointed to
the barman. 'This's Steam Train John's fireman.'

'Is he old enough for in here?' The barman lifted his clootie
cloth like a signalman and slapped it to rest on his shoulder.

'You cannie be taking railway custom then refuse Penalty's
fireman. The old yin himself'll be hobbling down the road and
hitting you with his stoking shovel.' Lawless winked at Simon.

'More like with his house crutch.'

Rudolf said, 'Lawless, threatening the barman. Again.'

'Aye, Penalty's taken a wee shine to the Young Fella right enough,
eh? He's on with you all the time now. Wait till you're on with
Shoutin' Darroch for a week, son. It's like trying to have a conversation with a switched-off telly.' Lawless pushed his head forward
on his neck.

'Switch that one off then. It's getting Hannan too riled up.'
Walker the walker hoisted the dregs in his pint glass towards the
pub telly.

Hannan waved Simon in towards him, so he crossed over to the man, nodding and smiling to the others.

'Aye, the Young Fella,' Lawless shouted, placing his hands flat on his thighs. 'The only millionaire on the fucking railway.'

'Big Ian's no far behind.'

Though Hannan was clearly drunk, he had an amiable smile.

'Fuck sake, look. He wears his railway jacket on his days aff; are you away to chapel, son?'

Simon shrugged. 'It's a warm jacket. Might as well wear out the railway's clothes and no my own.'

'Och, he loves being a wee train driver, doesn't he, boys? That'll soon fucking wear off in a few year. Are you looking for a train to drive on the Sabbath, sonny? He's keen.' Rudolf's eyes were all watery.

'No he's naw,' said Hannan in a low voice and he jammed his thumb upward to the television which sat high, marooned on a shelf against the painted brown ceiling. 'Had you telt at new year there, son, and that's it now.'

'Give it a break, Erchie.'

'What?' Simon looked up.

'Mick McGahey. He called in the army, man. It's revolution.'

'Right enough?' Simon smiled.

Lawless laughed. 'Is it fuck. Only in Erchie Hannan's mental brainbox.'

Hannan leaned back, so he could see beyond Simon and the fisherman. 'Lawless, nae more duty on beer after the revolution.'

'Beer's always a duty.'

Simon crossed to a chair and put his helmet down on it.

The fisherman spoke. 'You wanting a new motorbike, son?'

Hannan laughed.

'Pulled one up out of fifteen fathom in the Sound. A three fifty. Must of come off a boat itself.'

'It was the Icelandic traffic police.'

'Evel Knievel, trying to jump the Sound.'

'Works too. Runs like a dream. Spouts the odd cooked prawn out the exhaust.'

Hannan and the men laughed.

Simon smiled. 'Are you serious? A three fifty?'

Hannan laughed even louder and put a hand on Simon's shoulder. 'He's kidding you on, son.'

'No I'm no.'

From up the bar, Lawless shouted, 'Are you getting a round in, Young Fella, or are you just here for the scenery?'

Simon nodded and he pointed at Rudolf and Lawless.

'A heavy, son. Please.' Rudolf looked at the floor and his shoulders jumped the one time with a silent belch. 'Oh. There was a dislodgement there.' He swallowed.

Lawless nodded quickly.

Simon got in pints of heavy for every man – one for himself and one for the fisherman and for Walker too. He paid with a ten-pound note.

'Thanks, son. That's some round.'

Simon said, 'Aye. I'm surprised that Walker's dug didn't ask for a pint too.'

The men all laughed.

Lawless said, 'Leading Railman Mutt, the only one you can get sense out of on the railway.'

'He's no so slow, the Young Fella.'

'Aye. He's a character right enough,' said Lawless.

'So he is. He is a comic,' said Rudolph.

'No like Young Colin. You wonder if the lights is on in there with that yin. Young Colin must be related to Darroch in some way.'

'Nobody's related to Darroch. Nae even his mither.'

Hannan said, 'Now you pay attention to the news. Heath must be near hanging hisself.'

Simon sipped the top off his pint, eyes peering upward at the telly. 'What's happened?'

'Carrington says there could be two-and-a-half-day week.'

'Suits me.'

'Ya cunt, Lawless. You've been on a two-and-a-half-day week for twenty year.'

'Two-and-a-half-bottle week,' Walker said.

Hannan clapped his hands delightedly. 'Fucking McGahey said the army should come in on the miners' side. That was brilliant.'

The fisherman put his head back. 'That'll be right. The miners.'

Hannan looked at him. 'What are you laughing at? You're just a miner of the deep, ya cunt.'

Rudolf told them, 'Canna knock the miners as workers. Scottish and English. Every morn, a thoosand foot down and five mile out before I've scratched the wife's fanny.'

'Fuck sake, man. You're putting me off my pint.'

Hannan said, 'This is fucking revolution, boys, an we've waited long enough.'

'It's incitement to revolution; that's true.'

Rudolf turned round on his bar stool and said, 'Aye. The army'll help Mick McGahey right enough. Fucking shoot him. A Bloody Sunday all to hisself. Put him out his misery.'

'Drink up, Rudolf.' Hannan lifted his own new pint. 'I'm the Minister of Loyalty now and you're first against the fucking wall.'

The barman laughed behind the beer pumps. 'The only wall he's against is the yin he's pishing on.'

'The Tories've had it, man. That's for sure. It's a general election.'

'Feel that breeze – is that the red flag waving?'

'Nah. It's Lawless opening his wallet.'

'It's the wife's legs open.'

Hannan turned to Simon. 'McGahey told the army to disobey orders, man. He's saying the army should side with the miners. They'll be fucking tanks in Downing Street, man. Miners and soldiers thegether on them, waving the hammer and sickle. I telt you it would come to this. It's brilliant. Fuck Gormley. He's a good Communist, McGahey. Doesn't give a fuck about any of them, Gormley, Heath *or* Wilson.'

Simon nodded and sipped again from his first ever pint of heavy. He cleared his throat, and in a voice gauged for public statement Simon said, 'Revolutions are the locomotives of history.'

Hannan turned to face him and the other men went quiet. Oddly reverent.

Simon said, 'Karl Marx wrote it. For train drivers, it's no a bad quote, eh?'

'Fuck me. Never heard that one before and I've read a bit of old Marx.' Hannan shook his head.

'Aye. Marks and Spencer.'

Hannan looked stricken. 'Revolutions are the locomotives of history. That's a beauty. Away get a pot of emulsion and we'll daub it across the front of yon engine over on Platform Three.'

They all laughed.

'What is it? Revolutions are the locomotives of history? Imagine the faces on the big white chiefs when that pulled into Glasgow Queen Street.'

'Young Fella knows his books.'

'Good for you, laddie.'

'He's smart. Aren't ya, ya young fucker?' Hannan smiled sadly. 'See you've bought your wee tin peace badge, like the rest of the hippies.'

'Aye, son. Get your hair cut, or Lawless'll mistake you for lass, try and shag you in his sleep one of these nights.'

'Fuck off,' Lawless quietly said.

The fisherman leaned in and he peered at the CND badge. 'I thought that was the SNP badge. I've been misled all these years.'

'I joined up. By post,' Simon said.

The fisherman frowned. 'You've got to have the atom bomb, son. Keeps the population down.'

The older men laughed.

Simon smiled and nodded tolerantly, sipping his pint.

Hannan said, 'Leave the laddie. He's against the bomb and quite right too, but I'll tell yous what I think, boys.'

'Is there a door open round here?'

Lawless spoke the words, 'To dream the impossible dream.'

'Often thought to myself, we should get some gelignite from the granite quarries along at Inverarnan. The boys have it over there, left back from all the hydro work in the Pass. They still use it at the quarry. We's should get some ourselves and do yous know what we's should go and do?'

'Stuff it up your arse?'

'Go halfway down the line on a Sunday when there's nae trains and put gelignite in under one of the viaducts. I'm serious. The bridge at the top of the Lochy bank or the Nine Mile bank. Blow the fucker and bring her down. I can see it in the *Port Star*. "Sabotage suspected. Fifth columnists in the hills." We'd all be like commandos. Saboteurs. Darting from rock to rock, faces blacked out with engine oil.'

'Fuck sake.'

'We'll be up between them rocks like the Bonny Prince hisself, dodging the redcoats.'

'You're fucking mental, Hannan. You should try for a doctor's line for insanity. You'd get it.'

Hannan shook his head. 'Rudolf himself will light the fuse. We'll use the tip of his nose.'

'Fuck off.'

'You've the steadiest hand right enough, Rudolf.'

They all laughed – even Rudolf who held out his hand in front of him, shaking it theatrically.

'One bridge down, lads, and this line would be knocked out for six month.'

'They'd close it for good. Perfect excuse.'

'Longer in the pub.'

'Naw they wouldnie, boys. They'd rebuild the bridge. But it would take six month. They cannie pay us off, lads. Nae redundancies on the railway. Just nothing. Fucking nothing. Union would back us up and we'd all be on full pay for nothing.'

'We are.'

'Think about it, boys. Going to propose it as new business at the next branch meeting. Volunteers please, for a nice wee bombing party to head out into the hills and blow up a viaduct. We'll take a packed lunch with us then be sat on our arse on full pay for half a year, nae night shift or nothing. Pure bliss. We could take up hobbies!'

'Aye. Epic drinking.'

Hannan told them, 'We'd create the people's own railway. Free lollies for children, bonny lassies sunbathing in a special coal wagon pulled behind the engine, filled with sand, so's they had a wee beach to lie on, wearing bikinis like Torremolinos. Plastered in that suntan lotion. Ambre Solaire.'

Lawless laughed.

'No more Red Star Parcels. Red Hammer & Sickle Parcels we'll call it. There'll be an engine or two stuck this side of the bombed-out bridge, so's we'd name them the *Brezhnev* and the *Andropov*. And we's'd have painted on the side "Revolution is the". What is it, Young Fella?'

'Revolutions are the locomotives of history.'

'There you go, ya bastards. Feed on that thought, why don't yous?'

And strangely, the men did go quiet and think of it all, for a moment, as they raised their pints.

Tuesday 5 March 1974

Over the miles back and forth, Penalty always told Simon railway stories from the steam days. How with coal shortages during the war they ran out, and the passengers themselves had once climbed down from Penalty's train and fanned out into the trees – looking for fallen wood to burn in the firebox so they could reach the station. Once at the Fort Junction when they were delayed an hour, an impatient Penalty had stated, 'Young Fella, I'll show you what the real railway's all about,' and he undid his trousers. Simon got such a fright he backed himself against the side of the cab.

As they scooped over the saucer of the evening lands, darkness grew around their train in one vast covering dome, and cracks of wearied sun blinked at the horizons. Simon had been driving but he'd lost time and they were eleven minutes down as they came round onto 3 where he and Penalty gave it over to the backshift: The Englishman and Lawless. Standing in the open cab door of the engine, Simon watched all the passengers coming off, nodding to some.

In the bothy, Simon had pulled his jerkin on over his uniform, stared up at the rucksack in his locker then lifted it down. Back over on 4 he unchained his Yamaha; the small dent on the petrol tank always drew his finger. Lawless and Rudolf were shouting – and coupling up the two locomotives to form a double-headed formation to make up that night's 17.40.

With his headlight on, Simon crossed the square, detoured round the McAdam statue and accelerated in front of Our Lady's, the girls' Catholic school, then towards the golf course.

The lights of the Cona Estate were on the ridge above, beyond the invisibled railway. He squinted behind the visor up the far hill to see if he could pick out the lonely and singular electric lamp of the distant signal which he had passed in the locomotive only nine or ten minutes before. Through some articulation of the darkness, he could see nothing.

He bent forward to accelerate the bike up the steep hill then took the right. He turned off his engine at the car park exit, and since he'd been reprimanded before, he wheeled the bike in silence to the entrance and chained it there.

Helmet held under his arm, Simon nodded at the reception ladies and walked through the warm corridors until he came to the wee snug bothy, but nobody was in there – though a cup of tea sat in its olive-coloured saucer. He leaned against the edge of the door. After a wait Matron Randall came out the swing doors.

'Hello there, dear.'

'Hiya. Karen about?'

'She's across the huts. Wanting in?'

'Well, if it's okay with you. I know it's not visiting hours proper.'

'Och, the ladies don't mind, I'm sure. Off you go in to see her, pet, but just for a wee while.'

Simon walked into the ladies' ward. He had to pass the other beds.

'Oh, here he is, girls, it's the one who gave her the kissing disease.'

Simon smiled and stopped. He'd taught himself not to go red. 'Hello, ladies.'

Mrs McLaren turned aside in her bed and said to nobody in particular, 'He comes every day. Sometimes twice; he's a wee sweetheart.'

'When's the baby due now?' said Mrs Laurison.

'Lorrie!' that younger lady laughed.

'Where's my flowers then, son?'

'I leaned down and grabbed a thistle for you.'

The other ladies laughed.

Simon lifted the chart off the bottom of Mrs Laurison's bed. He pretended to study it. 'More cod liver oil for you, Mrs Laurison. We'll double the dose.' He pointed and re-clipped the chart.

They all laughed.

'He's a holy terror, so he is.'

'My wee grandladdies' wanting a hurl on your train one day, mind, son.'

Simon walked on. 'Aye.'

They watched him move away and beyond the occupied bed with the lady who always slept.

Nikki was in one of the top beds with empty ones all round her. Sat up with pillows in behind her back, all her school books were spread on the bed as always – the Beta maths one he recognised and others too. Their familiar covers seemed to him like a long-ago and grim memory with all their troublesome responsibilities; there were her tidy jotters too. That horrible pink nightie with the frilly neckline was across her flat upper chest and he saw the slippers on the polished lino by the bedside; they were yellow with the face of Dougal from *The Magic Roundabout* on the toes.

'Hey there.'

She smiled. 'Hiya.'

He held his own motorbike helmet above the crown of her head. She closed her eyes, giving him permission to lower the helmet down beyond her fringe so it covered her head and face. Simon stepped back so the ladies down at the bottom of the ward could see Nikki; she looked funny in the pink nightie with the big black motorbike helmet on.

'Och, will you look at that now?' one of the ladies laughed from down there.

From inside the helmet, Nikki's muffled voice said, 'Right. That's me away home now.'

Mrs Laurison's loud laugh was bouncing off those yellowish walls, marbled green to halfway up.

Simon lifted the helmet off Nikki and it pulled some golden hair with it so strands fell around her face, 'I wish I was,' she said and touched hair ends away from her mouth.

'Been up?'

'Went along the corridor to look at the telly for a wee while. I went up and down the corridors then I was tired enough to sleep a week.'

'Och, shame. You've to eat.'

'I'm trying,' she said, annoyed.

'I've got your present. We shouldn't wait any longer. It's just daft the months they've kept you in. I'll be giving you it next Christmas at this rate.'

She looked straight at the rucksack he'd put down and smiled. 'They'll let me home sometime. Have you brought it right enough?'

'Aye. You'll guess in a jiffy but it's not a dressing gown.' He gave her the rucksack and she unzipped it and lifted out the helmet shape still in the Christmas wrapping paper. 'Oh, Simon.' She tore away at the paper then she lifted it and put this one over her head.

'Does it fit good?'

The pink helmet with the black circle on the top nodded then she lifted it off and she studied it just a moment. He saw the end of her nose had gone red and in seconds some tears shot down her cheeks.

'Nikki.'

Normally they never even touched in the hospital but he held out his hand and took her fingers lightly. 'What's the latest the doc's saying?'

'Och, he hasn't been round today. He never comes to see me. Karen says they're still watching the spleen. It affects folk all different.' She held up the helmet and admired it. 'It's beautiful. How's work?'

'Och. Pffff.'

'That old John guy?'

'Ach, it's no the guy's fault he's elderly.'

'Too right. Sounds like they all are.'

'A guy says a while back that the railway's like an old folks' home on wheels.'

She laughed and under her breath said, 'Serves you right. We're both out of school now. Eh? Thought I'd get back for start of term but no chance, I reckon. Seen Karen?'

'She's over at the huts. What's the huts?'

'Och, the stores. She's away soon anyway.'

'Is she?'

'Where have you been today?'

'Down to Ardencaple and back.'

'My God. You do a lot of travelling, Simon Crimmons, but you never get anywhere except back here.'

Simon chuckled. 'Aye. You're right enough there. There was snow still up past Nine Mile. We're a thousand foot up there.'

She shrugged.

'The river was still all icicles and everything; pretty amazing. I did sixty-two miles an hour there.'

'Mmm.' She had lost interest already. 'I'm so behind in maths it's going to be impossible.'

He nodded. They looked at each other. She smiled at him and he smiled back.

'Does Matron know you're in outside visiting hours?'

'Aye. Saw her back there.'

Nikki had abandoned a passion for the rules and strictures of school to replace them with the rules of the hospital, Simon thought.

'What are you doing the night then?'

'Nothing. I'm off tomorrow.'

'You're always off.'

'No really. Just two days then I'm on the midnight freight till five in the morn. It's a spare shift tomorrow so you just don't go in. They've fiddled it so's the other shifts cover it and you get it off.'

'So you told me. Easy life on the railways, it seems.'

'Don't be telling people though. Fortnight off every six weeks. Four months a year, man. That's brilliant, better than school.'

Nikki gave him an oddly knowing look that reminded him of her mother's warning glances. 'You'll all go and get caught one day.'

'Some of the guys have other jobs as well as driving trains. It's mental, man. You can hardly call them lazy; they're doing two professions. One boy's got his wee fishing boat, one's driving vans – Shoutin Darroch's brother has the butcher so he's helping out there.'

'Karen's out at five in the morn. Goodness me, it's a wonder the trains don't know how to drive themselves.' She sighed and looked at the helmet.

'Do you want me to take your helmet away?'

'It's not going to fit in there, is it?' She nodded to the bedside cabinet.

He felt he was being reprimanded.

When he left the ward, Karen Caine was in the wee room with that other nurse – the chubby teuchter one from Skye. Simon smiled.

251

Karen called out, 'Look who's here. It's Ivor the Engine Driver,' and she laughed.

'We meet again. That's actually a song by The Who.'

Karen ignored him. 'How's ma wee glandular sister then?'

The girl from Skye smiled.

'A bit dour. How's the doctors say she's doing?'

'Fine if she'd stop worrying about school.'

'She says she's still so tired.'

'I've telt you that's normal with glandular fever. She'll be grand in another month, probably back in the house in a fortnight. Look. How sweet. He's got her a motorbike helmet too. She was telling me she thought you'd get her that. You'd better no let Mum and Dad know. They don't like her up on your bike.'

'I know fine. I was keeping it hid at the station.'

Karen reached out, took Nikki's helmet, pulled her paper cap off her hair and put the helmet onto her own head. Simon and the girl from Skye laughed at the sight of the pink helmet with the nurse's blue dress and white apron. Inside the helmet, the muffled voice spoke. 'It fits me too despite ma wee sister's big brainbox. Oh, this is grand. I've a taxi home at nights now, Lynne.'

Simon asked, 'Can I mooch a fag?'

Karen tutted. She turned away with the helmet still on.

Lynne said, 'You'd best take that off; if Matron saw you'd get hell.'

Karen reached out for her handbag that was hanging from the door of a tall locker on its strap. She took out a pack of Embassy Regal and a small box of matches then handed them over. She lifted off the helmet and gave Simon a stare. 'It does fit me fine,' she told him.

The Skye girl stared. She was always looking with those clear eyes and it annoyed Simon and gave him nasty thoughts that her eyes had only ever seen hills and cow shit. Like nothing ever happened in front of her private face, so she was always goggling outwards at other people, demanding spectacle – the drama of nursing and suffering would suit her fine, Simon thought. 'I'll be out front.'

'Here. Only smoke one of them now. I'm trusting you with the whole packet.' She put the new helmet down on a chair in the nurses' wee bothy.

'You can trust me,' Simon said, walking up towards the outside doors. Karen stood in the corridor, fitting her nurse cap back up onto her hair, her fingers moving and touching there – her arms held up. She watched him go.

Outside by the pillars at the porch of the cottage hospital, Simon stood with his back to the bushes. He lit a cigarette, flicked the dead match ahead of him and exhaled, his eyes following the mix of smoke and cold breath out into the darkness. When he'd smoked the cigarette and flicked the butt away he simply took out another and smoked it.

Karen Caine appeared below the portico carrying Nikki's motorcycle helmet in one hand. She was still in her nurse dress, tights and shoes but the apron and paper cap were gone and she had an unbuttoned duffel coat round her. Karen did not advance but stood by the pillars staring at Simon. 'That's me finished,' she said.

Simon walked towards her and handed her the cigarette packet and the matches. She checked her fag packet. 'You took two, you bastard.' Suddenly she dropped her voice. 'Are you goan give us a hurl home on the bike then?'

'Seriously?'

'Aye.'

Simon smiled. 'If you want. Use Nikki's helmet.'

They crossed over towards the bike.

Simon unchained it. Karen pulled on the new helmet with a muffled laugh. She must have had hairspray in her hair by the rustling, crunchy sound it made. He put on his own helmet and pushed the bike all the way forward till they were at the car park exit then he swung his left leg over the bike. 'You have to hang onto me tight now.'

'Don't go too fast.'

'I won't.'

'Christ,' she said and she made a noise as she swung her leg over the saddle behind him.

'The bike's no powerful enough to take us up the brae itself. Nikki and I go up the King's Way and walk down the back path to your place.'

'Do yous now? That's why yous are aye sneaking around in the back green, you randy wee bastards. Come on then.'

Karen's hands were held much tighter than Nikki's – and perhaps lower. He could feel an actual woman-bust pushed against the back of his jerkin. Simon drove slowly through the town, across the square, past Our Lady's school with its spooky statue on top and way down the esplanade. The buoys for the ferries blinked coldly out in the night bay. There was a car right up behind them on the King's Way and he slowed and waved it on so it could overtake, then he geared down for the hairpin.

Karen was heavier than Nikki because the bike really struggled on the last corner, the kerb crawling beside them so slow, he thought you could lean down and place a cup upright on the pavement – they almost stalled until they were round and picked up a few miles an hour, then he pulled in to the parking place near the gate.

He kept the engine ticking over as Karen climbed off, removed the helmet and pushed it out into Simon's arms. 'That bloody wind went right up ma skirt. What must yous both do in the rain – you'd be drookit?'

'We've got cagoules.'

'Is it any wonder Nikki's ill?'

Simon frowned.

'Och, sorry. Glandular fever is viral. It's nothing to do with the bike. Or kissing,' she smiled. 'I'm in a rotten mood. Hellish day.'

'Aye. I'll see you then.'

'No way José. Where's your manners? You can get us down that hill in the dark too. If the Prowler doesn't get me I might skid on my arse and I'm no sure if Mum's done my other uniform. I hope so. This one stinks of Mr McPhee's skitters.'

Simon didn't object and killed the engine. He took the padlock out of his rucksack and crouched, chaining the wheel while Karen stood beside him. She sighed impatiently then lit a cigarette, not offering one.

Simon put the pink helmet in the rucksack and carried his own. When they came to the gate, Karen bluntly said, 'Do I have to climb this bloody thing?'

'Aye. It was open for a while but someone padlocked it.'

'Probably the farmer did cause you two are aye opening it at all hours.'

Simon went first, passing his helmet through the spars and placing it on the ground then quickly nipping over.

The blue dress of the nurse uniform made it difficult for Karen to chuck her legs in black tights over the the top spar and her bag slung across her and swung about. She turned in the darkness as she came down on his side. He looked at her good legs through the bad light. 'See that bag. I don't remember it having a long strap.'

'What?'

'The night we went down the short cut.'

'Oh aye.' He saw her white teeth in a smile. 'Remember that, do you?'

'Your bag didn't have a strap.'

'Oh, you dopey docus; that was another bag. I've more than one handbag, you know.'

'Oh.'

'Where's this bloody path? Christ, you cannie see a thing.'

'Down here.' He walked ahead until they came to the point where the slighter path came off the worn one. He took a step. She stood above him and stretched out her arm so he had to lift his arm above and take her hand. He led her down towards their back green. She made a lot of dramatic noises and was none too steady on her feet.

'Fuck me. Are you sure that bloody bike contraption will no take me to ma front door? I'm no doing this again.'

'I'll be getting a better bike next year. I'm saving.'

'Will you now?'

Even when he got to the tiny jump down the brick ridge into the drying green he had to turn and hold up his free hand to her as if she were a queen stepping down from a horse-drawn carriage.

They walked in the dark towards the dark windows of the flat. Simon made for the back-green access door but Karen hissed, 'Hoi.'

'What?' he automatically whispered though he didn't know why. Because he and Nikki always did?

She whispered sharply back, 'Hush. I use the window so's the folks don't know if I'm in or out. They could be out themselves anyway. Dad's on the late and Mum's at the bingo club as usual. Maybe.'

'Oh, right.'

She went to the window. Simon stood a little back while she used her fingernails to grip and tug the window frame. The window swung open outwards. Now showing familiarity with the technique, Karen hoisted herself on the sill, twisted her leg so the sky-blue material slid far up her dark thigh again, and she swung her leg in, straddled on the outer wall. Her left leg reached and she sat to get a good stance, then drew her other leg up and into the bedroom.

'Come on in.'

'Eh?'

He saw her inside their bedroom, pulling off her duffel and tossing it over into the dark towards the bunk he knew was there. 'Come in a wee minute.'

'In? Nut. I'd better get going.'

'Shush. No so loud. What's the big rush?' She stood at the window.

He shrugged outside and stepped up to the opened space by the window. 'Nothing. I just best get home.'

It was so dark inside the room it was difficult to see Karen standing there. He could distinguish she had that belligerent face though.

'Can you see me?'

'What?'

'It's freezing with the window open, you know. Can you see me?'

He was unsure if he was meant to confirm in the negative or the positive.

She said, 'It's just, I'm taking off my uniform, cause it's humming. It mings.' She swiftly pulled the shortish blue dress up over her hair and dropped it, standing, and looking towards him. He stared but he did not move. She kicked off her shoes and peeled the tights down from her waist – they were like a skin of shadow, some contributory fabric to the darkness itself, another layer to its sootiness, so her pale legs came suddenly more visible as she bent and drew the black nylon clear of each foot. She stood up straight and again she paused. Then she reached behind and freed the black brassiere which fell away. As if she were doing some keep-fit exercise, she dipped, pushing the underwear along her thighs to her feet, and she rose again to face Simon, standing in the window space.

'What are you doing?' he whispered.

'Just changing. Since you can't see me. You're only sixteen so it doesn't matter. My folks aren't in. Or I can't hear them.'

He only nodded slowly and looked as she stood there.

'I'll have to close the window now,' and she came closer. He almost stepped back but held his ground. She reached her naked arm beyond him – he was sure it was shaking – and she pulled the window almost closed, but not quite. Holding it firm by the handle she placed her bare left breast against the glass and she whispered to him through the slim gap, 'If we kissed through glass it's not real kissing. It's not bad. I won't tell her.'

He made an involuntary noise in his throat. Karen's nipple was a brown nut against the glass, with white and flattened skin around it, like a microscope slide sample from school.

He raised his gaze to her face and she put the lips of her mouth against the inside glass so they too flattened out – undoubtedly like the undersides of slugs. Simon dropped his helmet on the grass, leaned in and gently touched his own lips against the cold and slightly gritty glass, exactly where her mouth was. Her right palm came up companionably against the inside glass and he mirrored this by placing his own there – hand against hand but no sense of human heat. They kissed through the flat and thin barrier of glass, their noses mutilated and splayed, then he mimed, touching and kneading first one, then both breasts which were flatly offered to him against the glass, but she suddenly made a pained noise and leaned backwards so her full frontal curved away into the blackness. The window suctioned closed – her hand had pulled it as she fell into the darkness, then she had moved some-where away into the deeper and unlit recess of the room. Possibly she lay on the linoleum floor? He dropped his arms and squinted, even put his hands quickly up against the glass to shield outside light, but he could not see her in there. He raised the cuffs of his jerkin and wiped unsuccessfully at his saliva on the glass, smearing it.

He picked up his helmet and retreated backwards across the green a short way then he turned and moved a distance up the small path. He studied the rear facade of the flats and the other apartment windows as well as the Caines'. Several windows were illuminated behind thin curtains of bright pastel patterns, some showing the outline of the lamp behind. He sat down on the path, dazed for some time, looking to that specific dark window, but nothing more showed from it. The ration of moon came clear of cloud tumble, its light banging over the smoky roundels up there and onto the roof slates. He knew she was on that top bunk mired in the obscurities, touching herself.

When a naked light came on in some previously darkened third-floor window, showing the corner of a wooden wardrobe, he sprang to his feet and began making up the path. Each breath was a curse, again and again, as he climbed back towards his motorbike.

Tuesday 19 March 1974

Inside the workshop the roof spots were on and the Albion Reiver had its cab canted forward, exposing the radiator and engine. Simon's father, Billy Strachan and Des – that young new mechanic from Glasgow – were stood together talking at the top end. Tools, hoses and equipment were hung on the corrugated-iron walls.

'It'll take the angle grinder,' said Des.

Billy and Simon's father looked at each other.

'You'll fucking snap it with the grinder.' Simon's father stood still.

Simon remembered that his father swore bad words at work but he'd never, ever heard him 'F' or 'C' once in their house in front of Jeff or his mother.

'Naw way.'

'I'm telling you, you will.' Simon's father looked up the long space between the lorry and the wall, saw Simon there. 'Oh-oh. Here's more trouble.'

Billy Strachan looked up. 'Och, we're okay now. We'll get the railway on it.'

Simon's father chuckled and that Des guy gave Simon a twisted mouth.

Simon's dad walked up towards him, leaving the two men behind him.

'Hiya.'

'What are you up to, Professor?'

'Nothing. I'm backshift. Thought I'd pop in and see you. I've hardly been seeing you on this shift.'

'Aye, well. I wouldn't know you lived in the house sometimes these days. I can't keep up with your coming and going.'

Simon followed him out of the shop and into the Portakabin. His father slopped down in the leather swivel chair behind the desk. He looked at Simon again. 'Well, I've phone calls to make. Away home, you, and help your mother in the garden.'

'I said. I've the train to drive at six.'

'Oh aye. Still got the biggest toy train set in the world, eh? At least I didn't have to buy you that.'

'Aye,' Simon laughed, came further in and sat down on the white plastic garden furniture chair from the ironmonger's.

Simon asked, 'Hey. Did you ever come across the Bultitudes? I met the son a while back. And the daughter. They're nice but a bit on the eccentric side.'

'The Bultitudes? How're you pally with the Bultitudes' son? I never knew they were ever up the high school.'

'Just know him from around.'

'I'd of thought he'd be a boy sent away to a boarding school.'

'He is and she's at the university in Edinburgh.'

'The university, eh? So she'll get papers and letters after her name, will she, like you should be doing?'

'Suppose. She's studying Geology.'

'What's that? I thought she'd be going for the Law with a full-time job defending the father in court. Bloody old bandit. Sold his lands to the government and we had to pay for it. He made a mint.'

'You know, rocks and mountains and all that, but I think she wants to, like, find petrol.'

'Oh Christ. They'll be digging up their lands next for oil wells. Ach, good for her. Wish you were at a bloody university.'

'Aye. I might go to night classes to get a few Highers, I was sort of thinking.'

'Oh, you're seeing sense now, are you? That'd be a good idea.' His father looked up and laughed and he threw down the invoice he'd been studying. 'Andrew Bultitude was in Italy when I was. Saw him in the distance once. In a staff car, headed for where the bullets don't fly. Officer of course.'

'He was talking about that.'

'Who?'

'Andrew Bultitude.'

'Christ, have you met him too in your travels? You fair hobnob with the high society for a firebrand railwayman.'

'He knew about you.'

'What about me?' He frowned.

'About you having the lorries and being in the army too. About your medals.'

'Oh Christ. He would have his nose into everything.'

'The daughter, Varie. She's fair bonny.'

'Is she now? Well, you can't afford her, laddie. Learn to know your place. How's *your* poor wee lassie anyway? With this fever?'

'Crabbit. She hates being up in hospital.'

'I'm not surprised, poor wee thing. She's a nice lassie. She'll end up down in the those universities as well, you mark my words. Have you took her flowers?'

'Course. Twice. She told me to stop.'

'Good laddie. See and take some to Matron for the ward as well. Butter them up, boy. Always keep on the right side of a matron. I learned that in the army.' Just then there was an audible crack from the direction of the shop. 'In the name of God.' His father dropped his reading glasses onto the desk, shook his head and leaned back in his chair.

Simon looked at him.

'I told that cheeky Glasgow bugger.' He shook his head.

Sure enough, in a few moments they heard footsteps crunching on the stone chips outside. Billy put his head in the door and looked straight at Simon's father. 'That's him gone broke it.'

His father stared at Billy and shook his head slowly.

Billy sighed. 'You told him. I told him. Hopeless.'

'Go fetch him.'

Billy's footsteps went away.

His father did not speak. Des took a long time coming then the steps approached. Double steps. Billy was behind him. The new guy stepped in and he said, 'What?' There was a long silence. Des admitted, 'Aye, it broke, but I can rejam it up tomorrow.'

From behind his desk, Simon's father chuckled and told him, 'You can rejam it up now.'

'Naw ah cannie. I'm away home.'

'I told you it would snap and so did Billy.'

Des said nothing. He turned a glance on Simon and so Simon looked away and pretended to concentrate upward at new lorry posters which came with the sales brochures.

'You can rejam it now.'

'No I cannie.'

'Is that right? You're cheesing me off now, son.'

'Aye,' Des replied in a practical way and coughed.

'Well, I'll tell you what. How about this wee arrangement? You can rejam it or go up the road?'

'*Up* up the road?'

'And you can take your books with you.'

'You serious?'

'I told you last week with the radiator and you buggered that and Billy and me both told you now not to force it and that's it gone. Two hundred pound squandered. That comes out my pocket.'

'Aye, well. Win some, lose some.'

Slowly Simon's father said, 'And you've lost.'

'I'll be in in the morn.'

'No you won't. You'll fix it tonight or you can be on the train to Glasgow, son. Your choice.'

'Och away and fuck.'

A tenseness came into the thick sound of the cabin. Billy had been outside listening and now he stepped up; just his presence was a warning.

Simon's father said, 'What was that?'

Des stared Simon's father down. He shifted the way he stood on his feet. 'I says, away and fuck, man.'

Simon turned and witnessed the curious frown on Des.

Behind, Billy said flatly, 'Don't be speaking to Mr Crimmons like that, son.'

But Simon's father held up his hand.

Des smiled. 'I'm a week in lieu.'

'It's here in the cash box waiting for you.'

Des shrugged. 'Have it your way then.'

Simon's father nodded. 'I will. So you're no longer employed by me. You accept that?'

'So you say.'

'I do say. I'll give you your books and back pay. That's fine but. Now. What was that you just said to me?'

'When?'

'Just a moment ago.'

Des said, 'What?'

'You told me where to go. Where was it again? I can't remember.'

Des tried to chuckle now. Simon made the mistake of shifting slightly and Des put his eyes on him, and out of the blue, Des said, 'What are you looking at?'

'Uh-uh.' Now the voice of Simon's father fell very low. 'Don't you look at him. You're talking to me.' He pointed to his own chest.

'Aye, I know. And it's a fucking drag.'

Simon's dad said, 'I want you to make me go where you just told me to go. You told me to go to fuck. Make me.'

Something else beyond tension came into the cabin at that moment.

'What?'

'Make me. If you're a man.' A quite twisted face had come on his father; with surprise, Simon read it as a mix of glee and anticipation.

'Aye, I telt you and I'll tell you again. Fuck off. You're an old cunt. You're an old English cunt with a shitey wee shop. Away, in your big fucking car and get tae fuck.' Des made a small movement forward for emphasis.

Simon swallowed and his father stood, and before anyone moved, his father was round the desk – amazingly quick in a way Simon had never seen – and he slapped the younger guy loudly across his face the way a woman would slap a man's face.

'Ya old cunt.' Des held his hand to his cheek. 'You old fucking cunt. I'll have polis on you raisin a hand to me.'

'You're not employed here, son. Get outside just a wee minute.'

Des looked at Simon's father then he turned and he stepped outside. Simon's stomach dipped and he noticed the young man's eyes go down precisely to negotiate the steps.

'Stay.' Billy pointed at Simon sat in his chair as he went out after the two other men but Simon didn't obey. He stood up and went to the doorway where he stood and looked out. Des's younger face smiled calmly, standing in the turning space. Simon looked down to the left and a mad panic arose in him. His father was slowly taking off his cardigan with the bone buttons, and he lay it down carefully on the cleaner stones by the side of the Portakabin and then his father's hand went up to his own mouth and the fingers picked inside. He lifted out his lower dentures then reached up, pulled down the upper false teeth, a silver string of saliva briefly following then snapping, and his father's lower face fell into an aged shape. He put the dentures down gently on the cardigan.

From the doorway Simon said, 'Dad.' He was ignored.

Des shook his head and smiled. 'Pass us your walking stick.'

Simon's father stood very still and he slowly undid each button on his orange shirt, all the time looking at the younger man – as if absorbing obscure information. He dropped the shirt without looking where it fell. The hairs on his chest were grey but his upper body was still slim, muscled but maybe some hanging skin was there, around the pectorals. Then he walked forward.

Simon repeated, 'Dad,' but in a beaten voice.

His father lifted his arms in that terribly old-fashioned army boxing style and Des stood awaiting him, arms loosed at his side, looking no more than amused by it all, then suddenly he dirtily kicked out Bruce Lee-style, ducking so the full force of the kick hit Simon's father on the side of the thigh.

Simon wasn't a fighter but he could not believe that even though Des's whole body came so close in, with arms loose at his sides, his father never used that opportunity for a first punch. The much older man calmly stepped backwards, putting weight on the leg, testing it, then he looked down. 'You've dirtied my clean slacks, you wee cunt.'

The younger man came ahead again and a vicious kick went the other way but Simon's father stepped back and the toe of the boot just skiffed through the flannel trouser by the knee. His father had moved round spryly – so he happened to face Simon and Billy. The toothless mouth was pulled tight in concentration, the gammy gums showing, and Simon felt tears forcing into his eyes; he gripped his own hands and something frantic came into his breathing. Simon wanted to say 'Stop' but no sound came out.

Mr Crimmons was circling as Des came forward to try and grapple, but Simon's father twisted and this time, again so quickly Simon didn't see it, Des's head flicked back hard.

Then Simon's father did a bizarre thing. He dropped his arms as if he were abandoning the fight and he began to stroll over to the far verge with his back to his opponent; his bony shoulder blades working, he looked down at the grass verge and frowned; he even stuck out a toe of his work boot to touch at a piece of waste paper.

Des watched this in puzzlement. They were at least thirty feet apart. 'You quitting?' Des asked, but in the pause Simon saw the guy quickly lift a finger to his lip and then glance down at it with a whiff of shock in his eyes.

Now Simon's father moved directly back towards Des – straight – walking at speed with his arms at his sides so Des couldn't predict the type of attack and the young man had decisions to make: to advance, to move aside, or to stand his ground. He wasn't foolish, he sensed the older man had some kind of obscure but higher mindset. Des lifted his fists – still stained with black oil – and moved aside. Simon's father dropped his fists and Des struck at Mr Crimmons's face very hard, close to the ear – Simon held in a yelp and winced as he saw his father's head jerk aside – but even as his neck returned from the blow his father's left fist also came, caught Des just below the ribs and then a right went hard to the stomach. Everybody heard the breath come out as Des's face bumped once onto the older man's grey chest hair, before he stumbled badly backwards.

The younger man tried to make good face.

Simon's father repeated the long walk routine, as if marking out the harmless dimension of a pitch for some obscure ball game – moving in a huge circle across the turning place, his boots scraping casually on the stone chips. Des wasn't letting himself be teased; he took big quick breaths for himself, trying to recover, then he advanced, almost running. Simon's father came quickly back to meet him, so Des's feet scuffled on the ground trying to react effectively. The older man raised himself up on his tiptoes and Des ducked to try and come in under but his opponent just danced aside.

He saw blood on his father's lip, and Simon realised he was sobbing, jerking sudden breaths. He tried to control it but could not, so his entire body was soon shaking.

Des lifted his arms – imitating the older man – but he seemed uncertain. Simon's father straightened, conforming a defensive move.

But suddenly he changed his whole style, the bare arms dropped, his entire body jumped while he kicked and his boot hit very hard right between Des's legs.

Billy let out a casual whistle of air.

Des's head swished forward and as he helplessly paused too long, a fast fist hit his cheek so his head snapped aside and spittle shot out to meet the hook of an arm coming hard the other way. The younger man lost a leg and fell to one knee.

Des's head found itself weirdly close to Mr Crimmons's groin, swaying there a moment as a right fist drove into his jaw. He was still kneeling. Another right.

Des fell over heavily onto his side. Simon's father kicked Des in the chest then he stepped round him – a hand shot out and tried to snatch an ankle but it was stamped on hard like a rat and then Mr Crimmons kicked very, very hard into the kidneys at the bottom of the spine and the curled body jerked, the legs straightening, and both Des's work boots shoved up a pointless ridge of stone chips.

'That'll do it, Bertie,' Billy Strachan shouted and he walked forward. 'That'll do it.'

Simon's father lifted his face. His eyes appeared different – with a new fury Simon had never seen, the eyes looked down as if surprised by this man at his feet. He spat out diluted blood and saliva over the purple ridge of his gums and onto the curled figure, then he walked back towards the Portakabin. 'If I'd had a decent drink I'd piss on you,' Mr Crimmons's gummy voice said.

Simon's shoulders were jumping up and down in convulsions and he used both hands to try and wipe away the tears upon his face. His father looked at him for the first time since the fight began. 'What are you bubbling about? I'll bring you up the hard way, son.' His father bent, pulled on his shirt but didn't button it, then carefully, with his back to the man on the ground, he put his false teeth back in his mouth with a frowning expression which Simon found heartbreaking.

Now Simon wept in the direction of the injured man; his fear shifted from his father being hurt to the terror that Des had been murdered. His father stepped past Simon into the Portakabin but put out his hand, ruffling his son's hair as he went.

Simon took a few deeper breaths and pulled at the sides of his eyes with the sleeves of his jerkin.

Billy was standing over Des. 'Get up, son. It's all done.'

Des suddenly pushed himself up on one arm as if he was late for something, his face looking around – one eye puffed up already. He nodded but said nothing. He didn't seem to know where he was.

Simon's father came back out of the Portakabin. He had a flat, small bottle of Teacher's whisky in his hand. 'Get that bum what we owe him and his week in lieu from the cash box, Billy. C'mon, you.' His father nodded at Simon and put his arm round his shoulders for a moment then dropped it.

Just at the edge of the garage yard, a small burn ducked under the boundary fence. When the brambles and young birch sprouted here in summer it could be a pleasant wee dell to sit in for some of the lorry drivers – but not in March. The wooden boxes were gone and the plastic chair had migrated into the Portakabin; yet it was here his father led Simon and they sat down together on the ground at the burn edge. His father wasn't even breathing heavily.

'Don't you tell your mother about that.'

Simon nodded and sniffed. 'Are you okay?' Simon put out his finger and gently touched his father's lips which showed a rustiness of blood. He remembered Varie touching her own father's mouth with a similar tenderness. His father blinked and turned slightly away.

'I'm fine. You look worse than me, boy.'

'You'll get cold, Dad.'

'No, but my slacks'll get more filthy. Your mother'll be moaning.' He chuckled, unscrewed the scratchy top of the small whisky bottle and took a sip, then he looked at his knuckles. Two were skinned off. One had a silver sliver of skin stuck up off it. His father sucked at it then looked at Simon and he spoke as if he had food in his mouth. 'It's not like the fistfights in the cowboy films, eh? I don't think that was clever, son, but sometimes you've to put the edge on a fellow. I'm no having a bloody hippy talk to me like that. Wee Nazi.'

'Aye.'

'Well, don't be snivelling.'

'I just thought you were going to get hurt.'

'Boxed in the army.'

'I know.'

'Nothing special. Plenty better than me. Coulter whipped me good and proper once. I'm older now.'

'Aye.'

He smiled. 'You make them think you're trying it one way then do it another.' He looked at Simon and said, 'Like with a lassie, eh?' and he laughed.

Simon was unsure about this but said, 'Aye.'

'Stop saying aye.'

Suddenly Simon shivered and a single choke of sob came up then he was better-feeling.

'It's the way of the world, son. Fighting.'

'Doesn't need to be. I don't like violence.'

His father chuckled. 'I see your daft wee badge there. I know what that means.'

'It's against war.'

'Well, I don't like war either.' He paused. 'Fighting and war aren't the same thing. I was bloody drafted, no choice; I fought but I didn't like the war. These dafty buggers the day join up. I never asked them to. Hitler was Hitler.'

Simon nodded. He took another breath. 'Dad, know what I think's sad?'

'What now?'

'Your medals.'

'What about them?'

'You just don't seem to care about them.'

His father smiled. 'I don't. I shouldn't have got them in the first place. Other men should have.'

Simon sniffed yet again and wiped his sleeve. 'Well, if I had them I'd always keep them.'

'Would you?'

'Aye. Course.'

'Why didn't you say?'

Simon shrugged. 'What were they again?'

'Ach. Nothing, most of them. Italy, North African Star – me

268

and Erwin Rommel had a wee boxing match too. They're just campaign medals, son. Do you know, in Tunisia, you could put some lard on the top of a tank and fry a bloody egg on it? I tell you, that's how hot it was.' He looked up at the grey sky where fate had landed him.

'But there's a special medal too. Mum says.'

Mr Crimmons looked down at the burn. He took a swallow of whisky and passed the flat golden lozenge of glass to Simon. 'Take a dram of the hard stuff but don't get stuck on it.'

Simon took the bottle. 'I'm not meant to. I'm driving the train.'

'Dry your tears then, or your railway pals will see. You told me a few of them railway fellows were using whisky instead of diesel to run on.' He nodded at the bottle and chuckled. 'The other's a DCM and bar.'

'A what?'

'Distinguished Conduct Medal and bar. You know what soldiers said in the army, son?'

'What?'

'Oh, you got the DCM? You mean the bullet just missed you and you just missed the Victoria Cross.'

Simon laughed. 'Was that what it was like?'

He shrugged. 'Pretty much.'

'Bar means you got it twice, Dad, doesn't it?'

'Yes.'

'You never, ever talk to me or Jeff about it but we think it's brilliant.'

'It wasn't brilliant. There was just this tower after Salerno. Watched it come down into itself. What a sight. Jerries had a right fucking smart boy up on top with binocs, bringing in eighty-eights on our column. Binocs *and* a rifle. He was bloody good too. I'll say that. Me and wee Smithy, Coulter and Collins the Taffy went up. Made our way there with ordinance. Up through that shite. Open ground, flattened houses, fuck all shelter, I tell you that. Run our way. Nearly got me, the bastard did. Bullet hit rubble beside my foot, bounced up and touched my leg. It was flat, shiny. It just looked like a coin falling off my puttees. Not a bruise. You'll never see your father move quicker than that two hundred yards.' He shook his head and continued. 'I got that wee Fritz cunt up there on his tower though.

269

Brought him right down in his own frightened shite.' He nodded back. 'See that lazy wee bugger I curled up back there? I saw boys curled up like that all day, Stukas coming in at us. Dive-bombers, they had a siren under the wing that screamed as they came down to bomb on you. It got stuck in some of the boys' heads that sound. They were hearing it forever inside their heads. One fellow, he got curled up in a ball like that and never did come out of it.' Simon's father frowned and whispered, 'The Wheel they called him. Two of us had to shift him about on a stretcher,' he chuckled, and looked out over the glade. 'The Wheel, I remember him fine. That boy stayed curled up in a ball for the rest of his life. They took him home to Hathersage outside Sheffield; he was just a farm boy. Never came out of that curl. Some days, I just can't believe I'm safe. Sometimes being safe doesn't feel right to me.' He turned and looked at his son. 'When you've been as scared as I was, the rest of your days should be joy, son, pure joy, but sometimes you actually forget. How in Christ's name I forget some days, I don't really know. I disappoint myself and I don't like any bum like that fella clouding my day.'

Simon nodded. 'But why don't you ever tell us?'

He raised his voice into a cheery tone. 'You think you have a good time, yous young ones today, don't you? The Beatles and your long hair and skinny lassies in wee skirts. I tell you, we had one hell of a time after they surrendered. Up through Italy in the Bren carriers, then in an armoured car with the bloody REME; Jesus, they were good boys, the REME. Smart cunts that stayed up back and volunteered for nothing. That's who I got my first lorry off back in England after the war. Buckshee, you know, off some REME boys I knew. But comin up Italy there. You went in a village and, well, I'll tell you, son, but don't tell your mother. The young girls was pleased to see us – if you know what I mean?'

Simon smiled and took a manly swig of the whisky but his mouth went on fire. He kept it down and he laughed, using it as an excuse to blow out the hot fumes. 'Aye,' he croaked.

'I'd say a blonde on one side and brunette on the other but they was all Italian. All brunette.'

Simon smiled, but was a little shocked.

'I went in at eighteen and I'd turned twenty-three by the end.'

Simon nodded. 'Right.'

'After the surrender the fighting stopped more or less and we were coming up on this road. You should of seen the mess of Italy and that road, laddie. Dead Jerries all along it doused in lime, just boys your age, looking up at the sky with their eyes still open. There was no enemy planes any more so every piece of junk was out on that bastarding road. Narrow. Nothing could get passed nothing. The British REME, the Yanks, staff cars, an Italian family in a big black car and chickens on the roof. Some Yanks helped themselves to the chickens. You should of heard the boy screaming but you knew fine the bugger was supporting Mussolini a few years before. Trucks, jeeps, Bren carriers, Shermans. A ten-mile queue and it had stopped moving. Hundred yards an hour. I was in an armoured car with Coulter and Taffy Collins who'd been at the tower with me. We lost Smithy at the tower. That bad wee cunt got him good; right in the head. Had another boy from armoured driving us. We'd come through a village that morning and got plates of spaghetti. It's never tasted good as that again. About six bottles of wine and cause we were inside an armoured car we could drink it all morning and no bugger saw us – and we drank the lot too. The four of us pissing out the slit.' He chuckled. 'We were stuck so long, and I was youngest, so Coulter sent me back up, walking to the village along the convoy fu' as a whelk I was, and I kissed the lassie bye-bye a second time. Eighteen, with hair down to here. Wonder what she's doing now? Took four more bottles of vino and I headed back up the convoy. It had moved about fifty feet in a whole bloody hour.

'When I got there, the driver boy from armoured was so drunk – even though he's only gone fifty foot, he'd turned the armoured car right over, upside down into the bloody ditch.' Simon's father laughed and looked at Simon. His face with the blooded lip was bright and happy.

Simon laughed.

'Wheels in the air with a crowd round. Everyone was laughing. Me too. Banging on the sides and making jokes. They'd try to dig them out the top of the armoured car where it rested but the bottom of that ditch was all solid stone. They said it was Roman and they built good. I was sat down there beside the top opening of the armoured car, chatting and joking with my pals in there for a bit. You could pass through a cigarette to them and the staff officer was squealing not to smoke in case there was spilled fuel. I can hear his plummy fucking voice to this day. Coulter and Taffy and the driver wanted the wine passed in but I couldn't while the officer was stood there.

'There was an escape hatch in the bottom of them armoured cars but it was jammed solid. They reckoned it had got stuck over burning debris and that it had welded shut. We went at the hatch with a sledgehammer but Coulter inside was laughing to give over, that it was deafening him. They were trying to bring a crane up or even just a bloody oxyacetylene but the road was barely wide enough to get anything passed anything.

'After an hour the rain came. Mediterranean rain battering down like the clappers. It didn't stop. Started to fill up that ditch quick. We tried everything but that water kept coming up. I could hear Coulter and the Taffy inside. Screaming. Then they went quiet. There was tapping. We though it was one of them but it was the empty bottles floating and touching against the insides. They'd drowned inside the armoured car, son.'

Simon's father looked out again across the burn. 'Coulter and the Taffy. He wasn't even Welsh. Just loved leek soup. Both of them killed by the bloody weather after all they dodged. That just wasn't fair. It wasn't fair. At least they got a last bloody cigarette.'

Sunday 31 March 1974

On a Sunday of rain showers, Simon had been in the County again with the boys: Lawless, Hannan and the bevy merchant crew.

He was a bit late up the hospital. Simon walked down to the nurses' station and his new pull-on waterproof trousers crackled. Karen Caine was standing there with Matron and both of them moved their heads towards him. Matron looked down at her clipboard as she stepped forward and walked away down the other corridor without saying hello.

'Aye,' said Simon. As usual, the ghost of Karen's naked body was there beneath her uniform, between them both, like a half-recalled map. But today she had the strangest face on her. Simon was amazed by it. Like she was angry at him and never herself.

'You had better go see her. I'm away home,' said Karen.

'Is she all right?'

'She's getting out.'

'Oh. Fantastic.'

'But she's not okay. Jeezo.' Karen turned her head aside and lowered her voice. 'You honk of beer.'

'What's wrong?' Simon's stomach moved further downward.

'Nikki was bloody greeting. All day.'

Simon frowned and he whispered, 'Why? Have you went and told her about that night?'

'What? No.' She spoke with huge anger and stepped into the nurses' station with her back to him. She reached out for her duffel coat and didn't speak.

Simon pushed the swing doors into the ladies' ward. None of the women in the beds talked to him. They didn't even look at him.

273

They kept their heads down, suddenly glued to *People's Friend* and the *Scots* magazine.

He walked up the ward length – even that bloody lady who always slept was now awake; her grey eyes followed him with a sudden liveliness.

Nikki was sat up in bed as usual with the Beta maths book, but she didn't lift her head and smile – as she always did.

He arrived by the bedside and looked down upon her. 'Hey, Karen says you're getting out? That's so brilliant.'

She looked up. 'Is it now? Who's this Varie thing then?'

'What?'

'Don't you dare. You heard fine.'

'Varie? Alex's sister. Younger sister. The guy you met that time.'

'That weirdo's even weirder sister?'

'Aye. Eh, nut. Not really. She's not that weird. Well, a bit, aye. Yeah. Maybe. Sort of.'

'What was she doing round at your house then?'

'What?'

'Was she not then? You heard just fine.'

'Who told you that? That was donks ago. Last September or something. Before she went away to university. In Edinburgh, and I've not seen her since.' He tutted. 'What are you on about, Nikki?'

Nikki looked at him.

'I mean, she worked at the stables beside our house Saturdays. She came round one day.'

'What for?'

'Nothing, Nikki. Nothing. Just for a ceilidh. We played records.'

'Oh, I hear you had a right wee ceilidh.'

'Who told you all this?'

'Just never you mind.' She edged up in bed a bit more with her book in her lap and her blue eyes looking into him. 'Och, you smell all of beer. God, Simon, are you drunk as well with your old railway daddies?'

His voice became defensive. 'What do you mean? As well? As well as what? Has that wee horse-nut Fiona been spreading gossip? She's just a daft wee yap. The stable's gossiper. She's a yappity-yap blether of a clipe.'

'Talking of drink, I was told you were once drinking with her in the Marine Hotel too.'

Simon snorted. 'Aye. And her brother was there too, like donks ago. You know what a gossipy wee town this is. I'm not knowing what you're getting at.'

'Did you two-time me?'

'Nikki, I've met the lassie two times in my whole bloody life.'

'And that's twice too much. You never told me once you'd been hanging around with her.'

Simon now found blood roaring in his ears from indignation and from shame. 'You don't like Alex. I get the feeling you don't approve of him cause he's all posh and the way. His clothes. You judged him more than he judges ordinary folk. I know you don't like him, so's I just didn't say.'

'I hear she's really bloody gorgeous too. That wouldn't have anything to do with it, would it? Typical. Brigitte Bardot with black hair is what I hear.' Her voice went soft. 'I don't even know who Brigitte Bardot *is*.' Tears, like a squeezed and clear ointment, appeared in her eyes.

The swiftness of these tears pricked Simon and he looked elsewhere, giving a huff of air. 'Huh, hardly.' Yet out of helpless vanity he also quickly enquired, 'Who says she looks like Brigitte Bardot then?'

Nikki looked down her slight body under the covers, to her feet, and she wiggled her toes. Her two fists tightened on the bedcover. 'Did you tell her about me then?'

'Course. Told her we ride round on the bike.'

'What else?'

'Can't remember.'

'Charming. I must make a big impression on you. You told her you and me was going together?'

'Course. What's this all about?'

'Your friend *Varie* told wee Fiona at the stables that she snogged you. Fiona told Lorrie McCallum and she was up here the day. How do you think I feel? It's probably been all round the school for donks.'

He said the wrong thing. 'You're no even in the school.' Simon felt himself going red. He'd been caught but he felt violent towards

Varie – yet what right had he? Bizarrely, Simon suddenly said, 'Highers is all you seem to care about.'

She frowned and said sharply, 'What? Aye, I do care about my Highers. I have to cause my daddy isn't rich. I've to get out the Brae Estate in this lifetime. It's all right for you. Answer what I asked you.' She lowered her voice. 'Did she? Did yous do anything?'

'I think I should come see you when you're back home.'

'So that's a yes then.' She impacted both clenched fists down onto the bedcover but the springs squeaked and the bed bounced a little. She looked up at him.

'I'm sorry,' he managed.

She started to wail – a completely unfamiliar sound, keening pain and anger. 'Why would you do that when I'm months in a bloody hospital?'

He didn't point out she had not been in hospital at that particular time. It was not much of a defence. He turned and walked down the ward length. He looked straight ahead at the swing doors, trying to reach them. His waterproof trousers rustled ridiculously with each long step and behind him were Nikki's chokes and sniffing inhalations. He didn't look aside at the women in their beds. One tutted. He swung the doors open.

Thursday 11 April 1974

Simon relished the late-night shifts and the touch of macho attached to those witching hours; home on his motorbike by twenty past four in the mornings while his family slept. When the rest of the house rose, his mum made Jeff tiptoe around out of respect. When Simon arose around one or two in the afternoon, the macho man's mum made his lunch for him which he ate in his pyjamas.

The weekday mail trains didn't meet the midnight freights up on that dark, marshal glen of Ardencaple. The Glasgow boys brought the mail train forward, on down till they met the freights in the Fort Junction at 3 a.m. – on the saddle of land between the mountains where that other branch line headed out, for the far north-west.

For two miles on the opposite side of the Strath, you sometimes tagged the priority London sleeper, or a late-running train north-headed, trying to equal you across that glen – its chain of soft coach windows – and out front in the dark was the orange flare of the pumping Sulzer exhaust up on the engine's roof – or maybe just the fly-red spot of the brake van's paraffin tail lamp, seemingly unmoving.

The midnight mail trains for the port were always two coaches – a compartment coach with a few passengers, sometimes none at all midweek, and a BG mail van with GPO canvas bags and parcels scattered across its concrete floor, as well as a bale of that morning's *Daily Record*. Over Christmas an extra bogie-less parcels van had been added for Yuletide mail. The red GPO van would meet them on Platform 3 each night.

On the day before Easter, Simon, Penalty and the guard Breck had brought in the mail train to the town at ten to four in the morn. They'd put the engine round about those two coaches, then when the mail was chucked out into the back of the postie van, they'd taken the train over onto the bay platform of 2, putting the coaches on top of the others there to form that morning's 07.40.

Simon was on the yellow Yamaha, up past the King's Way, going under the trees before the town's cemetery. He accelerated into that corner then braked, looking backwards quick over his left shoulder. He turned into the cemetery car park, circled slowly on the gravelly surface, pulled out onto the main road and headed back in towards town; he U-turned at once, moving slowly – at walking pace – alongside the kerb edge of the pavement beneath the trees. The pedestrian hadn't stopped walking though. She was completely ignoring him, striding straight along the pavement without turning her head, taking him for any cheeky male rider on a motorbike chancing his luck. He had to keep the bike going along slowly beside her, the exhaust spitting a little, him wobbling the handlebars to stay upright. She was looking straight ahead, wearing a dress with a flower pattern but the skirt of it was very short.

Inside the helmet he shouted.

Immediately the girl stopped walking and turned her head towards him on his bike. He put his leg out to stop the bike and pulled his helmet up then switched off the bike's engine. 'What are you doing out here all on your own? There could be weirdos about.'

She didn't smile, just looked directly at him. 'Yes. You.' She stared him and the bike up and down. 'So the cavalry has arrived. Of sorts.' She didn't seem at all surprised to find him there.

'Is Alex back for Easter too?'

Varie held out a bare arm and slapped Simon half playfully on the shoulder. 'Yes, but you should be asking after me. Anyway, we both have to leave the day after tomorrow. I'm going to spend more of my holidays in Edinburgh.'

She seemed odd; drunk but not drunk. Simon said, 'Och. Why do yous never phone? You never got in touch over Christmas either.'

She shoved out a fattened lower lip. 'Oh Soppy. But I wasn't here at Christmas. I have a flat in Edinburgh now with two other girls. Annoying nosy bitches.' Her tone changed. 'Be a good egg and give us a lift on your little scooter then.' She hoisted up one bare leg, like a dog against a lamp post.

Sternly he said, 'It's not a scooter. And I've only got one helmet.'

She dropped her leather boot back to the pavement. 'What do I need a helmet for?'

'It's strict law. Where are you going anyway? Were you really walking home? It's fifteen mile.'

'Where else?'

'Where have you been?'

'That it's your business, I've been down into your awful town with a mutt of a man.' A clot of her hair was across her face.

'What man?'

She shrugged. 'Gudrun, Goodwin, Good One, Gordon? Dunno. He touched my bottom in a council house, so I got up and left. He followed me down the hill, shouting. At this hour. Curtains moved. He did not offer to fund a taxi and I have no money. As usual. Goodness gracious me, your town is like a stew in a coombe. Do you know what a coombe is? Your town is like a sweaty dumpling stuck in a coombe.' Varie Bultitude leaned straight over and kissed Simon full on his lips. It was so unexpected to him, he pretty much fluffed responding. His helmet was clenched there between them like a baby in a papoose as they began to turn their faces against each other. The bike wobbled a little with her enthusiasm. As she kissed, Varie casually rested both her forearms on his shoulders without embracing him then she finally pulled away.

Simon asked, 'Haven't been riding your horses today, have you?'

She laughed out loud. Perfectly pleased with herself. 'No. You won't come out in blisters. This is a new dress. Isn't it beautiful?'

Simon looked one way then the other and he passed his helmet to her. 'Put this on and do up the strap thing tight under your chin. If there's a police car I'm in for it. But there never is a police car about at this time.'

She looked down at the helmet and seemed confused. 'What are *you* doing here at this time, Si? Master Simon Crimmons of the trucking dynasty? Have you been making love with your girlfriend.' Her voice went sad and needy. 'Your little ray of golden sunshine?'

Simon was impressed that she had retained all her insulting lexicon from the previous summer. 'No, I haven't.'

He did not mention the rupture Varie herself had caused. He

perceived Nikki was of more significance to Varie if she believed he was still involved with her. Simon pointed his finger to the west, across the fields. 'She lives just down the hill there, in the council estate. Her bedroom has a back window that she climbs in and out of.'

'Really? Oh now really?' Varie actually turned and looked across the fields. The back of the dress fell loose and short over her bum. 'And could we – you and I – take a little peek in through that window and watch her sleep? Oh, I'd love to watch her sleep.'

'Would you?' Simon was alarmed.

'Of course. She must be adorable. Like a little kitten. We could even climb in the window and join her. I'm sleepy.' She laughed nastily. 'You'd be like that valet when he was caught in the hotel with Lady Bolton and her maid.' A laugh barked out and echoed across the fields and as far as the rigid boredom of the graveyard where you could see the tops of the largest mausoleums.

Simon frowned. 'She shares her room with her sister.'

The famous white brow shuttered into trenches of shadow. 'That would complicate things. Might exhaust you.' She laughed a dirty laugh.

Simon coughed and answered the original question. 'I've been at my work.'

'Your work. At this time?'

He unzipped the bomber jacket, pointed to the British Rail insignia badge pinned on the lapel of his railway blazer, below the NUR and CND badges. 'We work all kinds of hours.'

'Oh yes. I hear the trains every day from across the river. When my granddaddy was at Broken Moan we had our very own little railway station; did you know that? I could tell a train to stop just like I've told you to stop now.' She held up her palm vertically.

It was true, there were the remains of an excavated old platform just before the horseshoe curve which used to serve the big house. Simon objected, 'You never told me to stop. I just did because I recognised you.'

'Did you? Ever so sweet. You always were a sweetie. How do you go on one of these?'

'Put your helmet on.'

She manoeuvred the helmet over her hair and pressed it on her head by placing her palm on the top. 'Oh goodness, this won't do.'

Simon reached out his fingers and she cooperated, lifting her long neck upward as he fastened the buckle there; the tips of his fingers touched the skin of her pale throat.

'Get on then.'

She swung her leg over as if onto a horse and sat across the saddle in Nikki's former place, pushing her body hard against his back.

Simon said, 'If I knew when you were in your house, I'd blow the train horn every time I went by.'

'Would you? Will you in the summer, when I'm back for the holidays?'

'Of course I will.'

'Would you really? I'd love that. Toooot-toot.'

She seemed to imagine herself already in her bed and lay the side of the motorcycle helmet against Simon's shoulders. She yawned then sighed sadly. 'But that's all too romantic, isn't it?' Her voice vibrated through Simon's shoulders. 'Tooting your train whistle for me. It would be like we had a midnight tryst, you signalling to me from over the other side of the river. One toot and you can't sneak over but two toots and you can so I've to take off my T-shirt. I would say, "Father, that sound is my working-class lover Si, driving his train, and we are going to elope together and there's nothing you or the Church can ever do."'

Simon couldn't turn all the way round to look at her, so he spoke facing forwards, 'Perhaps we should?'

'What?'

'Elope?' He zipped up the bomber jacket.

'But your little ray of golden sunshine? What would we do with the little soul? Will we take her with us? As our maid?'

'I'm not working class.'

'Yes you are.'

'No I'm not. You were going on about my folks' big house and how you liked it.'

'I do like it. But you work on the railways. So you're Scottish working class. Your accent is too.' She laughed and tutted. 'My father would never allow it. But it doesn't matter. I only believe in free love. I'll just share you with your little ray of golden sunshine.'

'Will you now?'

Varie moved her arm beyond his face and pointed ahead. 'Or do you have enough petrol for Gretna Green?'

'No need. You know how a ship's captain can marry people on his ship? Well, a train driver can do the same to his passengers.'

'Never?'

'Aye. It's even in the British Rail Regulations Book. My driver could certainly marry us.'

'Really? That's the loveliest thing I've ever heard. I really like you and I can't think why. I think you're clever. The student boys are dreadful. Are you asking me to marry you on a dirty train engine then? A marriage unrecognised by the Church but blessed by British Railways?'

Simon said, 'If you wear white dungarees, aye.' He'd turned now to look at her.

She made a wondrous thing with her eyes through the helmet visor and laughed.

Simon said, 'Go on then. I dare you.'

'I'll really think about it.'

'Is that us engaged to be married then?'

She sighed and tried out the phrase – presumably directed at her peers down in Edinburgh. 'Girls, may I present: my fiancé? An honest working boy. Oh, that would shock them. But I don't have a ring.'

Simon reached for the side pocket of the railway blazer underneath his bomber jacket. He turned and took her hand. He put the pulled tab from a can of Fanta on her wedding-ring finger. It slid about loosely.

She admired the ring pull on her finger. 'I suppose we are engaged to be married now.' She said harshly, 'Come on. Go as fast as you can. I want you to make me scream.'

Hoping it wouldn't rain, Simon raced the moon across the miles and Varie Bultitude gripped him around the waist. Unlike Nikki she looked over his shoulder at the meagre story the road offered in single headlight. They slewed left and right down the descending swerves to the new street lights of Donan which gave the village an unfamiliar look, like the outskirts of some strange city.

It felt illicit and liberating for Simon not to have his helmet on; the steady plate of air against his face made his eyes water and blew his lengthening hair backwards in the slipstream – sometimes strands were slapping against the hard front of Varie's helmet.

As they came up the long straight towards Tulloch Ferry he managed forty-five miles per hour. A lone night heron sensing dawn flew slow-winged and magnetic to the water's surface, crossing the small bay.

They moved slowly through his sleeping village and past the stables – his family home in darkness – beyond Jeff's primary school, by the level crossing for the loop road, then they were away again, out of the speed limit and accelerating by the loch islets, their pale shores and chokes of rich seaweed just visible.

The railway embankment towards Black Lochs Tunnel was up above them. Simon was so used to travelling on the train engines now, the dual route on the road had grown unfamiliar to him. It was disorientating for him to see the railway above, from down at the road's angle. His mind was up there at his natural elevation, familiar with every tree and bush close to the silver lines which had their shy blush of rust along their tops every Monday morning.

At Abbot's Isle they leaned the curves by meadow sides. Virgilian tongues of grass were there, reaching out into the still sea loch and the salty ghost mark of the tideline. Out towards the vertical cliffs, below the rock star's supposed holiday house, Simon pointed one arm. He felt Varie's helmet nod in some obscure agreement.

The motorbike slowed embarrassingly towards the top of the hill after they had passed beneath the railway bridge. Simon felt ashamed at the underpowered machine so he opened out the throttle full on the flat, across the clearing and down the hill into the bush country of Little Australia.

When they came to the village in the Back Settlement's 30 limit, he could make out the red spot of the signal aspect suspended high in the night air, and some smoke showed from the station chimneys where Davey kept three fires burning all night – in the waiting rooms and his office. He had been there driving the train through less than an hour before.

On the far side of the Back Settlement, the roofs of the council houses at Jericho Road showed across the railway embankment.

The Creich ben above was inked out as they downhilled towards the Glen mouth, alongside the bucking and ducking top stones of the long, long wall which marked the Bultitude lands to the south.

Down at river level where the railway came close again – although they had not met a single other vehicle in his helmet-free, fourteen-mile dash – Simon indicated for the right-hand turn; the flashing orange light from the fitted indicators lit up and then blacked out the verge growth along the right-hand side of the road.

He turned the handlebars in past Varie's childhood shelter. Closer up than on the train engines, he now noticed how the roof lining was warped upward on the little sentry box; he caught a glimpse of Mickey Mouse's faded trophy-handle ears, spotted the lively jape of a dwarf in his robes. The tall wrought-iron gates were jammed open and grabbed by cindered reachings of last year's brambles and by those new and fresh sprouts.

The verges of the three-quarter-mile driveway up to Broken Moan were marked with freshly whitewashed stones at regular intervals – grass blades around the stones had also been daubed with recent whiteness. Simon screwed his wrist and gave a burst of acceleration which jerked them ahead in the direction of the big house. The noise rattled out across the pastures and back from the dark windows of the disused lodge cottage.

Immediately Varie began to poke aggressively with a hard finger on his shoulder. He both braked and turned his head.

'Stop,' she shouted.

He wondered if she was being sick until they came to a halt.

'Stop.'

'I have.'

'The engine thing.'

He killed the engine.

'Put off your light things. Can't let old Mrs Mac or Father hear a bloody motorbike dropping me off.' She swung her bare leg back off the bike, pulled the helmet away and shook her hair. It was very dark now with the headlight off.

'Any chance I can see you tomorrow then?' he said.

'Don't be so silly.'

'Why not?'

'I mean come now.'

'Up the drive?'

'Yes. Don't you wish to?'

He got off the bike and began pushing it along.

'No. You need to leave it.'

'Leave it?'

'You can't take it up to the house. Hide it in the grass there.'

'In the grass?'

'Stop repeating everything I say. If you don't wish to then don't.' She shrugged.

He heaved the bike up into the low verge, pushed it a short distance from the metalled surface into the longer grass before the white iron railings, and here he gently let the motorbike down onto its handlebars and side. The way it lay in the scrub reminded him of the night he had crashed the bike with Nikki.

Varie snorted and she tossed his helmet over the bike and beyond the metal fence – far out into the overgrown meadow.

'Hoi, man. I'll never find that now.'

'Oh, shush. Come along.'

'If it's upside down and it rains, it'll fill with water.'

She laughed, her head held back. 'You can keep a goldfish in it. The kind you win when the fair comes to town.'

They walked up the driveway side by side, passing the luminescent sequences of stones towards the great and famed house. Simon couldn't see a damned thing. Varie took his hand as they stepped onward.

He whispered, 'Where are we going?'

Neither of them talked and soon his eyes adjusted. They were walking beneath a roof of great trees which overhung the upper driveway. The shadows and dimensions of the house gradually emerged to the left but Varie turned them away into a sudden tunnel. It was a long arbour of mature creeping branches, staunchly trimmed and trained over decades into a beautiful long cavern. When they emerged from the other end, he could hear the gentle shush of water over rocks from the tributary to the river which snaked round and encircled Broken Moan.

She walked to the left, down a gravel path, and he followed.

'If you meet a creature don't be alarmed, it would just be one of our badgers.'

He became nervous. Sure enough, walls and the shape of a very small chapel came out from the murk. She slid aside a bolt on a wrought-iron gate in the wall. 'This is the resting place of Mummy and my relatives. Ancestors too over there.'

'Oh.'

'Come in then.'

The ground became soft grass under his work brogues until she stopped ahead of him. He saw ornate, high headstones and conventional grave plots but he was aware of several flat pallets on the ground before him. He did not look down but turned and stared in Varie's face.

'Do you see what they are?' she whispered.

He knew fine. 'What?'

'They are glass graves. Thick glass.'

'The graves are?'

'Yes. No coffins either.' She spoke in a matter-of-fact manner. 'That's Mummy. That's Grandfather over there and this one is my uncle.'

'That's a bit bloody eerie.'

She laughed. 'Don't be afraid. Even if you had a torch you really can't see anything inside. Any more.'

He whispered, 'No?'

'Some sort of condensation and moss has got in and built up on the undersides of the glass. I'm told it was really only for the first few years you could look down on them, and when I was a little girl Alex and I were forbidden to come in here. Father had it padlocked. But I still come here and, well, I do this. Lie down with her.' Varie's head ducked, and with a restful and calm sigh she lay down on the glass grave of her mother, her pale legs out with the boots crossed over in leisurely form.

'Won't it break?'

She chuckled, a low sick sound. 'No-no-no. It's much too thick. It's like bulletproof glass. Though she was terribly ill, Mummy took a big boulder from the river and raised it above her head then smashed it down. She wanted to pull her brother out and be with him again.'

'God.'

'She only chipped the glass a bit. I was just a little girl but the gardeners told Alex and me all about it. My uncle took his own life, you know, and it was wholly ghastly for our mother. Lie down with me. I do this all the time when no one's about. Lie down.'

Simon fixed his gaze to the starlessness above, and he reluctantly crouched then lay out his body beside Varie Bultitude. Half of him – his right half – was on the hard glass beneath and his left half on the damp, thick turf, and though he again had a girl beside him he felt very far from the Glasgow hotel room. She lay still at his side breathing in their strange marriage bed.

'Isn't it peaceful? I could fall into a nap, I really could.' She chuckled again. 'You're brave. No one else would ever do this with me. Alex refuses. I come here and talk to her and she talks to me. I hear her voice all the time. Not just here – anywhere.' She laughed and she suddenly sprang forward and was standing above him – she moved close to his feet and Simon sat straight up at his waist, squinting at her though there was little light. She swung aside and walked away back towards the gate. He exhaled again, rose up and followed behind her, his hands automatically sweeping at the seat of his trousers.

She moved back up the path, leaning slightly forwards into the gradient; he followed behind the walking shapes of her pale legs, stepping until he could see some low buildings ahead.

It was a row of artisan cottages; the roof eaves came down so low, Simon could have reached up and scraped out the guttering with his hand. Varie crouched showing both bared legs and scratched aside a flowerpot. She came up with a key and unlocked the front door.

'What's this?'

'This is the groom's old cottage.'

'Eh? Where's your dad then?'

'Oh, I wouldn't concern yourself with him. He's away up in the house with his boring old friend whom he was at university with. They'll be blotto and oblivious by now. They drink themselves through the war and back again. That's why I went out this evening. He won't have the foggiest idea when I got back in and this is my little secret den. Even Alex isn't allowed in here. No one is.'

'You even have your own wee house?' Simon ducked under the lintel and within, below the painted boards of the ceiling, and

he had to stand helplessly as Varie moved around him in the darknesses. She had locked the door from the inside. It smelled damp
and there was a clicking sound then a burst of match light. She
was lighting a paraffin storm lamp on a long table. Once the wick
caught, she held the base down and pushed the spring catch which
lowered the glass bulb; smoke trembled out of the top vent and
the burned paraffin scent reminded Simon of the tail lamps on the
trains. He looked to see if the can ring pull was still on her finger.
It wasn't and this pained him.

A low, curtained window was opposite an old dressing table and
fitted mirror, with all the drawers gone. There was an armchair
with the stuffing knocked out of it and the long table. Upon this
table there were books, their covers and initial pages slightly curled
at the corners by dampness. And there were small lumps of chipped
rock all over that table, presumably from Varie's studies. On a small
bedside cabinet pulled up close to the arm of the chair was an
ashtray and a dinner plate, an old and partly eaten meal still on it.
Salad! 'What a great place.' He noted an open door into another
dark chamber where the greasy, slithering light of the storm lamp
light did not penetrate.

She opened the drawer on the small cabinet. 'Want to take a
puff? On a little reefer thing?'

He was shocked but quickly replied, 'Aye. Go on then.'

She flopped on the armchair so he was forced to stand. She
looked up at him. 'Smoked reefer before?'

'Tons,' he lied.

'I got turned on to it in first term. Then we'll do the ritual.'

'What?'

'The ritual that I told you of. Remember?'

'Oh, aye.'

'I'd give you this chair, dear, but it's filthy with horsehair.' It was
a threatening look now.

He chuckled but with caution and idly lifted two books: technical geology manuals, stamped 'The University of Edinburgh'. His
hand was shaking and he put the book down and shoved his fist
in his bomber jacket's side pocket.

Sitting there with her legs crossed she lit the thin, already rolled
cigarette which seemed just like one of Penalty's. She inhaled, held

288

in an absurdly long time as if it were a challenge, then blew out smoke with a strangely rich, oily scent. Not unpleasant. She took three other long draws, looking enormously solemn about the whole endeavour. Then she passed the lit cigarette over to him. He had noted her technique of holding the smoke down in her lungs in that therapeutic manner before exhaling it. He copied this. When he blew out he didn't cough as he was now used to inhaling cigarettes.

'Don't tell anyone that Alex and I like grass. Gossipy little parish round here.'

Simon nodded.

'The last thing we need is policemen coming up the drive to see Father.'

He nodded more and he took another inhalation. It didn't seem to be having any effect on him.

She leaned forward and she pulled off one boot then the other, letting them fall aside to the floorboards. No socks as usual. The painted toenails had changed colour. Simon looked down at the bare floor and he frowned. It needed to be swept. His mouth felt oddly soft – blubbery – and his voice sounded out as a distant thing from where he was within his head. 'You'll get skelfs in your feet,' he boomed and yawned.

She seemed to be ignoring him and opened that bedside cupboard, standing and leaning over then pacing in a circle as she poured a thick line of white sugar from a bag onto the floor. Simon watched. He tried to speak but the words were slow to manifest and he laughed. She walked around there, leaving the thick trail as a large circle, and just before the ends joined, she stepped outside its interior.

'This is salt. Bad spirits can't cross after I consecrate. We have to stay inside. Don't even put an arm outwith its circumference.'

Simon nodded. 'Oh, right, aye.' He felt oddly sleepy and looked towards the curtained window. Involuntarily, he thought of that gruesome burial ground. He could wrench a ring off one of the rotted fingers and give it to her.

She didn't enter the salt circle after she had created it, her bare feet tiptoed around the outside to return to the armchair. Simon and Varie looked at each other.

He glanced at the ceiling. Had a bird had just flown over the place? A goose? 'What?'

'Didn't say a thing. I always do what I say I'll do, Si.'

He nodded. 'You said we might get married.'

She laughed. 'Do you want to?'

'Course. You're completely beautiful. You must be the most beautiful lassie over fifty mountain tops. At least.'

She laughed. She was fumbling with a piece of paper and tore a scrap off. 'I write your name and you write mine and we put a symbol which is a memento of the calling.'

'Right.' He had no idea what she was on about.

She leaned forward, a university book resting in her lap to write on and all hair hung down.

'What are we calling for?'

'A message.'

'What message? From satellites going over?'

'A word. When you do the ritual you'll hear words.'

Simon held the reefer before his face and curled his nose. 'Is it not this, doing the talking?'

She chuckled and wrote more on the scrap of paper. When she passed it to him it had on odd rune inscribed and the letters: S I M O N. He leaned over to the table edge and wrote: M H A I R I, as she watched carefully.

'What are you doing?'

'Putting your name.'

'You can't even spell my name. You don't spell it like that.' She nicked the reefer back off him and looked at it then took a drag.

'What? How do you spell it?'

She blew out smoke. 'As it sounds. Vee, ay, are, eye, ee.'

'That's no right. Your name's Gaelic. Mhairi. M, H.'

'I know all that. I assure you I can spell my own name correctly. Nobody in England can pronounce Gaelic anyway so we spelled it the way it sounds.'

'Phonetically.'

'Yes. Phonetically. Clever train driver. You should be on *Top of the Form*. That is how my Christian name is spelled and do you know what the older girls used to tease at my school about my

290

surname? Bultitude – they used to say – that's the only name with "tit" in the middle and you don't have any.'

Simon said, 'It's still spelled wrong.' He paused a moment. 'The need to dominate. Always trying to change things before you even understand them.'

'I beg your pardon?'

'Yous posh English folk. That's what colonisation is. The need to dominate and impose without any understanding of the place you're colonising. Wiping out Scottish life to suit yourselves. That's a prime example.'

'I'm Scottish thank you very much. And do you speak the Gaelic since you are so clever?'

'Eh, nut. A wee bit Learner's Gaelic from the school. I like the word for "pardon". It's like, atishoo. When you sneeze.'

'Shut up then, Macduff.'

'It's a fact, and by the way, here's another. I've got the whole railway telling me I'm not working class enough and I've got you telling me I'm not middle class enough. This country needs to sort out the class question. As far as it applies to me.'

She laughed. Her eyebrows suddenly rose and she smiled. She wasn't offended – more excited. She relished antagonism and dropped the smoked-down butt onto the plate of food. 'That is making you belligerent. How interesting. Write my name the proper way.'

He looked away from her, tutted and wrote for the first time: V A R I E, then handed the rune back.

'We have to get into the circle now. To purify it.' She stood and with great ease she elevated the short dress up over her hair as Karen Caine had. She wasn't wearing a brassiere just a sort of slip and it slinked up over her face too. She shuffled down from her knees then straightened, looking directly at Simon as she lifted one foot then the other to shake off her pants. She watched as he slid off his bomber jacket and undressed before her. The reefer had made him uncaring.

'Hurry,' she said, in a surprisingly bored voice as if they undressed in full view of each other regularly.

He piled his clothes in a heap to the side. The CND badge on his railway blazer lapel clicked as it touched the floorboards.

'Your wristwatch too. Step in and sit with your legs crossed.'

From the cabinet she had taken a long white bird feather. She then stepped in too and sat on the floorboards facing him with her own legs crossed. She had a very straight back and a lonesome mole between her right shoulder and her little breast. She held that feather in her fingers and he thought she was like a tall pale feather herself. She said, in a voice suddenly shy, 'You're meant to be doing all this at dawn. Um. It's not dawn yet. Takes hours for the sun to get over that hill behind here anyway.' She jerked her head to the east.

There was sandiness and grit on the floor and Simon didn't like the sensation of it against his folded calves and his buttocks.

'You're skinny.'

'So are you,' he said.

'Nice though.'

'Mmm. You too.' He was actually cold. He had thought he'd be hard with her naked there, but he wasn't.

'No laughing.' She turned to face east and said in a louder and very formal voice, 'A matutinal invocation to all gods of the east. I bless this consecrated space.' She was very serious about it; a struggle for him not to smirk. She did the same for north, west and south, then told him, 'That's the circle consecrated. Nothing can cross it and get in.'

He nodded, smiling. 'I hope earwigs and other creepy-crawlies can't.'

'Be serious.' She flicked up the feather between them both and their faces came close in together again – as they had rehearsed in his bedroom the September before. She told him the magic word and he repeated it. Each time they said that word, their breath moved the sharp spears of the feather.

'What kind of bird is that from then?'

'A swan of course. Be quiet.'

He nodded. They kept saying that magical word back and forth: she, then he, she, then he – so it began to sound hypnotic. Their warm breath on one another's lips. Simon tried not to smile. He wondered if he should pretend to hear something.

There was a singular, trickly sound on the roof above them, like one tiny pebble coming loose, tapping down the slates. Her head shot up. 'What was that, Si?'

'I don't know. You got mice?'

There was another dribble across the roof.

'Oh my God. It's demons' claws.'

There was a scrabbling on the roof, as if several small, lithe creatures slithered about irritably after descending through the air and attaching themselves up there – then suddenly the roof began to hammer with excited vibration. She threw out her arms and embraced his shoulders, dropped her head so hair fell on his thighs. Her fingers were ice cold on his shoulders. He heard the familiar pingings on the glass panes of the curtained window.

'It's all right.'

'What is it?'

'Just hailstones, Varie. It's just hailstones.'

A richer crop of hail came down; some made the familiar sound of rattling down a chimney into a fireplace in that next room and they heard hail picking against the wooden door and jumping around frantic outside.

She leaned back and laughed. 'God, I was scared.'

He said, 'That's my motorcycle helmet full of a pound of ice then. You can send me home with a fresh salmon out your river in it.' He nodded, looking at her. Another batch of hailstones hurtled down, so loud they had to raise their voices.

'My goodness.'

'Thought it was a bit nippy. Glad we missed it on the bike.'

'I've told you not to be so Scotchly prosaic.' She leaned over aggressively so he flinched, shoved her fingers through his long hair as if suggesting a new style of cut. They kissed, legs still crossed, bare knees pushed hard against each other and preventing them coming closer, then she opened her legs and slid them swiftly ahead, past his knees, her thighs gripping his waist. Her right heel skidded forward and smeared through the salt circle behind him. 'Oh no. I've broken the circle.'

Simon slowly turned his head and sneered, 'Now you're in for it. The hailstones will charge but the salt'll melt them.'

'Seriously. Should seal it.'

Simon leaned backwards and used a finger to smear the salt back into place, sealing the little wall. She ran a finger lower down his belly which made his legs shiver. He whispered, 'All we need is some vinegar and chips.'

'Shut *up*, you; with always joking.' She looked in his eyes, playfully slapped the side of his head softly. They kissed again, relays of breathing going through them. She put her hand down between his legs and simultaneously nicked his earlobe with her teeth. It was sharply sore. She whispered, 'I want you to hurt me.'

'What?'

She grabbed his fingers and quickly pulled them down – the tops of her inner thighs were so wettened he glanced down. When she lay back, inky hair flopped onto the salt and splayed there, white grains tumbled in among individual moving black strands. He pushed into her almost straight away – just so he could say he done it with her for always. Words came out of her mouth with intervals between. 'Hard. Don't tell Alex but I'm on the pill. I want you to really hurt me.'

He did not want to hurt her and only continued to push gently so her fingernails went across his shoulder blades like bramble hooks and he felt his skin burst, ruck up and burn. His pelvis slid on her again and again, in retaliation, much more forceful. He pushed himself up on his arms to free himself from the nails and – as he used to with Nikki – to see her all the better. He pummelled in at her as if trying to slide her across the floor. Varie lifted a hand to her left breast, Simon's blood was on one of her knuckles, and she twisted her nipple herself, hard. The other breast – small and conical – vibrated like Christmas jelly each time he came to the repetitive stops. 'I'm just all yours,' she told him and he took advantage of that.

Soon enough her lips and breasts, the wet ridges and deeply private enfoldments of her tasted of saltiness, just as though he had pulled her naked from the sea.

All the time, Varie retained a slightly angered, displeasured twist around her nostrils, and much later, when she stood, the circle had been smeared in all directions, as if the salt had merely been flung haphazardly across the floorboards. Her shoulder blades, the backs of her thighs and her white buttocks were scarred with impregnated floorboard chips and worm-swirls of dust. She jerked the closed curtains apart. The glass was glossy, oil black, and it was still dark outside although the sky was by then draining into a washed-out blue, chilled with puffing white stars.

She crossed to the table, fiddled with the storm lamp and blew out the wick so it was almost completely dark but for that lighter square segment of outside sky. She began to adjust that mirror over on the old drawerless dressing table – as Nikki had once allowed the mirror in the Glasgow hotel room to reflect them. The glass returned Varie and Simon's position on the salted floor and the black window.

'The mirror is reflecting the starlight onto me,' she claimed, as she curled back down to him. 'If I wasn't on the pill, you could give me a star child.'

'A what?' Simon was uneasy about doing all this with curtains open.

'The starlight penetrates my belly and you have an astral child together; though bad spirits could come into our child because we broke the circle.'

Simon replied, 'Really? A star child? We'll put him up on the next Apollo mission then.'

Between the bouts of ecstasy, outside birds began to sing to them. Several times she cried out and this permitted him to sigh also, as when she pulled back her knees and pressured her fist into the bottom of his spine while that lactic light grew on them until he lost patience and stood to pull the curtains. She smiled up at this timidity, rising to her knees and making him stay standing there.

Cruel light was behind the curtains and the volume of birds calling out was quite extreme by the time they both dressed; Simon's shirt stuck onto the blood of his scratched shoulder blade which stung hysterically through his tiredness. There was salt in the scratch too.

Sitting in the armchair Varie picked at the flecks of dirt adhered to her bare thighs below the dress, and she brushed at her lower legs while her hair spilled down in front of her white skin like fast, wet coal on a chute.

When they emerged outside it was bright and cold. Simon saw how the tree twigs had water droplets which hung in tiny lenses and inverted the trunks reflected through them; light seemed to reflect from everything. She had put the key back under the flowerpot and then led him down by the riverside and its subtle deafening – they both squinted against the dawn sun which was lifting up behind the treeless hill which her dead mother once deforested.

'Don't watch me, if you please,' she primly told him, removing her boots again then shoving them out at his chest for him to hold. The leather above the soles glistened with smears from the damp morning grass.

Varie picked gingerly forward but he watched all the same, her bare shoulders between the straps of the dress. She curved her toes onto rocks then sat on a larger boulder at the river edge, pulled up the skirt of her dress and bit her lips at the chill while she scooped palm after palm of water between her opened legs. She occasionally looked up and around suspiciously but across the river to the opposite bank not towards Simon. His ears hummed and buzzed with fatigue but he loved the beauty of the sight which looked to him like achievement.

They didn't walk back up that arbour which Simon recalled from the night but instead approached towards the great house through fir trees. She had taken Simon by his hand and she sometimes swung their arms together. Through the wood, each tree trunk had a cat fur of green moss; pelts of vertically dropped needles circled the deciduous pines, orange, like rusty iron filings. Simon noted the new pine needles faced up in bunches yet on other trees they hung down. Broken Moan's full size, the precipitous drama of its towered baronial wing, struck him only then.

She pointed to a series of burrow entrances on a banking, the soil scraped and worn at the mouths. 'These are the badger setts that go right in under the lawn. Sometimes I meet them. Late one night a fat devil refused to get off the path for me and I had to step aside while he went on by. He sniffed my foot. Cheeky beggar.'

They stepped onto a wide lawn shaded in at the sides by more tall firs. They were in full view of the windows and Varie blatantly dropped Simon's hand. In the shade, the grass was still dressed in white hail, like rice thrown at a wedding. They moved towards some back door in the Victorian wing, built in pink sandstone. Simon squinted at his digital watch.

'Suppose I should be going.'

'Don't be silly. We'll wake up Alex for a scream and he'll be dazzled you're here. He's leaving for school.'

'We must stink. Your dad will know fine and be going mental with you, home at this time.'

'They'll be asleep in bed. And Alex wouldn't know what sex smells like.' She glanced at him with – rather late in the day – a flirtatious look and she led him through an unlocked arched door. Inside was a huge old kitchen with broad metallic work surfaces, like a works canteen but holding the rich blood scent of freshly butchered meat and game.

Walking down a corridor with gloss mustard walls and red linoleum they came out into a hallway. It really was an enormous place inside, which went up and up. Tartan carpets, wooden wall panelling, targes and swords hung above shuttered fireplaces, mounted steers' heads and stuffed birds with single, wet caviar eyes.

Varie gave Simon a sad look. 'It's like a stuffy old hotel, isn't it?'

There was a vast stairway with ornate baronial banisters which widened out at the bottom. He could see a wall of stained-glass windows at the first landing. It was all as big as some city museum.

Varie put her hands on both handles of two screen doors with frames in them – crystal glass with bevelled edging. She paused suddenly then whispered, 'Hush. Stay hidden right there.' She entered a long parlour ending in a set of double bay windows which must have faced the front turning place, the main river and then, on the far side, the railway – if huge curtains hadn't been drawn across. The room was so shadowy Simon jumped when he noticed the two adult figures. Each man slumbered as if dead in front of a huge fireplace filled with silver ash – both men completely asleep in old leather armchairs with brass studs. They wore tweed jackets, checked shirts and neckties – not even loosened in their sleep.

Varie came back out, tutted and whispered to Simon, 'They must have been up later than Mrs Mac and they haven't even blankets. That's terrible.'

Simon recognised Varie's father. He looked younger with his face relaxed and stretched out, despite the very silver hair. Simon frowned at the second figure and then recognised him from photographs in the *Port Star* – he was even familiar from blue campaign posters on telegraph poles. It was William Coutts, Conservative Party candidate for the constituency.

Varie walked away into a corridor and he saw her reach up to a shallow cupboard. She came back with dark rugs draped over her arm and she placed one across her father's thighs and torso and tucked it in. Then she turned to William Coutts and did the same for him. Simon watched the paper-white back of her thighs as she bent, the skirt of her short dress hoisting. Then she pointed to the way out. She quietly closed the screen doors behind them.

Disappointingly they did not use that grand staircase; they walked down a long corridor with marble sculptures – the frozen faces of historical figures – and sequences of windows with no curtains gave out onto the vista. Between three monkey puzzle trees, Simon could look right across the far river in the bright morning with the colours: the emeralds of new leaves, the rusts and reds of old bracken and the limes of the new sprouts, all magnificent above the railway's horseshoe curve.

They climbed some secondary staircase, Varie leading without looking back, her ringless hand out on the solid banister. The stairs were carpeted in the old-fashioned manner, with brass bars securing the thin, worn fabric into the lee of each step. There were more corridors upstairs leading in differing directions. But they were going further up to a second floor. They came to an oak door with a brass plate screwed into the wood: *Genius at Work*.

Varie knocked none too considerately and gave Simon a pained glance. 'Can't barge in and tickle him any more. He had a new lock fitted.'

Quite quickly the door was unlocked and jerked open. Alex stood there in semi-darkness. He was wearing striped pyjamas, and some kind of cloth eye mask was lifted up on his forehead. He had what appeared to be socks on his hands.

He spoke in a loud voice. 'Have you two been fornicating?'

Varie pushed into the dark bedroom. 'Jesus, Alex. Keep your voice down.'

'What are you actually wearing?'

'It's a railway uniform.'

'Well, I hope you used the tradesman's entrance.' Alex returned into the bedroom and Simon followed.

At the far end, Varie reached up and opened the curtains to a window made from small ornate panes. Alex pulled the blindfold back down on his eyes, and with his arms out like a sleepwalker, he paced in circles in the middle of the huge room, moaning. There were white plaster ceilings at differing heights with dark wooden roof beams. Plastic Airfix model kit aircraft – some of them with shattered wings and hanging parts – were suspended from threads. Simon saw that the poster which came with *Master of Reality* was pinned up on one wall. There was an uneven, spreading pile of *Melody Makers* underneath, against the skirting board.

'Where are my sunglasses, my sunglasses, you fornicators? Modern man does two things: fornicates and reads the newspapers; well, I can't manage either round here.' He lifted the blindfold on one side and held up his muffled hands in the socks. 'Serious burns at Le Mans this year.' He smiled at Simon. 'I wear socks on my hands or I scratch myself during the night.'

'It runs in the family.'

Varie gave Simon a smoky look.

Alex nodded. 'I saw that coming a clear mile off. Tried to avoid you, to save my rock-chipper's heart, but that was another uphill task. That might be a geological pun.' He sighed. 'And that poor little mermaid of yours. Never mind. You have my sort of blessing.' He sliced a tightly socked hand down, up and across Simon's face and chest, in the sign of the cross, then pulled both socks off and threw them at the bed. 'You should have seen the queue. Menial second-raters all.'

'Alex.'

'And what did Father say, dear?'

Varie called out cheerily across the large bedroom, 'They're still asleep. Even the Mac isn't up.'

Alex rubbed his eyes. 'I left them at four. Must have drunk half a decanter of malt. That really good stuff. I was going to sleep at the bottom of the stairs but it appears I made it up here after all. Oh. My bloody head.'

'Stop shouting. Take out your ear things.'

He picked a white earplug out of each ear and looked at Simon. He sniffed at the earplugs. 'It's the birds. *To Kill a Mockingbird*. Father took my airgun away and locked it up with the real guns. A point two-two. I used to take a fairly accurate potshot out the window at my feathered friends. And when I was drunk, at the Second World War air forces.' He pointed up at the model aeroplanes. A few were well shattered with hanging wings. Sure enough there were a few lead BB slugs embedded up in the noble beams.

'Any Stukas?' Simon asked.

'Of course. That's one next to the Messerschmitt. Minus a wing. The Germans had fab planes; better than dreary Spitfires. My God. You really do work on the railways. You've all your togs.'

'I'm the train driver.'

'Yes, Alex. He actually *drives* the trains along and he's going to go toot-toot on his horn for me all summer long each time he passes. Aren't you, Si? It's romantic. We might even be engaged to be married. He gave me a ring from a can of pop.'

Alex looked startled. 'I guess on your wage. I'm going back to bed.' And he did climb onto it. It was a strange sort of four-poster – one side seemed to emerge out of the wall, the upper frame built into the roof. He whipped the bedspread up to his neck but kept a close eye on things.

'Can I look at your albums? I've still got those ones you lent me.'

'Be my guest.'

'See you've got a guitar,' Simon stated; he just touched the top of the guitar and one string made a long dull drone.

'Just an acoustic. I want an electric. We should form a band.'

Simon got down on his knees flicking through the first of the two deep columns of records which were leaning against the tall skirting board. There was Hendrix, The Doors, Cream and The Nice – but there was odd stuff that made his lip purse. Stackridge, Spooky Tooth, *Ringo* by Ringo Starr, Wizzard, the Strawbs; tons and tons of Dylan too.

Alex was keeping an eye on the albums. Simon had come to all the Fear Taker albums. In a bored voice Alex said, 'They say Mark Morrell the guitarist from Fear Taker has that house at Abbot's Isle as a holiday home. He bought through Pered's, I believe. I saw a Ferrari there once, hugging the road.'

Simon nodded. 'Aye. If that's true it's fantastic. *Pascal's Moon*. He's a brilliant guitarist. Do you know Jack Bruce owns a whole island near Campbeltown too?'

'Yes. That is right. And Paul McCartney's down there. Too many of them.' A groan came from Alex in the bed. He'd found his sunglasses and they were on.

'Can I ask something? That guy down there with your dad – he's William Coutts, eh? The Tory?'

'Yes. That's Creepy Coutts. He's all for shagging my sister too. Isn't he, dear?'

'You have got repulsive.'

'It's that school. It corrupted me.'

'Are yous just all Tories then? I mean, it's not very imaginative.'

Alex's black lenses trembled over towards Varie. 'Well, of course we are. Father is.'

'I'm not any more. I'm for Scottish Nationalists now. They're magnificent.' Varie was looking out of the little windows, down towards the trees.

'Just, I thought you were sort of hippies. Rebels.'

Alex said, 'Seems to me all the hippies have become capitalists anyway. It's like prostitution versus free love. Might as well get paid for it.' His tone changed. 'Anyway, what else could we be? After Father kicks the bucket I'm not giving this house away to coal miners for weekend union conferences. You wouldn't either were it yours. Which it probably will be with the speed you move at.'

Simon turned his shoulders. 'What do you mean?'

'Well, you know? I'm doomed; a touch of Percy Shelley, a touch of Hendrix. Or is it a touch of Morecambe and a touch of Wise? If you get Varie proper you'll end up getting this lot one day. After Father and I are concreted into the yard down there. I'll tell you now. Watch for the plumbing.'

Varie laughed but Simon thought it had a nervous trill at the blasphemy. He said, 'What are you talking about? We're only young, man.'

'Oh, come on.'

'What?'

Varie interrupted. 'Alex believes he's doomed to die young because he has a hangover right now and the occasional touch of hay fever in August.'

The lenses held still on Varie and he said, 'Well, look at Mummy. And Uncle.' He turned back to Simon. 'Do you have expectations,

Simon? It's healthy and proper primogeniture, my friend. The Commander of the Pass is a simple sinecure to the sovereign but the house is tied up with it. Always goes to the eldest male. Never to the daughter. Thus if I wasn't here, it would go to Varie's husband. Not to Varie. You two marry and elbow me out in a rowing boat or hit me behind the left ear with a candelabra on the stairs and it's all yours, cock. Parvenu will be your middle name and your great expectations will be fulfilled.'

Simon turned his head between the siblings. He looked straight at him. 'You're confusing *The Prince* with some other Penguin Classic this morning, Alex. *Waverley* maybe by the look of this place, and I couldn't ever finish that.'

Alex laughed appreciatively. 'The thing about paranoia is it makes you too trusting. No. It really does. You think to yourself, gosh, I am paranoid. So you over-correct yourself, then one day you're caught out, right under your nose.'

'I have no interest in all this big house shite.'

'Oh, really?'

'I just think Varie's great and did the minute I saw her.'

'Great?' He raised his brow and looked across at Varie.

'And beautiful.'

'He's so sweet.'

'Ah.' Alex nodded with cynical exaggeration. 'It's an aesthetic thing.'

Simon spoke slowly. 'That's your word for it. People have emotions.'

'Yes. And what happened to your little ray of golden sunshine? Perhaps you'll pass her on to me?'

'Boys. It's too early in the morning to fight over us lucky girls.'

Alex said – with real venom, 'You love it, you mad bitch. It's just the kind of thing you would do. Marry him.'

'Crikey.' Varie spoke in a low voice and looked away. 'You'd better cover for me with Daddy when we go downstairs.'

'Always do, dear. I have since you were fifteen, you slut. Now we're not going to have some horrible political falling-out at this hour of the morning, are we?'

Varie tried to stir things up again. 'Alex, he called us posh English colonials.'

'I'm Scottish. More Scots than you. You told me your mother's from round here but your father, the lorry man, is English. That's treason, cock. We could have you hanged on private ground. We could set the army from Blair Atholl marching on you. I've met the chap who commands it. You'd have to scatter them with your train.'

Simon laughed.

Alex looked up at the ceiling and the small aircraft hung reflected in the black lenses. 'It's you that's the curious one, Simon; not us or anyone else. Little boy lost. Not sufficiently Scotch. Driving railway trains when your father has a lorry company. Scoffing at Tories and romping with the daughter from the big house.'

'He doesn't realise he's working class either.'

'Huh!' Alex blew out air. 'He's our only connection with the psychology of the working man. We'd be lost without him.' He laughed.

Simon held up *A Saucerful of Secrets.* 'Brilliant!'

Alex looked happier. 'Put "Remember a Day" on and we'll all sing it together now. I've got cigarettes.'

Varie called out, 'Hurrah.'

They listened to the sad song again and again – Simon supervising the stylus – without understanding its nostalgia, the volume turned up so loud the three of them didn't hear the morning passenger train across the river heading on down the Pass.

Despite the vast interiors of Broken Moan, the definite smell of cooked breakfast started to seep up. The three of them ventured downstairs. Alex was wearing slippers and one of his father's discarded dressing gowns lined with something shiny; it was too short for Alex. Simon took the precaution of zipping up his bomber jacket so his uniform blazer with its CND and NUR badges were concealed beneath. Varie had brushed her hair and she'd changed out of her dress – into jeans and those same riding boots. She claimed she was going to go and feed her horse. Simon couldn't understand where she got her energy from.

Simon had expected some grand dining room but Andrew Bultitude and William Coutts actually sat among shadows, deep into the huge cold kitchen, opposite each other at a long wooden table in the corner. Coutts was eating fried eggs, sausages and bacon which looked appallingly underdone with snow-white strips of fat. Varie's father appeared to be eating toast alone, taking it from two silver racks. There was a huge teapot on the table – an old aluminium one with black plastic handles and sooty carbon markings up the sides. Both men drank the tea from delicate china cups, still wearing the clothes they slept in, neckties rigid and maintained.

'Well.' Andrew Bultitude looked up straight at his daughter. 'Hello, Anne of Bohemia. Tea?'

'Good morning. Hello, William.'

Willie Coutts nodded, chewing. 'Now where were you last night, darling? Out gallivanting on the randan when you could have chatted with your Willie? I really only visit to see you.' He had an accent from the North of Ireland and each word came out of his mouth with a definite forward jut of his head – as if he were about to spit.

'Out with the girls. Again.'

'Your father tells me you're doing grand at the university?'

'I find the course amazing, yes.'

'And all grown up now and staying in digs, I hear. Gosh, I wouldn't like to know what goes on there, my love. We'll need to have lunch at the Café Royal when I'm in Edinburgh.'

There was a pause.

Andrew Bultitude held his look a moment longer on his daughter then glanced down to butter his toast. 'What does the polite and starved student say, darling?'

Varie smiled. 'That's very kind, Willie. That would be lovely.'

Bultitude was not looking at her. 'Home late, darling?'

'It was getting a little late on. I came in the front door.'

'Really? Where were you gadding about?'

'I was at Jennifer Pastor's. You know? Jennifer who knew the Appin horse girls. And then at her digs in town. She gave me a lift out in her dear little car.'

'Her digs? Who's Jennifer?'

'Just a girl.'

'Mmmm.'

Varie told them, 'You two were asleep in the parlour and I put blankets on you.'

'Oh.' This seemed to shame both men into a short silence. Alex made to speak.

'Take off those ridiculous sunglasses inside the house.'

Coutts laughed. 'Och, no. I might ask for a shot of those. He takes a dram, the boy, he takes a dram. Good for a man to learn to hold his drink, so it is.'

But Alex took off the sunglasses. 'You remember my local friend Simon Crimmons. You met him in town once.'

'Oh yes. Your father. Italy. The lorries.' Bultitude nodded, tossed his finger around and looked across at Coutts.

'Hello, Mr Bultitude.'

Coutts dived in. 'Your father has all the lorries we see, does he? Vera good, vera good. Credit to the county. So it is!'

Simon smiled slimly. He wasn't taking any compliments direct from a Tory political candidate. Imagine if Hannan could see him now, stood there with this conglomeration!

'Here bright and early, Simon?' Bultitude glanced at his wristwatch. 'Are we all up to some grand dangerous manoeuvres on that loch today?'

Alex said, 'No. But Simon was just leaving. He was in the red bedroom last night. Don't you recall me saying? We were cataloguing our record collections alphabetically. He's a stickler for detail so he didn't join us for whisky.' Alex added smartly, 'We're still only crawling through the Ms.'

'Oh?' Bultitude shrugged and bit into toast. He nodded. 'That bloody music of yours. I'm going to get the bell system reconnected but it's going to work in the other direction.'

Coutts laughed.

'I'll pull the cords down here and the bloody bells will ring up in your bedrooms – get you out of bed in the morning and tell you to turn that awful music off.' Bultitude looked at Coutts, chuckled and shook his head.

Simon had thought Alex's tale was a ridiculous and far-fetched suggestion, but then Bultitude said in a resigned voice, 'I never quite know who's staying in this bloody house, Willie. Mr Crimmons's son is very welcome but there was a fellow here once. What was his name? Stupid fellow. From Alex's school. The one before the one before.' He gave Alex a glance. 'He'd been here days before I found him taking bad shots in the billiards room. I asked who on earth he was and he said, "I am Alex's house guest and can I have something to eat?"'

Alex sighed. 'That was Gordon Sutherland. He thought you were the Mac's husband.'

'Yes he did. Asked if I could recommend some good walks and I told him to go to the edge of the loch and keep walking straight ahead.'

Coutts laughed loudly. But Simon intuited that Coutts was more delighted with the generous dimensions of Broken Moan – which could hide a guest for days – than with the anecdote.

Varie said, 'Do you know, Daddy, that Simon is violently allergic to horses? He's so hopeless. He can't step within forty feet of me if I've been riding.'

Bultitude smiled. 'She's horse mad, Simon. You're safe with Alex though. He couldn't stay on his rocking horse as a laddie. Could you? And your bloody ancestors rode in the Scots Greys as well.'

Coutts and Mr Bultitude chuckled slowly, like syrup going down the side of the pot.

Varie yawned. 'I'm going to feed Mr Peggy a last time. Will you do him from tomorrow night please?'

Bultitude nodded and said, 'Good girl. Good girl,' deluded that Simon could not be involved around his daughter.

Willie Coutts frowned. 'And how are you getting back to town young man? Would you like a lift? I'm off within the hour.'

'No thanks. Ah. I know the rough times of my father's lorries down the country. It's handy. I just hitch lifts all over in the things. Sort of personal taxis.'

Bultitude said – in a threatening but protective way, 'Be careful on that road. There are no pavements out here. We could do with a pavement, Willie. Take that one to Westminster.'

'I'll just wait at the bottom of your drive, if that's okay.'

'Yes, of course. What happened to your motorbike?'

'I left it at home. Alex said there might be drink.'

'Aye. There was that. We make it a tradition here once a month. Bring yourself downstairs next time.'

Simon was aware Coutts was staring at him. The man seemed

to have noticed Simon's railway dress trousers with the crease ironed in by his mother. 'And how is business for your father? Going well despite it all?'

'It's all right.'

'How many articulated lorries does your father have now?'

Simon paused insolently then replied, 'Ten. At last count.'

Alex yawned. 'I'll have a breakfast then. If Mrs Mac would make me one.'

Bultitude tutted. 'Easier for her if you'd all come down here on time. She has better things to do than line your stomachs as each of you crawl from a corner. She's not the Galloping Gourmet.'

'I'll gnaw on the end of a carpet then,' Alex said and ushered Varie and Simon out of the kitchen.

Simon turned to look at the two men. 'Bye.'

The three youths walked out the kitchen while Coutts and Bultiude fell back into conversation.

In the extravagant front-door porch of Corinthian columns with a white cast-iron shelter, Alex put his sunglasses back on.

Simon asked, 'When do you both go then?'

'Tomorrow or later today.'

Simon said, 'That's a shame.'

Varie mocked, 'Awww.'

Simon hated the way she blew hot and cold like that.

Alex stated, 'We shall be at your disposal all summer. This will be the celebrated summer of the sub-aqua descent. The Undersea World of Alex Cousteau.' Alex saluted in a formal, military way, then as he dropped his hand he looked at Varie. 'You can tell me everthing later.' He would not come out as far as the gravel and turned back into the shadows of the house.

Simon and Varie crossed the crunching stones. There was a car there. A coffee-coloured Hillman Avenger which must have been Coutts's vehicle.

'Don't get seen, getting your motorbike thing out the grass, or they'll know we lied,' she whispered.

'Okay. Will you get in touch?'

She nodded.

He leaned in to kiss her but she jerked back. 'Don't. Anyone could be watching.'

Simon turned and looked up at the huge old house behind them. He remembered what Big Davie had once said about there being a window for every day of the year. 'Who? How many people are actually wandering around inside your house?'

'Mmm. Nobody knows. The Mac could be.'

'I really want to kiss you.'

She looked at him and wrinkled her nose disgustedly. 'I go this way. Bye,' and she walked off between the fuzzy reachings of the monkey puzzle trees, towards the lower paddocks, yet she did turn to lift a hand in a little wave then smiled.

Simon slowly sauntered back up the long driveway beyond the trees, squinting at the new day around him. Despite the earlier hailstones, flies and buzzing insects were crossing the drive at speed in bright light. It was difficult to work out precisely where the bike and helmet had been abandoned on the left-hand side. Eventually he spotted the very top of a black handgrip. He looked back up the drive then climbed over the solid metal Victorian fencing into the field and soon found the helmet in the grass. Of course it was wet and damp-feeling on the inside lining. Even though it had only been ten minutes since he left the kitchens, he heard the sound of a vehicle on the gravel then its quieter approach through the trees from the direction of the big house. Simon fell to the ground and flattened himself among the wet, long wild grasses, listening to his heart beat.

The car got louder and hidden there he felt a great sense of illicit excitement over what he and Varie had done together. He was piratical and subversive. He wasn't sure if he loved Varie or had exploited her body but he enjoyed that confusion – he even told himself that his penis had struck a blow in the class war.

The tyres of Coutts's car suctioned along the tarmac on the other side of the white metal fencing. Simon bit his teeth together but the car passed without hesitation. 'Tory bastard,' he whispered and waited till he presumed it had reached the far end of the driveway when he cautiously arose.

Simon trotted holding the handlebars, wheeling his bike very quickly down the drive, watching both ways. In the dell by Varie's little sentry box, he finally kicked the engine into life and pulled on the sweaty, unpleasant helmet.

He was very tired and drove unsteadily uphill towards the Back Settlement. As he came up onto the flatness by the bogs, he sighted the morning goods train travelling in his direction, dragging excited exhaust from the engine roof. She was five tanks, a plywood van and two mineral wagons of coal with a brake van – moving tall, over on the embankments towards the Jericho Road houses. He could see how the eddying heat from the exhaust had dried the wet roof for a length behind it. It would be the two Ians on the early.

At Tulloch Villa, his father had already driven off to work and Jeff was still in bed. He was cagey around his mum in the kitchen and he told more lies about a traction motor burning out and the mail train not finally arriving into the town till an hour before.

His mum said, 'You don't blow the train horn like you used to. If that bike doesn't then you'll end up killed on that railway.'

'I've told you not to worry if I'm in late. The evening passenger was thirteen hours late in here once, you have to expect that.'

His mother offered to cook him a breakfast but he refused and she went out to work in the garden.

He climbed upstairs to have a bath which made the scratches on his back sting like fury. His white work shirt was a rusted palimpsest with long repeated lines of blood from his back and he hid it – he'd throw it out later.

He pulled the bedroom curtains and went to bed. It was difficult to get to sleep, his back stung, his head crackled busily. When he did drop off, his dreams were full of reptiles which grasped claws out of shadowy graves, Varie screaming, strange undersea echoes – like Hendrix's guitar feeding back, words all mixed in with them. William Coutts lifted the back of Varie's little flower dress. Her hard buttocks were spattered in glistening sweat beads and Coutts's fingers writhed inside a black sock, then snatched upward.

Simon woke. He got out of bed and sat in his reading armchair which Varie had once occupied. He smoked a cigarette then went back to bed and slept soundly right through till he got up for his midnight shift.

Simon blew the train horn opposite Broken Moan that night

and Penalty glowered at him and as late May developed into June he occasionally sounded it again but as usual neither Alex nor Varie ever got in touch and the horn sounded like a defeated echo going down the Pass.

Wednesday 12 June 1974

He was on midnight freight shift. On the Monday and Tuesday it had been clear and gentle and by Wednesday night it was still mild, but raining very hard when he got into the station bothy just before midnight.

Paul Breck was rostered guard. Simon and Breck made the usual sweet tea from the water heater, but by twenty past there was no sign of Penalty. Simon shook free his digital watch from his cuff and pressed the button.

Breck responded, 'John's a bit late, eh? No like him.'

'A bit, aye. What's on the night then?'

'Yous'll be nifty on the gradients. She's a double-heider. Two engines on, cause there was an engineering train up this afternoon – ballasting – and they've to get the engine back down. Left hoppers in the sidings at the Back Settlement and Nine Mile for a Sunday working. There'll be a wee bitty time-and-a-half overtime there if you're looking for it. Maybe next Sunday; you'll need to ask McGarry to get in there. If Hannan hasn't.'

Simon nodded. 'I heard about the ballast. Darroch and Jonty had to come in off the spare to do it, eh?'

'Aye. Big deal. It must've broken their hearts. Wouldn't want the railway to get in the way of the butcher's shop, eh? So we're two engines, four empty tanks on, I think, and two vans. Telling you, I'll be glad to be sat in the back cab of an engine the night. Gets a bummer horsing around in a brake van every fucking night.'

'Aye, it must be too.'

'No so bad the now. It's the winters. Woof. You need to get that stove going or it gets like a fucking fridge in the brake vans. Did we's tell you Rudolf burned down a brake van in '63?

'Naw? Was he drunk? Even in 1963?'

'That boy came out his mother with the hiccups. Cold winter, '63. Rudolf got that van warm enough. He'd parked and braked it up in the old goods yard that's all gone now since the mart went. Next to your faither's garages up there. Rudolf was fu' as usual and it was warmer in that van than up in his tip of a bachelor flat so he was sat in there alone for a few hours banging off the sides. Reckon he'd got the stove so fucking stoked, the chimney stack was red hot. He must been burning everything that wasnie bolted down in there, tipping glots of brandy in to keep it going. Next thing didn't he put his whole fucking arm up in flames. They saw him come flying out the van in the night, running across the yard with his arm all up in blue flames like a fucking Christmas pudding, but the cunt wouldnie let go that half brandy bottle. He doused his arm under the water tower for the steam engines. We had the two fire brigade tenders up in the old yard all nicht. All the boys came out and warmed themselves round the brake van while it burned.'

Simon laughed.

'Big melted ring of snow round her. Only the wheel base left in the morn so it was cut up on the yard. The fire burned the sleepers underneath as well, so the whole siding track had to be relaid. They should of sent Rudolf the bill.'

'Rudolf strikes again.'

'Aye. Donald Destruction. The army should use him. Nothing that man cannie destroy. Aye. Between you and me son, I cannie be fucked with goods and brake vans no more. I aye try to swap shift onto a passenger but Kellan wouldn't swap this week. Hassle on a heavy train with coals on it, so it is, pinning the brake in the van down on the banks. Jeezo, son. Ten year back we used to get fifteen and twenty wagons a day in, shunting two hour in the yards.'

'That many?'

'Oh aye. Had the mart animals and all the fish out and every house in this town with a coal fire. Think about it. No a bit of this central heating lark to warm your arse on. You'd get eight wagons of coals in twice a week and more in winter. Now I'm no getting at you, cause your old man has the lorries. But ten year ago almost every single thing you bought over a counter in the shops of this town had came up on the fucking train. Lipton's, grocers, ironmongers. The furniture, the clothes in the shops, the coal. Even the cars the garages was starting to sell come up on flat bogies by train to the old yard. All gone in ten year onto the roads. And the road is getting better. Christ knows all what'll be coming up in another ten year? Just a sack of fucking transistor radios made in Hong Kong.'

Simon nodded.

'Aye aye. Lonesome Gulch here these days, eh?'

Both their heads turned. There was gentle, almost pathetic chapping upon the bothy door. Maybe it had gone before, unheard over Breck's talking and the steady drum of the rain hitting the plates of the glass station roof outside. Breck and Simon frowned towards it. Breck stood, crossed and opened the door. There was a small old woman there. Hair in curlers covered with a scarf.

'Sorry to bother yous, boys. John's no so well the night.'

It was Doreen, Penalty's wee old wife.

'Ach.' Breck looked at his wristwatch. 'Nae bother, Doreen. Don't worry yourself, love. We can try and pull a spare body out. Tosh'll come down with the Young Fella here. I'll try get in the office and give him a tinkle.'

'Naw, naw. John's right here with me the now, it's just – he's worried about getting over to the train in the yard and climbing up on it.'

Breck looked round her. 'Where's he now?'

'In the car outside. I've drove him down the road.'

'Och, there's an easy solution to that; nae bother. Young Fella, away up the yard and get that train going. Tell Musty to put you back onto 3 road and John can get aboard on the platform there.'

'Righto.' Simon stood up quick, enjoying the sudden drama and responsibility of it. He left his second full cup of tea, grabbed his torch, and as he passed Mrs Penalty, he smiled.

'Thanks now, son,' she said, quite shyly.

The rain was thrumming on the glass of the canted station roof. Beneath the familiar leaks – even though the strip lights were only half switched on at this hour – puddles where the drips fell on the concourse glistened like patches of melted lard.

With his hat on, Simon trudged quick up 3 and right along the track to the box with his illuminated torch. The rain tapped on the peak of his hat. Musty was at the window but would only slide it two inches open – as if it was pure acid coming down – while Simon shouted up what was what then crossed the top yard to the fence road, where those dual-coupled engines sat on top of the formed goods train. By pure coincidence they were in numerical order; 27006 was on top and behind was James Bond itself: old 27007. They'd had James Bond down, the Monday night. The two engines were connected by the jumper cables so both could be operated from the front cab.

Simon climbed the ladder looking upwards, grunting, blinking in the rain, and he shoved in the door, started the engines and after the reservoir had built, took the train slowly up under the bridge with the windscreen wiper moving jerkily. He was finally solo – having to think of everything for himself. He was sure he'd forgot something important but in his nerviness he couldn't fathom what.

Up the cutting he opened the vacuum brake to hold her, crossed the cab and leaned from the secondman's seat, far out the engine window, almost to his waist, suspicious Musty wouldn't pull off the home – but Musty gave him a full signal and he saw that momentary slide of the glass aspect in front of the lantern from jam red to aqua green. The platform indicator lit and gave '3' – those white bulbs casting their frosty light down onto the wet roofs of the vans, across the gantries and ladders and the reflective flanks of the tank wagons behind him.

He slowly took it all down towards 3, his head out the cab window, looking backwards as he reversed, eyes blinking in the rain, his hand lapping at the air brake – making it hiss at will – crawling the wagons backwards into the curvature of that platform, squinting his forehead under the dripping peak of his hat. That excited sense of responsibility and self-importance was in him – going solo – the trembling certainty of the engine through the polished levers on his fingers; a stupid pride too.

Breck was stood at the far end there, invisible to Simon, but the disc of the white torch face circled in a rhythm as the engine came in alongside the granolithic coping of the platform edge, its patterns moving beside Simon. Rainwater poured from the concrete edging, down into that dark space between the train and the platform. Breck clicked his torch to red.

Simon twisted his wrist in a motion to shove the vacuum open and a gush of air blew down the valve, then with his right hand he chugged the master handle to *Engine Only*, opened the cab door and jumped to the darkened platform. Through the rain he saw they'd unlocked the main gates at the bottom and car headlights came slowly up and along 3 towards him. The car stopped by the wooden box of the water hose and the headlights went out, the filaments sinking away to nothing. He could see Penalty sat there in the passenger seat. He looked just the same – even a fag in the corner of his mouth. His wife was behind the steering wheel, now wearing glasses.

The passenger door swung out and Penalty's voice said, 'You never put a tail lamp on the back of that train, son. Christ sake. Breck'll do it now. Never conduct a train movement at night without a tail lamp on. Even on this yard.'

Straight away Simon bit his lip. 'Oh aye. Sorry.'

'Give us a lift out then, lad.' Penalty leaned over and spat his fag butt down by Simon's brogues. The old man did a painful smile as he swung both legs from the car. Simon leaned in, embracing him right under his arms – as he lifted the heavy fellow up, onto one leg, Penalty shot out an arm across the wet car roof to support himself then he hopped once.

Breck had walked up to them. 'Away and take a sickie, John. Back home and in your bed. We'll get Tosh out.'

The old man replied in a sure voice, 'No.' It was all the more forceful in its unusual thoughtfulness.

Breck was a small man – and old too. He looked at Simon and said, 'Are you all right with managing him?'

'Aye.'

'Just get us up on yon bloody thing.' Penalty nodded to the top engine.

'No bother. I'll give you a buck-up at the door.'

Penalty looked at Simon and he shook his head. 'It no just into the engine though, son. I can't fucking walk over there.'

'Oh.'

Penalty slapped his thigh. 'It's seized up total the night. That's it gone on me good and proper. Won't loosen up till tomorrow, and when we get to the Fort Junction the night, you'll need to load me on the fucking luggage trolley and pull me down the platform to get me up on the mail engine. Hope there's nae bloody nosy parker passengers the night.'

'Get on my back then.' Simon turned round.

'Eh?'

'Get up on my back.'

'On your back; can you take me?'

'Aye.' Simon bent at his knees and hooked his arms like stirrups, thinking of the night Karen Caine had mounted up on his front.

'Mind yourself,' said Breck.

Mrs Penalty had come out of the car into the rain to watch all of this. She had raised a finger to her mouth and she held it there, biting on it.

Old Penalty leaned himself in against Simon's back. The young man bent further and wrapped his arms around the short, thick legs and lifted under the burden of weight. Penalty grunted. With unsteady, scrunching feet, Simon started to piggyback Penalty slowly forward, across the platform surface and towards the cab door of the top locomotive, his face gurned up in exertion.

Breck and Mrs Penalty walked slowly behind as the two men moved through the darkness – a small procession moving towards a strange Golgotha.

On Simon's back – the breath and voice close to his ear – Penalty said, 'I hope none of them houses there is watching. They'll be thinking, "Aye. There goes that bloody Lawless again. So drunk they've a team for carrying him onto his train these days."'

Apart from Doreen, they chuckled. Simon felt his knees droop slightly and had to bite his tongue and lift more. By the side of the cab he turned round, legs shaking. 'Can you get your foot up in there, John?'

The cab floor inside the door was raised about two and a half feet off the platform – awkward in this position. Simon had his doubts. He shouted quick, 'Paul, get up in.'

Breck stepped up into the cab and turned round, arms held out a little inadequately to grab Penalty from behind. Faced away from the engine, Simon backed in more, raising himself as high as he could. Penalty's good foot jumped about nervily for gain and finally got onto the cab floor. The other leg was hanging useless – as if half shot off.

'Got him?'

'Yup.' Breck had his arms in round Penalty's big belly, his fists on the brass-buttoned waistcoat, and he was able to haul him onto the engine cab. Penalty supported himself on one leg within the doorway and he moved a little further back then flattened against the pipes and electrical equipment of the bulkhead. Simon had room to squeeze up, his own chest pushed against Penalty who was gasping heavily.

'I'll drive.' Simon wiped the rainwater away from his own face with the sleeve of his coupling jacket.

'Nah, son.' Penalty took a breath. 'I'll take her down. Better if I've something to keep ma mind on. Ignore the pain that way.' He stood there with all his weight on one leg, leaning against the back of the cab. 'Wind that fucking seat down a bit for me to get in it then. There's been some giant on it. You.'

Simon crouched on the floor and rapidly wound the seat elevation lever underneath to lower it, then he spun it round. Breck and Simon watched as Penalty put his hands on the armrests and hopped himself backwards onto the seat with a shove of his good leg. He yelped. Breck and Simon jumped.

'Wind us up a bitty then so my feet are good for the deadman's.'

Simon had to crouch again and he wound the handle using both hands with the weight of Penalty in the seat above. As he slowly ascended, Penalty stated, 'A short back and sides please. There we go. Perfect.' Penalty turned the knob to set the windscreen wiper to a faster setting then looked at his watch. 'Right, ten past one. Let's get this bloody show on the road, boys.' He pulled the vacuum lever off.

'Sure you're okay now, John?' Breck placed his hand on Penalty's shoulder.

'Aye. Fuck sake, man. Got that tail lamp on the back there?'

'Aye.'

'Away and get yourself in that second engine for a sleep.'

'Right. See yous at the Junction.' Breck opted to make his

departure towards the rear locomotive through the engine room – perhaps to avoid Mrs Penalty. The din suddenly grew very loud as the guard stepped through then the noise closed off with a shutter-like cut as he slammed the door closed behind him.

All this while, Mrs Penalty had stood down on the platform in the pouring rain beside the cab, looking in through the open door. She passed something up to Penalty through his window – a kind of package which he tossed indifferently into the circular dipped indent behind the vacuum brake handle, the dip designed as a sort of sunken refuge for drinks and other objects – so they would not be shaken off a driver's desk by the engine vibrations.

Mrs Penalty came back to the open door and handed up a tartan-banded Thermos flask to Simon. 'Ta, son. That's his water mixed with milk of magnesia.'

'Okay, Mrs Penalty.'

'Hear that, Doreen? Mrs Penalty. That's the manners of the firemen they're giving me these days. Calls me Mr Penalty all the time. He's out the polite school this one. It's Mr Penalty this, Mr Penalty that. Isn't it, son?'

Simon replied, 'Aye, Mr Penalty.'

The lady smiled but she seemed close to tears.

Penalty said, 'Right, love. Back at quarter past four.'

'I'll bring the car back down for you, John.'

'Mind yourself reversing there and don't go bang it, cause we can't afford the garage.'

'Aye, John.'

Simon stood in the open cab doorway as Penalty shoved the master in, opened out the throttle, and as both engines chuntered more excitedly, the night freight drew ahead. Simon continued to stand in the open doorway, holding on with one hand as the dark grit of platform surface sped up below by his feet. Mrs Penalty's small figure receded down the platform until she walked slowly to the car. Simon slammed the door and crossed the cab.

Musty was up there on his dark pulpit, tweed cap and overcoat on, holding the tablet hoop high. Simon leaned down out of his window, held his arm as if about to loop a partner in some Highland country dance, but instead of a young woman's birling arm, the hard leather hoop slapped onto his biceps, he pulled the token into

318

the cab and slammed the window shut while the engine exhausts battered on up and under the bridge. With two engines and such a light load on, Simon noted how Penalty only had the power handle opened up to around halfway and he even notched it forward on the higher curves.

Simon adjusted his own windscreen wiper at the secondman's desk to a speed which cleared the rain quick enough, the air hissing up on the cylinder above the windscreen. As had become customary between the two of them, Simon undid the strap buckle and lifted out the metal token. In the dark cab he had to lift the leather pouch right up to his eyes to decipher what was branded on the leather there. Penalty lifted his cigarette lighter and lit his fag. Simon was able quote out loud in the jerking shadows: '"For a Scottish Republic."' He returned the token to the pouch.

Penalty nodded. 'Quite right.'

As the locomotive climbed higher into the night, Penalty stared ahead thoughtfully. 'Aye, you've come on grand, son.' He was blowing out smoke. 'You're handling these things better on the hills, learning to feel the road – how to accelerate with different tonnage and no snick the corners.'

'Aye.'

'You're learning that a train's no a car. It's just a big bloody metal ball you roll down one hill and up another. You know every corner on this bloody railway now, eh, even at night? Bet you know this line better than you know the arse on that wee bird of yours.'

Simon glumly said, 'Aye.'

Penalty nodded rapidly. 'You're a grafter too. No like some of the lazy bastards on this line.'

'Aye.' Simon asked, 'Is your leg okay on the deadman's?'

'My good one is. Puts a bit of strain on it. Once both my legs go, I'll be jiggered. I'll have to hold a crutch in my teeth to push down on the pedal, eh?'

Simon chuckled carefully.

'The fucking deadman's pedal wasn't made for a peg leg like me. This pedal will have me chucked off the railway before anything else.'

Up by the distant signal was that young ash tree which grew close to the line and had been known to Simon all of that first winter. Now, on that June night, it was flourished up with fresh leaves and their pale undersides dashed in an irritated flick at the black glass of Penalty's side window – like a brief and intimate flash of some sea creature's underside, turning over near the surface of an inky depth.

Penalty reached forwards for that small package out the desk indent and placed it right before him by the *Exhauster Speed Up* button. His short fingers began unfolding. It was a torn-off colour front page of a *Daily Record* newspaper and Simon squinted in the light cast back from the dimmed gauges.

'See here?'

Simon stood and crossed to the driving desk. The train was just curving on the long swerves at the back-road bridge – above where he and Nikki had encountered the oil-covered swan. Simon put an arm out and held onto the bulkhead below the dirty little central window. He saw the twisted newspaper contained a colourful pile of Penalty's little pills. With eyes still ahead, Penalty put his forefinger into the pills and stirred them around and around.

'It's ma fucking Smarties. Twice a day, eleven of the wee buggers.'

'Eleven? Jeezo.'

'Aye. Some breakfast that. Used to be a man for my bacon and eggs.'

'What are they all for?'

Penalty said nothing, then, 'Guts and my leg. This one's to keep my hair growing, this one stops me from farting in my bed. This red one is an anti-Hannan tranquilliser. So the cunt doesn't nip ma heid.'

Simon laughed.

'I'm meant to swally them down with that muck in the flask for my belly, but you know what, son?' Penalty's hand went to the window by his shoulder; he slid the window open and Simon felt the draught and the noise from the two exhausts trailing behind. Penalty dipped his fingertips in among the pills, took a sprinkling and cast them out the window into the darkness.

'John!'

'Fucking fat lot of good they do me.' Penalty lifted the newspaper, held it out the window and snapped several times so the pills were cast away, free into the rainy night, then he slammed the window closed. He scrunched the page of the paper and tossed it into the indent.

'Will you be all right without them?'

'Shite weather, eh?' He nodded straight ahead.

It was as Penalty said. On the locomotives now, Simon had the night roads all up in his mind. He too could close his eyes and divine exactly where he was throughout these blinded lands – the swoosh of overbridges like loops around them at their ears, then gone, thrown to the rear.

On a dry night at Black Lochs Tunnel you merely exchange one darkness for another – the sucking air in the tunnel softens perceptibly as the engine pulls free at the far mouth, but no lights anywhere outside to define. That night, blots of rain on the wind-screens vanished as they entered the tunnel, then the sharp drops ripped back across the glass as they came free of the eastern mouth. But the blackness was just the same.

The drum of a bridge beneath, the brush of a bush that hadn't been cut back. When Simon closed his eyes, he could now have held out each arm like a night bird, flying over the lands to and from the outlying station. While he rode the midnight trains, Simon screwed his eyes tight shut, imagined every girl from his old school now fast asleep far across all these places, fair heads on pillows in some massive feminine dreamland. When he opened his eyes minutes later he still knew exactly where he was, in what field or waste – the lone spangle of some distant dwelling's porch light told him everything. The speckled frost of trackside hawthorn blossoms blushed out like a conference of ghosts in the black sweep ahead.

They moved steadily on through the darkened stations – as if on a pioneer train venturing up some long-forgotten line: the forlorn Beeching platform of Abbot's Isle, the hang of its roof with scalloped tiles, like a huge withered leaf. They came slowly along the platform of the Back Settlement where Davey stood out on the very edge, like a fisherman in a glistening sou'wester, wordlessly exchanging the token with Simon who leaned from the window of the cab door behind Penalty's shoulders.

In the heavy rain the train crossed the bog meadows along the raised embankments beyond the Back Settlement; the fields were in puddles reflecting some street lights as if the council houses at Jericho Road were marooned in a sequence of lagoons or rice paddies. Both their eyes only caught the stone edges of the bridge carrying the Black Stank Road out west. Down at the end of the two long straights was the gated driveway to Broken Moan; Simon put his face against the vibrating glass of his side window and looked over at the passing outline of Varie's childhood shelter. The big house was lightless up ahead.

Below the Creach mountain on the horseshoe curve, the house lights of the garage and small clachan below had all been extinguished. As the train carried itself around the curve, the engine swayed woozily from side to side. Simon reached down his fingers between his legs to the *Horn Valve* lever; he eased it up letting out a single, brief and low honk.

'Why you aye doing that here, man? You'll wake the deid. You'll have folk complaining.'

'Ach, you never know who's on the track,' Simon lied.

Penalty shook his head.

The goods train was now aimed east, through the gap of the Pass and the loch narrows – the road and the railway squeezed tight together at different elevations; the high pass sides sheer on either bank.

Penalty suddenly yanked the master handle back to *Engine Only* so some air spat in the switch box below. 'Young Fella. Leg's bloody killing me. Take her for a wee bit.'

Simon jumped up. The deadman's pedal had been disconnected by placing the master into neutral, so he took Penalty's arm and briefly helped him across as the train ran – driverless – into the black ahead. In one hop the older man was at the vacated seat so Simon jumped into the driver's position and leaned ahead, frowning, shoving the master into *Forward* and putting his feet hard down on the metal pedal. The seat was too low for him but he ignored this. 'You all right?'

'Aye aye. Fine, son. The leg's bad the night; knackering me.' Penalty took a few big breaths, then he lit two of his pre-rolled papers and handed one across to Simon who found them far too strong but he took it in his outstretched hand. 'Take it canny now, lad, cause this rain's filthy – keep her at thirty-five all the way to Nine Mile.'

The Pass proper had closed about them; out in blacknesses around were invisible walls of high crags, embedded rocks the size of houses and waterfalls right above – on either side of the loch's profundity. Often on the far shoreline in daylight were the crumpled, fleecy bulks of dead ewes and naive lambs who had tumbled the heights in the darkness, carcasses reducing to withered grey bags.

In the rain, the steep burns were plush and tightened, racing through culverts beneath the railway track in whiteness.

Their train passed onwards along the uneven edge of the disused Falls Platform; the Turbines Bar and the main Creach power station were below.

The Pass had fully opened out but rousty gusts of wind came straight in, strapping raindrops across the front of the engine. The wiper blades smeared aside the unctions from the glass. Simon sat himself forward in the driver's seat, moving his nose further from then closer to the windscreen, to time his opportunistic gaze. They passed where their idling exhausts came briefly level with the stained-glass window of the chapel at the uphill burial ground. The coffins in the moss and roots were quaked vigorously nine times a day by each passing train. There must have only been one second of bafflement and by then it was too late.

Like some ghostly marauder, the woman stood tall and weirdly angled in the middle of the railway track ahead, resigned to receive the force of the train, hands held up, raised to her face – and yet the glimpse of her was beatific, lit by the weak light from the route indicator on the front of the engine, combined with sudden head-lights leaking up from some halted late vehicle down on the road below. Her pale, pale face rushed closer.

A click alone came from Simon's throat – with his whole arm he pushed the vacuum brake forwards to *Emergency* and the air whooshed madly; his fingers never even reached the *Horn Valve* lever. He sensed Penalty suddenly look up but even he had no time to exclaim.

There was an impact with the woman's flesh, sickeningly loud down by the deadman's pedal – Simon felt the thump travel up into his legs and something new came up against the windscreen, like liquid chocolate, waves of it, hitting out from darkness, washing up the black glass then moved aside by the wiper blade for a second before slithering down and recoating. Blood.

'Christ.' Penalty had jabbed out an arm to steady himself as the engine began to shudder and to yaw; from the wheels and undersides came the strangest rattling and some heavy thing thumped high up against the side of the cab.

The blood was again swept clear from the window in the wiper segment but the rest of the glass was fully plastered.

'We're off the road. You've gone and put us off the fucking road, ya silly young bastard.'

Simon shouted, 'We hit a woman.'

'What? Oh Christ.' Penalty's despairing voice frightened Simon. The train had almost completely stopped, but the mysterious thumps and the grindings continued in beneath.

As they halted, Simon's windscreen pushed in against something that could not possibly have been there: twigs and leaves of a silver birch tree were wiping and pressing through that gore of windscreen, directly in front of him. Then, as if moved by human hands outside, the tree slid aside and was gone. Simon frowned.

'Wait up, man. Wait.' Penalty switched on the inside cab lights and both men blinked their eyes in adjustment. He grabbed Simon's metal torch off the sill in front of him then slammed back his side window. Wet muck immediately dripped in onto the arm of Penalty's jacket. He leaned out, shining the torch down and backwards along the stopped train. 'Aww, fuck sake.'

Simon had taken the other torch off his sill and he jumped to the loch-side door behind Penalty. He pulled down the window and directed his light below onto the track.

Below them, through whitened spots of rain, a dark river was shooting directly out from underneath their locomotive as if from a dam sluice gate – and in that racing gush they could distinguish the swift whip of broken and leafy branches tearing free from the pressurised gap beneath the loco then taking off, the water cascading outwards, flailing through trees then pouring downward onto the main road below. The rattling sounds were the stone ballast which supported and cushioned the track being sieved out by the water's force, rattling crazily on the undersides of the fuel and water tanks before the stones were catapulted away in long shots with other debris: mud, long snarled tree roots and unidentifiable clods.

'It's a landslide. Fucking stream has burst its banks up above. It's taking the track from under us.' Penalty stated it in a grim, certain voice.

'What'll we do?'

'Back up? But if it takes too much from under us, we'll be over and the whole train with us, down onto the main road and into that fucking loch. We'll be down there ourselves, in sunken Badan.'

'I hit a woman. Tall white woman with her arms up at her face.'

Penalty looked at him and ripped a single laugh. 'Daft bugger. That was the marble statue of the Virgin Mary from the cemetery up the hill. The whole land top has went and slid down over the track.'

There was a falling, crunching lurch and the nose of the loco dipped a few inches.

'Hang on to something, boy.'

But then the locomotive maintained its position.

'Thought that was us dead,' Simon said.

'Aye. It's going to roll over. You need to get out.'

Simon stepped and opened the driver's side window, leaning out with the torch; perhaps he half thought of jumping. 27006 was functioning as a huge barrier to a downhill flood and flotsam was being crammed against its sides. A swirl of mucky water – way above six feet in depth – had built up below the exit ladder from their cab before the water shallowed but poured out round in front of the engine. Along the locomotive flanks, an entire sapling was afloat, spinning round there in a whirlpool, its leaves dripping as it shuddered.

Simon couldn't see how far along and towards the rear of the train this deep torrent was affecting. He tugged his head in and pulled the vacuum brake lever back to *Off*. The gauge needle did lift towards 21 in. and the air brakes were climbing to 70 lb/sq. in. – as they should, so the brake pipe was still intact.

Penalty shook his head. 'Makes no difference even if the brake pipe's no busted, son. Traction motors won't work with the water that height above the rails and we might be off the road anyway. You can't reverse us back. Shut her down, kill some of the electric.'

They looked at each other. Simon nodded and began to think of his father's comrades, upside down in their armoured car – being slowly drowned. He pushed the *Engine Stop* button and both engines died out, the noise replaced by the uncontrollable sounds of the water. 'Let's get the fuck out of here, John. Right now,' and he shoved the brake back, *Full On* again.

'Aye. But there's no ways I can get down at the back and up into yon next engine. No way. That water'll just take me away. You'll need to leave us here.'

'No fucking way. Get on my back.'

With the engine-room lights on, his torch hooked on his knuckles and old Penalty's arms around him, Simon stooped and carried him on his back straight through the engine room on the gangway. The warm claustrophobia in there made Simon afraid for the first time. He did not want the locomotive to tip and roll over down into the loch with them in there – among the last sparks of electrics and the cooling sheets of hot engine metal as they sunk down to the drowned village of Varie's youth. The watch-like mechanism of the coil voltage regulator flashed at them behind its glass and Penalty's knees impacted on the narrow bulkheads; Simon could feel the man wince but he shuffled his way onward.

Simon turned the latch and kicked the engine-room door inward to the back cab, turned himself round and slid Penalty down off his back like a sack of coal onto the rear-facing driver's seat. Penalty sat up there, a child in its feeding chair and Simon switched on the cab lights.

Breck was behind them – across and through the glass wind-screens – in the next lit-up cab of the second engine. Their guard looked alarmed, wide-eyed, and he shrugged his shoulders. Simon opened the secondman's window and leaned out while Breck went to the corresponding window in his cab. They both had to shout over the rushing sound of the water between the locos below.

'Fuck sake,' Breck bawled across. 'I came out my seat. Are yous off the road?'

'The whole thing's going to go. Away back.'

'What?'

Simon shouted again, 'The whole thing could go, Paul; get yourself off the engine and away from the whole train – get out the back cab.'

'I'll fucking drown, man. I cannie swim.'

'Can you get out at the other end?'

'It's about knee-high. What about John? How'll we get him out?'

Simon called to Breck, 'Smash out your driver's window. Use your torch and I'll get this one.'

Simon raised his metal torch and smacked it onto the middle of the secondman's windscreen. It was strengthened safety glass with defroster filaments through it and did not break easy, but with rapid, continual blows he developed a pained distortion and finally a small hole until a crack ran along to the rubber sealant. Then Simon sat back in the secondman's seat, retracted both of his knees up under his chin and booted the windscreen with both soles of his brogues very hard, again and again. Each time the force of impact against the stubborn glass travelled up through Simon's legs; it tried to swing the swivel chair aside to the left or to the right. A last kick pushed the bent glass outward and tipped it away where it hung down out of sight. From below, the vast sound of the flood water became very vivid, powerfully gushing across the connecting screw coupling, jumper cables and the brake pipe down between the two locomotives. Simon broke away the shattered cubes of glass at the edges with his hand.

Breck had made similar progress busting out his window. He used the end of the wooden shaft of his green flag to penetrate until he could shove the shattered glass fully outwards with his palms and it fell away in one piece; Simon noted Breck had sensibly donned his coupling gloves.

Simon helped poor wincing Penalty across the cab and lifted him up to sit side-saddle on the desk edge, then Simon squeezed past his driver and climbed out of the glassless window space. His shoulder caught on the stowed wiper blade and he shoved it aside aggressively, bending the drive spar. There was a fitted handrail outside, just below the window, and the small footplate below by the Oleo hydraulic buffer, so he was able to lower both his brogues down onto that plate and stand outside there. Light flashed on the mucky water only inches beneath, gushing through, between both engines.

Penalty shouted, 'Christ sake, careful, Young Fella. Fall down there and you're away.'

'Aye, c'mon out.'

Old Penalty's head and shoulders came forward, through the broken window, propelling himself on his elbows, grimacing as if he was crawling up some escape tunnel. His hat fell off and away down into the torrent, showing his bald head. They encouraged him on and Simon turned, bending across to the handrail on 27007, forming a bridge so Penalty crawled on out and across his shoulders. Simon stared down at the bucking, frothing slime, moving just below the buffers. Breck leaned forward from his broken window, took hold of Penalty's arms, then quite easily – in one heave – pulled, sliding Penalty's bulk over, across Simon's bent shoulders until only the old man's legs still stuck out the rearmost loco. Simon straightened and unfortunately – as Penalty's bad leg and foot bounced in over the lip of the broken window – his black shoe jumped off his left foot; Simon grabbed for the shoe but it fell down, vanishing immediately into the rush of water below.

Simon stepped across then shimmied up and into that back locomotive as well. Then he continued to piggyback Penalty on through the second engine room to the very back cab of the rear engine.

Simon went down first. The muddy water felt strange around the legs of his trousers, instantly making the fabric heavy and slow-moving. The surface came up to above his knees but sometimes a higher wash came down from the hillside behind, lifting the cold water and adhering fabric onto his thighs.

The noise of the water washing through and under the locomotive was much louder down at ground level. Holding the handrails, Penalty came hopping down the ladder from the cab with surprising ease, one step at a time, putting all his weight on his good leg and gripping tight. Simon grabbed him from behind and lowered him down into the water.

Penalty said, 'Jeez, cold for a swim.' Penalty got on Simon's back and slowly he was carried away along the track beside the empty oil tanks and goods wagons then into the darkness towards the rear. Breck followed up behind, swinging his legs through the water and holding both torches up above his head to illuminate their way forward. Along by the oil tanks, the water dropped to ankle level and by the last van they were actually walking on the cinders and grush of a water-free trackside.

A train thoughtlessly follows the track before it in seemingly faithful obedience. To all three railwaymen it was strangely neglectful to leave their unmanned train behind them, abandoned on an active running track.

Simon almost collapsed crossing the rails but they finally came to the ramp of the old Falls Platform, and once up on it, he lowered Penalty who simply sank down to slump on his arse on the disused platform surface, his legs and arms out, leaning back on his palms like an exhausted sportsman. Penalty gasped, 'Lost my fucking shoe and I'd just had it reheeled.' In moments he had his baccy tin out and began rolling by torchlight, the hem of his jacket below the pocket was shite brown. Simon's trousers were caked in this same muck.

'Need to get down there to Turbines Bar and phone the police, eh?' Breck said. He was breathing heavily.

'That road must be well blocked too.'

'I see car headlights down there. Someone's been stopped by it.'

Penalty said, 'You need to get folk in cars clear. Case that train comes down on top of them. Leave me and both of yous get away on down the path there and get to a telephone. Walker and the track walkers have a sort of path down there to get a sly pint.'

Breck stood. 'Young Fella, you stay with John. I'll leave this torch. Thank fuck we've a young fella like you, son. There's nae way one of us could've got you out of there, John.'

'That's right enough. Mind yourself, Paul,' Penalty shouted at Breck's back as the man swished off through the brush below the platform edge.

They both listened to Breck descending away through the wet bushes then Simon spoke. 'See, with the screw coupling off, if the front engine fell it would just go on its own. It would tear out the bags and the jumpers but it wouldn't pull the rest of the train with it.' He said it almost excitedly.

'That's no your problem.'

'Aye. But if I could just get the screw coupling off from between the two engines, John?'

'That's a fucking daft idea. I'll no allow it. I'm your driver.'

'The water level was dropping.'

'You need a rope to tie yourself to something and we've none, and even if we did, you might as well just hang yourself with it.'

'Just let me walk up and take a look. If it's too high I'll quit.' Simon stood.

In a pained voice Penalty said, 'Don't, son. Don't you dare. I've told you. It's really dangerous. It's deadly and the train could go at any moment. There's nae ballast support under it. You felt it shift fine same way I did.'

'I'll keep this side of the train, John.' Simon took the torch and began walking back, leaving Penalty sat alone in the darkness.

'Don't, son,' he yelled in anger. 'You don't have to try and be all like your faither.'

Simon called, 'Just stay there.'

'Where the fuck would I go, ya daftie?' Penalty shouted. 'Be careful. I'm no away to tell your faither you were drowned, I tell you that. Don't expect that of me.'

Simon stepped back up the track towards the trembling red of the paraffin tail lamp which was clipped onto the back of the rearmost van. He moved freely without Penalty's bulk on his back and shone the single torch beam ahead, up the side of the train; the steep and wooded land was to his left and he moved cautiously along the narrow side of the wagons.

The rushing of the water was ahead and getting louder. As he passed the end of the rear loco, he was surprised to realise that while the water level was not as high as when they first struck the landslide, it had grown higher in the minutes since they made their escape. The fact that the water level was fluctuating moodily according to the strange burst up the hill made him uneasy. He aimed his torch ahead and stepped deeper into the water. His feet could feel the deep gaps between the wooden sleepers – like hollowed teeth – where all the stone ballast had already been completely sucked out.

A dislodged and floating whin bush still showing its yellow flowers was vibrating against the top locomotive. Water still was sweeping steadily down the hillside but not fiercely, collecting and then powering through the gap between the two engines.

In at the top of the second engine, the greater depth of cold water seeped in around his groin and he clenched his teeth. He keeked around the corner between the two locomotives and shone the torch in there. He could hear the waterfall from the torrent falling off the drop on the far trackside.

The coupling, brake pipes and jumper cables were festooned with tree twigs and green bracken stalks, the debris bound like wattle around anything it could wrap onto.

Simon very gingerly stepped forward and felt ahead with his submerged foot. It was as Penalty said. Where there should have been ballast under the track, it had all been excavated out by the torrent and there was just sunken depth – maybe to the naked rock – the track only held in place by the weight of the train upon it.

He tore away some weeds and bracken from the main jumper cable then he ducked underneath it, his face coming close to the surface. The battery isolation switches hadn't been thrown in either engine so he thought about the possibility of electrocution from the jumpers, but found he could reach over the engine control and main reservoir pipes to grab the metal coupling. To create slack he wound the screw bar round four times, dipping his chin near the surface to complete each revolution, then he balanced his brogues, took the chain in both hands and lifted – but his ungloved hand slipped, the torch hooked upon his thumb bounced once, slid off and was away into the water.

'Damn and shit it.'

Everything darkened around him but there was still some shadowy illumination from the switched-on lights in the two driving cabs above with their busted-out windows. He repositioned, balancing his submerged feet, craned his two arms in, gritted his teeth and lifted the coupling; it came free off the hook and fell down with a weirdly cushioned drop – slowed by the gush of muddy water.

Simon turned aside and as he quickly made to step over the jumper cable and escape, he felt a heave upward in the water level. A current swirled around him and he grabbed onto the jumper. Something very large and heavy hit the cab almost beside him. Intact and frighteningly clean, a varnished coffin was there, floating along against the side of the locomotive, seeking its gaunt passage. It creaked against the metal then the current sucked it slowly in among the trapped trees at the loco side.

331

Simon's eyes glanced higher up. Another coffin was coming down the torrent, trembling slightly as if in excitement, like a downhill toboggan. It hit the locomotive straight on but this time the older, streaked wooden side, wet earth still clinging there, splintered open and the invisible interior flooded – this coffin sank under the black surface very quickly.

Simon stepped over the jumper cable, but his foot missed the sleeper on the far side, his leg plunged deeper, then face first he was beneath the surface.

Unspeakable elements touched him down there until his mouth came free. He was stood in water now up to his chest and he lunged forward in panic. Two bright and demonic eyes faced him, the corneas glowing with a yellowy-green tinge. Simon let out a shout and punched a fist ahead. The satyr-like head of a drowned sheep vibrated at him then impacted his shoulder. He grabbed the wet fleece with both arms and swung the beast away from him, using it to force himself into shallower water, amazed at its sodden weight. He pushed ahead, up the side of the second engine as the water level fell away.

Beyond the wagon sides he flicked his filled, sodden sleeves downward and spat, crossing to the other side of the track. He walked along in the torchless dark but something shone bright, like a huge ostrich egg in the track mud. He had to crouch and lift it free with both hands where he held it in against his sodden groin until he approached the Falls Platform.

'All right, son? Are you all right?'

'Aye. Got the screw coupling off but I'm drooked. My head went right under. You wouldn't believe it, John. Fucking coffins floating down the hill from that graveyard. A dead sheep. It's like Halloween gone wrong up there. Bloody ghost train.' Simon shed the burden from his hands onto the platform surface where it plonked and sunk in the grit.

It was the severed marble head of the Virgin Mary, all white, her cheeks smeared in watery grime.

Penalty looked at the marble face and blew out smoke. 'Give us a kiss, love.'

There was a fundamental moaning sound. Both of them turned as the wet trees along the bank made a vast whooshing sound.

They saw the sad, yellow face of 27006 unnaturally canting sideways, the cab windows still illuminated – the interior lights faithfully lit; the front locomotive kept tipping on its own then slid sideways, gathering a catastrophic momentum down the steep embankment. It hit the tarmac road below with a sound they had never heard before, which echoed with calamity far across the New Loch to the Concession Lands and then back up the three miles of the dark Pass, to Broken Moan where it awoke the masters and the servants alike.

Saturday 15 June 1974

The National Union of Railwaymen branch meetings took place in the flat-roofed community hall in behind the Port cathedral and this is where the emergency meeting took place.

NUR meetings weren't usually well attended – often the committee of seven outnumbered the ordinary members – but when Simon parked his motorbike round the side and went in through the front doors with his helmet under his arm, the hall was completely stowed out with railway employees. Many folk were standing since there weren't enough seats, but not just that – every head in the place turned at once towards Simon. Through the cigarette smoke, some cheers went off.

People who had never been at an NUR meeting were there. Even conciliation grades who had a separate clerks union were in attendance. Though he wasn't NUR, Hannan himself was leaning against the back wall with the only other two ASLEF members: Lawless and Coll. The three of them usually held their own secretive, vaguely Masonic meetings in the County – if at all. Hannan returned written minutes to Central Office which were largely fictitious, verging on imaginative.

Hannan shouted and pointed. 'Here he is, everybody. It's the railway wrecker himself. God bless this man; blew up the railway single-handed.'

A few people cheered.

Young Colin the guard stood close to Simon and he shouted across, 'Saw your name in the paper. You'll need to autograph it for me.'

Simon flicked him a smile and nodded. It was true. Simon's name had been mentioned – in heroic terms – on the front page of the *Port Star.* Simon wished he'd left his helmet on. A few lone hands clapped and gradually a small but significant hive of applause built up for him then died out. Others just laughed.

English Elliot's voice came from down front, where NUR committee members sat behind the row of tables which had been pulled together. 'This lad, Brother Crimmons here, is a bloody hero. Pulled Brother Penalty to safety.'

Boney the clerk said, 'He is a hero. If you're going to tell us we're getting six months idle on full pay. If we're getting paid off, he's not.' He was only half joking.

People laughed.

English Elliot sounded quite annoyed and pointed. 'Excuse me there. Doesn't matter who was driving the train, that track was blocked and it could have happened to any of us. Nothing could be done, and under the circumstances, young Brother Crimmons did wonderfully.'

Simon put up his hand as he would have back at school. The cramped room went silent. He had never spoken in public before apart from in English class. 'Um, I didn't pull him to safety, Paul Breck, Brother Breck pulled him. John just slid across my back.'

All heads turned to Paul Breck who was seated over on the far left. 'Aye, that's right enough, but it was the Young Fella's bright spark to smash out the windows to get John out between the engines. And it was him went back in all that water to uncouple the top engine or the whole train would be down there on the road.'

Rudolf stood. Shakily. 'Can I ask committee a question? John lost one of his shoes and his hat. That hat's railway property but the shoe was his own. Can he claim it back, cause I lost a shoe once and I don't even know where?'

A big laugh went up, the committee touched cigarettes to their line of ashtrays and diligently ignored the question. Wee Ian went, 'You'll need to ask that when last month's minutes have been read.'

'Brother Penalty would tell you how well the boy done if he was here.'

'Where is John?'

'Brother Penalty's absent the day and sends his apologies. He's a wee bit shocked and at home the day. We'll enter that in the new minutes.'

A voice shouted from the side, 'Yous mean he doesn't know whether to go on the sick or not, till he hears if we're all getting kept on full pay?'

People booed the comment.

Hannan shouted – his voice dominating everything as usual, 'Folks, we cannie accuse the Young Fella of doing an inside job for his faither to help the lorry empire, cause he's went and bollixed the main road as well. Nice one, son.'

Now the laughter was louder than ever.

Simon smiled. He noted that although no trains were running into or from the Port, every person except him was now dressed in uniform, including some figures in mothballed blazers who never wore them – even Walker the track walker and Rudolf had brushed down and donned the full garb. The concern about continuing to be paid had brought out a sudden new pride for railway dress regulations and sartorial appearance.

Wee Ian – who was Branch Chairman – shot up from his seat behind the front table, though that didn't make too much difference. He called out, 'Hoi. Quiet it all down now. Brothers. Sisters too. Please. Order!' Ian turned his head and frowned down at Musty the signalman. 'We don't ever get Sisters here. Isn't that something?'

Isobel the Ticket was stood beside Diesel Mary, the station and carriage cleaner. Isobel called, 'Away and don't be calling us your sisters, we don't even look similar.'

'And if yous are all so bloody brotherly, how about a seat for me and Isobel?'

'Aye, boys,' Walker shouted. 'Shift your arses for the bonny Sisters,' and his dog barked with excitement.

'Does the dug get a branch vote too?' a clerk shouted.

'Away. They're no NUR. These seats is reserved for NUR members only.'

'Yous should take a vote on that, Ian. First point of order for the day. Are these seats for NUR members only?' Hannan looked at his wristwatch. 'We should be out of here by nightfall at this rate.'

One of the clerks called, 'Put the Red Hannan in charge.'

'I second that motion,' Hannan shouted.

Wee Ian squeaked, 'This meeting's no called to order yet. We've got everyone but the bloody Salvation Army in here the day. I must say, Brothers and Sisters, that I wish meetings were this well attended every month.'

This got a lone, pious nod of agreement along the committee.

Hannan shouted, 'Oh, but there is some of the Sally Army in here, Ian,' and he pretended to play a slide trombone, making a loud flatulent sound.

Most folk laughed, even some of the committee smiled, but the female clerks tutted.

Coll said, 'Aye. Where *are* the bogs round here?'

Hannan shouted, 'Through there. Lincoln's cooried down in one, listening.'

This got the biggest laugh yet.

Wee Ian yelped, 'This's no protocol at all. Not protocol. Brothers. ASLEF Brothers, yous're no even in this union. Clerical grades too. You all know fine yous shouldn't be in here. Jeezo.' Everyone saw wee Ian's head jerk to observe someone at the back of the hall and other heads turned. 'Stronach.' Wee Ian spoke forcefully. 'You're no even on the railway any more, man. You've retired. What are you *doing* here?'

The Stronach called out, 'I take an interest. And I've nothing on the day.'

'Give us a tune,' someone shouted.

Wee Ian turned to the Branch Secretary, Guard Thomson. 'Don't be writing this down, Tommy. Don't write it down.'

Thomson held up his hands. 'I wouldn't have enough paper. Besides, what note was that you blew; just for the sake of keeping accurate minutes, Hannan? Was that a B flat, Stronach?'

People laughed.

Hannan shouted, 'Just tell us all the facts before you call to order and we're off to the County bar.'

Folk laughed but people also called out, 'Aye. Tell us the facts.'

'Aye. How long's the railway shutting down for? What's the engineers say?'

'Is it true the railway could close down for ever?'

'That's just a daft rumour about the town. There's a legal obligation to keep the railway open.'

'What's happening with pay?'

Wee Ian squeaked, 'Quiet. Quiet please. Well.' He looked around. 'Look, folks, we really can't have this.'

'How no?'

'This isn't a public meeting. Is there anyone from the *Star* here as well – nae doubt? We can't have members of the public in here. Next thing there'll be bloody Shutters Stuart from the paper in here taking his silly photies.'

'Who cares? Everyone needs to know, Ian. And we're all going to know soon enough.'

Big Ian the driver was down the front. 'Bugger the railway. When'll the bloody main road be open? I've got prawns and lobsters needing sent to Glasgow.'

Everyone laughed.

'Okey-doke, right. Look. I can't talk specifics for those of yous in other unions, but I'll go so far as to say, I know this'll apply all round.'

'What about the conciliation grades? Are we's getting kept on pay?' It was Gemmell talking.

A female clerk voice went, 'Och, of all the people to be fussing; you've been on the sick. You should be the last one asking.'

Gemmell whipped his head round to the speaker. 'Aye, so? So? I've a doctor's line.'

Hannan shouted, 'Aye. Spend at least eight hour a day in the fucking pub.'

People laughed but the female clerk tutted again. 'The language in here. I'll no be back.'

Wee Ian shouted, 'All righty, all right. Settle down and I'll speak.' It grew quiet.

'Big Ian does have a point. This town can't take being cut off by road and rail and with tourist season just getting on the go. According to the police, despite the engine come down on it, the road is basically sound and they can set up traffic lights even before the engine is hauled away.'

Tosh shouted, 'They should tip the engine into the loch; 006 always was a heap of scrap anyway.'

Some of the other engine drivers laughed.

Hannan shouted, 'Right. First off, we should estimate the engine's

338

scrap value and divvy it all up atween us the now, eh?' He reached into his railway trouser pocket and he pulled a handful of coins out which he pretended to share with his ASLEF Brothers.

Folk laughed.

Wee Ian announced, 'Okay. I can only speak with regard to specifics on behalf of members. But generally.' Wee Ian put on his reading glasses and sometimes glanced down at written notes on the table below him. 'Eh, just past Falls Platform about three hundred feet above the line, two deep streams overflowed and joined together. It was exceptional rainfall. The downhill torrent destroyed the top access road to the cemetery and the mass of water caused landslip. The Chief Engineer from Glasgow says the railway embanking seems secure, but they'll have to shore it up on supporting walls to be sure, then replace whole track sections. However, seventy yards further down from this incident, two culverts have been torn out and the whole three spans of Bridge 98 – which is, ah, a low bridge of original stone construction – are destroyed.'

Murmurs began.

Wee Ian looked up from his notes. 'So it's just as well the landslip stopped the train where it did, or the Brothers would have hit the missing bridge. Now, young Brother Crimmons here uncoupled the front locomotive without regard to his own safety – and a statement about his action will be going in the minutes to Central Office. Tosh, Brother Toshack, got the other engine up on the line started last night and the engineers allowed him to reverse her up to the Back Settlement. So we have one operating locomotive now, downside of the occurrence. The other locomotive, as you'll know from the photo on the front of the *Star*, is rested on its side on the main road, blocking it. She's writ off. Police are undertaking an operation but think they can get the road opened tomorrow or the next day, even before the engine gets low-loaded away. Just divert traffic round it.'

Breck said, 'See if you can get John's tea flask out of it. He was saying the wife is asking and she's right annoyed he's gone and lost it.'

Folk chuckled but others sheeshed him.

Wee Ian looked down at his papers. 'Now, the Chief Engineer

from Glasgow makes an estimate of two to three months the line will need to be closed for repair.'

A hubbub arose.

'That means four to five month,' Walker told them all. 'Four to five month, I'm telling yous. Permanent Way never done a job to time in their lives.'

'So the proposal is to keep the station itself open as normal. Lincoln thought about running a shuttle train service from here to the Back Settlement, but it's been decided instead to run trains from Glasgow to Nine Mile House then from Nine Mile to here and back by bus.'

'Hurray.'

Hannan shouted out, 'What crews'll operate the trains up to Nine Mile?'

Ian looked over at him and smiled. 'Glasgow crews only of course.'

Hannan punched his fist into his palm. 'Yes! Nay trains to drive and the World Cup's on.'

'But we've all got our jobs?'

'Officially I can only speak for my members but aye. The long and the short of it is that yous are expected to report for duty as normal though it's looking like a very easy summer for all of us on full pay.'

Folk clapped and a cheer roared up.

'The Permanent Way, huh? More like it'll be like a permanent holiday,' Killan announced. 'Talk about a three-day week, we's train men are on a no-day week.'

Clarky, another of the Port signalmen, told Killan, 'Aye. Just like you and the drivers always have been for bloody years, with them spare shifts of yours.'

'Aye, that's right enough,' Gemmell added.

Ian went on. 'All the conciliation grades will operate a normal shift system.'

Now there were boos.

'Tickets will still be sold for the bus and train link as normal. Those of you in the parcel office, parcels will come and go by road to the parcels office. Freight, oil and coal will need to come up by road. National Carriers should be involved in the replacement freight services.' Ian looked over at Simon. 'And there might be some private work for road haulage put out to tender. You can tell your father.'

Everyone laughed and looked at Simon.

Hannan clapped his hands and shouted, 'Boy oh boy, the Young Fella will be getting extra servings of his pudding the night, eh, folks?'

Everyone laughed.

'Drivers and guards and signalmen are to turn up as per shift.'

'That'll be right.' Gemmell shook his head. 'Signalmen and nae trains.'

'But that's Irish. There's nothing for us to drive. What's the point in us coming to work?' Hannan pointed out.

'We've all been wondering that for years,' Big Ian shouted from down front.

Wee Ian said, 'Aye, but eventually there'll be engineering trains operating from this side of the occurrence, with the loco.'

Isobel shouted, 'That'll no keep these drivers out of mischief.'

Hannan looked around. 'Yous're right. We's should all be sent to Tenerife on account of the shock.'

Wee Ian coughed and said, 'And it's been suggested the station building be repainted during the shutdown.'

Folk laughed cynically.

'Aye. And Lincoln'll be expecting us drivers and guards to do it.'

'So we should,' said Hannan. 'Paint it red. Aye wanted to see Lawless on the top of a ladder.'

There was a gabble of gladsome talk and some people even started moving towards the door – even NUR members.

Wee Ian shouted, 'Hoi. Hoi. We've to call the proper meeting to order now.'

'Och, what's the point of that, Ian? The railway's went on holiday and so have we.'

'What's the police operation?' someone asked.

'What?'

'Yous said there was a police operation.'

'Did yous no hear about that?'

The congested movement towards the exit door now stopped in a synchronised manner; people held back to listen.

Wee Ian told them, 'The flood water came down through the old

Catholic graveyard and across that wee top road. Water came right through the resting chapel there, blew out every piece of stained glass, knocked down the gravestones, but then all the topsoil slipped away down the hillside, coffins started popping up here and there and floating down the hill. Some were very old and were busting open. Eh, part of a skeleton was found hanging on a tree branch.'

'I thought I hadn't seen McGarry about,' Hannan shouted.

A lot of people hooted.

'And some human skulls were found down on the road.'

'That's just the locals.'

'Good God,' said Isobel the Ticket and she crossed herself.

'Aye. A few coffins have been swept right out into the New Loch. One of them apparently,' Ian coughed, 'Is quite, current. There was a very recent interment – last Wednesday in fact – and the police are concerned there could be a body or a coffin washed up on the shores, so it's important for them to scour the loch and be able to identify it. The coastguard have a dinghy out on the loch.'

'Jings. He'll just be away down to the drowned village for a last pint,' Lawless called.

Hannan laughed but Isobel – a stickler for midnight Mass – gave Lawless a turbulent scowl.

'And that reminds me,' said Wee Ian. 'Young Simon. Ah, Brother Crimmons. We've had a request for the return of church property.'

Hannan laughed. 'Oh, that's brilliant. The Young Fella took home the heid off of the Virgin Mary.'

Young Colin the guard chanted, 'Rangers, Rangers, Rangers.'

'Shut it, you idiot.'

Simon shrugged. 'It all smashed to bits when we hit it. I did take the head bit home, as a sort of good-luck souvenir. Her nose has broke off.'

'You been practising kissing it?' Rudolf shouted.

Folk laughed.

'Och, that's just terrible talk.' Isobel the Ticket shook her head.

'Shame you didn't get her arse and give the lassie a good spanking for wandering about on the railway at night.' Hannan looked directly at Isobel.

Simon said, 'I'll bring it in.'

'Dinna get it mixed up with one of the skulls or you'll give the Father a heart attack.'

'Will yous just shut it for once?'

'Well, don't bring it to us in the station for God's sake. Take it to the cathedral here.' Wee Ian nodded his head.

'Are the church going to stick her all back together again?'

'Aye. Like Humpty-Dumpty.' Then in a quieter voice Hannan said, 'They should have a go at John Penalty too.'

'Right then. Hoi. I'm calling our meeting to order.'

'Ach, leave it, man.'

'Aye. What's the rush now?'

'We'll do it in a few month.' There was another mass squeeze towards the doors and this time most folk exited through them. Soon there were just the hardcore regulars left for the NUR meeting. The committee outnumbered them.

Wee Ian was left shaking his head, staring down at his notes.

Simon himself couldn't be bothered sitting through another round of last month's business and the True Account, so he snuck away with all the others.

Outside the hall, Hannan stepped straight over to Simon, talking quickly. 'What did I tell yous, eh? Just as if I'd blown up one of the bridges myself. Bloody good luck, eh? It's like communism has happened and we're living in paradise now, boys. And the World Cup too. Good job the other night, son, by the way. You're a hero. Was Penalty okay, eh? I bet he was going off his rocker. And I'd have paid good money to see the wee barrel getting shoved from one cab to another through the bloody windscreen.'

Lawless chuckled. 'It would be like *It's a Knockout.*'

Simon frowned. 'Aye, but old John, y'know, he's suffering a bit.'

'Aye.' Hannan shrugged then looked a bit uncomfortable. 'What are you up to yourself?'

Simon smiled. 'Looks like the summer of love, eh?'

'Aye. For you, you lucky young bastard. And that wee Nicola Caine.'

'I'm no going with her any more.'

'Are you no going with Caine's wee lassie? How no?'

'Seeing someone else.'

343

'Are you now? Take nae prisoners you, eh? Randy big bastard.'

'Who's that you're stepping out with now?' Lawless asked.

'It isnie Caine's older lassie, the sister, is it?'

'No,' Simon replied sharply.

'Keep it in the family?' Hannan laughed and turned to Lawless.

Lawless went, 'Oh, her, the nurse? Oooo. Ever seen her come in the Modern Lounge on a Saturday night, man? Fuck me, if I was twenty year younger.'

'Don't you mean thirty, ya old cunt? You enjoy yourself, Young Fella. You no coming to the pub the now and we'll get you in the ASLEF, 'stead of that circus in there?'

'Nah.' Simon asked, 'What are we all going to do for the next months?'

'Fuck all, boy. Enjoy it.'

'Stick your head in the County some day for the games,' said Lawless.

'Aye, I will.'

Lawless and Hannan moved away. But then Hannan walked back to Simon. He turned his head to Lawless and he gave him a look. Hannan put his arm around Simon's shoulder. 'Look, son, I might as well say. We don't want you getting a fright.'

'What?'

'It's John.'

'What about him?'

'He's no keeping so well, son. Doctors, you know. The old sawbones have been at him again, saying it's no looking so good.'

'What's wrong? His leg?'

'It's no just his leg. He's no a well man, son. He's got other ailments too. The stomach. Aye. He's got an ailment. I don't want you getting a fright. I'm no going to say it wasnie worth your while getting him out the engine the other night but it's not at all looking like he's got long, the crabbit auld bugger. Yous know we're all secretly fond of him. Fond as hell, son. He was talking to me a few weeks ago. He invited me up the house to talk about it. He's the cancer, son. In his belly and in his guts and all the bloody way through him.'

Simon frowned, he felt outraged tears coming, but also he felt possessive about John Penalty. He was hurt that John had confided

344

in Hannan of all people before himself. It made him feel like a child unworthy of such knowledge and also as if he was still not part of their community. He heard a crack in his voice. 'He never says nothing to me and he's my driver, man.'

'He'll not be with us much longer. Get me? I don't want it spoiling your summer.'

Simon nodded curtly.

'You take it easy.' Hannan removed his arm from Simon's shoulders and he walked quickly away.

Tuesday 18 June 1974

Simon swayed as if drunk – but he wasn't – across the drive and into the walled garden where his mother toiled, pulling weeds in the middle of the potato rows. She straightened when Simon came across the soil towards her, beyond the strawberries now covered in their green nets where the odd sparrow would get stuck.

'Watch the carrots.'

He looked to his feet, missing the tall feathers of the carrot leaves, then stepping between the bushes of tatties in the lazy beds.

His mother frowned. She was wearing that anorak and had those old PE leggings tucked roughly into her wellies.

'I know fine you're smoking up in your room, Simon Crimmons. I see puffs of smoke appearing from out the gap in the window.'

'Only one or two.'

'Give me one then. Bloody midgies.'

He pulled the pack of Embassy from his bomber jacket with an accompanying box of matches then held out the pack to her.

She grunted, 'I hope you collect the coupons.'

'If I'm finally killed off on the trains next time, you'll find them hid in my old penny box under the bed.'

She smiled. He leaned over but it was a windless eve and simple to light her cigarette and then his own with the same match. They both began smoking.

'Oh gosh,' his mother said. 'That's good.' They made a show of blowing the smoke around them at the midgies.

'How long have you been stopped now, Mum?'

'Since I was expecting with Jeff. It's a bad, bad habit. But I tell you, it was these bliddie midgies that started me.'

'Aye, gardening. It's dangerous for the health.'

'I'll be knocking off soon and we'll have a nice pot of tea. What's the matter?'

He groaned and suddenly he let himself fall to the soil, in a sitting motion. He looked at the lumps of freshly tilled soil beside his track shoe, rich and black earth — it almost looked like a pile of freshly cooked mince.

'Now your jeans will be filthy and that's more washing for me. What's wrong with you? Are the pressures of fame too much?'

Simon chuckled as his mother looked down at him.

'I'm so sorry, Mum.'

'What?'

'The last year. It's been the silly season. You and Dad were right. I never should have left the school.'

'What's the matter? You're a quiet one, but I know when something's wrong.'

'I've ruined my life.'

She laughed. 'You can stop this railway and work with Daddy any time. He's just all bark and no bite. He takes spells. Notions. Besides, has railways not turned into the ideal job? Paid to do nothing?'

Simon blew out air and smoke, looked up at his mother. 'I've gone and got a girl into trouble.'

'Oh for God's sake.'

Days before he had just been playing records, so Jeff came all the way up the stairs and banged on his door. Simon took the chair back out from under the door handle, as if they were in on something together as brothers. Jeff said, 'It's a girl on the phone. I think it's that horse one with the toes.'

Simon smiled. 'Right. Thanks.' Simon took the stairs down fast, turned slightly to the side, angling his shoes round for grip on the carpet; the hall receiver was off the hook, lying flat on its side on the shelf. Jeff was walking up the corridor and Simon paused until he had gone away round the corner. Then he waited again till he heard his wee brother shut the door to the living room.

'Hello.'

'Simon?' Varie was whispering.

His heart sank. She wasn't even certain of recognising his own voice. He said, 'Hiya. Are you back then?' He wondered if she was going to bring up the story about him on the front page of the local newspaper.

'I'm expecting.'

'What?'

She didn't speak for a moment. 'I'm expecting for sure.'

'How? Are you all right?'

She made a noise. 'Oh, sure.'

'How?' He whispered, 'You said you took. You know.' Simon looked up the corridor – he was sure Jeff would be listening; he even frowned, ready for the click of the receiver in the kitchen being softly lifted.

'I was joking.'

'Joking? How can you joke that? Is it even humanly possible? Just one time in one night?'

'We did it more than once, Si.'

'Yes, but that shouldn't matter, it's the time. When you're, what the time in your cycle stuff is.'

'I know I shouldn't have. But you were just there on your motorbike. It was fate. It was meant to happen.'

'I don't believe that, Varie.'

She was annoyed. 'I can't be on –' she dropped her voice to almost nothing to say the two words – '*the pill*. My father would find out.'

'Fuck sake, was that no all a bit silly then?'

'That's right. Go and swear at me. Daddy swore at me too.'

'Aww, naw. Naw. What're we going to do?'

She didn't suggest a thing.

Simon said, 'You told anyone else?'

'Who could I tell except my father? I'm so lonely I cry at night. I couldn't finish my coursework.'

'Oh, Varie. I'll come pick you up on the bike.'

'I can't ride on a motorbike. The way I am. In my state. I might fall off and lose the baby. I'll take the bus. Or your silly train.'

'Take the bus. You haven't been reading the paper about the train, I guess.'

'Si, that's not all.'

'What?'

'It might be a cursed baby. Demonic. Because we broke the salt.'

'Why are you so –? Always. Don't say daft things on top of everything else.'

The only place they could devise to meet was in the town, outside the Marine Hotel which they had got drunk at the year before. Her appearance was the same – maybe even thinner. She refused to go in so they leaned suspiciously on the wall outside, going silent when any hotel guest entered or departed the building. They both looked across the bay, watching the putt-putts annoyingly circle, rarely looking at each other's face. She told how she had been physically sick, retching each morning for a week, and had been lingering in Edinburgh seeing a judgemental doctor twice, to be sure.

She constantly looked close to tears and said she felt worse because she had doubts.

Simon shook his head. 'What is a person who doesn't hesitate about decisions? I say a Nazi. Doubt is a great thing.'

Nobody spoke in the car on the Tuesday following. Simon looked up from the back seat of his father's second-hand Jaguar, towards the railway embankments, across the fields beneath the cliff of Abbot's Isle House, where that bloody rock star supposedly came in the summers. He could see the pale, flesh-coloured chimney pots but all else was mysteriously concealed beneath the treetops.

The car swished under the railway bridge and up onto the clearing. The same route he and Varie had taken on his motorbike that night.

His heart began to pound and he moved his fingers nervously when the car turned to the right into the drive, passing Varie's innocent school shelter, then they headed on down the driveway of white stones.

It was a bright day again and the grass and growth of the meadow where he had lain hidden was now efficiently mowed flat; unlike the wild free mountain heights all around above them, these ordained lands were controlled.

Simon's father spoke to his mother – somehow not including Simon. 'At least the neighbours won't be gossiping, it's too massive to have any.'

His mum's head didn't move. The car tyres frothed on the gravel at the front door and they came to a stop. That rough old Ford Transit van was parked a little further up ahead.

His mother and father climbed out of the car and then Simon did. His polished black shoes sank in the stone chips and became dusty straight away. The many windows of Broken Moan reflected his figure back as if consuming him in some way.

Simon was wearing the blazer from Forsyth's in Edinburgh which had been bought for the wedding of the big cousin almost two years before. The sleeves were too short. He also wore ironed slacks, a blue shirt and a mustard-coloured tie with a big ungainly knot. He saw his image in the ground-floor bow windows, possibly the ones to that long parlour where Bultiude and Coutts had slumbered. Simon recognised what he looked like: some hopelessly implicated peasant torn from the outland, brought to a grand court beyond his minimal sophistication.

Very quickly, Andrew Bultitude appeared in the large porch flanked by slim Corinthian marble columns on either side which supported the roof. He was dressed as usual: tweed jacket with the thin tie. Simon's father walked towards him and held out his hand first. Bultitude took it quite willingly. After all, both men had been having very long phone conversations.

'Albert,' said Bultitude.

Now he was facing Bultitude, Simon's father said in his still-strong Yorkshire accent, 'Bert will do.'

Making it sound like a bad piece of meat in his mouth, Andrew Bultitude tested out the word 'Bert' uneasily.

'This is my wife Agnes.'

Simon's mother was less sure of herself. Her own father had drained land and planted trees for the gentry and the usual psychic damage was ingrained. She dipped her head slightly and helplessly as they shook hands. She was also wearing what she'd worn at the big cousin's wedding.

Now Bultitude looked towards Simon and to escape the indignity of shaking his hand, he said, with a surprising edge of wry humour, 'And I've had the pleasure of already meeting your son. On two very brief occasions.' But he added, 'As has my daughter.' Then he changed tone, nodded towards the Jaguar. 'The Mark Four.' The clipped fact was of course also an accusation of concern with appearances beyond one's station.

Simon's father said quickly, 'One of the better models.'

Bultitude nodded and turned immediately, his house itself testament enough to how he soared above flimsy showings.

They went in among the shadows which size engineered; the dutiful furniture polish smell of Broken Moan was a wearying thing to Simon already.

Sure enough the four of them trailed into that same dawn parlour. Pinioned in a huge armchair as if tied down, Varie sat. She was wearing a white blouse which came up tight on her neck and a matronly long skirt which came down close to her ankles. All of which succeeded at least in making her look slightly older. Gone were the bohemian flourishes of wild black hair. It had been adamantly brushed down into a controlled frizz, secured in tightly at the back – though she looked as pale as ever. If anyone's eyes dropped to scrutinise her flat belly, it wasn't obvious. She rose up but stood uncertainly, trying not to fold one foot in behind the other ankle as was her habit.

Simon's mother made sure to reach her first and took her offered hand. 'Hello, Varie,' then she added, 'It's nice to meet you.' It was all said in a disgracefully misplaced and civilised tone of voice, meant for entirely different circumstances.

'Yes, you too,' Varie squeaked in a defeated way.

Simon's father nodded to the teenage girl and said, 'Hello, Varie,' in a resigned way but with a gentleness. Almost as if he already knew her.

'Mmm. How do you do?' The foot shot in behind the ankle and pressed there a moment.

'Take a seat and tea is just coming. Or would you like something stronger, Bert?'

As if the beverage was already guaranteed, Simon's father said, 'I'll have a stiff one.'

Bultitude was magnanimous. 'I'll join you there.'

The seating had been arranged in a political way. Bultitude dropped silently into Varie's armchair, leaving her stranded in front of Simon's parents. Two other armchairs – surprisingly not matching types – were arranged to face him across a round table. Blatantly, there were no seats available for Varie or Simon. But they were not to be relieved of their suffering so easily. Bultitude said in a condescending manner, 'So, Simon. No trains for the moment?'

'Eh, nut. No.' A silence hung in the huge room so Simon casually added, 'It's looking like four months or something. Maybe even more.'

Bultitude stared towards the windows and nodded. He said, 'I didn't possess the strength of knowledge that you were an employee of British Rail. Until more recently.'

Simon blinked. 'I suppose you could call it a more interesting summer job.'

Bultitude laughed very briefly. 'I *suppose* you could call it that.'

Simon's father abruptly and coldly said, 'The laddie works hard.'

Simon was shocked and touched but at the same time he sensed that air he had experienced in the Portakabin. It was suppressed violence, so he became afraid.

Bultitude said softly, 'Sit down please,' addressing Simon's parents. He seemed to retrieve the upper hand for a moment and Simon's parents had to sit obediently, leaving Simon stranded in the open like that first day in the station bothy. His father wasn't having it though, and immediately looked at Varie. 'Studying your books, love?'

She nodded her head quickly. 'Oh yes.'

Bultitude cut in, 'And I read too about your heroic efforts.'

'It's nothing. I was dead scared.'

'No need to be modest. It's all quite interesting. Tell me. Didn't the fabled rock signals warn you? Aren't the old piano wires which famously sing in the wind, strung along the slopes there, tripped by rock falls?'

Confident on this ground, Simon went on. 'They reckon, eh, think that when we passed the rock signal for our section it was off, eh, it was at green, cause it was just water flowing through the wires, it was only when we'd passed the signal at green something heavier, thicker mud and tree branches, finally tripped it, so it did fall down to danger behind us but too late.' Simon was afraid of going on but there wasn't much else to say. His voice faded a bit.

Bultitude nodded again but finally showed that he had lost interest by looking down at his polished oxford shoes and Simon immediately shut up.

Bultitude raised his eyes quickly at the two adults in the seats before him and said, 'Well, I think, as we all used to say, it's a lovely day and time for the children to go out and play in the garden.'

Simon's father said, 'They aren't children.'

'Show Simon around the gardens a little; don't wander far though.'

Varie nodded and looked at Simon then he followed her out, not through the kitchen but down the hallway to another grand back porch. Through an inviting archway with no doors, Simon glimpsed the huge billiard table in a wood-panelled room and he wanted to go in but accepted it wasn't an appropriate moment. Neither of them spoke. Even when they were outside in hopeful air, Varie led him across the mowed grass towards the long bower which was alive like a huge marquee, smothered in blue flowers. Simon was afraid she was returning him back to the groom's cottage but almost the moment they stepped under the shade of the wrangling trunks above, Varie stopped and she put her arms of white lace sleeves around his neck and dropped her forehead on his shoulder.

'Are you all right? Has your dad given you hell?'

'No. Yes. You look funny in your shirt and tie.' She spoke without looking up.

Simon sighed at the irrelevancy. 'It'll be all okay, Varie.'

'Will it? Your parents seem nice. Do you mean we will be okay?' Her weary voice physically trembled up to his head.

'Yes.'

'And that matters?' She would not look up at him.

'To me it does.'

'Me too. I won't be able to go back to the university in September and I love it.'

'No. It doesn't look like it. Not this year.'

She glanced up. 'Oh. You mean I might be able to go back the year after?'

'Maybe sooner. If the baby comes in the new year. You might get back after Easter.'

'And you wouldn't mind me going back? I don't know how to look after a little bouncing baby anyway.'

'I don't either; we'll learn. My mum'll help us.'

'You mean she would be willing?'

'Course.'

'And you'll work on your railway. But now it's broken?'

'What?'

'Your railway.'

'No, no. I'm getting paid every month while it's off. I can work for Dad and get spare money for the baby and it'll all be back running in the autumn. It's looking to be a great summer. If we can be together.'

She sighed. 'Look how they treat us though. That is going to get worse.'

'Aye, I know. It's like Robbie Burns. You know, we're on the stool in the kirk?'

'What do you mean? I don't understand Robert Burns, all the strange words about haggis.'

'Ach. You know? We're in the doghouse for a good while.'

'What alarms me most are my father's hints we won't be allowed to be together. Ever. It appears they wish to split us up already. If we didn't have the telephone we wouldn't even have spoken until now.'

'Well, they won't. If they fuck with us we'll get somewhere to live in town.'

'What?'

'In the town. We can live somewhere in the town.'

'Really? How?'

'There are some places we could rent with my wages or there's other cheaper places.'

'What do you mean?'

He did not want to say the word but he had to. 'Council places.' He thought she would faint but he was surprised.

'Ooooo. Little flats on council estates with coal fires?'

'Yes.'

'Like where your Nikki lives?'

'Eh, aye. Like I told you though, me and Nikki don't see each other any more.'

'Like that place I was in with that man – the night you took me here on the motorbike?'

'A lassie goes to top of the waiting list when she's expecting.'

She laughed and she held out a palm like the dancing Indian

goddess on the cover of the Penguin *Upanishads* – the hand indicated the differing wings and architectural styles of the house behind her. 'But I come from a home like this.'

'So? You saying it's not good enough for you?'

She frowned, hurt. 'No, no. Not at all. I mean other people have greater need than me.'

'Oh. Nut. That's not true. If it's the only way we can be together; like if our folks flung us out, that in a way – emotionally – they're doing, then you've as much right as any lassie to a flat. The council can't judge who you are or aren't. Just your need. My pal Galbraith explained it all to me once. His folks always lived with the council.'

She smiled slyly. 'Father would be black-affronted.'

'Aye, I know.' Simon smiled too, cementing it as a conspiracy.

'Gosh, imagine. It'd be lovely. We'd have a double bed and I'd make it like my bedroom here. And my Edinburgh room. I'd have imitation Persian rugs flung on the floor and hung on the walls and candles everywhere and it would be our little nest. With baby. I'd make you a sandwich when you went out to work.'

'It's called a piece.'

'A piece.' She tried to say it – badly – in his accent.

'Aye, well, we'll see. Not too sure about carpets nailed to the walls. The council might have something to say about that.'

She laughed, excited already about the possibilities of upsetting any staid neighbourhood rulings. He had a sudden image of an obscenely young Varie, leaning out the window to the front drying green, a scarf over her hair and a reefer in the corner of her mouth, shouting to the other old shawly wifies.

Varie said, 'There are disposable nappies now. You don't have to boil them like Mother did.'

He laughed. 'Aye, my mum still boiled them when Jeff was a wee-er little shit arse.'

'It's going to be fine, isn't it?' she said, then suddenly she burst out bubbling in a greet. It was remarkable to see her cry as the tears were very clear, scampering; they didn't show on her white cheeks unless you watched their brief, trickly descent, but her eyes became extremely red all around the black pupils. He touched the tears away with his forefinger. Her eyelashes had jumped together in sharp clusters, black and shining, as if coated in glue.

'Now now. Don't, Varie. You look like I'd be after I've went on your horse.'

She laughed and whimpered. 'And I bet I can't keep Peggy tied up outside in a council house.'

'No, no, you can't do that, and he'd be handy too, for you popping down the town to get the messages.'

She laughed, moved her hand and gently pushed his finger away from her cheek where he was stroking; she shook her head and sniffed, then said perceptively, 'It will look suitably remorseful if they can see I've been crying. They want that.'

Simon nodded. 'What is Alex saying?'

'He's not impressed. He feels he's lost two playmates in one swoop. And the first thing he pointed out was, that I can no longer be his scuba-diving partner any more this summer, so he's furious. He'll cool it eventually.'

'When's he back from school?'

'He's back.'

'He's back?'

'He's upstairs now. He refuses to see you.'

'Oh.'

'He's angry and I think he's a little afraid of you. He thinks you're a roughie toughie at heart.'

'I'm not.'

'He's scared he'll get cross and you'll just biff him one. Oh. He told me to tell you he wants those records and books he gave you back.'

Simon said nothing about such pettiness.

Varie said, 'You're so broody and quiet.'

'Quiet? Me?'

'Yes. You never give much away. I know what you are, Si. You're a thinker and a watcher. A clever one. That's what I liked about you from the moment I first met you in that hotel.'

'I didn't think you even remembered me from that day.'

'I did. Your eyes, watching. You're sure who you are and you don't trust the world; you think the world might spoil your plans for you. I'm like that. And here we are spoiling it for each other for ever.'

'Och, don't say that, it's not true.'

'It seems to me you're still making up your mind about everything. Even me. Reading your books.'

'Well, my books aren't much help to me now, are they? There's not much about getting a council flat in the Penguin Classics.'

She laughed and sniffed.

'And if I'm a watcher, it looks like all I'll be watching is the wee baby.'

Varie must have been operating on secret orders. After nattering and cuddling and even kissing – in a way that didn't build sexual passion – beneath that bower where the petals quivered, she led Simon back up to the house without explanation.

His strength slumped and he didn't want to go back inside there. But they went.

The three parents were talking, in measured tones, rational and without any heat. Yet they fell silent as they heard the two guilty teenagers approach and the moment Varie and Simon entered the room, Bultitude stood up.

'Varie, you take a seat with Mr and Mrs Crimmons and if I could have a word with the young man.'

Simon turned his head towards his parents but his father told him, 'On you go, son.'

Bultitude walked towards Simon and he made that motion of solicitude which teachers at school used – holding out an arm behind someone, both as a gesture of protection but also of control, without physical contact but ushering a figure forward. Such gestures were doubtless used in Belsen, Simon thought, and stepped out and back down the hallway and behind him Bultitude followed, saying, 'On your left if you please.' Simon turned down another corridor – longer and narrower – until Bultitude said, 'And on your left again if you please.'

Simon entered a very large study; the walls were hung with intricate engineering plans and technical drawings which had been framed in wood and glass. 'I trained as a structural engineer but I don't practise any more,' Bultitude stated and closed the door behind them. There was a huge and ornate working desk and behind it a modern chair which didn't fit with the rest of the furniture. The chair was a bit like his father's in the Portakabin but fancier. A

357

window was behind this chair with ivy bunching in over the outside frames, almost swarming across the glass. The ivy quivered in the outside breeze.

Bultitude said, 'Do you take an adequate interest in your history?' The man turned and indicated a much smaller frame than others hanging on the wall. Behind glass was an ancient letter, its folds appearing withered, almost opposite Simon's nose. 'This is an electronic facsimile. Do you know what a facsimile is?'

'A copy.'

'Yes. An exact copy based on a photograph. The original is locked there in the safe with not much else. I used to have the original hung here but a fellow – a historian – told me I was ruining it by having it exposed to the light. Nonsense. My father and my grandfather had the original hung.'

Simon frowned at the letter. It had been written by hand, in what looked like quill ink.

Nivel by Charlesoix jun 19

Mother Father,

Thanks this finds me well unlike many good men.

And yesterday a great battle here and two or three the same and B'parte put to run. With us now behind in what looks to be a fine chase.

One ear sings from gun to our left y'day but unharmed in all other ways and god be to remain as more must come.

Today safe, my love and duty ever

Yr son

Andrew

'Do you know where that was written?'

Simon shook his head. 'Nope.'

'Battle of Waterloo.'

'Right enough?'

'Yes. Right enough. The author was my great-great-something-grandfather. I told Varie when she was just a little girl that her forebears rode in the Scots Greys but I'm afraid that was a little bit of ornamentation. A damn wee fib. I told her to encourage the horsemanship and it worked. That Andrew Bultitude was in Byng's lot. He would have had his Waterloo with both boots on the ground.'

'Right.' Simon smiled cautiously and looked to the left. Here was an old, long, framed colour photograph. He was amazed to see it was the bloody Queen of England standing outside the front entrance of Broken Moan by those marble columns. Simon noted the cast-iron shelter above the front porch was painted a different colour back then. There was Bultitude himself, younger with the shorter haircut that all the men modelled – but he was not hugely changed, standing right next to the Queen who was in a greenish tweed get-up; a long complement of staff and others all stood formally in line.

Even at a time like this, Bultitude was unable to stop pride coming into his voice. 'That was when the Queen visited me,' he claimed. Then he pointed to a striking, slim woman in a long blue dress who looked like an Italian film star, and standing on either side of her were two children – a little boy and a little girl.

'That's Varie there with her late mother.'

'Oh, wow,' Simon said and he looked closely at the childhood features trying to compare them to what he knew. He studied the mother as well.

'And that is Alex.'

Alex was tiny. Simon scanned the other figures trying to identify the dead uncle, but he could not.

Suddenly Bultitude nodded back at the letter and said, 'Clearly you're a young man who hasn't kept his boots on the ground?'

Simon tried forlornly, steering matters to – of all things – the local cinema. 'I've seen a film about Waterloo.'

'Yes. I'm sure you spend a great deal of time in the back row of the local cinema. Take a seat and I won't charge you for it.'

Simon conformed, sat on the side of the desk he knew he was expected to sit on, while Bultitude went behind where he lowered himself into the modern chair. Yet Simon thought Bultitude was just a man like other men; his shit travelled through the same sewers as everyone and Simon would not defer to him.

For just a moment, Andrew Bultitude considered Simon there, where he wanted him. Where he paid off and took on estate employees and gardeners. He pointed, using his pinkie which for some reason annoyed Simon even more. 'You know, I bet you even sleep well at night. One always does at your age. The things I did in my youth – but when my head hit the pillow, nine solid hours without a flicker. When you hit forty that changes. The doubts start to creep in. The sweaty nights.'

Simon thought that Bultitude seemed to sleep well enough when he was blootered. He immediately said, 'I'm sorry for what's happened but it doesn't show how I feel about Varie.'

'I think the facts display very well how you feel.'

'It must seem to you I don't respect Varie but that's not true, Mr Bultitude. I respect her very much.'

'Noble words with an air of rehearsal about them.'

It was true he'd said his bit but he breathed out and repeated, 'It's how I feel.'

'How you feel has nothing to do with it. The ruination of the rest of my daughter's life is the issue, and you're off to a sterling start on it.'

'It won't be her ruination.'

'Already is. And both of you just damned children.'

'Yes,' Simon said.

'Well, at least you accept that. Varie was a flourishing student at the Edinburgh University and you've ruined this.'

'I was just talking about that with her.'

'Were you?'

'We were thinking.'

'Stop. Two terms we can dispense with. One is We and the other, Thinking. There is no We, and your parents – who seem reasonable sorts – and myself will do all the thinking. It's clear neither you nor my daughter can do it for yourselves.'

Simon toughed up. 'Look. We, Varie and me, are not being split because of what's happened. We're facing up to it and we'll deal with it. I've got a job and she can go back to the university. After.'

'I'll tell you how we are going to deal with it. Luckily Varie is protected and cared for.' Bultitude seemed to be thinking aloud only to himself. 'She can return next year. Yes. That can be arranged easily with the university authorities. Meanwhile she'll live here in what we once called the privilege of her confinement.' The voice was certain, considering, as if stating events which had already occurred. 'You won't be welcome anywhere near this house again. You must have known that she lost her own mother at a vulnerable age. You must have conceived – bad choice of word – comprehended how that's affected her.'

'I know. And I'm very sorry. But I just don't feel I took deliberate advantage of her; she's clever and her own person.'

Suddenly Bultitude looked outraged and seemed to be in actual despair as he looked across at Simon. 'And you must have known we're also a religious family. We are Catholic. You must have known that and how it explains our tolerance?'

'Yes,' he answered, deciding to let that claim go.

'You must have known what that meant in our terms?'

'I do. Yes. Though I'm not a Catholic.' Simon stiffened up. 'And while there are history lessons going on, Mr Bultitude, it isn't the first time in history this has happened to a Catholic girl.'

The man held him in very steady gaze. 'Now you insult us.'

Simon was unsure if he meant the family or the Church. 'No. That's just a fact. And you can't break me and Varie up either. Sir. That's for us to decide, not you or my parents.'

Bultitude leaned forward. 'I play a long game, son. You're young. You're impatient. You think you know how the corn ripens but you do not.'

'There's no longer game than a child, Mr Bultitude.' Simon saw that bolt strike home. 'It'll be my baby as well as hers. I'm not asking anything from you.'

'It appears to me you are asking a very great deal.' Bultitude put both his palms down on the desk. 'Don't try to fight me, young man. Because I'll win if you try to fight me.'

Now Simon leaned back and he took a breath. 'Then we'll just have to get married, won't we?' Simon saw the result of this. The older man actually blinked and those words came back to Simon. The ones Penalty had said that night on the engine. That there needed to be a man who would bring Bultitude down to size one day.

Slowly, a little unsure, Bultitude said, 'If you think that could ever happen then you are dafter than I presumed.'

'I don't think you can stop us, sir. I think you need to give us a chance to deal with this and if you are so upset then we'll get married. I've talked about it with Varie.'

Bultitude was quiet for a long time and his voice changed. It was suddenly reasonable. 'There will be no need for that.'

'Really? Oh, really? I thought you believed in it? You're not aware of how much I care for Varie. That's your mistake. So we'll just have to get married.'

He became angry again. 'You don't know the meaning of it. No man does before forty.'

'Is that like sleeping well too?'

'It's like faith, which you can know nothing about at the age of seventeen.'

'I'm seventeen next month.'

'Good for you, bloody Methuselah. Your father and I had been through wars by the time we were twenty-one and we still knew nothing.'

'I think he knew plenty by then.'

'Self-knowledge is a long battle, won over time. What will you know in a few years? Nothing. Then you'll move on. Other girls, other cries and whispers to compare in the night. I've lived.'

'But —' Simon paused and Bultitude actually waited to hear what was next as Simon flicked his hand about the grand study — 'you're too tied up in all this, and you've let it affect her happiness.'

A dismissive snort.

'Some people don't want all this.'

'My goodness. You are a young saint. Varie did claim you should be in the university too. Not the University of British Railways. Since you're speaking so frankly without need of a dram like me, the Church doesn't blind me. You aren't the first boy to go to bed with her. I know that fine. She's been a wee holy terror with no mother to guide her.' Now he lowered his voice down. 'And I'll tell you this, each boy that's looked into her face has seen this house in her eyes. You too, and don't think you'll get your hands on a single bit of it. It all goes to Alexander. Every damn bit, down to the horse shit in the paddocks. Varie gets nothing. I need you to know that and to think about it.'

Simon stood up. 'I don't care. I've no interest in all this.' He shook his head to dismiss everything around him. 'You're obviously obsessed with it.'

If Bultitude hadn't been surprised he wouldn't have moved but he betrayed distress by shifting the swivel chair round an inch or two then tried to look casual. Finally Bultitude said, 'It's inevitable that I'll beat you.'

Simon started walking and opened the office door; the man repeated quietly, measured, without explaining, 'It's all inevitable,' and oddly, he added, as if admitting he should at least remember his name, 'Simon, you won't get married to each other. I'll make sure of it. I'll do anything to stop it. Anything.'

Politely and gently, Simon closed the study door behind him, feeling its weight and the heavy efficient click of the smooth lock mechanism.

He had planned to walk straight out and sit in the back of his father's car, but Varie was talking with his parents in the parlour and he could not pass by without kissing her. It was a steady, polite conversation and to his horror he couldn't interrupt as Varie explained, in a less forthright voice than usual, the seasonal move-ment of horses from one paddock to another, and in a moment Bultitude had caught up with him and, creepily, he put an arm onto Simon's shoulder and lied, 'We had a nice little chat.'

Yet Simon nodded – a strangely masculine act for the sake of the others.

Soon enough the Crimmons family was retreating towards their car. Bultitude remained glued to his daughter's left side. It was a cruel stance and Simon didn't have the nerve to lean across and try even to kiss Varie's cheek, so all he could risk by way of a farewell was to stretch out his hand, take her arm in its lace sleeve and squeeze it gently. He got the usual mild fizz of an electric shock from her blouse. After all their gothic intimacies they were reduced to this. They had been unsexed. Varie didn't even respond in her face, though her slim bicep was as tensed as back in April when she had bent her spine upward from the dirty floorboards.

Bultitude stood a moment under the canopy of the porch then ushered his daughter back inside and closed the double doors before the Jaguar had even started its engine. Herb Alpert's Tijuana Brass trumpeted into life and his father angrily jammed the volume off. Simon had undone his tie and tugged it off through the collar of the shirt by the time they had reached Varie's shelter at the bottom of the drive. Simon undid his top shirt button, twisting his neck to the side and he casually said, 'That wee hut there was for her when she was up at the primary and caught the bus. See, it's got all Donald Duck and *Jungle Book* cartoons painted in it.'

'Oh yes,' his mother said in a kindly way.

His father muttered, 'And she might be living in it soon enough too.'

His mum added, 'Oh, Simon, she's an awful bonny-looking lassie.'

'Christ, Agnes. He knows that.'

'I'm just saying.'

'It'll be a pretty baby. Am I surrounded by idiots?' Simon's father was silent all the way to the Back Settlement until he said, 'And what did the Duke of Wellington have to say to you, Casanova?'

'Funnily enough he had a letter from the Battle of Waterloo itself in there that he was bumming on about.'

Mr Crimmons blew out air. 'I'm surprised he didn't take a sword to you and chop your block off. Did he get you to clean his shoes?'

'Nut.'

'Should have. You complete bloody idiot.'

'He had a photo of them with the Queen.'

'Oh, we can remember that. When she came to open the Hydro thing.' His mother absorbed the tensions, visibly sitting more erect in the front passenger seat, voice climbing higher as she made compliment after compliment about Varie and when she ran out of things to say about the pregnant girl she found laudatory aspects about the garden of Broken Moan to comment upon until Simon's father said, 'Put a sock in your mouth, woman.'

The rest of the journey was a silent one. When they parked in front of Tulloch Villa, Simon climbed out and made for the back door.

'Don't you be running upstairs to greet or laugh or whatever you do in that bloody bedroom, you wicked wee bastard. You get here with me.'

'Bertie, hush.' His mother could read the pitch of the anger.

'Come along here.' His father walked down towards the garage at the bottom of the drive. Simon followed. He soon fathomed it. His father was heading for his motorbike which was parked in at the side of the garage and he was going to smash it to pieces with the sledgehammer. Sure enough, his father veered for the tool-shed door adjoining the garage. Simon held back. It was ridiculous – as if the bloody motorbike itself had had sex with Varie. His father opened the tool-shed door, turned his head and saw him stopped there.

'Come here at once.'

He hadn't been in the tool shed for a couple of years. Inside, the smell was overwhelming and he had forgotten it – the musty pepperiness of a potting shed, dusty air, fibrous from dried soil. The sets of rakes and hoes, shovels and spades, hayforks, picks and sledgehammers, all propped erect inside the row of fragile, strained tea chests. All inherited from the previous owner. The chests' tin edging was rusted and the thin wood sides were rotted, frayed and broken open like wafers. The cobwebbed, two-handed scythe, which fascinated him as a child, still hung on the dull and blistered white-wash. It all reminded Simon of his simpler childhood when the tool shed and the sand pile were adventure enough, before girls' differing bodies became a realm of wonder – as Andrew Bultitude had warned.

His father reached over and started lifting then rejecting the smoothed wooden handles of tools which sprouted up in tangled confusions from the tea chests.

'What are you doing?'

They both looked at each other. His father hadn't put on the electric light in the tool shed and it was shadowy, lit only from the door. Dust filaments still moved in the natural light – like blemishes within the eye itself.

'Here.' His dad passed tools to him, holding them with one single hand. A pick was crashed noisily out then a rusted crowbar. His father said, 'We'll need the Stanley knife from over there.'

Simon followed, hulking the pick and the crowbar over the driveway as they moved back up towards the car. Simon wondered if they were going to attack the Jaguar for some perverse reason, then finally he realised what his father intended.

The formal front door which they never used, with its amusingly wonky HS∩d electric doorbell button, was not locked. His father shoved in the door and Simon followed him through the hallway into Tulloch Villa's long blue room.

'Don't, Dad,' Simon said. 'It doesn't matter.'

'Oh, doesn't matter now, does it?' Simon's father stared at him and he nodded the knife at him like a teacher's ruler. 'Tell you what you are, son. Do you know? A bum. A useless good-for-nothing bum.'

'I know I am.' Simon put down the tools carefully, propping them on the tiles in front of the fireplace, gently leaning the crowbar's rusty height against the smoky white marble of the mantel.

His father got down on his knees in the middle of the floor as if about to pray, but he took the Stanley knife blade to the blue carpet with both hands. Men from Wylie & Lochhead in Glasgow had come up in a big van to fit that carpet, but his father slashed the fine wool in one long cut.

Simon could see the blade judder, resisting its travel over the uneven, sturdy floorboards beneath that inch of pile. His father dropped the knife, put his fingers into the slash and dug, then using his body weight he heaved backwards; the carpet lifted two inches but tugged tightly at both ends of the cut, refusing to tear. He shifted into a crawling position on all fours then his fingers went in underneath; some final resisting threads gave sharply and a triangle of fabric tore up, revealing the varnished but paint-flecked boards beneath.

Now nosy wee Jeff had appeared at the door. 'Daddy, what are you doing?' He spoke with a mix of caution and delight. Jeff looked at Simon standing there, dressed in the curious clothes.

'Away upstairs, Jeff,' their father said patiently.

'You've ripped the good carpet.' Jeff pointed and he giggled. 'Why didn't you roll it up all careful?'

Simon turned to Jeff. 'It's your bloody fault, you wee git.'

Their father shouted, 'Now, Jeff. Jeff! Upstairs now, and it is not your fault, son. It's this idiot here. Away upstairs.'

Jeff had suddenly taken in the atmosphere of the room, he became confused and afraid, then started to cry.

'Ah, for God's sake, bubble face,' Simon shouted.

'Would you go upstairs?'

Jeff wailed and the howls receded, with some intervals on specific stairs to make sure his mother had a better chance to overhear his distress.

Simon's father stood and grabbed the pick. He hoisted the tool so the handle was up by his face and he brought it down hard. Simon flinched. The impact made a crack – violent and odd in the domestic surroundings – and the floorboard immediately split along its length. But they could feel he had struck exactly where there was a supporting floor beam beneath. He adjusted his feet and the next blow hit the board where hollowness lay under it. With a squeaking sound the pick penetrated the wood and stuck. Simon's father stumbled forward a little. Then he forced the lodged pick handle upward. The floorboard creaked and resisted and the tool jammed again – against another underfloor beam. He twisted it free and let the pick fall onto the carpet.

Simon's mother stepped in the room. He knew she'd been boiling the electric kettle. 'For God's *sake*, Bertie, what on earth are you doing? You're wrecking the house. What's wrong with Jeff?'

Neither of them answered her.

'You've gone and cut the good carpet – it's spoiled.'

'What the hell does anything matter in this family of nutters that I work my arse off for?' Simon's father moved to the crowbar. He tried out the weight of its length in his hands then crossed and forced it hard into that breach in the floorboards.

Simon's mother turned and looked through the back windows and up the short tarred driveway. 'Folk from the village are going to see, Bertie. They'll go and call the police.' She strode to the bottom of the room and pulled both sides of the curtains closed.

Simon's father walked round the lodged metal bar then placed both hands on the rod and used his full weight to heave the floorboard up; the way Simon pulled back a points' lever on a siding. The crowbar shook with resistance then came a loud crack as the wood broke in one place; a further loud squeak and the floorboard yawed up along its length, revealing a row of angry, exposed nails.

Upstairs they could all now hear Jeff howling, seemingly reacting to each noise of his home's destruction, his legs kicking in tantrum as he lay face down pummelling the mattress of his bed. But no one went up to him.

Watched by his wife, Simon's father got down on his chest and reached in under the floorboards. Simon's mother shook her head.

'Jeff was just a wee crawler. He didn't understand. Why did you just go and let them lay the carpet on top then?'

Simon's father shouted, 'Because I wanted to forget. It's only old snobs like Bultitude wants to remember cause they did fuck all.' He reached in and lifted out what looked like a coin attached to a bright piece of cloth. 'Here's your fucking medals for you, you useless sponging shit.' He tossed the medal at Simon who went to grab it but missed and it fell to the intact carpet by his feet.

'Oh my goodness.' Simon's mother shook her head. 'I thought the spiders would have eaten them. The colours haven't faded at all.' She turned to Simon. 'Near eight or nine years since this carpet went in. It was just bare floorboards. The old carpet was lifted and I left Jeff crawling around in here just for a wee jiffy, while I went to the kitchen to boil the kettle. I came back and the empty medal box was lying next to a crack in the floorboards. The wee mischievous bugger had dropped each medal in. The carpet men were coming the next day and your father didn't care. I begged him to get his medals out but he wouldn't. You should have listened to me.'

Mr Crimmons actually nodded.

Simon said, 'Isn't even dust on them. It's like time stood still.'

His father roughly tossed the three other medals and they landed on the carpet by Simon's feet. Then the man just sat there breathing on the ruined floor.

Simon bent over then held the last one up to his face. The ribbon was fantastically bright. Almost fluorescent in quality.

'That's the Africa Star and that's the Distinguished Conduct and bar,' his mother said.

His father told him, 'Give that to your wee bastard child to remind it of Grandad, cause you'll get bugger all else out of me. Clown.'

Thursday 27 June 1974

Simon drove the yellow motorbike past the cathedral and he turned up the Brae Estate hill towards where Nikki and Karen's house was; leaning forward he down-geared. Aye, even on his own, yon bam of a bike struggled uphill. If he lived up here he'd be better off parking it at the bottom. There was going to be nae money for a bigger bike either.

He looked at the street numbers then let the bike perform the inevitable largo of its own slowing and he put both feet out. There was a wee car park up the crescent where he'd walked with Karen Caine that time. He parked there and chained, walked back downhill with the helmet under his arm to the close at 17.

Kiddies were playing out the back drying green, running through hanging sheets; hiding behind them like screens, their voices echoed through the corridor and up the stairs as he sprinted to the first floor. A red door with a plastic mother-of-pearl-imitation name sign: PENALTY. There was a loose-fitted buzzer button in the middle of the door. He began repeatedly wiping his trainers on the doormat.

Penalty answered looking just normal – rolly in the corner of his mush, the heid top baldy and grey hair straggles with no railway hat. He wore a loose cardigan with brown buttons over a shirt – a walking stick supported him. 'Well I never. Come away, son, into the body of the kirk.'

'Thought I'd see how you're doing.'

Penalty yelled down the corridor, 'It's only my wee fireman, Doreen. The yin you sent me away with the night he went and wrecked the whole bloody railway.'

Simon laughed.

In the front room, Muhammad Ali was on the old black-and-white television set. They didn't seem to have a colour one like Simon's parents. Penalty pointed to the telly and said, 'There's a good man, we could do with him in Scotland. Cassius Clay, eh? He'd sort us out.' But Penalty crossed slowly and leaned cautiously to the side of the television where he turned the knob and switched it off.

'Aye, he would,' Simon said.

Mrs Penalty came down the corner from what must have been two back bedrooms and said cheerily, 'Hello there, son.'

'Hello, Mrs Penalty. Sorry to drop by without saying. I couldn't find yous in the phone book.'

Penalty went, 'No on the phone, son. Get on the phone and it's nothing but trouble. Pest of a thing; Lincoln gabbing on to come out for late shifts or our son, down in bloody Plymouth with his crazy wife, on for an hour. I got it tooken out. There'll come a day when the phone's compulsory, son, I'm telling you now.'

'You just howd your horses, John Penalty, and don't be getting worked up in two minutes.' His wife smiled. She was leaning against the wall at the corner of the corridor and Simon noted how the wallpaper was indeed a bit shiny there. 'John's told me all about how you got him out them engines.'

'Ach.'

'Oh, now don't be modest with your auntie Doreen, you should be up for a medal.'

Simon grimaced. 'I've got a few of those already.'

She just laughed. 'Aye, for putting up with John every day.'

Simon smiled and nodded as Penalty sat in an armchair and balanced his walking stick across his knees.

'Sit down, son.'

Simon stepped over and sat on the armchair at Penalty's right side. The armchair was scattered with loads of wee cushions and they were a bit uncomfy but he just ignored them – he didn't want to start shifting them all. Simon nodded. 'You seem fair speedy on that stick.'

'Oh aye. This's what I need.'

'Why don't you use it at the work?'

Penalty looked round at Doreen and they both laughed. 'I can't come down on the bloody railway with a big bloomin walking stick like I was ninety-five, son. I'm a driver. If an inspector or that seen me hobbling round on this up to an engine, I'd be taken oot and shot like a racehorse. Got to keep my pin on the deadman's. If I was sent to a bloody medical they'd fail me for sure. I've more faults than the *Titanic* on me. Lincoln and McGarry turn a blind eye to me, which is good of them. They know I've only a few year to run till retirement.'

Simon nodded. 'I'll pretend to use it then and carry it for you.'

Mr and Mrs Penalty laughed.

'You wanting a cup of tea, son?'

'No thanks, no. I just popped round for a wee minute.'

'Well, it's nice to see you. I'm ironing in the back room,' the lady smiled at him in a kindly way and she disappeared up the corridor.

Penalty went, 'I hear the meeting was a bloody bourach.'

Simon laughed. 'Aye. Everyone marched out after they found we were closing down but getting full pay. Wee Ian was squeaking like a balloon.'

Penalty laughed. 'The buggers are dafties. Run to the union when theys're wanting their holiday dates sorted but they're gone the rest of the bloody year. One day there'll be nae union and they'll be shovelling the management's shite from under their arses as it comes out. Then they'll be told to tip it over their own heids, and they will.'

Simon smiled and nodded.

He mumbled, 'Probably around the same time the telephone becomes compulsory.'

Simon smiled again. 'You seem on grand form.'

'I am. Three or four month off, lad. It's a bloody lifesaver for me. I'll rest up. Maybe a fortnight away somewhere. The races at Ayr on ma travel passes and get my strength back.'

'Aye.'

'Look.' He pointed the stick out horizontal. 'There's yon book I was telling you about.'

'Eh?'

'The book I was telling you about. The Johnston book. *Our Scots 'Noble' Families.*'

'Oh aye.'

'It's right there, away and take a wee deech at it.'

Simon sprang up and went over to a small furniture unit. There was a long row of the *Scots Magazine*, all squeezed together with their spines rigid, *Scottish Birds, Scottish Wildlife, British Rail Diesel Traction Manual for Enginemen.* There was the *British Rail Rule Book.* An old edition of *Signalling Regulations,* a book of stories that looked dead interesting, called *Outlaws and Tramps.* A Hugh MacDiarmid. *Poems* of Robert Burns, *The Ragged Trousered Philanthropists, Love on the Dole, Tales of the Toddy, History of the Scottish Working Classes,* some Penguin Spike Milligans. Simon pulled out the '*Noble' Families.* He couldn't stop himself standing there and turning straight to the start of the entry for the Bultitudes.

Broken Moan is a natural defensive position and it was out here in the meadows, by the dam chase where the cairns supposedly mark the site, that Robert the Bruce surrounded and ambushed the MacDougalls of Lorn – allies of Balliol – in 1309. The small watch castle was built around this time and a Commander of the Pass appointed and given ouster-le-main until the times of the Hanovarian Campbells. In the title-greedy nineteenth century, the Commander's role was anglicised, enshrined by Highland-loving Victoria and Albert and set as sinecure to the sons and son-in-laws of the Bultitudes.

The curious name of the seat is supposedly explained by the seasonal winds which howl up the Pass from October to April, playing over the arrow slits and loop holes of the medieval tower, singing the disquiet and the melancholy of the Bultitudes.

Their first recorded rascally begins in . . .

Penalty was watching him. 'Are you reading it, son?' He looked away. 'Aye, and that isnie even up to date. He wrote that in the thirties but then he went and disowned it when he got respectable, but he was a great man. And a socialist. He wisnie a good nationalist though. I shook his hand once.'

Simon closed the book and put it in his bomber jacket pocket. 'I'll get it back to you. Thanks.'

Penalty looked down at the carpet between his legs. 'You keep it for yourself, son. You keep it, as long as you read it. Promise me that.'

Simon nodded. 'I will. I've something I need to tell you about.'
Simon crossed and sat down beside him again.

Penalty turned aside slowly. His baccy tin was on a wee table
next him and he began making a rolly. 'Fire away.'

Simon leaned towards Penalty and dropped his voice to a whisper,
his eyes going up the corridor to where Mrs Penalty had gone.
'I've gone and got a lassie into trouble.'

'Oh naw, laddie.'

Simon nodded.

'Oh naw. That's no funny. Christ, there goes your wages. Caine's
wee lassie? He'll scalp ye now, man. You're way too young for
bairns. You're just a bairn yourself and that's a whole new ball game.'

'It's another lass.'

'Another? Oh Christ. I thought you were goed with her? Well,
Jeez, what do you want me to tell you? I'm a bit late in saying use
a good rubber. Is she for keeping the bairn?'

'Aye. She's Catholic.'

'You're getting deeper and deeper here. You marrying her?'

'Maybe. I'm not saying to you who she is.'

'No. I understand that, son. It's none of my business.'

'But you'll be finding out soon enough. I'll tell you myself when
the time's right. And when I do, well, I think you might take a
view on it.'

Penalty frowned. 'It's no a relation, is it? That Peggy Grierson.
The lassie at that Our Lady's is Doreen's niece; she's bonny and
they're Catholics. It had better not be.'

Simon laughed. 'She's no relation of yours, John. That's for sure.
What I wanted to ask you about—'

'Aye?'

'—was council flats.'

'Oh, right. Oh. You serious? Thinking of making a go of it up
here in Boom Town?'

'Aye. Why not?'

Penalty said, 'Well, they're building a fucking new primary school
just for the likes of yous, aren't they?'

Simon laughed.

'What's your pappy going to say to this?'

'Not much. How's it work?'

'Well, it had better no be a ground floor yous get, ya wee shit. With this leg, I've been greeted at the council to rehouse us in a ground floor for three year now, but that's what happens, they all go to the young yins. If she's in the family way, you go to the top of the list. There's a flat up there on the corner of the crescent right now.'

'Really?'

'Aye. Get her on the list. You'd be welcomed into the bosom of the community, you poor cunt.' He laughed and so did Simon. 'Want to go see it? Come on then.'

Penalty had done up his cardigan and he shouted down the corridor. 'Just popping out a sec, love.'

Simon took the old man's arm down the stairs and out the close onto the brae. A car was going downhill and whoever was inside tooted the horn; Penalty tipped up his walking stick in acknowledgement.

Up the crescent, Penalty pointed the end of his walking stick at a third-floor flat on the second close. 'That yin. Paradise, eh? You might think the view out to the islands is beautiful but you're best no facing west. The winter gales hit you. The windows whistle and leak and you'll have damp on the back walls. Never get no sun. But that one's free.'

'Well.'

'Get yourselves down the council building and her name on the list. Are yous wanting to come bide with us?'

'Eh?'

'There's a spare room in the back there. That son of mine is never back. Christ the last time he was here, the cheeky bugger booked into bed and breakfast. Bloody McGarry himself. His sister-in-law runs a place and the bugger gets Isobel the Ticket to recommend it when folk are asking at the ticket office. Cheeky bugger. The bloody son stayed at a guest house with the wife rather than listening to his faither's view on things.'

'John, that's kind but I couldn't.'

'You got enough of me at the work, eh? Lucky escape.'

'No, man. It'd be an honour. I'd learn something living with you, but we couldn't bother you.'

'Well, you keep it in mind, son, if things hot up for you at home. The offer stands.'

Simon nodded. They both stood on the crescent corner and Simon said, 'I will, John. Thanks.' Penalty gave Simon his arm and they slowly began their move back down the brae together.

Simon drove down through town from Penalty's flat on the Brae Estate and pulled in towards the bus garage then along by the mart and the Mart Hotel. He considered popping in to see Galbraith at the carpenter's where he'd taken a summer job. Galbraith was suddenly threatening to keep the job and also not return to school. Simon got enough interrogation from Galbraith about Nikki and he had been very careful to hide his acquaintance with Alex and Varie, so that day it did not seem wise to see Galbraith.

Instead he drove on past the bus park and the blaise pitches; beyond the cash and carry he chained the bike outside his father's garages but he didn't go into the compound. He walked across the humped railway bridge and looked down on the track there. Already from lack of use, the silver rail tops were rusted the same orange as the football pitches.

He put his helmet into his rucksack then Simon began the climb up through the trestles and stages of leaf, breathing deeply, shooting his hands out to clutch at holds. He could feel the book Penalty had given him banging against his side in the jacket pocket.

When he reached the swing, the ground around it looked recently disturbed. A new generation of wee kids must have discovered the place at last.

He ducked by the thorn tree and out onto the rock, right there where he'd been with Nikki. The table and chairs were gone; the tarpaulin and all the stuff in the cave too, including his mum's blanket. When he stood at the edge and looked out and down he saw the distinct shape of the table legs – the whole thing was on its side, twisted and suspended high up in the air, resting in tree branches forty feet above the slope surface below. Leaves seemed to have grown up and folded around the furniture, almost concealing it. He tutted out loud.

Simon sat down on the big rock. The silent railway underneath troubled him. He felt something was due and it wasn't any train.

Something huge and final, like the Russian rockets shouldered down in their silos, pointed at Ardencaple Glen. But it wasn't that. It was something else. A spoiling was coming to this place.

It was something to do with Varie, how she had talked that night in the groom's cottage about the rocks, opening the fundament itself and allowing to rise up old powers and beings which lurked down there, loosing them upon these lands. And a child. He could barely cope with Jeff.

He shook his head at it all, looking out through the splayed leaves across the Port — and to the inner summer lands, going eastward, backboned by roads, veined with single tracks and passing places, the railway and all he knew.